DESCENDANT OF THE ELDERS

DESCENDANT OF THE ELDERS

REALM BLENDER
BOOK ONE

Gary Swaby

REDITAL

PART I

Chapter 1

IT WASN'T THE PAIN that rippled through my body that prevented me from being a competent space marine. It was the fear of being less of a man in the eyes of my comrades, because of my condition. Regardless, I did myself no favors by forgetting to take my medicine. It was a daily requirement for me; but still I would forget. Some days it was deliberate, because I'd lost motivation to be healthy. On days like this, it was because I let the mission become my only concern.

"Remember Sergeant, you're headed to an uncharted world. There are no oxygen mills so you'll need to carry your breathers," came Administrator Blake's voice through my Comm-link.

"Understood," I told him.

"If you see anything suspicious, radio it in. Don't engage if you encounter native lifeforms," he added.

"Roger," I said, glancing at my partner, Joe Elentos.

"Let's do this," he nodded in response.

We stepped into our shuttle and I typed the location into the navigation. Once the system registered that we'd buckled up, it began its descent down from the spaceship.

Our destination would be the last known location of some missing space marines. It was our job to investigate their disappearance.

"So, Wardson, is this the first time you've been on an uncharted world?" Elentos asked.

"It's not my first time, but nowadays they assign me to the local systems," I said. This was because the Alliance viewed a marine with a medical condition as a liability.

Elentos rubbed his neck. "So," he continued, while gazing through the window behind me. I turned to see if there was anything there, I saw nothing but the dull red skies. "One of the missing marines is Natalya Carrick, right?" he asked.

"Affirmative."

"Didn't you..."

"Yes." I replied. I already knew what he was about to ask and I didn't want to talk about it. Taking the hint, he decided to read the mission brief on his Comm-link. I did the same.

Nurvoa was home to a species that showed no signs of communication. From the images on the Comm-link they appeared to be giant reptiles that could walk on two feet. They could switch between movement on two feet and all fours. The latter formation allowed them to cross large distances in seconds. This species—named Drekarth—were aware of other races in space, including humans.

"These Drekarth don't even attempt to communicate with other species," Elentos said, as if reading my mind. "They just stare at you if you're in front of them."

"And then they go about their business as if you're not even there." I added.

"Yep, and it says they had a conflict with the Garrues years ago. But the Garrues' attempt to wipe them out was unsuccessful."

"And nobody knows why, or how the Drekarth even fought back," I said. "Going by their previous behavior, I doubt the Drekarth have anything to do with the disappearances." I added.

We continued scrolling through our Comm-link interfaces. "Research says that the only thing the Drekarth are concerned with is hunting, gathering the fruits of the land and building towns and structures for their growing population."

"Yeah," he said, rubbing his chin before popping down the visor on his helmet. When landing on planets with no oxygen zones, it was essential that we protected our skin with a visor. Our suits contained built in breathers, which were small masks that locked in over the nose and mouth and pumped out oxygen.

"The mission that our marines were on is classified, but I have a feeling it wasn't Drekarth related." Elentos continued. "And I doubt they would have opened fire on them for no reason."

"Carrick and Flurwick aren't that reckless," I said. "Natalya plays by the book. Climbing the ladder is the only thing she's concerned with." It was a truth that stung.

"But is Flurwick obedient?" he asked. This, I had to think about.

Jonathan Flurwick was recently promoted and had the respect of many marines inside the Galactic Alliance. On the few occasions that I'd worked with him, I hadn't enjoyed it. He was stern, impatient and his attitude towards other species was questionable. For a man who aimed to be a high ranking official in the Galactic Alliance, he didn't enjoy mixing with other species. Flurwick was as condescending as they came.

Before I could answer the question, the shuttle bleeped twice to notify us that we were five minutes away from our landing.

It was time to ready our equipment. At a base level, every marine wore skinsuits made from a fusion of latex and synthetic fabrics that were discovered in space after first-contact between humans and the Stowyth species. Over these skinsuits we wore modular pieces of armor that we could customize as needed. Because I was susceptible to getting sick in cold conditions, I wore combat pants over the bottom half of my skinsuit, I needed an extra layer of warmth. I then installed leg armor over my combat pants. On my upper body, I installed a chest and abdomen piece and arm pieces that had a special cutout to make them compatible with my Comm-link.

Nurvoa was an area with heights so we assisted each other in installing our Jet Boosters—also known as jetpacks. Elentos holstered his Burst-fire Blaster and a Rifle. I chose my trusted Radox Blaster that could extend into a long-range rifle for sniping. All I had to do was press down the pop-lock and pull on the levered handle and my blaster would transform into a sniper rifle on the fly. A scope would even flip out of the top for me. It was my favorite piece of Alliance artillery and it was lightweight.

My hope was that we would have no use for these weapons. It had been a while since I'd had to shoot on the job. There was just one more thing I needed with me. I slid my personal smartphone into my boot. Admins urged us not to carry personal devices on missions because our Comm-link could radio in any support we needed. But every marine broke this rule.

"Approaching destination. Conditions seem normal. Please observe the area before leaving the shuttle." The system told us.

Elentos put a round in his blaster and nodded at me. "Alright Brandon, let's go get your ex-girl back."

CHAPTER 2

"DO ME A FAVOR, Elentos," I said, as I pushed the shuttle door open. "Call her, Carrick."

"Heh," he grunted, "I understand, bro."

We hopped out of the shuttle and saw that we were at the base of a huge monolith. The dirt surrounding us was a bright shade of red that contrasted against the dark burgundy sky.

"I see footsteps over there," said Elentos. I examined the footprints and saw that they were the exact shape and design of the standard space marine boot. I looked around to see if the footprints were of two different sizes but there was clearly only one size.

"Flurwick and Carrick must have split up," I said.

"Isn't it weird calling Natalya by her surname even though you dated her?" Elentos asked. "You shouldn't have to be so formal about it right?"

"Get serious, Joe," I said, shaking my head. "I thought you were dropping it? Anyway, I guess we'll just follow these footsteps for now, but be on your guard. Something doesn't sit right with me here."

My shoulder erupted with sharp throbs as we moved

forward. I took a deep breath and remembered just how differently it felt to breathe oxygen through a breather. Typically, on planets in the Milky Way, oxygen mills were set up to provide fresh air over a certain radius. In that case there was no need to use a breather. But with Nurvoa being an uncharted world with no colonies, there were no mills set up to provide oxygen. My body could always tell the difference between oxygen from the mills versus from the suit. On these occasions, the difference in oxygen would cause my joints to ache.

"You alright, Wardson?" Elentos asked. "I didn't piss you off, did I?"

"No, you're alright," I said as we came to a stop. "It's just my body reacting to the difference in oxygen." I looked up at the large rock deposit where the footprints ended. I could see that there were paths above us, likely leading right inside the monolith. "I guess Flurwick boosted up here."

"Let's go for it," he said. We both tapped our shoulder switches to turn our Jet Boosters on and pressed in the button on both of our palms with our two middle fingers. Then it was just a case of holding onto the buttons for as long as we needed to and hovering forward, using our body's weight to direct us where we wanted to go. "I can't wait till they roll out the updated models of these. I heard we'll be able to hover for longer and mobility will be vastly improved.”

“As long as you’re the beta tester, man.” I smirked. “AMG Systems always messes up their first releases.”

“That’s true. Commander Pearson almost lost an arm firing one of those on-arm rockets,” said Elentos.

As we touched ground again, my Comm-link bleeped and detected a fellow marine’s dog tag. It caught my eye as it sparkled on the ground by a heap of rocks. I held the dog tag in my palm and wiped dirt from it with my opposite gloved hand. Dirt was stuck in the engravings, making it difficult to read through my visor. I scanned the tag with my Comm-link.

“This dog tag belongs to Lance Corporal, Simon Cunningham,” said the A.I.

“What was Cunningham doing here?” Elentos asked.

“Comm, tell me his current status.”

It took a few seconds for the Comm to look up this information. “Simon Cunningham’s last orders were from Lieutenant-commander Jonathan Flurwick. These orders are classified.”

“Shit!” I looked over to Elentos.

“That’s weird that we’re just hearing about Cunningham being here,” he said.

“We should inform Administrator Blake,” I said.

“Wait,” Elentos held his hand up. “Simon Cunningham has a twin brother named Charlie who just made Private First Class."

"Now that you mention it, I think I've seen him around at Earth base."

"Maybe we can ask the Administrator to patch us through to Charlie so we can see what he knows. I've seen Charlie around since Flurwick and Carrick went missing and he didn't seem like he was missing a brother."

"Good thinking," I said. "Let's hope that Charlie isn't on a mission." I put a call through to our administrator and he answered in seconds. "Administrator Blake, sir. We would like to be put in touch with Charlie Cunningham as we believe he may have some useful Intel on the whereabouts of our missing marines." I didn't mention the dog tag just yet. My hope was that Blake would patch us through to Charlie, no questions asked. If we hit a brick wall then I would tell the Administrator about the dog tag, and he would then be forced to do some digging.

"Trying to reach him now," he said. "So, what have you guys—HUH!?"

"Blake, what's wrong?" I asked.

"According to the system, Charlie Cunningham is on Nurvoa with you."

"What!?" said Elentos, repelling in shock.

"I'll send you his Comm-ID. You should be able to reach him directly." But I never got the ID, because just then the Comm-link system on my arm was shot with a laser. The screen cracked open, smoke and battery acid oozed from the shattered opening.

"Put the gun down, Cunningham!" Elentos pointed his blaster at a huge rock just above us. There was no mistaking it. Charlie Cunningham was standing on top of the rock with his gun pointed right at us.

CHAPTER 3

"**WHAT ARE YOU** playing at, Cunningham?" said Elentos. "Stand down, now!"

Charlie's eyelids thinned. "I don't wanna kill you, so do as I say."

"Charlie, what is this? What kind of Private shoots a fellow marine?" I asked.

"I'm giving you five seconds to lower your weapon." Elentos yelled.

"What are you going to do, Elentos? Shoot me?" Charlie asked. He cupped his left hand under his right to steady his aim. He then positioned his body to eat recoil.

I raised my own blaster in response. "Why was your brother here? And where are Flurwick and Carrick?" I asked, wanting to keep him talking.

Charlie's wrist twitched, "none of your business."

"Need I remind you that we outrank you? Answer the question, Private." My hands tightened around the blaster.

"Go to hell!" Charlie fired another shot. The beam whizzed past Elentos' helmet. Elentos, acting on reflex, shot the edge of the rock below Cunningham's feet. The rocks scattered beneath him, causing him to lose footing and come crashing down on the same level of rock we stood on. It was the exact shot I was thinking of making, but my blaster wouldn't have had the same power as Elentos' weapon.

I ran to Cunningham and aimed my blaster over his face. "Tell us what we need to know, Cunningham, or you'll never see the line of duty again."

Cunningham panted. "Alright, I'll tell you what's going on here. Just give me a hand will you?" He extended his arm.

Something in my mind told me not to trust him, but my devotion to my fellow marines betrayed me. As I went for Cunningham's hand it closed into a fist. He retracted blades from between the knuckles of his gloves and slammed them into my chest. The impact floored me and my suit buzzed as my electronics malfunctioned.

I was dazed momentarily, but not long enough to miss Elentos dashing towards Cunningham. My eyes refocused themselves just in time to witness Cunningham's blades shattering the side of Elentos' visor. With Elentos' visor glass busted, Cunningham slammed the blades into the side of his breather. Elentos' body hit the ground next to me.

"Elentos!" I cried. I needed to find his backup breather as soon as possible.

Cunningham stared down at Elentos, as if realizing the consequences of his actions. He shot me a glance and then he dashed forward. I raised my blaster, ready to defend myself. But before he came within the range of physical contact, he took off into the air with his boosters. I watched him elevate up the monolith, disappearing under the darkening burgundy sky.

The clock was ticking. I crawled to Elentos who was gasping for air. "No, no, no," I cried, as I searched his utility belt for another breather, but it wasn't there. "Elentos, you didn't pack a backup?" He'd instead decided to pack additional ammo. I grabbed my own backup breather and placed it carefully over his nose and mouth before hitting the switch. "Breathe Elentos, breathe." He palpitated as he took in the oxygen.

"Thank you, Wardson," he said, once his breathing had stabilized.

"Come on, let's get you out of here," I threw his arm over my shoulders and felt a sharp pain in them as I took his weight. My electronics were down, but luckily my Jet Booster had a separate power supply.

Ten minutes later, we were back at the shuttle. Elentos breathed in a fresh supply of oxygen from the inside. Our breathers pumped oxygen from a small replaceable cartridge. This meant that it was best for us to preserve the cartridge whenever we had the chance to breathe from another oxygen source.

"We need to reach Blake and let him know what's happened here," I said. "Call the Administrator," I told the shuttle.

"Sorry, Administrator Blake is on another call."

"Shit.' I looked back at Elentos, who was sitting still, breathing in the fresh air. Having no oxygen in space—for any length of time—was enough to cause long lasting trauma in the body.

"Elentos, I'm sending you back to the station." He eyed me as I spoke. "Alone," I added. He looked ready to protest but he perhaps didn't have the energy for it. "Make sure you fill in the Administrator. I don't have Comms, so send reinforcements as soon as possible, okay?"

"You shouldn't go out there alone," he struggled.

"Don't worry about me. I can hold on until you send reinforcements. I want to find out what that asshole is up to."

Elentos nodded. We saluted each other.

"Head back to the station." I told the shuttle car as I stepped out. It was much darker now, so I activated my suit's battery powered flashlights as the shuttle's light went out of range.

I heard footsteps coming from different directions that caused me to circle on the spot. Soon enough, I found myself surrounded by several Drekarth. Instinctively, my hand found the handle of my blaster. While continuing to circle on the spot, I held up the blaster to show them I was armed and ready to fire. The Drekarth stood in a circle around me, making clicking noises. The lizard-like species stood on their two hind legs with their eyes gradually glowing brighter. One of them stepped forward, its tail trailing behind it. It clicked rapidly and pointed somewhere behind me. At first, I was reluctant to take my eyes off of the lizard. That changed when I heard a mechanical sound somewhere in the distance. Charlie Cunningham was high up on the monolith, aiming a rocket launcher in the air. Aiming at the shuttle I'd just sent Joe away in.

"Stop!" I yelled. I ran towards the monolith, as if by some miracle I would be able to stop him. I heard the Drekarth moving behind me and I didn't know if they were following or chasing. I didn't even care.

My stomach turned as Charlie fired the rocket. Seconds later there was a heart shattering crash. The sky was lit up with a ball of flame. I fell to the floor, defeated by the realization that Joe Elentos was gone.

Chapter 4

A WAVE OF EMOTIONS overtook me. My hands tightened into fists as I turned to look up at Charlie, high up on the monolith. He stared down at me for a moment before walking away in the opposite direction until I could no longer see him.

Mentally, I had thrown away all camaraderie. Charlie had crossed the line and I wanted to punish him. I barged past the Drekarth that were still stood around me, and then I dashed towards the monolith, picking up enough speed to be hurled far above by my Jet Boosters. I landed a few levels short of where Charlie had stood moments ago. I continued running and jumping, making my way further up the giant rock. Charlie's loud curses filled the air as I got closer to him. He growled as though something had pissed him off. *You have no right to be upset,* I thought.

I cleared the last piece of rock with my Jet Boosters and made it to flat ground. Charlie was kneeling with his back towards me. In front of him was a glistening swirl of mist. It was like a shimmering black cloud and I'd never seen anything like it.

"Unfortunately for you, Brandon, I cannot get through," he said. "This means I have no choice but to kill you." He stood with a rifle in hand. The rocket launcher lay on the floor beside him.

I raised my blaster in response to his weapon. "Well, if this is how it ends, Cunningham, I at least need answers. I need to know what was worth murdering your own comrades for. I take it this has something to do with that cloud."

Charlie smirked. "Beyond this portal are our comrades. The ones you are looking for; including my brother, Simon."

"Are they in danger?"

Charlie shook his head. "Far from it; in fact, they will likely come back stronger than ever."

"What is it? What does it do? And why have you turned traitor for it?"

"You ask too many questions, Sergeant, and it's not my place to tell you."

"Then it's over for you, Private. You'll forfeit your pos..." Charlie fired his weapon before I could finish my sentence. The armor I'd chosen to attach to my skinsuit deflected the shot, but I knew I may not be so lucky the next time. Inside my head, I was thanking myself for equipping a heavy duty armor piece.

Charlie sensed I was about to return fire and rolled

away to avoid my reflex shot. The shot went right through the portal. I dashed forward with my boosters to close the distance between us. My intention was to engage him in close combat. He responded with more shots, which forced me to jump dodge with my boosters to avoid being hit.

Instinctively, Charlie rolled to avoid more fire. The lack of cover made us both vulnerable, to the point we had to keep moving for of fear of being hit. I needed to close the distance between us. The only chance I had was to fight him hand-to-hand. Using my boosters, I shot towards him two more times until he was almost within physical reach.

He readied his fist-blades and I made a mental note to protect my visor. Charlie tried his luck, throwing his fist my way. I side-stepped it and moved in to tackle him while his abdomen went unguarded. I was now bent over with my shoulder wrapped around his mid-section. With all my strength, I tried to take him off his feet, but he was rooting his weight to the ground. Charlie took the opportunity to slam his fist-blades into my back multiple times. The impact of these blows shredded the outer casing of my Jet Boosters and somehow he'd activated them so that they sent us flying forward into the dirt.

I was now lying on top of Charlie. The static from my malfunctioning boosters was deafening. I pressed my left forearm into Charlie's chest to hold him and then raised my right arm, ready to strike him.

Then I felt a stabbing pain rip through my shoulder that made me squirm—the same kind of pain that had plagued me my whole life.

Charlie seized the moment and rolled me to the side. He then stood and started slamming his chunky boots into my chest repeatedly. My armor had taken so much damage that his blows were piercing through to my skinsuit. I was winded, struggling to suck in the air from my breather. Pains rippled both inside and outside of my body. My eyes blurred, but not enough that I couldn't see Charlie raising his fist-blades above me. He was going to finish me. This would be the end of my legacy.

Before his blades could puncture me, a dozen Drekarth surrounded us.

Charlie spun around, realizing that they were making a stand against him. He stood; ready to take them on one by one as soon as one of them dared to approach him.

One of the Drekarth's tongues extended through the air and wrapped itself around Charlie's wrist. I heard him yell as the tongue tugged him off his feet. By now I'd caught my breath. My pain still remained, but I was able to struggle to my feet. When I'd managed to stand, I noticed that the Drekarth had somehow disassembled his fist-blades.

With Charlie disarmed, he was pushed to the center of the Drekarth formation. It was as though they were awaiting his next move. Perhaps they were giving him a chance to surrender.

"Just give up, Charlie," I said. "If you cooperate now, you can still leave here with your life."

Charlie chuckled. "None of you matter. None of you are a part of the plan. The Galactic Alliance will fall once the true power of the Milky Way makes its way here."

"Cunningham," I said, stroking my shoulder. "I don't know what the hell you're talking about, but you have a lot to answer for. Make this easy and you won't have your entire family's name thrown through the wringer."

"Your lizard friends here can't save you," he said. And then he pulled something out of a pouch on his belt. He cupped it into the palm of his hand and slammed it into the dirt. It was a plasma mine. "I'll see you in hell someday, Sergeant."

Charlie sprinted past the crowd of Drekarth. When they realized what was about to happen they all followed suit and pelted on all fours. My speed was no match for theirs. There was only so far I could push my throbbing limbs before the blast lifted me off my feet and launched me across the rock. Right into the black mist that Charlie seemed to have trouble getting into. Whatever stopped

Charlie from getting into the portal didn't stop me.

Slowly, everything faded to black.

CHAPTER 5

THE DARKNESS SWALLOWED ME. My body felt like it was crushing under heavy weight. I closed my eyes, believing that this would be my demise. All of a sudden, the darkness turned into a dazzling brightness. I was unaware of how much time had passed when I felt my body slam against solid ground. My head spun as I opened my eyes. Through blurred vision I saw trees swaying under a midnight blue sky. Sharp pains stabbed my shoulders as I sat myself up and brushed dirt off of my visor. The visor was tight over my face and I wanted nothing more than to rip it off.

My vision corrected itself and my surroundings came into view. I was no longer on Nurvoa. Nothing in the briefings mentioned a forest as beautiful as this one.

Before me was a giant tree with branches that seemed to wind around its trunk. The branches intertwined at the trees' high points and extended outward. They segmented into portions of leaves. The other trees surrounding the towering oak one looked as though they were positioned to add contrast to the master. I'd found myself on some of the most alluring locations in our solar system, but something about this setting came across as surreal.

My body turned in response to a thunderous noise behind me. The black mist that I had come through was swirling, and it was fading as it did so. Bolts of lightning shot down over it and they came so close to me that I had to roll across the grass to get clear of them.

Everything went pitch black after that. The midnight blue sky was replaced by a blanket of darkness. I sat up trying to reach out and feel my way around like a blind person. I grabbed my blaster as a precaution. There were crackling noises close by and for the first time in years of galactic duty, I felt an uncanny fear.

The midnight sky gradually returned, bringing back its natural light. "Where the hell am I?" I said to myself.

"Good, you speak Anglish too then," came a voice. I turned to see another human. He was young, slim and had shaggy blond hair. His clothes looked homemade, his shorts were trimmed unevenly at the edges and the ends of his vested jacket were cut awkwardly. On his back I could see a bow and quiver.

I lowered my blaster. "Please, I need to know where I am."

"Is that a trick question? Your other folk seemed to know exactly where they were," he said.

"Other folk?" I realized that the man was breathing openly, meaning that there was oxygen. I popped off my visor and breather and felt relieved as the cold breeze lashed against my face. "By other folk, do you mean Natalya and the others?" I asked, sucking in the fresh air.

"I know not their names, but I saw those who wore these strange garments that you wear now," he pointed, "they weren't as friendly as you though."

Lieutenant-commander Flurwick and Natalya had been known to have stern personalities, so it wasn't wrong to assume that someone would find them unfriendly. I got the sense that something more was going on here though. "Please, I have some questions. I need to know exactly where this is and where I can find some communications." I needed to report to Administrator Blake as soon as possible.

The man scratched his head, looking slightly confused. "We're communicating right now are we not? As for where you are, you're in Relaun, of course."

"Relaun? Which planet is this? I've never heard of it."

"Planet? I'm sorry but I'm not understanding your nonsense," he said. He looked at the sky briefly before continuing. "Look, I'm not sure what all that darkness you caused was about, but my father might be worrying about me. I only came here to try understanding that thing you and your people came out of."

"Where did they go?" I dropped my visor onto the ground and rubbed my face. My eyes burned from dehydration, my mouth was dry and I ached all over.

"I don't have a clue; I haven't seen them since earlier." He turned towards the trees. "Look, I have to go. Good luck with whatever it is you're planning and thanks for not killing me with your weird looking staff. One of your other people didn't hesitate to use his."

He must have been referring to my blaster. Meaning that Flurwick, Natalya or Simon had fired theirs after coming here. This was too overwhelming and I was in no shape to figure out what was going on. My electronics were offline, my Jet Boosters were damaged and I needed rest. "Take me with you," I said. "I need to figure out what's going on here."

"Hmmph..." the man grunted. "I think bringing you back to me town will spook everyone out and me father might actually behead me."

I noted his accent. The use of 'me' instead of 'my' made him sound slightly Irish, but it wasn't quite Irish. "Please, I just need to figure out where I am and why those other marines came here. If I manage to call my Administrator then I can arrange to be extracted as soon as possible."

He shook his head. "Look, you're doing me head in with all this funny talk. Just follow me, alright?"

CHAPTER 6

THE MAN HELD HIS BOW in front of him with an arrow nocked as he walked at a slow pace. His calculated movements told me that he didn't want to create too much disruption in the environment. His precautions were enough to let me know that I should keep my blaster at my side. "So, you really have no idea what a planet is?" I asked him. "Does this place refer to worlds as something different?"

The man looked around at me with his eyebrow raised. "I can tell that bringing you to town is going to be a mistake. I have no idea what you're blabbering on about."

It struck me as strange that any number of intelligent beings on a planet could have zero knowledge of the Galactic Alliance. Every *known* habitable planet had been visited and documented by the Alliance and even the most hostile species were aware of the organization's existence. There were planets not explored to their full extent, such as Nurvoa, but there were always information and communications established, even if the Alliance had no outposts. This man appeared to be human, and all human colonies in the galaxy had to have knowledge of the

Alliance.

"Please, tell me about this place you call Relaun." I said. The man stopped for a moment and held something in his palm. He placed it upside his ear as if trying to listen to it. "What is it?"

"Never mind," he said, placing whatever was back in his pocket. "Thought I heard something; as for Relaun, I don't even know where to start. Maybe we should exchange names first before I go on?"

In all the confusion, I had forgotten to introduce myself. It was common protocol for marines to announce their name and rank to strangers. "I'm sorry; I'm Sergeant Brandon Wardson of the Alliance Marines."

"So, do I just call you Brandon? Or do I have to include all that other rubbish you said?"

"Brandon is fine."

"Alright Brandon, my name is Finian Glaed. Took me mother's name," said Finian.

"Father not around?" I asked.

"Actually, it's my mother who isn't around. Long story if you know nothing of our traditions," he said. We continued to progress through the long path. "Relaun is a mysterious world that is not always so clearly understood until you're willing to venture out into the wilds. There are myths and stories about how our land was formed. Most people believe that the magical crystals keep this world together."

"Magical crystals?" I had the urge to pinch myself.

"At the center of Relaun are a bunch of giant crystals. It is believed that they are what allow us to use magic here."

I stopped dead in my tracks. "Wait, hold on a sec. Are you trying to tell me that you can do magic?" Although various species in our galaxy had unique abilities, the thought of magic was preposterous. Science ruled everything, or so the Alliance believed. "Can you pull a rabbit out of the hat or something? Or turn me into a frog?"

"You misunderstand me. I don't mean that everyone can use magic. Not all of us on Relaun are born fortunate enough to use it. Only the lucky ones are born with the gift; unless you're Elven, of course."

"Elven?" I fought the temptation to laugh. "Is this a joke? because Natalya doesn't tend to take her jokes this far."

"You clearly..." he started, before we heard a beaming noise. There was a flash of red light through the abundance of trees to our left.

"That was an Alliance weapon, I'm sure of it."

"Sounded like an Amber Monkey to me," said Finian holding up his bow. I stared at him, not even wanting to ask.

"Wardson," I heard, and then Lieutenant-commander Jonathan Flurwick stepped out of the darkness.

"Lieutenant," I saluted. "You're here." I felt relief at seeing him here before me. It would surely mean the end of this preposterous mystery.

Flurwick surveyed me, looking closely at my damaged suit and the blaster I held at my side. "At ease, Sergeant," he said, with his thick British accent.

"You're the one from before," said Finian. "You didn't seem so friendly when I last saw you."

Flurwick looked sideways at Finian before turning back to me and ignoring him. "Making friends already, Wardson?"

"Sir, please let me know what's going on here. My partner Joe Elentos died at the hands of Charlie Cunningham. He mentioned that his brother, Simon was with you."

Flurwick scratched the gray stubble on his chin. "Sorry to hear about your partner, Sergeant." I noticed the lack of grief and displeasure on his face. "The truth is, Charlie was supposed to be standing here instead of you." I remembered how puzzled Charlie looked as he stood in front of the black mist. "Is he still alive?"

"Don't worry, your friend is still breathing, unlike mine," I said.

"Watch your mouth, Wardson," said Flurwick, but

suddenly I didn't give a shit about chain of command. "Look Brandon, I'm willing to recruit you to my unit. We're operating in private, away from the Alliance. But I assure you there will be long term benefits."

"Your mission," I said as my hands shook with rage. "Your mission seems traitorous if you'd permit the murder of a fellow marine. If that's the case, I want no part of your mission Lieutenant. Just tell me how to get out of here."

Flurwick laughed. The wickedness of the laughter shook me. "Wardson, I can't allow you to leave here without you being a part of my team. You'll make a great asset to me. If you're refusing to join me, then I have no choice but to force you."

Flurwick held his right hand up to my face and I lost all control of my body at that moment. All I remember is my head tightening as if my brain was enlarging at an alarming rate. Flurwick's desires were transferring themselves over to me. Everything became a blur but I remember seeing a beam of light from Flurwick's other hand, blast Finian to the ground. I saw what Flurwick wanted from me and I was willing to allow him to command me. I was about to tell him that I would join his cause but then we both fell to our knees simultaneously.

✳ ✳ ✳

My consciousness came back slowly. "Shit, I'm still too weak," said Flurwick on his knees.

"What the hell was that?" I panted.

Looking to my side, I saw Finian sitting up, groaning. "It's coming," he whispered. Whether he was whispering to himself or not, I had no idea.

Flurwick got back to his feet and gripped his blaster. "I suppose it's easier to just kill you." He pointed his blaster inches away from my face.

"Where's Natalya?" I snapped. If this was the end of my life then so be it. I was fully prepared to meet an untimely demise when I joined the marines. I wanted to at least know that Natalya was safe before I went out; even if we weren't on the best of terms.

"Oh yes, of course," he said, smirking under his gray pompadour. "You two used to have a thing. She talked about you often, Wardson." He slammed his foot into my chest, sending me to the floor. When I looked up, he still had his blaster pointed at my face. "She's safe and under my command now. Maybe you'll remember her in the afterlife, Sergeant."

I heard movement from Finian's direction and before

I knew it Flurwick was being knocked off his feet by some creature on all fours. The only sound that could be heard was Flurwick's yelling. The feline-like creature itself seemed to make no sound as it tussled with Flurwick, attempting to eat at his face. Flurwick had a forearm under the creature's neck, directing its fangs away from him. His other hand was reaching for his blaster. Still grounded, I managed to kick his blaster out of his reach before Finian pulled me up by the elbow. "We have to leave now," he said, pulling me to my feet. I was in serious pain as I stood. I would need to find some medicine soon. Somehow, I managed to force my legs into a limping sprint as Finian guided me ahead.

I had no idea how long we ran when I heard the blaster go off. I saw it register with Finian as he glanced behind us briefly, but he didn't let it slow him down.

We eventually met the edges of the forest and I saw an expanse of grass ahead. In the distance I could see a formation of buildings. "That's where we're headed," said Finian. "I hope your man didn't kill the Pardu."

I bent over to catch my breath. "Was that thing your pet?"

"Not quite, but I think I've developed a bond with it. It isn't trying to kill me anymore."

"I would like to move on so I can get some rest," I

said, breathing in deeply to slow the pounding in my chest. "I'm a wreck right now."

"You look it too."

"If I wake up and I'm somehow still in this place, then I'm going to need you to tell me what the hell is going on around here," I said.

"I have no problem explaining myself to you," his hands were behind him, fastening his bow to his back. "It's me dad I'm worried about."

"It seems like my colleagues have caused this mess, so I would like to formally apologize to you and your father in person, on behalf of the Alliance."

"There you go about this alliance again."

"I have to ask," I said. "But was that thing Flurwick was doing to me, magic?"

"It was indeed." Finian nodded. "I believe he was attempting mind magic on you. And what he hit me with is called force magic. If you pay close attention, you can sometimes see colorful auras being released into the air when magic is used. The colors can giveaway the type of magic that's being used, but I mix em' up all the time."

"How is it possible that he can do this? Magic doesn't exist where we come from."

"Look, let's carry on. We should reach home in about twenty to thirty minutes if we're quick. You can speak to my friend at the Mages Guild tomorrow if you want to learn about magic.”

Many questions needed answering, but it was essential that we got somewhere I could rest my body.

CHAPTER 7

MY EYES BURNED as they opened to the sounds of roosters in the barn. It had been almost midnight—on the local clock—when Finian and I arrived in Corwy town. Finian had taken me right to his house, where his father was sat reading at a candle lit desk. Finian's father, Kover Braggart had scolded Finian for bringing a stranger home. Kover inspected me with his eyes of judgment and concluded that I was trouble. Finian pleaded for his father to allow me a sleep for the night. I'd jumped in and apologized to both men, putting extra emphasis on the fact that Finian had saved my life. Kover Braggart had then gone back to his seat and sat down. He'd lit a pipe and inhaled before he made the call that I could sleep in the storage shed next to the barn for the night. He didn't trust me enough to stay in the house and I suspected that he had set up precautions.

I sat up, my body still in pain from the events of the previous day. When I had stripped down to my skinsuit, I'd remembered that my smartphone was in my boot.

I wasn't able to get any service here in Relaun. I had no way to communicate with Administrator Blake or the

Alliance, or anyone for that matter. Judging by the medieval architecture in Corwy, there was no Internet, and no satellites to connect to. It seemed that even electricity was a foreign concept here. Magic was their energy, as far-fetched as it sounds. Solar power would be able to keep my device charged, so I hoped that I would be able to find some use for it. I would also need to find a way to repair the equipment on my suit if I was to be able to protect myself here. I had a limited supply of blaster cartridges, which meant I had to be selective about firing my weapon from here on.

I thought about my exchange with Flurwick. He was harsh as a Lieutenant-commander, but this was another side to him that I had never seen before. Flurwick would no doubt try to kill me if he saw me again. On top of that, he seemed to be able to use the magic that Finian had spoken about. The black mist had been responsible for bringing Flurwick, Natalya, Simon and now me into this world, and the mist was gone. There would be no back up marine units and no way out of Relaun without finding Flurwick. My only hope of ending this was to seek him out and find a way to make him see reason.

It had been a rough night of sleep and I remembered dreaming of Flurwick a number of times. The context of the dreams weren't clear, but I remembered seeing him hold some kind of black crystal. His eyes had glowed with intent as he'd stared at a shiny object. His expression was as menacing as when he'd tried to play with my mind.

The shed door creaked open and Finian stepped inside, followed by his father. "Morning Brandon, I brought you some breakfast," said Finian. He carried over a wooden serving tray. On top was a bowl of soup, some bread and a hot drink.

"You'll need your strength," said Kover. "You're going to be helping Finian with his work today. If anyone talks to you, you don't say a word. Finian will talk for you. And for bleeding cry, make sure you take those strange clothes of yours off and put these on." He threw over a pile of homemade clothes. Kover said nothing more before leaving the shed.

Finian sat on a bag of hay across from me. "I'm sorry about me father. He's worried you're up to no good."

"It's alright, I understand his suspicions. I wouldn't trust me either," I said, biting into my bread. It was deliciously fluffy and I was even devouring the outer crust—something I rarely did. Kover was right, I needed my strength. "What type of work do you do?" I asked, spooning some soup into my mouth. It was thick and spicy. It tasted like tomato soup from Earth.

"I'm an assistant merchant. That's another reason why me old man is so grumpy. I had to take me mother's name."

"Why did you take your mother's name and what does that have to do with you being a merchant?"

"Well," he pulled a small piece of metal from his pocket, followed by a dagger. He proceeded to sharpen his dagger using the piece of metal. "Seeing as you don't seem to be from here, I'm guessing there's much to explain. I'll start with human traditions."

"Go for it," I said, picking up the mug full of tea.

"I'm not aware of how things work in your parts but around here a boy becomes a man at fourteen."

I spat out my tea, but it was less due to the shock of Finian's words and more to do with the bitterness of the tea. "What is this?" I asked.

"Its Gorvey bush tea," he chuckled. "It's good for you."

I braced myself for another sip. "Continue," I told him.

"When a boy reaches fourteen years of age, he must take the Trial of Becoming. Passing the test will mean you take your father's last name, but if you don't pass you take your mother's."

"So what is your last name before you take this test?" I asked.

"Nothing; you're registered with your first name and a set of numbers. After your trial the numbers change to reflect the result. But the townsfolk used to call me Finian of House Braggart before I did me Trial of Becoming. That made it seem even worse once I failed to earn the name."

"That's not right," I shook my head. "It's as if your people think only losers should take their mother's name."

"Well, they argue that there is no passing or failing. Your last name is what determines the types of jobs you're accepted for in the town. Those with their father's name tend to have interesting jobs like hunting, working in an armory or being a part of a guild."

"Are the poor girls in your town subject to these tests also?" I asked.

"Not at all, the test is for the men. Women tend to take the more mundane jobs here by default. And it's up to their parents which name they wish their daughters to take. Lately, there has been a rise in women in the guilds though."

"Well, at least the women have some choice," I said, scooping up the last crumbs of the bread.

"Usually, the test is something like hunting a creature, crafting a weapon or assisting one of the guilders on a dangerous outing. I was prepared to face whichever one it would be."

With my breakfast finished, I stood up to throw on the clothes Kover had provided. I would wear them over my skinsuit. My skinsuit was designed to hold in my body's warmth. Warmth was something I needed to keep me in good condition. I just needed to remember to drink plenty of water. "I take it that you didn't get the kind of test you were expecting," I said, ending a moment of silence.

"Well, the night before me Trial of Becoming came around, the Warriors Guild discovered an enemy outside of Corwy. They held him prisoner and tried to interrogate him, but he wouldn't say a word. Someone on the council decided that it would be a good idea for my test to become the execution of this prisoner."

"That's a tough responsibility to put on a young person," I said.

"Indeed. They blindfolded me and walked me to the platform. They put an axe in me hand and removed the blindfold. There was an audience watching me; me father included. The pressure was too much and as I looked into the eyes of the prisoner I felt as though he didn't deserve this. I ran off the stage in tears; spent the whole day in the woods. Me father has been ashamed of me ever since that day."

"That's terrible, man," I said, patting hay off of my new fabrics. Like Finian's clothes, the edges were uneven. I could see the sleeves of my skinsuit showing beneath them. My look was certain make me seem like a weirdo, but I was adamant on keeping my skinsuit underneath, because they also improved my my blood circulation.

"Who was this enemy anyway?" I asked.

Finian stood and slid his dagger in the waistband of his long-shorts. "He was a Mutano. They're a race here in Relaun who despise humans. Humans live in fear of them because of their incredible strength."

I shook my head. "This place seems as messed up as where I come from."

"While we work, I want you to tell me about where you're from. I must say that the armor you people wear is remarkable."

"And I'll have more questions for you," I said. "To start with, what exactly does an assistant merchant do anyway?"

"Follow me and I'll show you," he said.

Chapter 8

WE JOINED A PATH that led to a giant torch-like monument. It stood atop a block of steps, surrounded by various shops with banners. We'd seen the giant torch alight on my way into town last night.

"This is the town square, and the central meeting point in Corwy," said Finian. I remembered the magnificent glow across the town that had emanated from the torch. "It's called the Luxlevis. It's enchanted so that it will provide light across Corwy every night."

"So it lights itself?"

"Indeed it does. It was first lit by Lord Jerrus, one of The Elders, thousands of years ago. It has stood here ever since."

I made a mental note to ask who Lord Jerrus and The Elders were later on. "Yesterday, you mentioned that not everybody can cast magic. How is it that Flurwick can, despite being from where I'm from?"

"Patience, my friend, I plan to inquire about that at the Mages Guild later on." A large bell hung from a wooden frame a few feet away from the Luxlevis. Finian told me it was for alerting the town in times of emergency.

Aware that I was asking too many questions, I kept quiet. Finian led me down one of the paths from the Luxlevis. We came to a large cabin surrounded by trees. "The lady I work for lives here. It's also where she trades from. She's part of the Merchants Guild."

I followed Finian into the cabin. We entered a small shelved room. The most peculiar items resided in jars all along the walls. A barrier stood before us where the owner served her customers. "I'm here, Dalice," Finian called.

Strange insect-like creatures in jars caught my attention. Some were alive and some were lifeless. There were various plants and stones. On another side of the room were steel swords, daggers, shields and maces. I circled around to take everything in, until something shiny caught my attention. I walked forward to investigate. I was then looking at a large stone with symbols inscribed all over.

"Leave it." said Finian as I reached for it. "I wouldn't touch anything you don't understand here."

A cat jumped onto the surface and stared at us. What caught my eye the most about the cat was its unusual shade of green. For a moment the cat stared me up and down as if taking in every detail of my appearance. The cat then meowed as if communicating something.

"Is this cat magical too?" I asked.

"I'll explain later," he said, right before a woman

came walking out from the back room.

"What have I told you about bringing strangers from out of town, Finian? I have items that I do not wish to be spread all across Aldeen," said the tall woman. She had to be around the same height as me and I was over six-feet tall. Her creased skin told me she had a couple decades on me.

"He's not an out of towner, Dalice." Finian paused, as if reconsidering his words. "Well actually, he is, but it's a bit more complicated than that. I am trying to help him get back to where he needs to be."

Dalice raised her chin at me. "You, stranger, tell me where you come from and why you're here."

"Umm, I come from a planet called Earth in the local solar-system..."

Finian cut in before I could carry on. "Look Dalice, it's a long story, but I found him out in Corwy forest. Someone else tried to kill him. He's just following me and helping me out until he finds his way."

Dalice stroked her cat who then purred. "You say this man is going to help you. That's good, because I have four large sacks of Medius Stones to deliver to the Mages Guild. Between the two of you, you should be able to deliver them in one journey." The cat dribbled on the surface.

"That's perfect then, I was going there next anyway," said Finian.

"Don't go bothering the mages, boy. They're not allowed to share information with outsiders anymore."

Finian crossed his arms and curled his lip. "I'm not exactly going to ask them how to become a necromancer, am I?"

The fluffy green cat hissed at Finian. "Just you be careful, boy," said Dalice. "Go around back and I will pass them to you." She disappeared into the back room.

A while later we were walking along the outskirts of Corwy. Finian and I held two heavy sacks full of mysterious stones. I had only deduced that they were magical objects. "What do these things do?"

"Medius Stones are used to extract magic from crystal deposits all over Relaun. When they're charged up they can infuse weapons, armor and other objects with magic. They're valuable to the guilds," said Finian, as we tugged the sacks uphill.

"Didn't you say the magic crystals are at the center of the world?" I said, trying hard to maintain my breath control. Despite keeping myself in shape, I sometimes struggled with simple tasks due to my condition.

"The giant crystals that power Relaun, yes; but all

over Relaun you can find smaller crystals that pillar from the ground. They're full of magic energy. If you're not careful they can even kill you."

I readjusted my grip on one of the sacks for fear it would fall out of my hand. "I've been to many worlds in the Milky Way and I can honestly say that I've never been anywhere like this." Finian stared at me with a raised eyebrow. "By the way, that cat back in the cabin, was it magical?"

"Ah yes, Parsley," said Finian. "Parsley was born with some kind of mind magic that allows him to speak to his master through a bond that they share."

"I thought so."

"Of course, Parsley was also born with his head up his arse." he chuckled.

"What about your feline? You said you share a bond with it too, right?" I exhaled with relief as we found ourselves on even ground.

Finian let the sacks rest on the ground and wiped sweat from his forehead. "If you mean the Pardu, that's a little more complicated," he said. "See, the Pardu is a legendary creature and it's quite rare to see it. The fact that it makes no noise means it's never easy to know when it is close by. During one of my trips into Corwy forest, I saw it for the first time in my life and was mystified. While I was in awe, I fell from a tree. It heard me and ran over to attack; almost killed me."

"How did you manage to get out of that exchange alive?"

"Well, while I was wrestling with the Pardu, that black mist appeared and the people like you came out. The Pardu ran off as if it knew something that I didn't."

"How long ago was this?"

"Two days ago," said Finian. If time in Relaun was measured anything close to the time back in the Milky Way then these events that Finian spoke of aligned exactly with the time of Flurwick and Natalya's mission. The classified mission they never came back from. Each planet in the Milky Way had its own time scale, depending on how it rotated; but Universal Galaxy Time—UGT—had also been established for those traveling long distance across the galaxy to follow. In UGT, Flurwick and Natalya had gone missing exactly two days ago.

Something from the previous night occurred to me. Finian had known the Pardu was coming during my confrontation with Flurwick. "If the pardu makes no sound, how did you know it was coming when Flurwick was about to take me out?" I asked.

Finian's face lit up as though he was glad that I asked. "After me exchange with the Pardu, I had its hairs all over me. I later visited me friend at the Mages Guild. Me friend was shocked that I was so close to such a legendary creature. They enchanted pieces of the Pardu's fur so that I would be able to hear it when it was nearby." That explained why Finian had held a piece of fur to his ear back when we were in the forest.

"That sounds like some serious magic."

"My friend has advanced skills, but dislikes harmful magic." Finian grabbed his sacks and we continued on. "My friend is actually a gifted healer."

"Would your friend happen to have an Aspirin?"

Finian side-eyed me. "Uhh—what's asspurrin?" he asked.

"Nevermind," I shrugged. "It looked as though the Pardu came to your aid when it took down Flurwick. Did whatever your friend do, create a bond between you?"

"I'm not sure on that myself; I'll inquire about that today."

"I hope the shot we heard from Flurwick didn't harm it."

Finian pointed me towards an alley on our left. "I hope so too."

CHAPTER 9

THE RINGING OF A small bell triggered as we stepped through the gate. "The bell uses magic?" I asked.

"Ah, you're picking things up fast aren't you? There's also a separate bell that triggers if it detects magic," said Finian.

We walked into the building resembling a large medieval town house. A gaunt man wearing jeweled rings on each finger stared as we approached. His head was bald, but streaks of gray hairs extended out from the sides. He resembled some kind of mad scientist. "What you got fer us today, young Finian?" The man asked.

"Four sacks of Medius Stones," he said, setting down his two sacks on the surface next to where the man stood; I followed his lead. In the background, two separate chimes came from the bells outside; perfectly sequenced so that one bell chimed in between the other. "That will be two-hundred-and-thirty gold, please," said Finian.

The man raised his bushy white brows before removing a small sack full of coins from his tunic. "Young Finian, you will be sent to the gallows for trying to extort the guild. We already know that Dalice is charging two-hundred-gold."

"Oh, did I say two-thirty? My mistake, its two-hundred as you say," said Finian, staring at the chandeliers above. The man placed four golden pieces on the surface, each engraved with the number fifty. The numbers were surrounded by tiny shards of crystals. Finian scooped up the coins. "Cheers, Sir Gringham. Look after yerself."

Two individuals in singed robes barged past Finian as he approached the door. One of the men was dark skinned and looked around my age. The other was older, with gray streaks in his beard.

"Sir Gringham!" One of the men yelled in panic. "Send word to Highwell that the Master Conjurer has disappeared."

"Disappeared? Tell me how this came to be, Apprentice." Sir Gringham responded.

"We have no clue how it happened, good Sir,"

"One minute the three of us were riding our horses to Brenmore." The younger apprentice continued, cutting off his partner. "The next minute we were blasted from our saddles by a wave of fire. By the time we rolled off the flames, the master conjurer was nowhere to be found."

Sir Gringham looked troubled. "I must spread the news immediately. I'll need a search party." Sir Gringham looked down at Finian as if remembering he were there. "Young Finian, while on your daily travels, I must ask you to visit the Warriors Guild and repeat to them what you've heard. They are sending out a party to Highwell two hours from now, so I would like for them to extend this news to the capital."

"Yes sir," Finian nodded.

"Please excuse us now, Finian, we have much to plan," said Sir Gringham.

Finian and I walked outside, but before we reached the gate, Finian looked behind.

"What's wrong?" I asked.

He placed a finger over his lips. "This way," he pulled on my garments and led me down a side path, towards a beautiful garden. Cylinder shaped trees were aligned, bordering five squared ponds with lilypads and strange fork-headed fish. As we walked along the trees I heard the sounds of insects; there was screeching, along with the kind of chirping that crickets made.

"So beautiful," I said, as we reached the end of the path. I saw young faces in robes sat on benches. They were facing an olive skinned lady in white robes whose right hand was glowing with a white aura. She held it in the air as if demonstrating.

"Yeah, I guess she is nice looking, but she nags me too much for me to see her that way," said Finian.

I realized that he had misunderstood my comment. "No, I didn't mean..." I started.

"Mind if I sit in till the end, Eva?" Finian yelled.

The glow disappeared as she scowled in our direction. "That is all for today. Be sure to refer to the section on progressive healing in your tomes. Next week I will be piercing your fingers so you may heal your partners."

"Actually, I don't think I want to be anywhere near this class. I'd rather wrestle an ogre than let her put a blade to my finger." Several of the students roared with laughter while the healer's face turned red.

As the young students disappeared, Finian approached his friend and I followed on. I caught her glance for a moment and felt my chest rise. Her hair was tied into a bun; her face was round and her body curvy. Her hazel eyes had a gloss that demanded my attention and I had to stop myself staring into them.

"Finian, I told you not to disrupt my lessons," she said, as she packed up her accessories from the glass table. "I also told you not to bring others here. If word gets out that I'm passing on knowledge of the guild to you both, they'll have me exiled."

"I know, Evangeline, but I brought him here because he has something to do with the mist."

At the mention of the mist, Evangeline's eyes locked onto me. My insides turned jelly for a moment. "Follow me," she said.

We walked into a small shack with a pointed roof. The shack was cylinder shaped and had a staircase on the far side that twisted upwards to a second floor. There were medicine cabinets, bookshelves and units filled with stones of different shapes and sizes. There was a warm coziness to the place.

Evangeline walked over to a teapot and filled it with water from the pipe. She then sat the tea pot down on a metal plate with coal underneath it. Her hand waved around the coal and flames shot up.

"Evangeline, meet Brandon," Finian said, walking to the center of the room. "Brandon, this is Evangeline." She walked towards me and extended her hand. As I took it in my own I felt warmness from her palm because of the fire she had just conjured.

"My pleasure," I said, trying to avoid her eyes as I towered above her.

"So, tell me what you have to do with the mist," she said, walking back to the teapot.

"I have nothing to do with it. I'm from a world that is different to Relaun." I rubbed my neck, trying to think of the simplest way to describe what happened. "I'm what is called a Space Marine. I travel around planets and complete missions on behalf of a government organization."

"I have no knowledge of what you speak," she said.

She sprinkled the contents of a jar into three individual wooden cups.

"I'm sorry, it's difficult to explain," I said.

I told her that I had been on a mission to find my missing comrades. I explained about Charlie Cunningham attacking me and killing my partner. Then, I recalled the events that had led me to Relaun; following Charlie Cunningham while consumed with anger and getting blasted into the black mist. "When I regained consciousness, I was in the forest and I met Finian shortly after."

Evangeline walked over to us with two floating cups of tea, hovering over each hand. Impressed, I took the one she presented me with and smelled the contents. "Is this that Gorvey tea?"

"It's Botterbus tea. Try it." she said. The tea was as smooth as honey going down. I felt a light-headed sensation and then I had a sudden desire to tell Evangeline my innermost thoughts.

"Please, let me tell you everything. Ask me what you want to know." I told her.

"Wait, hold on a minute." Finian shot from beside me. "Did you just give him truth serum?" What he said registered to me, but I didn't care. I just wanted to talk.

"Finian, we cannot trust this man." She pushed him back as he attempted to walk over to me. "Something bad is coming, I can feel it inside." She got closer to me and stared me in the eyes. "Now, tell me what *really* happened and why your people are here."

"It happened as I told you. I am unsure why Jonathan Flurwick, Natalya Carrick and Simon Cunningham are in Relaun. I too am curious about Flurwick's ability to use the magic here. I am also unsure why I am unable to use the magic," I was speaking every unfiltered thought that entered my mind.

"You see Evangeline, he's not lying. You fed the man truth serum for no reason. How long will the effects last?"

"Until I say." she spat. "Tell me what you want from us right now. I want to know what you most desire here in Relaun."

"I want you both to help me track down Flurwick and the others so that I can learn what he's after and why my partner was killed. I want to know that my ex-girlfriend Natalya Carrick is safe. I want to find a way back home. I want to look into your eyes..."

"That's enough." she snapped.

"By The Elders! Is this really happening?" said Finian, shaking his head in his palm. My head swirled; I was enjoying the dream-like sensation. I felt like I was about to fly up into the clouds to find peace and happiness. Then, Evangeline pushed a soft ball of leaves into my mouth.

"Swallow please," she said, tilting my head back while

standing on tip-toes. As soon as I swallowed the sensation disappeared. I wiped my hand over my face, wondering if everything that had happened was real. "Before you say anything, I want to tell you that I am sorry I had to do that. When strange people appear, I must take precautions. I had no reason to trust you."

"Was Finian's judgment not enough to go by?" I blinked.

"Yea Eva, that's not a nice way to greet a companion of mine, you know."

She turned towards Finian and for the first time I noticed how her ears pointed upwards at the helix. "You told me of the one like him that was a wicked man, torturing harmless creatures in the wilds for no reason. You haven't even known this man for a day and you're so willing to trust him?"

"I was half expecting him to destroy Corwy when we got back, but he didn't. Nothing in his actions has shown me that he's up to something. It's the Elven blood in you that makes you not trust us humans, you know," said Finian.

"I am only half, and how many times must I tell you not to make assumptions about Elven ways." she snapped. I felt her eyes back on me. "We are wasting time. Clearly you're caught in some strange conspiracy, Brandon. You say that this man you know of is able to use our magic.

This would suggest that he is somehow connected to Relaun."

"You think he was born here?" I asked.

"It is possible. But if that is so, my next question would be how he made it to your..." she paused, "to your world and back. There is no magic in Relaun powerful enough to open a gate to somewhere like where you are from. Not even tales of The Elders speak of such magic. Furthermore, nobody even knew that other..." She seemed to have difficulty in thinking up the right words, "that other worlds existed."

"Interesting," I said. "And there is no documented history of a place called Relaun in the Milky Way." I paced back and forth, thinking of everything I'd learned that day. "Earlier, when speaking with Sir Gringham, two apprentices came in talking about a missing conjurer," I said.

Finian snapped his fingers. "Oh yeah, thanks for reminding me."

"Do you think this conjurer is capable of creating that mist?" I asked.

"No," said Evangeline. "The only magical gateways that exist are designed to transport you from one place in Relaun to another. And only The Elders were capable of constructing such magic. These gateways still exist today, but even they must be recharged by Medius Stones before they can work."

I thought about this before bringing up my next theory. "Remember last night, Finian? When Flurwick struggled to use his magic on me."

"Of course."

I recalled something that Charlie Cunningham had said. *'They will likely come back stronger than ever'*, he had told me while standing in front of the mist. "Do you think there's any chance that Flurwick is seeking help to enhance this magic he has?" I looked from Finian to Evangeline.

Finian and I quickly described the magic Flurwick had used on me to Evangeline. "Hmm," she said. "It can take somebody years to learn mind magic at that level. There's no way someone with no previous connection to Relaun can be that powerful." She sat down and crossed her legs; her chin perched on her fist as she stared into nothingness. Her dedication to the subject brought a smile to my face After a short, awkward silence, her eyes darted to us. "I need to think this through and see what is happening up at the guild hall," she said. "Please visit me tomorrow and we will revisit this conversation. We will have no choice but to call a town meeting and let Brandon speak of what has…"

"No, that can't happen," Finian snapped. "The Warriors Guild will throw him in the dungeons and forget about him."

She stood. "You mean like your other friend?"

"It's not happening, Eva. We need to figure out something else," he said, grabbing my arm. "Come, Brandon."

We left the shack and made our way back to the garden.

On our way to the Warriors' guild hall, Finian led me up a back alley and into a small shop full of live animals. There were rodents, snakes, kittens, and birds. They also had various lizards and poisonous spiders. Finian explained that none of the animals in this shop were magical, because magical animals caused trouble for the owner. Finian ordered a box of freshly dead mice. When I asked him which animal he planned to feed them to at his father's barn, he told me he'd explain later. We then joined the central pathway further up from the Luxlevis and made our way to the guild hall.

The warriors' guild hall was right alongside the far end of the city walls. A watchtower was erected high above the walls, giving scouts a view of what was lurking outside the city. Two armored guards with axes stood adjacent outside the caged gate leading into the hall. They demanded that we leave because a convoy carrying artifacts was about to head for the capital city. Finian pleaded with them to let him in, as he'd had news about the missing conjurer to pass on.

"I'll have you thrown in the dungeons if you don't listen, boy," said one of the guards.

"I know who you are Ander Gailen. When word gets back to Highwell that Corwy didn't respond to the disappearance of the Master Conjurer, I will let them know that it was your fault," Finian said.

"Wait here, boy," the man finally said.

Ander returned and reclaimed his position after five minutes. He said nothing more. During this time, the two guards kept eying me through their helmets.

When the gate opened, the guards turned to face each other. A dozen warriors on horses with darker shades of armor poured out from the gate. Then came a large steel chest placed on a wheeled pallet, carried by two horses.

Three more warriors, wearing shiny emblems on their breastplates followed behind the pallet. The convoy stopped. Then a warrior wearing gold armor addressed the guards.

"Anything to report?"

"Nothing suspicious, Master Retgar. The young chap who works with the merchant mentioned something about a missing conjurer." Ander pointed in our direction. The one called Master Retgar, trotted over to us on his horse. "Speak of the conjurer, boy." he said.

Finian gazed at the chest on wheels; I nudged him to respond.

"Sorry Sir. On my dealings with the Mages Guild, two apprentices mentioned an attack as they accompanied the Master Conjurer. By the time they'd rolled fire off themselves, the Master was nowhere in sight. They say he's been captured. Sir Gringham wanted you to send word to Highwell so they can assist in the search."

"Shit," said Master Retgar, raising the visor on his golden helmet. Through the gap in his helmet, I could see thick strands of beard hair. A large scar ran across his right eye. The eye was a solid ball of white. "That's not good news to hear before we set out to deliver an artifact." He climbed off of his horse and faced the guards. "Ander, go and send word that we need more men. We're not going to take any chances; also tell Aribella to send me fifty silver coins for the young man." Retgar turned to face Finian once more. "Thank you for relaying this news." He then set his good eye on me, as if noticing me for the first time. "And who is this man that you're with?"

"Oh er, he's a friend of mine from Brenmore," Finian lied.

"Speak your name, stranger," said Master Retgar,

raising his chin at me.

"Brandon, Brandon Wardson," I said. I immediately regretted my obedience. I may as well have saluted him, the way I answered him as if he were a higher ranking marine.

"Never heard a name like that in Aldeen, in all my years," he stared me down. "Did you take your mother's name too?" His good eye switched between Finian and I.

"What does it matter if I did?"

I saw what looked like a smirk above the helmet's mouth guard. "This one's got some fire in him," he said, tapping his hand against my chest. "I like that. If you were a Corwy resident then I may have asked you to try out for the guild," he said. Finian was twitching beside me, and then he diverted his gaze to the ground. A dozen more men on horseback trotted through the gates. One of the men tossed a coin sack at Finian's feet. "Tell Sir Gringham that we'll send word." Retgar turned to face Finian again. "The coins are for you. Spend it wisely, boy." Retgar climbed back up on horseback and charged away.

Finian picked up the sack and turned towards me. Something in his disposition was different as he moved closer. He made no eye contact. He snatched the box of mice that I had been holding for him. "Perhaps it's best we part. It's not a good idea for me to be keeping you around here." he said. "Go find yer people without me." And then he marched off towards the bushes without another word.

67

CHAPTER 10

I STOOD PERPLEXED. After knowing Finian for a day, I'd never imagine that he'd ditch me so abruptly. He'd seemed fascinated with my predicament and I was sure he was more obsessed with solving this mystery than I was.

After watching the convoy disappear into the distance, I snuck into the bushes that Finian had run into. Plants towered over me and leaves of all colors littered the dirt beneath my soles. I wandered around aimlessly, trying to get a sense of which direction Finian had gone. I activated the flashlight on my phone and saw crushed leaves on the path to my right. I followed the leaves, assuming this to be the path he had taken. Judging by the direction, this was a secret path inside the Warriors Guild fortress.

The bushes had grown so tall that I could no longer see what was above me. A couple of times I found myself a few feet shy of stepping on traps designed to capture wild life.

Soon enough, I was losing my sense of direction and I let out a heavy sigh. My mouth was dry and my body needed water, this was made abundantly clear by the throbs in my hips; signifying that my deformed blood cells were clogging up the joint. Hydrating my blood was often enough to help these joint pains pass, but there was always the risk of it escalating and sending me into what was known as a sickle cell crisis.

Should I give up? I thought. Even if I did, where would I go from here? Could I go back to Kover's barn? Knowing that both he and his son didn't want me there? Maybe it was finally time to face the music and seek out Flurwick on my own.

I was wasting time. As a marine, I should have been focusing on completing my mission, not chasing strangers. I decided to return to the barn and grab my equipment.

As I turned to go back, I dropped my phone and heard it collide with something solid. I rushed to pick up the phone, worried about damage. There was a small chip at the bottom corner, but besides that it was still intact. It had taken worse beatings than this. I pocketed the phone and felt the metal surface beneath me. Brushing away leaves, I quickly discovered that it was a trapdoor leading down into the uncanny depths of Corwy. I locked my fingernails into the crevices to lift it but it wouldn't budge. I rubbed my fingers over the surface again and felt some engravings. I reached for my phone and activated the light. A message was revealed...

It appeared that even in Relaun, passwords protected the darkest of secrets. Trying my luck with passwords in a foreign land was a sure path to failure. I decided that *spilling the drink of my soul* would be easier. At least back in the Milky Way the Alliance provided us with software to decipher security systems. Either that or they hired hackers.

I grabbed a small twig with a sharp end and opened up my left hand. I forced the twig into my palm and dragged it until I felt a stinging sensation and saw my blood leaking. "Wonder if they have tetanus shots here," I said to myself. I held my bleeding hand over the surface and readied myself for something to happen. The metal door creaked upwards in a mechanical fashion. Inside, a ladder led down into the chilling darkness. There was no way to be sure that Finian was down there, but my curiosity was enough to have me forcing my legs down the ladder.

Light revealed itself before I hit the floor. Stone walls surrounded me and wall sconces were mounted along pillars on the path ahead.

Before I could proceed, a fleet of critters swarmed me. They surrounded me until I was forced to close my eyes;

for fear that one of them would fly right into them. The pests clung to my skin and a prickling on my palm told me that they desired my blood. I clenched my fist tight and tried to pat them off with my free hand. In my moment of chaos, I felt my heel press onto something solid that slid down into the floor like a button.

Suddenly, I was netted against the wall right beside the ladder. The critters crawled over every inch of my body as I struggled to free myself. They were flocking down my arm, desperate to find the source of the blood.

"Get off me!" I cried, as I slammed my fist against the wall in frustration. Some of the critters had taken the opportunity to slip into my mouth and I blew air between my lips to spit them out.

The netted fabric was thick with tiny holes. I pressed my foot against the net in attempt to shift whatever was binding it to the walls.

After some time, I felt movement beside me and although I couldn't see anything, I felt a tear in the net. Then, my body fell forward against the stone floor.

Cold water splatted me; sending me into a fit of shivers. "Shouldn't have followed me here," said Finian, standing over me with a bucket. The critters were now reduced to black dots plastered all over my body.

"What the hell were they?" I asked.

"Blood Mites; put them down here meself," he said,

"same with the net."

"Why?" I stood.

"Well, once a trespasser sheds his blood, the Blood Mites will flock to them won't they?" He shrugged. "Nobody uses this entrance to the dungeons but me. And I want to keep it so."

"Well thank you for the bath," I said, through gritted teeth.

"It's Minus Water. It can be a real life saver in the worst of situations." Finian's mood seemed to have shifted.

"Why did you leave me? What did I do to deserve this?" I asked, removing my overcoat.

Finian placed the knife he had used to cut me free into a sack tied on his hip. "Look," he said. "I'm sorry about that, alright? It's just that all I've ever wanted to do is be in one of the guilds. It's been my dream since I was young. And then you come along and they're telling you that you should be part of the Warriors Guild. Meanwhile I'm treated like some scrub." He handed me a piece of cloth to wipe the mite remains off my skin.

"Finian, understand this," I straightened up and looked him in his eye. "It doesn't matter what anyone thinks of you. It's your actions that will shape how people view you in the end. If it wasn't for you, I wouldn't have lasted an hour here in Relaun. To me, you've shown nothing but bravery by trusting me; especially given the fact that your father judged you for it. You've shown more strength to me than anyone else I've met in this town so far."

"Why thank you." He scratched the back of his head. "That might change in a minute or two though."

"What will?"

"Me showing you the most strength."

"How so?"

"Follow me," he said. We walked alongside the pillared walls and turned at an intersection of corridors. "The reason I came here is to visit a friend of mine. The dead mice were for him and I'd given them to him when I heard you making a racket back there."

"Your friend is a prisoner?" I asked, registering the fact that we were in a dungeon.

"He's a forgotten prisoner actually," he said. We walked by a bunch of vacant cells. A couple of them were occupied only by chained skeletons. We stopped by the end of another corridor in front of a particularly large cell. I heard feral sounds of eating and as I gazed into the cell, I noticed a large shadowy outline. "Remember I told you that I was to execute an enemy for my trial?" Finian asked, as the figure walked into the light.

"He's still alive?" I gaped. The bulk of the prisoner was intimidating. His skin was a dark shade of blue and he was full of tribal tattoos. His face was human-like, with yellow eyes and a thick beard. Curled horns encircled either side of his head and dreadlocks draped down to his chest.

"Brandon, meet Blok," Finian said, as the beast growled.

"Why bring another?" Blok's voice vibrated through the corridor.

"Calm down, big fella, we can trust him. He's from somewhere far away from here, just like you. Except, you're still from Relaun, and he's from somewhere completely different." Finian's hands swayed as he tried to explain. "But that's beside the point."

"How is it that they kept him alive?" I asked. Blok roared at me as I asked the question. "Not that it's a bad thing, of course." I shrugged.

"Well, after me Trial of Becoming. I was the talk of the town. Everyone was so disappointed that I didn't kill him and that's all everyone was talking about. My guess is that after the test, they chucked him in here to deal with him later but then forgot about him. People started assuming that the guild had executed him."

Blok was revealing his black gritted teeth, as if willing me to try and do him harm. "How long have you been visiting him?"

"Well, me test was four years ago now." Based on the fact that children were forced to take the trail at fourteen, this meant that Finian was now eighteen. Two years younger than me. "I was an outsider after that day," he continued. "I wanted nothing more than to find somewhere to escape so nobody would find me. And I make it my business to know every hiding spot in Corwy, so I'd found the trap door leading down here when I was eleven. But after me test, I tried to figure out the secret word to get in. It took me two hours, but I figured out that the word was Rorith, the name of Lord Jerrus' eldest son. I made my way down here and found Blok," Blok grunted, his eyes following my every move. "He wasn't hostile towards me; probably sensed that I wasn't a threat."

"The boy is good human." His voice ripped through the hall and I wondered how all this noise didn't travel up to the guild hall above.

"I'm not a boy anymore, Blok." Finian rolled his eyes. "Anyway, from then on I decided to feed him and keep him company, since no one else would."

"What kind of creature is he?" This time I anticipated his roar so that it didn't catch me off guard.

Finian ignored Blok's display of anger, as if this was normal behavior for him. "Blok is a Mutano. He's not a creature. In Relaun, there are three types of beings; humans, Elves and Mutanos." Blok grunted again. "Elves believe that Mutanos aren't real beings because they can't use magic. Of course, there are also humans that can't do magic, but at least our species is capable of it to some degree. It's the fact that all Mutanos are unable to cast magic that makes the Elves see them as nothing more than animals." Finian looked over at Blok, who seemed willing to let him finish speaking. "And Mutanos dislike Elves because..."

"Because what?"

"Well, Elves are snobs. They're so gifted with magic that they feel superior. The tension between the two races went on for years, until war ensued. To be honest, it was the Mutanos who started the war." I waited for Blok to disapprove of Finian's claim but he was silent. "They invaded Aldeen to take the land from us humans. The Elves decided it was the perfect time to fight the Mutano tribes. They claim they did it for us, but I think they saw it as an opportunity to eradicate the Mutanos."

Being an Alliance marine, I was no stranger to warring species, but Finian had me hung on every word as if this was some juicy gossip. "Of course, humans sided with the Elves; and combined, we were able to push the Mutano tribes back to their lands in the north. The war ended when Elven forces went over to Ogesh and defeated their Chief. Since then, the Mutanos have despised Elves and humans. And humans have lived in fear of the Mutanos returning to Aldeen."

"Hence why your people were so spooked when he

showed up," I added.

"Spooked, yes," said Finian, as if not understanding the word. "Anyway, Mutanos usually murder humans on sight. And humans fear their raw strength."

"What exactly was he doing here?" I asked, and again Blok growled.

"You can ask him questions too you know, he won't bite."

"I will!" Blog slammed his palm against the bars and for a second they all shook.

How the hell hasn't he broken free? I thought to myself.

"Don't listen to him, he loves us humans. Blok's story is like mine you see. Blok's tribe exiled him for disagreeing with their blind hatred of humans. For whatever reason, Blok seems to like us and wishes to do no harm."

Watching Blok eye me with murderous intensity made me think otherwise. "Are you sure?"

"He doesn't trust you yet, that's all. You have to understand that I'm the only person he's spoken to for four years."

"Him smell different," Blok pointed at me.

"Well, I wore new cologne today," I smiled.

"What?" Finian asked. Blok's eyebrows creased as if he thought I'd insulted him.

"Nevermind," I shrugged. "I forgot where I was."

"Blok, I'm afraid it's getting late and I still need to figure out what to do about this one," he pointed at me. "Father didn't want you staying another night, to be honest." Finian was avoiding my eye even though the statement was directed at me.

Blok walked side to side in his cell. "Bring cat tomorrow and don't bring other man."

"How many times do I have to tell you that I'm not bringing you a dead cat? Cats are loved creatures here in Aldeen."

"Cat taste good."

Feeling brave, I walked over to Blok. He growled and showed his massive clawed nails as I got closer. "Look, I know you don't trust me. I want you to know that a friend of Finian's is a friend of mine. I have my own mission here in Relaun, but if there's any way I can get you out of here, I will do so."

"Blok not need other man."

I held up my hands. "I'm just being nice."

"Finian-boy is Blok only friend." He growled. It was a challenge trying not to laugh as he spoke his broken English.

Back in the Milky Way, our Comm-links had built in translators that could translate every language in realtime. Translators also cleaned up any misspoken words if a species was trying to speak a native language. But even if mine was functional, it wouldn't work in Relaun, because nothing about this realm existed in our databases.

"Come on, let's go, Brandon," said Finian. "See you tomorrow, Blok."

As we walked back up the corridor, I heard Blok repeat the words, *I want cat,* several times.

CHAPTER 11

I'M NOT SURE WHAT woke me. An uneasy feeling had come over me that told me something wasn't right. Finian found me a place at the local Inn, so I was more comfortable than the previous night. He'd used the coins he'd earned, even though I'd advised him against it. The room was small and full of wooden furnishings. Not exactly cozy, but comfortable enough given my situation.

Deciding that I couldn't get back to sleep, I activated the torchlight on my phone. My eyesight was usually good at night time, but not in this windowless matchbox of a room. We'd managed to haggle with the Inn Keeper because of the lack of a window. Finian had made sure the Inn Keeper knocked the price down a few silvers. The room was only illuminated by candles that sat in the corners of the walls and the two chandeliers that hung from the ceiling.

My intuition rarely failed me. Marine life had given me the instincts to know when something was brewing. I knew Flurwick was out there somewhere and that it would only be a matter of time before he made a move. It was these feelings that ensured I wasn't caught off guard when a shuddering crash brought me to my feet.

The Inn was north of the Luxlevis and my room was on the south side of the building. The point of impact had come from behind me, which told me the noise had come from the direction of the city gates.

I kicked my chest open to retrieve my equipment that Kover had packed for me. I stretched into my skinsuit and kitted myself with leg and arm pieces of armor. Something told me that I would need to be fast on my feet, so I refrained from equipping my chest piece and my visor, which would have piled on more weight.

I holstered my blaster and forced my hands into my combat gloves. There was one more energy cartridge at the bottom of the chest and my blaster already had a half full cartridge equipped. My shots would need to count.

As I entered the corridor I saw guests flocking outside their rooms to find out what the commotion was. Many residents eyed me as I flew down the stairs to the lobby. The Inn Keeper was watching through the open door that led outside.

His face shot towards me as he heard my footsteps. "Something bad is happening. It looks like the Undead are invading again, but even they don't possess the power to knock down our city gates."

"What exactly are these Undead?" I asked.

"What kind of question is that? And where do you

hale from young man?" His eyes looked up and down my body.

"Nevermind that; tell me if there's an easy way to take out these Undead." I asked.

"Fire or healing magic, and lots of it," he said. "But you can't do anything about it yourself. We'll have to ring the bell to notify the guilds." As he said it, another crash had us repelling in shock.

"I have to get out there. Trust me; I do this for a living where I'm from." The Inn Keeper's eye's bulged as I brushed past him and ran to where the Luxlevis stood in all its beauty. Ahead of me I saw flames dancing over crumbled heaps of giant stone. The level of destruction was unsettling.

A wave of mutilated and unconscious looking corpses was marching in my direction. Their eyes glowed like fireflies. Judging from their build, there was no way these Undead had destroyed the walls. They were just like zombies from popular fiction back in the Milky Way, except these ones were real. Seeing them ripping apart the surroundings, right before my eyes was surreal. It was like I had suddenly been warped inside of a video game.

I took my blaster from its holster and extended it out into a laser-rifle. Once the scope popped up on the top, I glanced through it and saw the wave of Undead had spread out towards Finian's farm. I had the urge to take out a few of them with precision shots, but ringing the bell was more urgent.

While dazzled by the light of the Luxlevis, I managed to reach under the body of the bell. I tried to swing the clapper, but it wouldn't budge. Only then did I notice the message carved into the wooden frame holding the bell.

"Place your hand on the frame and the bell will realize the danger that looms."

After a faint touch on the frame, the bell's vibration almost knocked me from my feet. The bell would wake anyone who had been able to sleep through the chaos.

Now it was time to face the Undead before they claimed any lives. I hoped the guilds would swing into action at any moment, but I wasn't going to stand and wait for them; especially when the Undead were so close to Finian's home.

My odds of surviving an assault on the Undead were slim, but with a vantage point I could control the hoard to keep them from spreading down the alleys. I just hoped I had enough shot capacity in my cartridge.

I picked up a ladder posted up horizontally along the walls of the Inn and then I set it up vertically along the wall. The ladder was a few inches short of the edge of the rooftop, but a long limbed guy like me would have no issue climbing up the rest of the way. The Inn Keeper came to the door below and stared up at me as I climbed the ladder, his mouth agape. "Get back inside, it's not safe." I yelled as I ascended onto the flat roof.

"Don't trouble my plants," he said, and then I heard the door slam. Only once I looked behind me did I notice the assortment of plants that he had been referring to. I took a kneeling position and rested my right arm aside my knee. Through the scope, I saw the Undead marching forward, getting closer to the Luxlevis. Some of the Undead were merely skeletons brandishing armor, shields and weapons. Others had torn flesh that was peeling away. There were many gruesome looking zombies with lopsided eyes, or eyeballs hanging out and other deformed body parts.

My scope hovered over one of the mangled monsters heading for Finian's farm and I pulled on the trigger. The beam hit its skull and I watched the monster disintegrate into glowing red particles. The Inn Keeper said that only fire or healing magic would work on them, but he knew nothing of advanced Milky Way artillery. I continued to fire upon the strays until only the central horde remained. Soon, the LED on my weapon told me that the cartridge was nearing emptiness. As the Undead approached the Luxlevis, I unloaded on the front lines, creating a pattern of red blemishes.

Suddenly, I heard battle cries coming from the direction of the guild halls. They had finally assembled to defend their town. I peeked over the corner of the rooftop and saw an army of warriors almost as big as the Undead's; many of them wielding flamed torches with round shields on their opposite arm. Mages in robes carried staffs, and archers took positions on rooftops on the surrounding buildings.

Judging by my outings with Finian earlier that day, Corwy had many side paths that could be used to flank the Undead horde. Part of me was hoping that the guild forces had put together flanking teams to help them quickly take control of the battle. To win a large battle, you needed to have control of the entire battlefield; I'd learned as much during my time in the Alliance. But the Undead had come unexpectedly, and the guild forces hadn't had much time to respond. Because of this, it was entirely possible that they were just planning to face the horde head on with brute force.

Fire arrows were beginning to tear into the front lines of the horde. Flames spread around their bodies, burning surrounding monsters. The warriors positioned themselves by the Luxlevis and knelt with their shields before them. Then, mages stood beside them aiming their staffs at the zombies. Seconds later, waves of flame devastated the monsters until only the backlines of the horde were seen. But more and more of them emerged through the gates.

I slammed a new cartridge into my blaster and pulled in the handle to morph it back into its pistol form. What I was planning to do next was join the warriors below, but before I could descend the ladder the normal way, a familiar whistle rang through the air. The kind of whistle I'd heard before seeing Joe Elentos blasted to smithereens.

My weight shifted from under me as a rocket came crashing into the Inn. For a moment I felt weightless as my body was lifted into the air. It felt like slow motion in a movie, because as I was falling I had enough time to wonder whether this fall would lead to my death, or whether I'd be crippled for the rest of my life. I also registered the fact that the rocket had come from an Alliance weapon, and that it was entirely possible that Simon, Natalya or Flurwick had seen me up on the roof.

My body hit something solid and I felt a secondary thud before realizing that I was no longer falling. Voices and footsteps surrounded me. When I looked up a bearded warrior had his blade pointed at my throat. "What in the name of Jerrus are you?" he yelled.

"I'm trying to help," I gasped. The fall had hurt, but I was so used to pain that I possessed an abnormal threshold. "I was sniping some of the Undead from the roof." I had to yell for him to hear me over the cries of battle. I was worried my uncommon appearance would lead him to think I was the enemy, and thus entice him to slit my throat.

The warrior held his hand out. "Not sure what sniping is, but if it's help you're offering, we may need it," he said. I took his hand and brought myself to my feet. "That's an odd choice of attire." He pointed.

"Yeah, I guess it is." I replied, knowing that our ideas on what constituted as armor differed.

The second blast had created space for the Undead to attack the front lines of the guilds. The enemies were pulling closer towards us. Some were actually climbing the Luxlevis. My stomach turned as I saw a few guild warriors having their flesh eaten.

My bearded ally and I found ourselves cornered into what remained of the Inn. "Let's see what you can do," he said. He bashed the approaching Undead in the chest, knocking it back and then he chopped off its left arm. I noticed that the arm was twitching on the ground. Another Undead lurched towards me but I swerved its arms and swept it from its feet by slamming my arm into its chest and tripping it on the back of my knee. I followed up with a shot from the blaster.

When I glanced at my bearded friend, I noticed flames dancing around his blade. A pulsating glow illuminated his hands where he held the hilt. The weapon was being enhanced by magic. He struck the armless Undead in the heart, and it fell into a bundle.

"I need to get me one of those." I said.

"Looks like you've got something that defies all knowledge of magic there, boy," he nodded at my hands.

It was then that I remembered the rocket. The reason I had come crashing down here to begin with. The reason I was stuck in Relaun to begin with. "I need to get behind the horde of Undead," I said. "They're being led by people I know." I regretted the statement as I was saying it. Sometimes I was too forthcoming for my own good.

The bearded man stepped towards me, blade first. "If I find out you've got something to do with this here invasion, I will behead you myself. Do you hear me?"

"I promise you that I didn't start this. But if you help me get close to the gate then we can get to the bottom of it."

Just then, an Undead creature jumped onto his back. His blade clanged on the floor and lost its flame. The man bent forward trying to flip the Undead body off of his back. The monster was desperately trying to chew into his neck. My shoulder throbbed once again as I held up my blaster, trying to find a shot that wouldn't harm my bearded companion.

For a split second, the monster's head was still, as his mouth opened wide to take a bite. Seizing the moment, I pressed the trigger and watched the monster dissolve. Relief brought the man to his knees once he realized the monster was no more.

The man panted on the ground for moment and then took his blade. "Baron is me name," he said, rising to his feet and approaching me.

"Brandon," I said, shaking his hand.

"Follow me and we'll take a side route that bends around to the gate. I expect that some of them would have spread around the town, so be on your guard."

Baron led me up a path behind the—now collapsed— Inn. As I saw the wreckage, I felt sorrow for how many people inside must have been crushed. I promised myself that I would claim justice for every last one of them.

CHAPTER 12

MY CURIOSITY WAS AT PLAY, as I watched the sword glisten in Baron's hands while marching down the side path. "How do you use the flames on your sword?" I asked.

Baron scowled at me. "Have you never seen a weapon enhanced by Medius Stones, boy?"

"I haven't," I replied. "And I am twenty years old now. I may have a baby face, but I no longer qualify as a boy."

Baron raised an eyebrow. "The mages issue these enchanted weapons to us, you see. This weapon is a bit special though. It's bound to me. It feels my spirit to know when I need its magic. They don't all work like that. Sometimes they're activated by a word. Sometimes they're activated by tightening your grip on the hilt. It all depends on the level of magic the one who carries out the enchantment possesses in them."

"That's fancy," I said.

"The real question is what in the name of The Elders are you wearing? And where'd you get that small staff you were using? You must know some advanced magic to be able to rid the Undead so effortlessly."

"It's a long story." I paused, believing I'd heard something.

"What's the matter?" Baron asked.

I held a finger to my lips to indicate silence. I paused my breathing to help enhance my hearing, all so that I could locate the source of the noise I'd heard over the rustling of the bushes beside us. I counted to thirty in my head before deciding that I must have been hearing things. "Guess I'm hearing things."

"We'll proceed slowly," he said.

We were now walking down a dirt path behind the aligned buildings of Corwy. On our left was a line of trees and bushes. Long poles alight with fire stood erect down the side of the path. We had good visibility and I figured we would be able to see anything approaching. How we managed to be ambushed, I didn't know. All I knew was that before I had time to register it, skeletons brandishing daggers, spikes and swords surrounded us.

They knocked us off our feet before we had time to react. We managed to force ourselves up, only to be backed against a wall.

"If I die, it shall not be by your hands, you filthy abominations!" yelled Baron. And then he removed something from his waist. I didn't see what he possessed, all I knew was that he threw it at the feet of the skeletons and then they stood frozen before us. I felt the chill emanating from them. Baron's blade lit up and then he swiped it across the entire line of skeletons, reducing them to shards of ice.

"I hope every guild warrior is this well-equipped," I said.

"Only the ones that know how to haggle enchantments from the mages," he said. And then we felt a vibration beneath our feet. I wondered if it was another rocket, until I saw a creature as tall as the trees emerging from a dimly lit side passage. Baron's mouth hung open as we looked upon what seemed to be a giant ape. I watched it stroll towards us with a vicious look in its solid white eyes. It walked on all fours and as it roared sparks flew from its mouth. "Mother help me, it's an Undead Amber Monkey."

"Looks more like an ape than a monkey," I said.

"This is no time for smart comments, boy. I will catch its attention from the front. While I do that, get around its back and start firing." He said, directing me with fluttery hand movements. "You hear me?"

"Roger, let's move."

"It's Baron, not Roger." He dashed forward, right into the path of the Amber Monkey. I pressed my back against the wall and crept along it, trying to go unnoticed. The Amber Monkey shot a burst of fire at Baron. He used his shield to protect his body from the fire, but by the looks of the shield, it would not survive another round. As I got into position, I saw the Amber Monkey hurl its gigantic fist at Baron. He evaded the assault and wedged his blade into its hand. The creature stood on its two feet and roared at the sky with the blade still stuck in its hand. Baron was now unarmed, unless he had something else up his sleeve. I aimed my blaster at the back of the ape's head and fired. Each shot deflected off the monster; what shocked me most, was that it showed no sign of realizing that it had been shot at.

Still on its two feet, the Amber Monkey combined both his fists together and slammed them down onto Baron.

"No!" I cried. There was no way he could have survived the attack. The Amber Monkey turned to acknowledge me after hearing my cry.

Realizing that it was ready to finish me next, I started to back up with my blaster aimed at it. I saw the bundle that was Baron's body behind its legs. "I'm sorry," I said.

With the monster facing me, I had two weak spots to target: its eyes.

The beast was getting so close that its stench clogged my throat as it revealed its teeth. Its eyes looked plain and distant, as if all its normal consciousness no longer existed. Its jittery movement made it difficult to aim, but I had to be fast and precise.

As it raised its arms for an attack, I took my shot and caught it in its right eye. The ground shook beneath me as the monster recoiled in pain. Its left hand cupped its right eye and fiery sparks fell from its open mouth.

I fired at the left eye but missed the shot because of its swayed movement. Although its eyes were solid, with no iris, I could sense the exact moment that it looked upon me with pure rage. Its teeth clenched together, its lips curled and its nose wrinkled. The beast swung on me with its right hand and I fell backwards to avoid it. My blaster was far out of my reach when I saw the ape's mouth open up wide. Flames emerged from the back of its throat and I realized that this blast would burn me alive.

"Not today, dead breath," someone yelled. An arrow jammed itself into the ape's neck, cancelling its attempt to rain fire down on me. The monster stumbled back and forth with its hand on its neck for half a minute; during which time I looked up to find Finian on top of one of the buildings with his bow in hand. After some time, the Amber Monkey fell backwards into a heap and became lifeless.

Finian held his thumb up to me and I saluted him. "Your timing is impeccable," I said.

Finian climbed down, using the fence below the building for a safe descent. "One of the perks of being an assistant merchant is having access to some of the deadliest poisons in Aldeen. That one was called Deathly Blight; brewed by a well-known alchemist in Highwell."

"Sounds impressive; but I must say that I owe you a great deal for saving my life again," I said embracing Finian in a handshake.

"We must..." Finian started before hitting something with his foot. It was Baron's sword.

I picked it up, "it must have fallen from the monster's fist." As I held the sword, I looked over at Baron's body, just feet away from where the ape laid sprawled. "He mentioned that this weapon was bound to him, he should be buried with it."

"I would actually suggest that you keep it. You may need it," said Finian. "If we survive this night then you can unite the sword with his body."

"Understood," I said in agreement.

"Brandon, you must follow me. I saw the ones like you. They were leading the Undead and they're looking for something."

"Lead the way," I said, picking up my blaster.

"I guess I finally know what an Amber Monkey is," I

said, following Finian down the path.

"That was the Undead version."

"Where do the Undead come from?"

Finian's head jerked in my direction. "It takes some powerful dark magic to create Undead. I am unsure on the actual process. I just know that the mage gives the bodies of the dead new life. For an army of Undead to be formed, they would either have been lurking for many years until they banded together, or a group of mages got together to create the army all at once."

I thought about that and what it could mean, until we came to a bend that went up hill. I could see the edge approaching and Finian told me that there was a small drop that would put us west of the Corwy entrance.

On the approach to the bushy drop point, we heard shouts not to far away. Finian held my shoulder, gently pushing me into a crawl. We proceeded forward on our knees, elbowing our way towards the edge of the path.

"I'm sure he's here. I could have sworn I saw him on that damn building. If he's here, I want you to deal with him." I heard. The voice was male. He was yelling as though he couldn't hear himself over the sounds of battle. "I'm going to find the artifact. I will bring the remaining apes with me for backup. That should be enough force to get me into the guild hall. You patrol the Square and be on the lookout for your boyfriend."

"He's not my boyfriend," said the voice that I hadn't heard in eight months.

"Natalya." I whispered. I felt Finian's glance beside me.

"Just obey your orders," said the man who could only be Simon Cunningham. That wasn't Flurwick's voice.

We heard footsteps fade away until only steel on flesh and the groans of the Undead could be heard. When the coast was clear, we rose to our feet. "The chest," said Finian.

"Come again?"

"Retgar and his escort were delivering an artifact to Highwell. That's what your friend is after."

"He's not my friend," I replied, "but your theory checks out." I had already forgotten about Retgar and the chest. It was a good thing that Finian was thinking on his feet. "That means they've caused all this chaos for nothing. Men and women are being murdered for something that isn't even in the town walls anymore. I've never known marines to be so carefree when it comes to civilizations. I have to get to the bottom of this and stop them."

"Well, I'm going to check on me dad. Last I saw him he was retrieving his old enchanted weapons from his underground hideout. He's so hard-headed and stubborn that he'll throw himself into the middle of the battle. He's too eager to die for Corwy."

"Like father, like son," I said. "You shouldn't have risked coming to save me. Anything could have happened to you."

"Oh, plagger-poop!" he said, and I raised a brow. "I make it my business to be where I shouldn't be."

"Well, you shouldn't be here. And I mean it." I approached the small drop. "I'm going to track down Natalya and find out what's going on here. You should try and alert some of the warriors about Simon's plan to infiltrate their guild hall. With any luck we'll be able to make them call off this attack and we'll interrogate them both."

"You sound like a guild master." He walked to the edge of the drop beside me. "Perhaps Retgar was right about you."

We dropped simultaneously to the path below, ready to separate and follow the plan.

My ex-girlfriend was perched atop arched tree branches within the perimeters of Kover's farm. She had a perfect sniping posture with the way she positioned herself. Her legs spread upon a branch underneath the bark that held the majority of her weight. Her upper body rested on her padded elbow, allowing her to aim down her scope. Natalya was well recognized for her sniping skills. As far as I knew, she'd never missed a shot. Administrators went out of their way to assign her missions in areas with large terrain.

Watching her now, made me sick to my stomach. I shook my head, watching her scanning Corwy, taking shots at warriors and mages.

Natalya had always been stern. Being born on a colony in Venus made her feel superior to Earth humans. Her snobbish view of the galaxy had created conflict in our relationship.

Even when considering all the things I disliked about her, I could never imagine her defying the morals of a marine. Watching her murder innocent people with no remorse was unfathomable.

I edged forward, knowing that if she was alerted to my presence, she would take my head off within seconds. My body felt shaky from the fear that a zombie would jump out at me and give away my position. My movements became more calculated to compensate for the shaky anxiety and the reoccurring joint pains.

My blaster ammo was tested on various materials. It couldn't burn through metals so easily, but it could put a dent in it. Tree bark on the other hand, could be cut through easily depending on its thickness. No matter the level of hatred I felt for Natalya at this moment, I didn't want to hurt her. I just needed her on the ground, where I could engage her up close, without drawing the attention of the horde and without her being able to blow my head off.

My arms twitched as I aimed to the left of her boot. It was rested on a branch curving outward. The way her body stretched across the branches made her resemble a spider in a web. Shooting out the branch that held most of her weight might cause her to hit the ground too hard and I wanted to ensure she landed safely; she definitely had the reflexes for it. But there was no way to make this any easier, the longer I deliberated, the more Corwy locals would pay for it. So I took the shot, feeling the sharp burst in my palm. For a split second she looked directly at me before the branch fell from under her. She fell flat on her front and a loud crash came from the wooden fence that she hit on her way to the ground.

I sprinted forward to grab her before she could recover. Before I could reach her, I felt the impact of something pelting my shoulder. She had shot me with her signature self-made revolver. During the second I took to register this, her legs twirled in the air. She lifted herself into a handstand and flipped her body back onto her feet.

"You always were a show off," I said. She took aim at me again with the revolver and I raised my blaster; my shoulder burning with pain. I could feel the blood trickling out of the wound. With my ailment, the last thing I needed was to lose blood.

"Die!" she said. The tone of voice didn't match the woman I knew.

As she charged at me, I was thankful that she wanted to engage in close combat. But my injury would give her the advantage, and she knew it. Luckily, I had Baron's secret weapon hooked on my utility belt. I would use it if necessary.

Natalya threw a left hook, which I blocked with my right forearm; the pain in my shoulder causing me to growl. Air spewed out my mouth at repeated intervals as she slammed her fist into my ribs. The mixture of blood loss and fatigue stunted the level of haemoglobin in my blood, and thus, I was weakening fast. Natalya knew of my flaws and she would use them well. All her moves were calculated.

I kicked her shin and threw my weight against her by barring my forearm across her throat. She fell backwards and I fell with her. True to her reflexes, she managed to place her boot to my crotch mid-fall and hurl me over her head.

We now laid head to head, our bodies adjacent.

Strands of her dark hair tickled my scalp. "Why are you doing this?" I asked. No answer came; instead she dug her nails into my face. Her two most middle fingers blocked my nostrils while her remaining fingers poked at my shut eyelids. Her weight was on me again as she rolled herself backwards onto me. It was the pain in my body that stopped me making the witty comment I wanted to make, as I watched her body rest on top of me. It felt intimate, but her eyes had the intensity of a cougar pouncing on a prey.

Natalya choked me and I gagged while looking up at her loose strands of hair, hanging from the bun that had been neatly tied before our scuffle. It pained me to have to hurt her, but this was a matter of life and death. I clocked her with a left hook and sent her falling sideways.

As I stood, I breathed in sharply, feeling the results of her handy work. "Natalya, I hate having to hurt you."

She looked up at me with pure hatred, before rolling backwards to her feet. "I see the gymnastics are paying off," I said. She shifted into a combat stance and I followed suit, ready for round two.

Before we could continue, a horrendous battle cry diverted our attention. In the distance, Undead bodies were now flying left and right through the air. The majority of the horde began circling a huge figure, which seemed to be making short work of them. I saw mages burning through the Undead while their attention had switched to this new threat. As the figure stepped closer the Luxlevis, I saw that it was Blok, the prisoner that Finian had befriended.

"Not good," said Natalya, who was now less concerned with me.

"That's the nicest thing I've heard you say all night," I said. And then I felt my body lose all strength. My legs turned to spaghetti and I fell to my knees.

"You will be dead within an hour," she said, looking down on me. "The bullet was coated with poison. I must go now. Farewell." She moved into a jog and I watched her through blurring vision.

"Wait!" I cried, reaching out to her. "I deserve an explanation."

At these words, she walked back towards me. She knelt in front of me and cupped my chin in her hand. As her face drew closer to mine, I realized how much I missed her intimacy. As her lips hovered before my own, she turned my face to the side and pressed her lips against my cheek. "Goodbye," she whispered, as she drew away.

And then, my heart skipped a beat. Not because of lust, but because she was blasted from her feet by a yellow wisp of light.

CHAPTER 13

WHEN MY EYES CAME INTO focus, I saw the hazel-eyes belonging to Evangeline. She was now brandishing a staff in her right hand. *Had Finian summoned both Evangeline and Blok himself?*

I feared for Evangeline's life when I saw Natalya's face contort with rage. Evangeline could be no match for Natalya on a physical level.

Natalya was fast on her feet, charging towards the mage. Evangeline held out her left hand and a glow emanated that caused Natalya to stop mid-charge. She stood, rooted to the spot. Evangeline's hand glowed and her eyebrows creased together.

"Evangeline," I called.

They remained like this for what felt like minutes; until Evangeline responded. "Quick!" she said. "I do not possess the level of magic to reverse her mind warp permanently. Please interrogate her and learn what you can. She will not stay like this."

Evangeline walked over to me and helped me to my feet; throwing my arm around her shoulder. I wasn't sure how much strength I had to stay on my feet, but I also didn't want the shame of asking her to set me back down.

Natalya turned to face us and she was at ease. She seemed more like the Natalya that I knew. That I had loved.

"Please, Eva," I said. "Dig into the side of my right boot; I have a device nested in there. I want to record what she says." Evangeline was confused at the request but she followed my instruction. First she eased my body down and rested me against something solid—phew!—and then I felt her fingers fishing for something at the side of my ankle. Soon enough she was handing me my phone. She gazed at it, as I unlocked it and started the voice recorder.

"Natalya, what is going on here?" I asked.

There was little pause before she started spewing her answer. "I am to assist Simon in attacking Corwy. We seek the Elder's artifact that is being kept here," said Natalya.

"Who asked you to do this?" I panted. My breathing became heavy as I felt burning sensations inside.

"Lieutenant-commander Jonathan Flurwick," came her answer, as expected.

With her free hand, Evangeline removed something from the inner breast of her leather robes and held it to my face. "You must chew this and swallow," she said. I did as she said. Whatever it was, it tasted rubbery. It took great effort to chew. My jaw ached as I struggled to break it down. Soon, it dissolved in my mouth and I swallowed the remains. "You will pass out within the next ten minutes. Please continue your interrogation. Ask her what they want with the artifacts and where the master conjurer is. Then find out if she can stop the Undead from attacking.'

Natalya was stood, staring at us as if waiting for direction. "What does Flurwick want with the artifact?" I asked, and I realized that Evangeline had referenced the artifacts as a plural. Meaning there was more of them.

"He hasn't told me his plans in full. Flurwick knows this world is full of magic and he's not stupid enough to tell me every detail. All I know is that Relaun is a vessel for his power. Relaun is the key to Flurwick unlocking his true gift. There will be nobody as powerful as he when he returns to the Milky Way. The artifact is merely a tool needed to fulfill his plans."

My focus waned as I felt beads of sweat drip down my forehead. I found myself looking into Evangeline's eyes for direction. "Ask her how many artifacts Flurwick knows of."

"How many of these artifacts does Flurwick know about? And what's his next move?" I asked.

"Flurwick has not told me how many there are. But I know that as we speak, he is building an army to oppose the Elves. They pose the biggest threat to his plans. Indoctrinating me is helpful for him because now he has a loyal subject to be wherever he can't be. But he is practicing his magic on me, so that he may use his mind magic to control the Mutano and other forces in Relaun; ones that will be helpful to him."

"Will he try to use the Elve—-" I started, but Evangeline cut in.

"There's no way he will be powerful enough to take on the Elven kingdom or indoctrinate them. But having an army of Mutano will give him strength. The Elves have artifacts in their region, so Flurwick will need to face them soon enough." Only some of her words were registering in my head. My body suddenly felt heavier. My vision became colorful swirls. Evangeline must have felt me slipping away as she placed her hand on my chest to keep me stable. "Can you still hear me, Brandon?"

"Yes," I said.

"She is only responding to you because of your connection to her. She remembers you. Before you pass out, please ask her where the master conjurer is."

"Natalya," I said, now slurring. "Where is the master conjurer?"

Natalya moved closer. "He is with Flurwick in a camp to the west of Brenmore. Flurwick is using him for his information and as a means to enhance his own abilities. The conjurer was also used to control the Undead army."

This time I knew what I wanted to ask. "How can

Flurwick do magic? Why can't we?" I struggled to get the words out. I wasn't sure if it was the haziness in my mind, but the sounds of the distant battle seemed to have died down now.

As I looked up at Natalya, something was changing on her face. The soft rounded brown eyes were creasing into slits. The lines arching from her nose were becoming more defined. "Flurwick is one with the—" she started. Instead of continuing her explanation, she covered her face with her hands.

Evangeline left my side. "Oh no!" she exclaimed. She picked up her staff and stood ready to contest Natalya. "Stay back," she said, as Natalya looked upon her with venom.

"Ready to die, freak?" she ambled towards Evangeline. Evangeline seemed reluctant to use more magic on Natalya. She stood with the end of her staff pointed at her, taking no offensive action. She was taking small steps backwards, but she would soon have nowhere to go.

Out of nowhere, Natalya broke down screaming, her hands clasped against her head as if suffering from a migraine. "Brandon," she cried. "Help me!"

"Natalya," I called, with whatever strength I had left.

"Her mind," said Evangeline. "It's confused."

And then, Natalya fell into a bundle before my eyes.

"Natalya!" I cried.

Evangeline crawled beside her, placing fingers on her neck. "She's alive; she's just had too much strain on her mind."

Footsteps were quickly making their way towards us and I worried about what would challenge us next. I turned my head to see Blok, with Finian on his shoulders. "Brandon, are you alright?" asked Finian.

"No." I whispered. It was all I could get out.

"We should be thankful that you had a Mutano on your side," said Evangeline, rising to her feet. She walked in my direction and knelt before me, feeling my bullet wound. "I wonder if your monstrous friend will be able to stand against these horrifying weapons that his people are carrying."

"Blok not like the Elf-girl's words," came the growl of the Mutano.

"I'm only half Elven. Try not to let your prejudices dictate how you address people," she said. She prodded my wound and I felt a sharp sting, but I lacked the energy to react.

Nearby, something clanged against the cobblestoned floor. Something shiny was rolling on the ground a few feet away and I soon recognized it as an Alliance grenade.

"It's going to explode in ten seconds." The words drained me.

Blok rushed in to scoop up the ball and Finian fell from his shoulders in the process. Blok's hands were so large that the grenade could have been a stress ball to him. I worried that the grenade would blow him to pieces, but his body spun in a circle and then he hurled the grenade into the sky, where seconds later it exploded. It was a fitting night for fireworks.

"Next time, give me some warning that you're about to save our lives, big man," said Finian, rubbing his back.

Another clanging sound followed, but I was unable to locate it. Thick waves of smoke quickly rose into the air and blinded us. I was all too familiar with this smoke. Smoke that would induce fits of coughing. And that's exactly what I heard from Finian and the others. By the time the smoke hit my lungs, my body was already so weakened that the coughing was shutting me down completely. The last thing I remembered seeing were the corners of Evangeline's eyes. They were obstructed by the hand she was using to suppress her gagging.

A blur came into focus behind her and as my eyes were closing I saw a silhouette stand above Natalya and pick up her body.

PART II

CHAPTER 14

DAYLIGHT STUNG MY EYES as they opened. The sun poured through the caged windows. I sat up on the bed, grunting with discomfort. My shoulder was bandaged; my chest felt tight and my joints gave their usual throb. My body never reacted well after days full of strenuous activity, but on this day there was also the fact that my head felt like it was going to split in two, adding an extra edge to the normal pain.

During times like this, I would question my own reasons for joining the Alliance marines. I'd had it good on Earth, despite the many misunderstandings from people who didn't know about my disease. But eventually a time had come when I'd felt so alienated from what was considered a normal life that I wanted to experience the galaxy. Joining the Alliance was just the cheapest ticket to the Milky Way.

But more than that, I wanted to prove to myself and others that no matter how sick you were, nothing could dominate pure determination and willpower. Being among the youngest of sergeants in the Alliance gave me some confidence that I could endure my inner anguish and persevere.

But on those days when the pain was too much, willpower mattered little. I needed to find some form of medical relief here, or I'd lose all hope on my ability to push on with the mission.

I looked around at the unfamiliar setting and came to the conclusion that I was on the top floor of Evangeline's shack. It was the only building I'd seen in Corwy with such a wide circumference.

"Hello?" I called. When no answer came I got up and searched around for my clothes. The only thing I had on was my underwear, and I wondered who had undressed me. Men's clothes were neatly folded on a dressing table. They weren't what I wanted to wear and they felt tight on me despite my slim build. There was no other choice than to make do with what I had. Wherever my gear was now, I hoped it was safe.

I ran down the spiraled staircase and marched right outside when I saw no one downstairs. Outside was vacant and peaceful, and I appreciated hearing the birds chirping after such a horrendous night.

Evangeline was at her teaching station. She was wearing leather robes, enclosed over a steel plated chest piece. She continued clearing up her glass desk without acknowledging my presence.

"Good morning, Evangeline," I waved. "I want to say thanks for looking out for me."

She looked up at me with those eyes. "I was going to make breakfast, but something else came up," she said. "You are wanted at the town square, but first I want to make sure you are have recovered." She walked over to me and I took a seat at the front bench.

First she felt my forehead with her palm. Then she checked my pulse through my wrist. "I'm sorry but I need to check your blood," she said, taking a small needle from her robe.

Needles were my worst friend. Every time doctors demanded blood from my veins, I had to mentally prepare myself, despite having put up with this unpleasantness since my youth. I was thankful that Evangeline was able to draw my blood on the first take. Most times, my veins would collapse at the first prick of the needle. She dripped my blood onto a small pane of glass for observation.

"First time, I'm impressed," I said. Evangeline was silent.

She placed her palm over my arm and I felt a stinging sensation. I realized that she had healed the small cut with magic. When she moved her hand, there was no mark blemishing my skin. Evangeline walked over to her desk and I watched her examine my blood through her microscope. "I take it the poison is gone?"

"Indeed," she said. "Even after receiving an antidote, a person may fall sick for at least a week after. But you seem to be fine." She now added something to my blood and examined it further. "What worries me is the unusual shape of—"

"My blood cells," I finished the sentence for her.

She looked up at me, "why are they like this?"

"I have a rare blood disorder called sickle cell anaemia. My cells produce in a sickled shape and that makes them block the flow of blood in my vessels."

"But those cells carry air around your body, they are important. You must suffer great pain from this," she said. There was no denying, this girl was really a healer. She knew things on a medical level and also had the magic abilities to help people. I wondered if there were many like her here in Relaun.

"I get chronic pains frequently," I said. "Sometimes it's more serious than others. But it's something I've had all my life. I've learned to cope with it." I was eager to change the subject. "What happened after they threw the smoke grenade last night?"

She breathed in as if it pained her to relive the events. "Some mages from the guild were able to dispel the smoke. The guild leaders saw you laying there and believed you were one of the enemies. Finian and I had to plead with them not to take you. I promised if they let me heal you that you would be ready to argue your case to them once you had awoken. They have confiscated your belongings."

"Man, that sucks."

Evangeline turned her head towards me and her eyes narrowed. "I mean, that sounds bad." I said.

"You can't even begin to imagine," she said.

"I'm sorry for all this trouble. And I want to thank you again for saving my life last night. Natalya would have killed me if you didn't step in when you did."

"Your girlfriend loves you," she looked me dead in the eyes as she said this. "Her love for you was helping her fight the indoctrination."

"She isn't my girlfriend. We had something, but that was so long ago that it seems like a different lifetime now."

"Regardless, you are the key to helping her," said

Evangeline. "She is not evil. She is a victim of this Flurwick character."

"I guess I'll keep that in mind," I said, realizing that I was now standing. "Shall we head over to the square?"

"You will go alone," she said. "It no longer concerns me." I was about to ask her why; before she threw a dagger at my feet. "Guards are still finding Undead throughout the town. You must be on your guard." I picked up the small dagger. "Tightening your grip on the dagger will summon healing magic." She continued.

"A blade with healing; what, do I stab myself so I can feel better?"

She looked at me with a chilling gaze. She wasn't in the mood for my snide remarks. "The healing magic is designed to kill the Undead. They are vulnerable to healing."

"Thank you, Eva," I said.

She placed a small sack on the glass table. "Take these herbs. They should help you produce healthier blood cells. It won't cure your pain, but it's something."

"You don't know how much I appreciate this. I don't have any medicine on me, so this helps." I picked up the sack and nodded to her. "One more thing," I said.

"Why did you say this no longer concerns you?"

She looked me over and sniffed before her answer came. "I have been removed from the Mages Guild." My eyes bulged. "I will be leaving Corwy today."

CHAPTER 15

THE ALLEYWAYS WERE VACANT on my trek to the square. Undead remains lay scattered by the central path; their bodies burned to a crisp. The stench almost brought bile to my throat. Memories of Baron came to mind; the poor man who had died trying to help me find a way to my former marine brethren. Whatever they did with his sword, I would see that he was buried with it.

The entire town was gathered around the Luxlevis. A group of people were stood on the steps beneath the structure. I could see that one of them was Blok. His large outline and blue skin could be made out at a distance. His hands were bound behind his back. Finian's slim frame and blond shaggy hair also came into view as I strolled closer. Several people stood in front of Finian and Blok, including Kover, Dalice and Sir Gringham. There were four others that I didn't recognize.

"This Mutano was living in the dungeons of the Warriors Guild without our knowledge. He was being kept alive and cared for by someone within these walls," came the nasally voice of the front most figure. He was a short man with a long pointy nose. "One can only assume that it was the same person looking out for the stranger in Corwy; the stranger that dressed like those who led the Undead last night; the same folk who blasted through our walls with little effort." The man turned and pointed at Finian. "This boy has a father that I respect. As Taskmaster of the Farmers Guild, I can even say that we have considered Kover's application to join the guild and reap our benefits." These were leaders of the Corwy guilds. Finian had mentioned to me that the leaders of each guild governed Aldeen. Each town in Aldeen had its own set of guild halls, and the leaders at these halls formed a council that called all the shots in town.

"This boy, however," he shook his fist towards Finian, "was unable to earn his father's name. It shows in his actions; for he is now aligning himself with scum." Kover stared expressionless at his son.

"Just yesterday, Finian introduced me to the stranger," said Dalice. "There was something suspicious about him. Even Parsley could figure that out."

Groans of confusion came from within the crowd as I barged through in attempt to reach the Luxlevis. Within the crowd, people whispered how they'd always known that Finian was up to something. Others even went as far as saying that his mother passed down bad genes.

"People of Corwy," came the voice of another person on the steps. The axe bound behind his back told me he was either a warrior or an executioner; perhaps both. "This Mutano was able to break free from his cell unassisted. The creature is dangerous and must be executed." Blok growled and the crowd repelled so hard that I was knocked back.

"You have this all wrong," I said, finally making my way to the front of the crowd. "These are innocent people and they only seek to defend this town," I walked up the steps towards the group of speakers. "They were defending everyone gathered here today."

"This is the stranger that was dressed like them," said another of the guild representatives. Her face was slender and her ears pointed. The woman's eyes were a glistening blue and they stood out in a similar way to Evangeline's. Based on description, the woman was of the Elven race. She wore a long green tunic and a sparkling necklace draped over her black collar. A thick plat of hair lay over her shoulder ending below the breast. It was astonishing to see real Elves, existing just like how they'd been fictionalized on Earth.

"Yes, I'm the one you're talking about." I said,

trying to avoid looking her in the eye. "Please, let me explain my story."

"We must execute the Mutano right away and then chain this stranger up for interrogation," said the axe man. His bald head had become a red bubble over his long gray beard. "We were caught off guard last night. We cannot give them another chance to strike." The crowd cheered at his words. They were eager to see an act of violence that would end their worries.

"I am human," I said. "Just like most of you here. I am as upset as all of you at the events that took place last night. If you give me some time to explain what has happened, we can form a plan of attack against those responsible."

"Let's hear the stranger out," said the Elf. The crowd broke out into chatter and the warrior's nose wrinkled.

Confusion showed itself on their faces as I explained the Milky Way. The crowd whispered among themselves when I spoke of coming through the portal. One of the guild leaders—wearing robes—eyed me, twirling the end of his beard around his fingers; he looked of Indian descent, which added to the diverse list of ethnicities I'd seen in Relaun so far.

The warrior sized up Finian as I explained how he'd found me and saved my life when I came face to face with Flurwick.

"It's easy to claim your innocence, but how are we to believe you?" The warrior said, cutting me off.

"You don't have to believe me, but I know where Flurwick set up camp and I know what he plans to do next." I turned to Sir Gringham and his companion in robes. "If you allow me to, I can tell you what I have learned about your missing conjurer."

Sir Gringham's eyes widened, "please continue."

Fear spread on their faces as I told them about Flurwick's plans to capture the artifacts and indoctrinate the Mutano tribes. "If it wasn't for your healer, Evangeline, we could not have learned what we know now. You need to rethink your decision of removing her from the guild." I said in closing.

"I am sorry, but because the healer didn't report any of her activities she took part in with Finian, she is unreliable," said the man in robes, twirling his beard. "We must however, rescue our master conjurer." He now turned to the man with the axe. "Jorn, could you supply some of your warriors to assist in a rescue party. I shall gather some mages at once."

Jorn the axe bearer shook his head. "I would love to Elbert, but Retgar took some of our best men with him on the convoy."

"If what the stranger says is true then Retgar may be in trouble," said the Elven lady.

"Exactly my thoughts," I added. "When I fought Natalya, she told me Flurwick and the conjurer was near Brenmore. But with Natalya and Simon's escape, it means we can no longer assume that Flurwick is still there. If Simon broke into the Warriors Guild looking for the artifact and found out that it was gone then there's no doubt that Retgar and his men are in danger."

"But they are going to Highwell. If the capital city is attacked then what hope will we have to combat this threat?" Sir Gringham asked.

"Let us warn Master Retgar." Several people gasped at hearing Finian speak.

"Pardon me, young man, but this is a serious conversation between guild leaders," came the nasally voice.

"Well, that's half the problem with Corwy; you people never listen to those with more than half a brain."

Finian countered.

"What did you say?" the short man approached Finian but Kover stepped forward, causing him to flinch. "You ought to be showing him some discipline, Kover," he said, looking up at Kover's stone expression.

"Only I will decide how to deal with my son, Sir Andras." Kover snarled. "Now, we shall let my son speak; for it was his Mutano friend here that defeated the Undead." The crowd was silent; hung on every word of the exchange.

Finian had a spring in his step as he pushed past Sir Andras. "People of Corwy, understand this. If we send out the best forces our guilds have to offer, then we have no defense should there be another attack. If you all want Blok and Brandon gone so much, then you should let the three of us find Master Retgar and then get help to rescue the conjurer."

People in the crowd broke into conversations of their own. "But you failed your Trial of Becoming, boy. You'll fall victim to the wilds as soon as you step outside the walls." came a shout from the crowd. There were too many people for me to locate the source of the comment, but the majority of the crowd responded with laughter.

"You're all so blinded by your traditions that you

can't see how Finian saved your asses last night." I spat. "When you look at him, all you can see is a boy failing this meaningless trial; instead of seeing the young man who saved my life. The same young man who kept the Mutano alive for four years; the same Mutano who cleared the horde that we were struggling to defeat. Ask yourselves what would've happened if the three of us weren't around last night." Silence followed.

"How dare you challenge our traditions," said Sir Andras.

"Sir Andras," said Kover. "Respectfully, I would like you to shut your mouth." An immature side of me chuckled inside at the comment. I had to bite my lip in order to not let the laugh escape me. Knowing that Kover was the kind of man to live and die by the laws of his town, I looked at him now with nothing but respect.

"By The Elders! Kover you're not making a good case to be accepted by the Farmers Guild."

"Screw your Farmers Guild," Kover spat. "Half me farm was destroyed by the Undead last night. What matters more is our safety. This threat will affect all of Aldeen if we don't stop it now. Finian is my son and my responsibility." Kover looked down at Sir Andras with pure venom. "Last night, innocent people were killed for something that is no longer in Corwy. My son's failure on his trial is what allowed the Mutano to be here today." Kover turned to address the crowd. "The same boy you all laughed at is now the reason you're all stood here breathing. So if my son wants to continue to help you useless brutes, then so be it."

"I do not like the Mutano's presence here," said the Elf. Through my peripheral vision I saw Blok's teeth become visible. "But it is true that he helped save us. Sending these three away to find Retgar will do nothing but help us while also getting rid of the Mutano. My vote is to hand this responsibility over to them so that we may focus on rebuilding the walls and evaluating our defenses."

"Getting our Master Conjurer back is important," said the man known as Elbert. "Finian and his friends will have our support in this matter." Sir Gringham nodded his agreement.

Jorn looked as though he was disappointed that he wouldn't get a chance to use his axe. "Listen Stranger; make sure you find Retgar before he reaches Highwell. If you do so, suggest that they split into two teams. One team can find the conjurer while the other can continue to escort the artifact to Highwell. Highwell cannot fall to attack," he pressed his finger into my chest. "Do you hear me?"

I knocked his hand off my chest. "Understood, Jorn," I looked him in the eyes until he turned away.

"The Hunters Guild is happy to share supplies with you, and I would like to suggest that the Warriors Guild does the same," said the Elf.

"Thank you, Ma'am," I said.

"Call me Sharia." She extended her hand.

"Brandon," I said, shaking it.

"Highwell is to the far North East of Corwy. By now, its likely Retgar's men are halfway to Highwell. I suggest you get three of our horses from the stable and take the path leading to the North. You are less likely to encounter beasts on that route."

"Unchain him please," said Finian, pointing at Blok. Jorn swallowed hard and his lip curled but he obeyed and moved towards the Mutano. Before he could get behind Blok, he found himself flinching as a growl escaped the Mutano. A grinding noise was heard and bits of twisted metal flew across the platform at odd angles. The Mutano's hands were now free, and he made it obvious by beating his chest.

"Bleeding cry! That beast cannot be controlled."

cried Sir Andras.

"He could have killed us any time he wanted to," said Kover, with an eyebrow raised at Blok. "He could have slaughtered us at any time; especially while you were slandering him. But he didn't."

The group parted cautiously as Blok walked forward to Finian's side. "This public hearing has concluded. Please go about your business." Sir Andras said to the crowd. No doubt eager to avoid further public humiliation.

Sharia turned to us. "You must leave at once. Please visit us and collect anything you require for your journey."

"Thank you," I said as the guild leaders began to walk down the steps.

I turned to face Finian's father and he smiled. "Kover, I wanted to let you know that I appreciate you speaking up for us," I said, extending my hand.

"I still don't trust you," he said, grabbing my hand. "But to see how my son responded to the threat last night, and to know that he had a hand in saving this town, makes me willing to accept that he's made friends with a stranger and a Mutano." Kover patted Finian on the shoulder. "I want you to have my set of armor. You've earned it my son."

"Wow, really?" Finian smiled. "I thought you sold them after I failed me trial."

"Come for them after you have visited the guilds. I would like to see you before you set out." Kover looked at the three of us in turn. "I must go and rebuild what's left of the farm."

As his father left, Finian clapped his hands together. "That was marvelous. Did you see all their faces?"

I waved Finian and Blok towards me as I descended the steps. "Let's go, we can't waste time."

CHAPTER 16

WE DECIDED TO VISIT the Hunters Guild first because Sharia had been the nicest of the guild leaders, but Sharia was not present at the guild hall when we arrived. Despite this, her assistants saw to it that we received all the hunting supplies we would need for our quest.

"Lady Sharia also asked that we feed you up so that you won't waste any time hunting for food." They told us.

A large dining table held various dishes, and my stomach responded to the sight by letting out a rumble that everyone heard. All kinds of meats were on trays for our choosing. Finian guided me on which creatures some of the meat dishes had come from; even going as far as to suggest which meats I should eat with the many vegetable dishes on offer.

Eventually, my insides felt ready to burst and the will to hold my fork waned. When my hunger was gone I looked up and saw that Blok was stood by the door watching us. "Why isn't Blok eating?" I asked.

"Mutanos don't eat warm food. They seem to prefer

eating their food raw. I'm no expert on how their bodies work, but I think cooked food affects their strength or something."

"Shall we try to get him something now?" I chewed on the last piece of potato and pushed my plate forward in submission. "Because the whole point of them feeding us is so we won't lose time hunting food."

"It's not necessary. The big man can look after himself. When we're in the wilds he'll likely disappear when he smells food. And then he'll catch up with us when he's done," said Finian with a ball of food in his cheeks. For such a scrawny man, he could sure eat. Looking around, I noticed how differently the hunter's hall was designed from the others. Etched on the walls, were hieroglyphic creatures with gold patterns shimmering around them. Many of them resembled cats. I felt like I was in Egypt.

"All done," said Finian, placing his utensils on his plate. "I beat me record of four plates in a day."

Inside the warrior's guild hall, was what looked like a museum exhibition. The interior walls were blocks of stone, overlaid with banners and paintings. Past battles were represented in paintings, with descriptions written beside them. Along the walls, displays of damaged armor from these various battles stood.

Finian and I waited in the guest hall for the warriors to hand over my things. Blok had refused to enter the walls of the Warriors Guild. He was unforgiving of them for keeping him prisoner for so long.

"So, Blok could have freed himself at any time?" I asked.

Finian shrugged. "Seems so."

"What made him stay there for four years?"

"Blok loves humans. He's fascinated by us. I suppose he was willing to succumb to the will of humans. Last night he knew we were in danger so I guess he decided it was the right time to free himself."

"I'm grateful he's on our side."

Footsteps came from the corridor and a stocky man came into the hall carrying a chest. When he placed it on the ground I opened it and scanned the contents to ensure all my belongings were there. Something shone from inside and after shuffling pieces of space armor I saw that it was Baron's sword. "I would like to request that the sword belonging to the warrior named Baron be buried with him," I told the man who brought the chest.

"Show me the sword, stranger," he said.

Upon holding the sword by its hilt, a warm tingle rippled inside of me. It was brief, but I felt a power from the sword transfer over to me. "What is happening?"

"Baron's sword has enough power from the Medius stones to last a decade. When it showed no signs of igniting for us, we figured it had been bound to a new soul," said the man winking. "Since we found it with your things, it was obvious that it had chosen you."

"So I should keep it?"

"I heard your speech at the square today, stranger. Something about how you carried yourself was admirable. For that reason I fought to ensure you would keep the sword. Others wanted to keep it for their own personal use. But I think you should honor Baron's memory by taking the sword and putting it to good use. He would have wanted that."

"Thank you," I saluted.

"Lucky you with all the fancy weapons," Finian said.

Aside from a few magical bombs, we left the Mages Guild empty handed. Sir Gringham apologized for the lack of supplies and I'd empathized with him, knowing they would need resources to keep themselves safe. Finian had cursed as if expecting more.

Sir Gringham wished us well on our journey and we walked back towards the gate with the magic bells. As I looked over at the cylinder shaped trees in the distance, my mind strayed elsewhere. Finian walked through the gate and patted Blok on the chest. "You alright, big fella?"

"Where are we going next?" I asked.

Finian looked over at me, "I want to stop by at Dalice's place. She owes me some silver."

"Go ahead, I will meet you there," I said walking away.

"Wait, Brandon!" I heard Finian cry.

My walk transitioned in a sprint as I saw the shack come into view, but her teaching space was vacant. None of her things remained. The shack door was wide open, showing a bold level of indifference. Evangeline was gone, and as I stared through the open door—at a number of empty jars on a table—I wondered why I felt such desolation.

A blazing row broke out inside Dalice's cabin. "I would have thought that after breaking my back for you all these years, you'd at least speak up for me in my time of need," came Finian's voice. Blok's large frame could be seen in the corner as I walked in. His arms were folded.

"You are careless, boy," said Dalice. Her eyes acknowledged my presence but she continued her argument with Finian. "A task so important shouldn't be put on your feeble shoulders. You couldn't even pass your Trial of Becoming."

Parsley the cat bolted from the back room across the work surface and out the open door. A gagging sound then came from the back of the cabin. Blok growled and positioned himself to attack.

"By The Elders! It's another attack." Dalice ran from behind the barrier and stood before us. "Do something! I cannot have my cabin destroyed."

Finian removed his dagger and I grabbed my sword. The Undead limped its way out of the back room. Foam bubbled from its mouth as it faltered its way towards us. The thick blue hand of the Mutano came across its neck and then it was lifted into the air. Blok then slammed the Undead to the floor in the way a professional wrestler would.

"You are damaging my flooring you stupid creature." Dalice yelled, as chunks of wood flew up from the impact. Dalice cowered into a corner as Blok looked up at her with his teeth exposed; the Undead still pinned beneath him.

My sword fired itself up, as if reading my mind that it

was time to finish of the Undead. "No, get it out of here before you burn the place down." Dalice cried.

Blok lifted the Unded back up by its neck and brought it outside. The Undead thrashed around as Blok carried it and it almost managed to scratch me in the face with its nails. Blok threw it on a patch of grass far enough away from the cabin to prevent the flames expanding. I knelt to impale the creature with my sword and Blok planted his foot over the creature's neck to prevent it getting up. As I brought my sword down into its flesh, over and over—causing dis-colored blood to spew everywhere—I turned on my mental filter so that I wouldn't commit this scene to memory. It was a trick I'd had to teach myself while being in the marines, because you had to be strong enough to put some of the things you saw behind you.

Soon enough, the creature's gagging stopped and the flames around its body grew so fierce that we had to back away.

Back inside, Dalice was composing herself. "What were you saying about me being careless?" said Finian.

Parsley ran back inside to join his master and he began purring at her side.

"Blok want cat," said the Mutano. Parsley hissed at him.

"While I would like nothing more than to see you eat Parsley, you can't have him I'm afraid," said Finian.

I had to suppress the desire to laugh at the absurdity. "Has Finian done enough to prove himself to you now?" I asked Dalice. "Not that anyone needs your approval, of course."

Dalice walked over to the work surface and pulled something from behind it. "Here's your coins, take them and a jar of health poultice with you and leave immediately."

* * *

"That's what she gets for leaving her back door open." Finian giggled, as we made our way to his farm. "The look on her face was priceless. It shut her right up seeing us take out the Undead like that."

"I figured you deserved more than some coins and medicine after that," I said.

"Ah, that's alright. I helped myself to a few items on the shelves when she wasn't looking anyway." He smiled.

From over Finian's shoulder, I saw something that

stopped me dead in my tracks. A young boy, perhaps in his early teens, was sitting beside a wall with his arms wrapped around his legs; his head planted into his knees. I could hear his sniffles. Without really being aware of my actions, I approached the boy and knelt beside him. "Hey, is everything good, young man?" I asked.

The boy looked up at me and twitched. He then turned to see Finian and Blok who were looking on with confusion. "It's you," the boy said, wiping his face with his wrist. "The stranger, the Mothernamed and the Mutano."

"Mothernamed?" I replied.

"Finian," the boy said, pointing towards the man himself. "Both him and I are Mothernamed. We both failed our Trial of Becoming."

Finian approached. "Ah, is that why you're sad? When did it happen? I didn't hear about any trials taking place this week."

"My trial was two months ago," the boy said, under his shaggy jet black hair.

"Ah, so you must be the boy that failed to slay the growing arachnid in the House of Healing."

The boy nodded. "That's not why I'm sad. My

parents were killed fighting the Undead. And now nobody wants to help me." The boy broke into hysterical cries.

"Hey," I said, placing a hand on the boy's shoulder. His arms and legs were covered in dirt as if he'd slept outside in the aftermath of the battle. "What's your name?"

"Filip." he sniffed.

"Don't worry, Filip. We're not going to leave here until we find someone to look after you."

"L-let me come with you," he said.

I looked up at Finian as he said it. I thought about honoring Filip's wish, but I knew it would do more harm than good to carry him on such an unpredictable mission.

Finian knelt in front of the boy. "We'd love to, Filip. I'd especially like to carry you along because we Mothernamed have to look out for one another. But we know not what we'll face out there. We can't endanger your life when your parents have already died trying to protect you."

Filip sniffed hard and I felt his body shake. "Actually," said Finian. "We're about to go to the perfect place where you can stay. How would you like to take over me own room? I've got all sorts of cool treasures stashed away there, and they'll all be yours."

At this, Filip looked up and I thought I saw the first inklings of a smile. He nodded.

We soon reached Finian's farm. When we got to the shattered gates, Filip turned and looked up towards Finian. "Please Mr. Glaed, will you get revenge for my parents. If you put a stop to it without the guilds help then they'll have no choice but to thank a Mothernamed for restoring order."

Finian glanced over at me with concern. It was as if he was being asked to do something he didn't believe he could achieve. "I'll try, Filip," he said, looking back down at the boy.

Once inside the farm, Kover came out to greet us. He eyed Filip with confusion. "Recruiting children for your quest now are you?"

"I'm not a child, I'm fourteen sir," said Filip.

Kover raised an eyebrow. "What's your name young sir?"

"Filip Widforss," he said.

"Ah," said Kover.

"Father, his parents died at the hands of the Undead.

As you know, this town has a poor reputation for looking after Mothernamed. For that reason, I would like for my room to be his while I am gone." Finian said. Kover merely nodded.

Finian knelt and whispered something to Filip. After a moment, Filip had bolted through the open door in excitement. Finian smiled as if he were a proud father.

But speaking of proud fathers, it was Kover who glowed with enthusiasm at the prospect of his son stepping up to defend Corwy. Inside their house, Kover supplied us with some treats to snack on during our travels. When Kover handed over the leather armor to his son, it was like watching a father prepare his son for his first football game. For a time, I sat snacking on some sausage rolls as I watched Kover demonstrate different stances and ways to handle daggers and blades. He also showed Finian the right away to throw a dagger so that it would hit its mark.

Finian and I changed into our gear while Kover offered Blok some dead animals to feast on. Kover had developed a strong level of tolerance for our Mutano companion; this was evident after Blok had broken several wooden furnishings by accident. "Blok sorry, Blok strong," the Mutano had said each time. Kover smiled at Blok's clumsiness and set aside the broken pieces of wood in a corner. No doubt he would repair them in his own time.

From Finian's room, we heard loud thuds indicating Filip's amusement. Once or twice, Kover had checked in on him. I was happy that Filip had a temporary place of residence where he would be looked after. Looking at my damaged Jet Boosters and the remains of my Comm-link at the bottom of my chest, I was beginning to feel the loss of my own home; a place where I belonged.

Once outside, Kover offered us a cart to attach on a horse so that we would be able to carry our things with ease.

"Father, do you have any advice to offer? This is the first time I'll be going so far from Corwy without you after all."

"Son," said Kover, placing a hand on his son's shoulder, "don't be a dick," he smiled. Finian chucked and then he shared a hug with his father. I shook Kover's hand and saluted him.

"Good human," said Blok. Kover nodded in response and we went on our way.

Outside the shattered walls, three horses stood by the stables waiting. "That's what I've been meaning to ask you," said Finian, looking up at Blok. "Do Mutanos even ride horses?"

"Blok use feet," said the Mutano. "Horse is food."

"No it's not. By The Elders! Is there anything that you don't want to eat?"

We fastened the cart to my horse and before long we were following the path ahead. As we set into fast gallops, Blok maintained a consistent speed while sprinting alongside us. Before long he'd disappeared completely and I inquired to Finian about his whereabouts.

"You needn't worry about Blok," he said. "I'm sure he'll find us."

CHAPTER 17

RAIN TURNED THE DIRT INTO a squishy puree that shot upwards as our horses marched across the large expanse. Along the way, vicious birds could be seen watching our disruptive presence. Once, I looked behind at the cart and saw what looked like a small gray bear clawing at the edges of the cart, as if sensing food. Finian had dropped back to knock it off the cart.

The Corwy locals had spoken of the wilds with such fear that I was expecting to encounter terrifying beasts at every turn, but so far I'd only seen what some may find cute and cuddly creatures.

"Some parts of the wilds are calmer than others." Finian told me when I'd brought up the subject. "It's likely we'll face the most danger at night."

Every now and then, Blok could be seen sprinting beside us, matching the speed of our horses; only to disappear again at random. When I asked Finian where he went, he shrugged and said Mutanos are a fascinating mystery that humans cannot understand.

Sometime in the late afternoon, we found ourselves surrounded by six-foot vines. The vines were so thick and so densely populated that it became unclear which direction we needed to be heading. During this time, I used my phone to determine which way was north-east. The compass spun and for a moment I figured the app wouldn't work in Relaun, until finally it settled and pointed to our right.

"What trickery is this?" Finian said, snatching the phone from my hand and flipping it front to back in his palm. His mouth opened as he frantically moved his hand around the screen.

"It's called a smartphone. It's a communications device that is popular back on Earth. Where I'm from," I said, reaching for it. He moved it further from my grasp.

"What can I do for you today?" said the A.I feature on the phone.

"It speaks," Finian yelled. "What is this magic?"

"Sorry, I am unable to find a connection to the network."

I snatched the phone back and slipped it into my pocket. "It's not magic, it's called technology."

"Can it be used as a weapon?"

"No. Think of it as a tool," I said, dropping down from my horse. "Since this path has low visibility, we should walk alongside the horses for some time."

"Agreed," Finian said, following suit. "I just hope we don't lose too much time."

We continued to feel our way through the vines. We were careful not to be stung by nettles that Finian had informed me were poisonous. After some time, I felt an indescribable energy radiating from something nearby. Finian confirmed that he felt it too and our curiosity led us to break our path.

Chopping down some vines on our left revealed the source of the energy. A crystal shard stood slanted from the ground and rose to around shoulder height. A purple aura surrounded it, and strands of lightning flickered all over. "Don't get too close," Finian said, as I found myself drawn to it. "Only those who can cast magic may get close to these deposits without being hurt."

"It's incredible," I said. Even with having explored the wonders of the Milky Way, I was in awe at the glowing crystal.

"Many times, I have come across a crystal deposit and wished that I was a mage."

"Are the crystals at the center of Relaun like this?" I asked.

"I've never seen them in person, but they are said to be gigantic. There are points to the west of Aldeen where you can see them from a distance. Of course, nobody has actually survived getting to the Island of Crystalline. People tend to look at them from a safe distance in their boats."

I was hardly the type of person that snapped a bunch of photos, but I couldn't resist capturing the crystals with my smartphone camera. "I guess we should continue moving," I said, looking at the photo I'd just taken.

The sky was darkening at a rapid rate, meaning we'd soon be at risk of attacks from feral creatures.

"Indeed," said Finian. "Once we make it through this forest of vines we may begin to join the path that the convoy are taking."

"How are you holding up?" I asked him as we walked back to our horses.

"You mean how I'm doing?" I nodded in response. "I'm fine. I love to explore as you may have noticed. How are you, stranger?" He smirked.

"I'm great," I said. "My arm still feels a little stiff from the shot, but whatever Evangeline did has healed it good."

Finian took a swig of his flask before speaking again. "I noticed you went looking for her before we left. Had she already departed?"

I nodded back as I pulled the horse by its collar. "She left abruptly; didn't even close her door. I feel bad that she was kicked out of the guild for helping us."

"Agreed," said Finian. "She had every right to yell at me while you were out of it. I don't think she actually blames us though. She was just upset. I can tell you one thing though."

"What's that?" I asked.

"She fought the council hard to ensure you were able to rest up at her place. They would have thrown you in a dungeon if it weren't for her."

This caused me to daydream about Evangeline tucking me into her bed. My mind wandered, until I became self-aware that I had created an awkward silence. "I am thankful. I hope she'll be okay. Where ever she is."

"She has family to the west, in a village named Mirarth. Perhaps she'll head back there for some time. In the future, I imagine she could sell her remedies or maybe even set up a house of healing."

"What are Elves like as a race? And do they mix with humans much?" I asked; letting out the questions that had been on my mind for a while.

"Most of them think highly of themselves because of how easily magic comes to them." He yawned. "They have their own languages and their culture is much different. They believe The Elders were all Elves. But it's certifiable that Lord Jerrus was a human." Finian began scratching his under arm. "As for mixing with humans, many Elves settled in Aldeen after the war. It then became more common for humans and Elves to become involved. Evangeline is the daughter of a mixed couple as you probably already know." I had thought about that detail more than I cared to admit to him. "You tend to see more Elves in Aldeen the further west you go. That's because their home land of Lainunia is across the river on that side."

"I see."

It was becoming clear that we were both fatigued. We fell silent for some time and Blok joined us, matching our slowing pace.

Vines transitioned into regular bushes and leaves, and soon we found an open forested patch of land covered by towering trees. "I can't go any farther," Finian said. "Can we rest for an hour?"

There was no objection.

My survival training skills were long out of practice,

so I let Finian guide me with starting a fire. We gathered dry grass, leaves and bark to build a tinder nest. When Finian began to twist the spindle in his hands, Blok stepped in without warning and took over the task. Ember soon came and Finian blew the flames onto the nest.

We ate some meaty snacks that Kover had provided for us and Finian asked me to explain about my origins and the Milky Way. Blok sat upright against a tree trunk, his eyes closed. Finian soon fell asleep after I recalled the difficulty in telling my parents that I had enlisted in the space marine program.

* * *

"With all that horse shit there must be others close by." I heard someone say.

"Did you see the lovely piece of arse they dragged in back at camp earlier? I want to get back and have some of that."

"Those ears will poke your eyes out if you're not careful with that one."

"Human or Elven, I don't complain. It's not often we capture a lady is it?"

"Ah, bleedin' cry! If it will shut you up then let's

head back. If we miss some loot then it's your fault."

I opened my eyes to pitch black darkness. The fire had burned out and a chill caused my body to stir. Being a light sleeper, I'd always been able to overhear conversations and I was grateful for it on that night.

When the sounds of footsteps were trailing away, I flashed my phone and saw that Finian and Blok were still sound asleep. Waking them would make too much noise and stealth would be needed to follow the strangers back to where they were headed. My eyes quickly adjusted to the darkness so that I could make out the outlines of trunks and stumps. I crept over to where I placed my things and bound the sword to my hip and holstered my blaster before creeping in the direction of the voices.

CHAPTER 18

MUD PLASTERED MY SUIT as I crouched low on a hill overlooking a camp. Small huts and tents littered the bowl of land that the two shady characters had led me to. The area resembled a crater, placed right in the middle of a large expanse and hidden by the woodlands. To the far end of the crater from where I was crouched, I could see that the area sloped right into a cave entrance. I wondered what kind of secrets they kept down in the cave, but it didn't matter given the current situation at hand.

At least thirteen men were walking around the crater, and I had no idea how many of them were inside the huts and tents. The two men I'd followed were now talking with a man wearing an eye-patch. They handed him their sacks; sacks that were surely full of stolen goods from their outings. The one-eyed man pushed one of the other men and laughed, before walking in the opposite direction. The two men turned and walked towards one of the huts.

After observing my surroundings, I figured that moving one-eighty degrees around the crater would allow me to drop down the slope and be behind the hut. From there, I could try to sneak in undetected. Most of the men were facing the opposite direction and I got the sense that they weren't often confronted; a fact that might make them lazy.

I positioned myself to slide down against the dirt, trying to make as little noise as possible. Voices could be heard from inside the hut that the men had entered, but I couldn't make out any of the conversation. I crept around it, taking one step at a time; trying to figure out their positions before proceeding.

"Look what we have here," came a voice behind me. My body fell backwards as a green glow filled the air. A knuckle slammed into my jaw before I could pick up my weapon. "What's this then?" said the man, with the eye-patch, holding my blaster.

"Be careful with that." I panted. "It's like nothing you've ever used before. It could kill you."

"Shut your hole!"

He pulled me up, put me into a headlock and then forced me into a walk until he'd reached the hut; at which point he pushed me through the door. "Look what the cat dragged in, lads. He must be looking for her," he said, pointing to the back of the room.

Tied to the front of a ladder was Evangeline. Her

arms were tied upwards to one of the steps and her hands were wrapped in bundles. A cloth ran its way around her mouth and was knotted at the back of her head. Her face was blood red. Strands of her hair hung at awkward angles, some of them stuck to her face with moisture. I hoped she hadn't been seriously harmed.

Her eyes bulged as she watched me be pushed to the floor by the man with the eye patch.

"What is he wearing? I've never seen anything like that before," said one of the men I had followed.

"My thoughts exactly," said the one with the eye-patch. "Let's strip him down, lads. Make sure you bundle his hands in case he does magic." The man pulled the sword from my hip and then one of his minions stretched my arms out in front of me. The other pulled on my dented chest plate, looking for a way to detach it.

I slapped away the first minion's hand and that allowed me plant my fist into his stomach. As he staggered back, I uppercutted the second man and pushed him to the floor; where I pulled a dagger from his waist. Turning to face the one-eyed man, I saw that he now held my sword to Evangeline's throat.

"Let her go," I said, eying my blaster on his waist. "If you untie her and hand her over, I have a hundred gold for you." I lied. I wasn't even sure if that was a worthy amount of gold.

"That is tempting," he said. "But I needn't give up my guest here to get the gold from you when I can take it from you." As he said this I noticed Evangeline's breathing intensify. She bit her lip as if enduring insufferable pain. I thought the sword had pierced her throat and for a second my insides plummeted. But above her head I could see that her hands were burning through the binding.

The man with the eye-patch sniffed profusely, as if he could smell it. "Bitch," he said as he realized what she was doing. The sword rose in his hand as he readied it to strike her. I launched the dagger, remembering the way in which Kover had taught Finian to throw one. It spun through the air and sliced through the man's shoulder. Blood splattered on the furnishings as he bellowed. He took to the floor and grabbed a piece of stray cloth to press against the cut.

Making my way over to Evangeline, I picked up my sword that he had dropped and cut her lose from her binding. Her hands were tender and she groaned every time my hands brushed against her own. When I removed the cloth obstructing her mouth, she took a number of deep breaths.

"Let's get out of here," I said, helping her up. My foot found its way into the man's chest and I took my blaster from him. We were halfway to the door when the ground shook so violently that I was almost knocked back. The man was now sitting up with his arm held out, casting his magic.

"Its surface magic," said Evangeline. She held her own hands out in response and shot pelleted balls of fire at the man. She bit her lip as she did so.

Mugs and utensils clanged on the floor. Chairs toppled and the dining table flipped over as the room continued to shake. My knees hit the floor hard as I tried to balance myself.

Looking up, I saw that Evangeline's pellets were missing their mark. She was struggling to aim them with the room shaking. The man was able to stand and walk towards us; immune to his own magic.

My eyes locked down the iron sights of my blaster. It would be hard to get a clear shot but I would try. His attention was on Evangeline; the opposing mage. My arm was unsteadied as I transformed the blaster into a rifle. I held the butt of the weapon under my arm to lock it into position and I fired at an angle. The red projectile hit him in the thigh and he fell back clenching his leg.

With the room now steady, Evangeline used her

magic to bind the man's hands to the floor with frost. "Come, let's be quick. My elemental magic is weak," she said.

Outside, the other men were just getting to their feet, after also falling victim to the earthquake. I let off a few warning shots in their direction as we ran uphill and cleared the camp.

"How are your hands?" I asked, as I led her back to our camp. She wore a beautiful laced necklace that caught my attention with its sparkle.

"They are sore. But they'll soon heal," she said. We were watching our steps to avoid tripping on fallen branches. "It's risky to use magic with your hands bundled. You can really hurt yourself. But as a healer, I was willing to take the risk," she said. A moment of silence followed in which we caught ourselves glancing at one another. "You didn't need to put yourself in danger. I would have found my own way out." she sighed.

"Clearly you're capable of holding your own," I said. "But since you saved my life last night, there's no way I could have ignored any sign of your capture." We stopped so that I could consider the path ahead. My memory told me that we needed to bend around to the left. "Besides, I wasn't even sure if they had captured you or another Elf. I would have attempted a rescue no matter who they had in there." I continued.

"Those ruffians have the last of my supplies." She let out a deep breath.

"Sorry to hear that. If you travel with us, we'll be happy to share."

"I had rare ingredients with me. Potions and antidotes that are difficult to replicate. All my alchemy supplies and my books, they're all gone." Tears fell from her eyes.

My hand rubbed against the leathers on her back. "Sorry to hear that. I'm just happy you're alright."

She looked up at me with those eyes that shimmered bright under the moonlight. "Why are you out here? What happened at the square?" she asked.

"Well, the council argued over our fates for a while. Listening to them blabber angered me, so I went up there to explain our side of the story. We made it clear to them that a man with an agenda led the attack, and that we must stop him. Finian persuaded them that it would be beneficial to send us out to find the warriors carrying the artifact to Highwell. Before Flurwick and the others have a chance to plan a second attack."

"I was also going to Highwell," she said. "Before they captured me, I saw fresh carriage markings and footprints in the dirt. The convoy has been traveling slowly. You may be able to catch up with them if you continue on without delay."

"Why don't you come with us?" I asked.

She walked out of my reach and continued around the bend. "So you can protect me?"

"So we can protect each other. There's strength in numbers, right? We're all heading the same way. It makes sense."

"Your eyes are yellow; you need water," she said, as informally as my doctor would. Usually when others saw my yellow eyes—caused by broken down blood cells in my system—they made snide comments and joked about it.

Evangeline must have seen the camp before I did, because she no longer needed to wait for me to direct her. She climbed over a large stump and dropped down across from where the Mutano slept. His eyes shot open, as bright as light bulbs.

"Hmph! The other man has Elf girl now." he grunted.

"You know Blok, you could just learn to say our

names," I said, jumping down from the stump. I walked over to our supply cart to find water. I offered Evangeline her own flask.

"Wait, what?" Finian yawned. "Eva, wha—what you doin' here?"

"It is not by choice, I can assure you." she snapped. "We must leave here at once if you are to catch up with the warriors."

"Alright, alright; I suppose we've had enough rest," he said, rising to his feet. "Let's get going, Blok." Our horses raised their heads as we approached them. "Who you sharing with, Eva?" asked Finian.

"Myself," she said, climbing the nearest horse.

"W-wait!" He grabbed after her horse, but she moved on ahead leaving us looking at one another.

I climbed the other horse and looked down at Finian. "You know I'm riding, right?"

"I can't believe this," said Finian, planting his face in his palm.

CHAPTER 19

EVANGELINE HAD GOOD SENSE of direction, so I trailed behind her while filling in Finian on what had occurred during the night. "You should have waked us," he said.

"I may have lost their trail if I did."

"What if they'd killed you? Me and Blok would have no clue what went on."

"It was a risk worth taking," I said. "Besides, my training gave me the edge over those men. It was the magical one with the eye-patch that was a challenge."

"Lucky for you, your damsel in distress ended up saving you" Evangeline shot back. It was the first inkling of a smile I had seen from her.

"There's no denying that. You saved my ass once again." I smiled.

Finian pointed over my shoulder, "halt!"

Ahead, Blok stood over a dozen bodies. We dismounted our horses to investigate.

"Blok find dead humans; fresh blood," said the

Mutano. Immediately, I recognized the dark shaded armor pieces they wore.

"That's guild armor." Finian pointed. The bodies lay maimed and mangled. A few of them had blades stuck in their chests. Among the bodies we saw who the warriors had been fighting. They wore leather gear outlined with fur. Steel pads covered their chest pieces. At a glance you could see the tailoring wasn't as elegant as the warrior's armor.

"Exul clan," Finian said, watching me stare at the bodies. "They act as a private legion; ready for hire by anyone who has the coin."

"Mercenaries, huh? Would they have reason to fight the warriors?" I asked.

"The guilds don't like the Exul. And I suppose it's the same the other way around. But they are not hostile towards each other unless there's a good reason."

Evangeline examined one of the Exul bodies, lifting the eyelids. "What are you doing? Don't touch him," said Finian.

She ignored him. "I see no signs of indoctrination," she said. She looked up and gasped, "Over there." she pointed. We saw a body struggling its way to us. Using the only arm left on its body to pull itself our way. Evangeline crouched beside the man who was wearing guild armor. "Stop moving, you are making things worse."

"We fought... so that Retgar could carry on to Highwell... with the artifact." He coughed. "Find him." The man's head rested on the ground and his fingers fell flat.

"Oh dear," said Finian.

"Let's keep moving, we can talk on the way," I said, mounting the horse. "They may try to ambush Retgar again before he reaches Highwell."

* * *

"I don't know what's worse." Finian said, behind me as we continued en route. "Retgar being ambushed on the way to Highwell, or Highwell itself being attacked. Highwell is our capital; if we lose it then we're in big trouble."

"Is there no fast means of communication in Relaun? Back where I'm from, we could have been telling Highwell to prepare for attack ahead of time."

"We used to have Bards that would travel around Aldeen using magic boots or horses. They'd pass on

164

information, but it became too risky for them. They were being attacked left and right by ruffians like the ones you fought last night. Not to mention the wild beasts lurking everywhere." Finian explained.

"There was a time where the guilds protected the Bards. And supplied them," said Evangeline, riding alongside us. "But Guilds started to find it difficult to manage supplies, leaving the Bards to operate independently."

"Sometimes you get folks who enjoy being on the roads and are willing to pass on messages and items for a few silvers. On one of my ventures out of Corwy, I even met an independent hunter named Callenhan who would slay beasts for the Hunters Guild. He was kind enough to pass on information to each town he visited. Soon enough, he was recruited by the Hunters Guild in Highwell for a stationary teaching position; all that talent going to waste."

The story reminded me of an infamous space merc who doubled as an advanced hacker. The Galactic Alliance had wanted him to enlist for years but he refused. "Is there no magical means of contacting others who are far away?" I asked.

"In Lainunia, the Elven region, there are sorcerers so

powerful that their mind magic is able to stretch incredible distances. They are able to relay information with mental images," said Evangeline.

This reminded me of something I had wanted to ask her. "Last night you mentioned that your ice magic was weak. Does this mean that mages have specialties?"

"Yes." She sighed, steering her horse to avoid large rocks on the dirt path. "It takes years of repetitive training to master each type of magic. Healing magic is my expertise but when it comes to elemental magic, I'm no match for other mages."

"That guy last night, was his level of magic advanced?" I asked.

"His surface magic was some of the best I've seen in years. Surface magic is not something that's often practiced in Aldeen."

"Humans prefer to shoot Fire, Ice and Lightning projectiles at each other all day." Finian added.

"I hear that. Where I'm from people would rather shoot guns than engage in hand to hand combat." As the path narrowed, I positioned myself behind Evangeline. We were still close enough to continue our conversation and I was grateful because it was important that I understood the magic of Relaun. Preparation was important for when I found myself face to face with Flurwick again. "I noticed you were using a staff the other night. Does that make your magic more powerful?"

"Staffs are a specialty of the Elves. Each one is designed to enhance your abilities in different ways. But magic is more powerful from the hands. Staffs and infused weapons simply focus the magic in a more precise way. Magic from the hand is powerful but difficult to focus in situations where you have many targets."

"I've been noticing that when magic is used there are usually colorful auras that release in the air," I said.

"Indeed," said Evangeline. "The colors represent the type of magic being used. Ruby for fire, Sapphire for ice, Amethyst for thunder, Emerald for surface magic, White for healing, Amber for mind magic and Citrine for force magic."

As I had the horse leap over a large heap of rocks and felt Finian's chest bump against my spine, I relayed this information in my mind; trying to commit it to memory for future reference. "I see. Thanks for the rundown."

"There's also Obsidian, for dark magic. But it's not something that can be easily used."

"Why's that?" I asked.

"A rare crystal must be in the possession of the mage for them to be able to cast it," she said.

We slowed down as we came to a lake. "We are getting close to Highwell now. Let's lookout for any sign of Retgar," Evangeline said.

We cleared the lake and allowed our horses a moment to drink. Blok appeared as if out of thin air and he too drank from the lake. During this time Evangeline forced me to take a swig of my flask and eat some of the herbs she'd given me for my blood.

Her regard for my health caught me off guard. Being a marine was tough, because succumbing to medical conditions only made you weak. You'd be seen as a liability. But having somebody who was urging me to look after myself, instead of exerting myself was something I wasn't used to.

"Has he not recovered from the poison yet?" Finian asked. Unaware of where Evangeline's concerns had come from.

Deciding to change the subject, I asked for an estimate on how many hours away from Highwell we were.

"Let's see," said Finian, rummaging his pockets. He then pulled out my smartphone. "Your clock isn't set to the right time, but two hours have passed since I last looked at it. So, since we've reached the river I think we should easily be in Highwell in about four hours."

I snatched my phone from his hands. "What are you doing with that?"

"Oh sorry, I took it to have another look at it. Guess I forgot to give it back."

"You would make a great thief, you know that?" I said.

"Would?" He raised an eyebrow.

"Enough," said Evangeline. "Let's continue."

We continued on for some time and the silence became suffocating. We were paying close attention to the path, looking for signs of Retgar. Blok was keeping pace alongside us as our speed slowed. I could hear him sniffing continuously, catching the scent of things we couldn't see.

Trees parted as the path expanded and when light sprinkled through the patches of leaves above us, we knew we were coming to an exit in the forest. "We are near Highwell now," said Evangeline.

After emerging from the forest, I was met with a view that could have been from a painting. The path ahead was a long wood bridge leading into a giant lump of land beside a mountain. On top of the land was a city. The city had an array of pointed roofs and towers. A giant waterfall was at the backdrop and its waters forked in many directions beneath the cliff we were now clearing. Another bridge arched out from the left hand side of the incredible city, leading onto a ravine.

"It's beautiful," I said as we cleared the bridge.

"That it is," said Finian from behind.

After we cleared the bridge, we were met with a sight that we had hoped not to find. Retgar's body lay sprawled across a patch of grass.

CHAPTER 20

AFTER SOME EXAMINATION, Evangeline found that Retgar wasn't beyond being saved. As long as his severe injuries were tended to with haste, he would live. She'd healed his wounds with magic the best she could, but he would need stitches. Finian ran ahead and banged on the gates, yelling through the peephole for the guards to open up. They were reluctant, until Finian threatened to have their jobs taken for allowing a master warrior to die.

We decided to place Retgar on the cart that his horse had been pulling the artifact on, so we could push him through the city without aggravating his injuries. When Finian had made his way back to us, we lifted the chest off of the cart. Blok carried Retgar and slammed him on the cart with so much force that we winced at the thud.

"Careful, Blok!" Evangeline snapped.

"Blok sorry." he grunted.

Highwell's streets were densely populated. "Please clear a path, we have a master warrior who is in serious need of help," yelled Finian.

Crowds of people parted as we pushed through. People stared, and I wasn't sure if they were more curious about the dying warrior with the golden armor, or the bunch of misfits pushing him forward. My skinsuit stood out among the leathers, tunics and common fabrics that the locals wore. And the sight of the Mutano caused many people to rush into buildings.

The urgency of the situation made it difficult to admire the city, but I could tell that Highwell was an architect's dream. We passed under bridged walkways and towering archways that were expertly crafted. At the center of the city was a giant bell tower with a golden clock face on the front. Finian had also pointed to a coliseum where gladiators collided for leisure.

Soon we reached the gates of the Warriors Guild to the far right side of the city.

"Master Retgar!" Came a cry from the gate. "What has happened to Master Retgar?" An armored man sprinted forward.

"We found him passed out outside the walls." Finian explained.

"He has multiple lacerations and has lost excessive amounts of blood. He needs immediate care. I am a former healer of the Mages Guild, ready to assist should you need me," said Evangeline.

More men had rushed out from the gates now and I moved aside to let them take the cart. "You better come with us then, me lady," said the man.

Blok startled the men as he dropped the chest containing the artifact at their feet. "What in the name of Jerrus is this Mutano doing here?" the man asked, reaching slowly for his blade.

"Relax." I held his arm. "Blok here helped rid Corwy of an entire horde of Undead." The man considered this and lowered his arm.

"I take it the Runes of Aktarth are inside? I forgot it was due back here so soon," he said.

"Runes of Aktarth you say?" said Finian.

"Forget I said that. You aren't to know that."

"It's not me you have to worry about." Finian replied. "Highwell may be in danger of attack over these runes. You must gather defenses from all guilds and set up scouts outside the walls. Corwy has already fallen victim to an attack from the Undead."

"The Undead? They are no match for the defenses of Highwell," said the man.

"May I ask your name?" I cut in, holding out a hand to embrace him.

"Danford," he replied, taking my hand. "And you are?" he asked, glancing at my armor.

"Brandon; I'm a traveler who knows the threat that lurks. It's important that you don't underestimate the enemy. Not only have they captured a Master Conjurer and led an Undead army, but their leader is attempting to mind warp the Mutanos.”

At this, Danford glanced at Blok with his mouth agape. “I'll take your word for it I suppose. But our priority right now is to get Retgar healthy again so that he may tell us the dangers that he faced.”

“We wish to be there once they revive Retgar,” said Finian.

“I suppose you've earned that.” Danford proceeded to give the three of us small orbs the size of marbles. “Take these; they will glow once we summon you.”

“I've never seen anything like it,” said Finian, twirling the orb around in his hands. Sparkling mists pulsated in different colors inside the glass orb.

“Highwell is a big place. The Elves at the Mages Guild created these orbs as a means to summon one another when needed. All I have to do is close my eyes, envision who I wish to summon and if they have an orb it will glow and emit an energy that will make them suddenly aware that the orb is glowing. Even if the orb is locked away in a draw in their study, they will suddenly have a need to seek it out. It's an efficient use of mind magic.”

“I suppose that's the closest thing to a smartphone you guys have,” I joked. Only Finian chuckled.

“I must head back inside,” said Danford, shaking our hands. He paused in front of the Mutano, rubbing his neck. Blok raised his hand; as if that was the only pleasantry he could offer. Danford nodded. "Please, try not to lose your orbs. If you get farther than two building lengths away, you'll no longer be drawn to them when you're summoned. For now, enjoy Highwell."

Before long, we found ourselves separated. Finian had disappeared among the mass of people navigating the streets. Blok and I were left trying to hold awkward conversations.

"Blok want mead," he said, pointing at a tavern on the corner of a narrow street.

"You drink?" I asked.

Blok grunted. "Other man thinks Blok is animal."

I had to avoid chuckling at the statement. "I suppose I could do with some myself." I shrugged, knowing that it was probably a bad idea, given my health risks.

Together, we walked towards the tavern door. An eerie silence came about as soon as we'd made it through the door. Several faces stared our way, mouths wide open. Eager to ignore the onlookers, I waked straight towards the bartender. Blok followed with loud audible stomps.

"Do you have brandy?" I asked the the bartender. She nodded in response. "I'll have a small glass of that and whatever he wants." I patted Blok on the back and he pointed to a bottle high up on a shelf behind the bartender.

"One glass?" she asked, eying Blok.

"Bottle," said Blok, in the least threatening grunt I had ever heard from him.

"That will run ye five gold and two silvers for the both. That mead is rare stuff," she said.

Finian and I had split our coins between us the day before, but looking through the sack I held, I realized that after paying, I would be left with only a few silvers. "Ugh, Blok. I don't mean to be a party pooper, but is there anything cheaper you could have?"

"Mmmph! Pooper." He grunted.

As I fumbled with coins, I felt a presence behind us. I turned to see a number of men staring. "I'm not sure where you hale from; but only humans are welcome in this tavern. You might want to take yer pet here somewhere else," said a man, positioned in front of three companions.

"Leave them be, Ulrik. Don't forget you still owe me yer tab so I won't appreciate you running off customers willing to pay." The bartender yelled.

"With all due respect, lady," I said, "Nobody will be run off in here. We have the right to drink; especially my friend here who has saved countless human lives."

"I don't give a shit who he saved. He's still a filthy abomination," said the one called Ulrik, pressing his finger into my chest. I knocked his hand away as the Mutano roared. Ulrik stepped back, his hand gripping the handle of the hammer at his waist.

"Come on boys, let's have them," said Ulrik. But little did he know, his backup had abandoned him. When he realized this he barked before swinging his hammer at Blok. Blok caught the man's wrist and flipped him over. Ulrik's weight came crashing down on a table, shattering it to pieces.

Blok then picked the man up by the neck and walked him to the door, before tossing him through the doors as easy as a plank of wood. A burst of applause erupted from inside the tavern as if the Mutano had just provided the daily entertainment. When Blok reached the bar again he slammed a gold coin down in front of the bartender. "Bottle," he said.

I couldn't contain my laughter. "I think you've been hanging with Finian for too long." I said, shaking my head at the theatrics. Blok's lip curved into what might have been a smile.

For some time, we sat enjoying our drinks. Although I realized just how out of place Blok seemed among us humans, it was nice to finally have some downtime; and to engage in something as casual as drinking alcohol. My plan was to limit myself to just one drink. I wasn't a lightweight, but the alcohol would dehydrate my body to dangerous levels; inviting the worst kinds of sickle cell pains.

I recalled countless nights in which I'd gone out drinking with marine buddies, only to be up all night suffering from excruciating pains. Drinking alcohol was always a risk, and it was a risk I shouldn't take in Relaun.

How hard the drink was hitting the Mutano, I didn't know, because his demeanor never changed in the slightest. But I had the feeling that the mead had triggered a sudden desire for him to communicate.

Slowly, it became clear that Blok wasn't as slow as I once thought. He told me of how Mutanos have the ability to communicate telepathically so there's never a need to speak English—or Anglish as it was called in Relaun. This meant that Blok's poor use of Anglish was the equivalent of a non-Anglish speaker learning the language for the first time.

I tried to train him to say my name. "Bran-don," I said. "It's just *bran* and then *don* at the end."

"Bran...Do," he mumbled.

"It's a start, we'll work on it. How long did it take for you to learn Finian's?"

"Finian teach Blok Anglish every day," he said. My eyes strayed beyond Blok's bulky shoulders to where a mysterious man with a thick mane of white hair was approaching us.

CHAPTER 21

"EXCUSE ME," SAID THE MAN. "Could I ask you two to assist with an important task? It's just that two of my judges have drunk themselves to oblivion and now I am in dire need of replacements."

"Judges?" I asked.

"Yes," he said, rubbing white strands of hair on his face. "Two of the most promising Highwell youths are to engage in their Trial of Becoming today and there must be only one winner."

Once I knew what he was asking, my ethics made me want to refuse. But, something one of my Lieutenants had said came to mind: *Change must occur from the inside.*

"I'll do it," I said, "you coming, Blok?"

"Blok stay here," said the Mutano.

"That's a shame. I thought a Mutano would make an excellent judge for this contest. Though I'm sure some of the committee would be against the idea," said the man. "The name is Arn. I'm head of the youth committee here in Highwell. And you are?"

"Brandon Wardson, a traveler," I shook his hand.

Arn remarked on how unique my skinsuit was as he

led me out of the tavern. "So, what kind of contest will this be anyway?" I asked.

"The boys must slay a beast. If one of them manages it and the other does not, then the winner will be clear and judging won't be necessary. If they both slay the beast or neither of them does, then we will need judges to determine who did it the best."

"Will it be dangerous?" I asked, as we turned down a sloping alley. The tall curves of the coliseum walls could be seen at the bottom of the street.

Arn glanced at me. "Of course, there is always the possibility of death. Have you not witnessed trials before? I suppose as a traveler you grew up in the wilds."

I shook my head. "Why am I the only one that sees a problem with subjecting innocent youths to something that can kill them?"

"With all due respect my friend, we are looking for a judge, not someone looking to preach their morals. You know how dangerous it is in Aldeen. We need to ensure that men are strong enough to cope with the threats that lie ahead. With respect to your friendly Mutano, the rest of them could decide to attack humans again at any time. We also have an increasing number of necromancer activity and the Elves have seen dragons flying over Thirion many times. In these times, we cannot let our young men cower."

"There are better ways to train them."

An older black man cut me off as we walked into the coliseum. "Arn, you have returned. Did you find the other judges?"

"Sorry Josef, but they weren't in any shape to judge. Luckily I found this mysterious looking traveler who goes by the name Brandon. He was with a Mutano, so I am sure he has the credentials to judge such a task," said Arn, patting my chest. "I suppose I will also fill in for the other missing judge."

Josef's eyeballs shifted between me and Arn. "I suppose it will have to do. We have no time left to linger. Follow me."

The coliseum was magnificent. Sitting at the judge's panel gave me an elevated view of the oval amphitheater. Rows of limestone panels were pillared in a circle, holding thousands of seats for spectators; but the coliseum wasn't full. A rough guess would have me at around two hundred people in attendance. Looking down, the stage itself was graveled with stone walls erected into a maze-like arrangement. "We decided we would have walls to obstruct the children's view of the monster. It will help them develop hunting skills if they must seek out their target before it finds them," said Arn.

Even being a product of the harshest training regimen in space wasn't as jarring as this. At least I'd had a choice in the matter.

"Ladies and gentlemen thank you for being in attendance for today's Trial of Becoming." came the voice of a young announcer. He wore brown robes with a red cape that draped behind him. The man was speaking into his hand. "Today, Highwell's most promising children will participate in a test of survival, to see who is worthy of carrying their father's name. We have three judges here today. The first is Master Warden, Jale Enchcroft of the Warriors Guild, who has promised a position at the guild for today's winner." To my right I saw the robed man sitting next to Arn raise his fist into the air. A scar curved at the side of his face like a crescent moon, he had a single strand of white hair that shot up among the brown strands from his forehead. He had a signature thick beard, which I now knew was a common trend of the warriors. "Also judging will be head of the youth committee here in Highwell, Arn Mathier." Arn stood and bowed towards the announcer. "Finally, we have a replacement judge. I'm told that this man travels with a Mutano which he has tamed. So there is no denying that this mysterious traveler has valuable experience of the wilds. Please welcome, Brandon." I nodded with little enthusiasm, unhappy with the introduction. They were making Blok sound as if he were a wild beast that I had conquered.

"Now, let us commence. Each contestant will enter

individually and they will have ten minutes to slay the best that shall be let loose at the other end of the stage. Both monsters will be different, and the contestants have no knowledge of what may lie ahead. First up will be young Oswald, son of Brent Haugen. Oswald has excelled far beyond his peers during his hunting lessons. He hopes to demonstrate his skill today and earn his father's name."

The young boy entered from behind the pillars at the opposite end of the coliseum. He wore a hooded leather robe with a quiver carrying arrows for the bow he held at his side. At the side of the stage closest to where we sat, two men pulled a cart with a large box shaped veil, concealing whatever was underneath. They lifted the box from the cart and removed the veil to reveal a creature that looked like a cross between a wolf and a crocodile. The creature's body was full of scales and its head was long and flat, leading to a fanged mouth that could snap shut before you could blink. It stood high on all fours with its long tail curling behind it. The beast's feet were webbed.

Arn leaned over to me, "a Dilowolf; fast-moving with a snappy bite. That's a cruel choice of beast for the young boy. He'll have to be particularly cunning to come out of this alive."

"And you still think this is okay?" I asked. Arn didn't answer as the men carrying the beast were now sliding the front of the cage open. The beast bolted out of the cage as soon as the gap was wide enough for it, and I saw the men run to the back of the coliseum. A line of fire shot up from the ground, preventing the beast from leaving the stage.

On the opposite side of the stage, the boy, Oswald, was creeping to the first stone wall, unaware of the danger awaiting him. Oswald then climbed the second wall he came to. This wall was much smaller in size than the first but he was still unable to see the beast.

The Dilowolf was beginning to walk in Oswald's direction as if sensing a prey nearby. Its broad snout swayed left to right after each step it took with its long legs and webbed paws. Oswald took an arrow from his quiver and nocked it. I heard gasps escape the audience as we all wondered what he was aiming at. The beast wasn't near enough for him to have seen it, let alone fire at it.

He shot an arrow that fell somewhere beneath him and shook his head before taking another arrow. We knew the second arrow had hit what he was aiming at because he leaped down from the wall and took his arrows back. Onlookers soon realized that Oswald had killed a rat and was now laying it by the edge of the stage as bait for the creature he could not see. With the bait in place, he scaled another wall and waited with an arrow in his bow.

"What a smart young lad. Putting those darn pests to

good use," said Arn. As we saw the Dilowolf approach Oswald's position we held our breaths in unison. The beast dashed forward as it smelled the dead rodent, and Oswald took his shot. The arrow hit the Dilowolf's hind leg and it moaned before turning to find the culprit. When it failed to find anyone to its left and right, it finally looked up at Oswald who had another arrow ready to fire. A sound of pity escaped the audience as Oswald missed the shot completely.

What came next had me shifting in my seat. The Dilowolf's tail extended over its head and whipped the boy's feet, causing him to lose balance and fall from the wall. "Damn, that was a hard fall. He needs help," I said, shooting up from my seat.

"Relax, Brandon, the boy must learn," said Arn. I turned to look at him and saw the Master Warden side-eying me.

"How will he learn if he's dead?" I yelled.

"Sit down, traveler, you're making a fool of yourself," said the Master Warden.

"Oh dear," said Arn, his eyes now back on the action. The Dilowolf was pouncing, as the boy struggled to his feet. Oswald managed to grab a dagger he'd had tied to his suit, but before he could use it, the Dilowolf's jaws had locked over his arm. The scream was heard throughout the entire coliseum and I had the sudden urge to jump down to the stage to help.

The only thing stopping me was a memory that haunted me. During one of my VR simulations I'd exerted my body to its limits and become breathless. My teammates had to abandon the mission to ensure that I was alright. It was an automatic fail for me and I'd had to sit out for an entire year before trying to get back into the marines. Being saved or rescued during a test would no doubt make the boy feel as though he was incapable of getting the job done on his own. It was what Finian must have felt after being unable to execute Blok. For that reason, I decided that I'd only jump in if he was on the brink of death. The boy still had a fighting chance.

For a minute, it seemed that brink of death moment might come as blood leaked from the boy's arm. His screams had become quiet and he now seemed determined to release himself from the beast's hold. Somehow, the boy managed to wrestle the beast onto the floor and grab the dagger he had dropped with his other hand. With his arm still locked between the beast's teeth, the boy brought the dagger up into the Dilowolf's throat three times until his arm came free.

"He's done it, that's a kill!" said the announcer, speaking into his hand. Oswald, who was distraught, continued to stab the creature until he was encouraged to get treated for his wounds.

"You see, Brandon? The adrenaline always helps them in the end," said Arn. I chose to ignore him. Instead, I hoped the next teenager would have an easier time than Oswald did.

The stage was cleared before the announcer came back to introduce the next contestant. "As a reminder to you all, the next contestant must slay his creature for this contest to go to the judges. If he fails to slay the creature within the time limit then Oswald will be our winner by default. Our next contestant goes by the name Erwin, and he is the son of Jared Glazur."

Erwin wore leather overalls over his bare chest. A spear was his choice of weapon and he wore skeletal face paint on one half of his face, giving him a menacing look. "He sure seems confident doesn't he?" said Arn.

Below us, another creature was being unleashed. This time it was a large arachnid, similar in size to the Dilowolf before it. "Let's hope it doesn't get its pincers on young Erwin. These spiders are venomous." I shot a blank look in response to Arn.

The spider showed more intelligence than the Dilowolf as it moved swiftly through the walls. It was leaving webs that stretched at all angles, creating traps for the poor unsuspecting teen. As Erwin approached the middle of the stage, the spider snuck along the outskirts, webbing up walls that Erwin had already passed. The spider then backtracked, creepily crawling along the outskirts until it was back in front of where Erwin was heading. It was as if the spider already knew the layout of the area the way it was plotting against the boy. There was webbing both behind and ahead of Erwin, and he would run into it once he turned the next corner.

And then, something none of us expected happened. The spider perched itself on the highest wall on the stage. It must have spotted the spectators, as it began to shoot venom into the audience.

"By The Elders!" Arn stood.

"How could you ever think this was a good idea?" I asked, standing alongside him. I watched as Erwin turned, figuring out the arachnid's position based on the cries from the crowd. Then, the spider leaped across two of the walls until it was at the center point of the stage. It then faced us, the judges. It was as if by standing up we had caught its attention.

To our shock, the spider came leaping at us. I held up my blaster and Jale unsheathed his sword as if ready to toss it at the spider. But—while in mid-air—the arachnid's body was struck by the spear that had been in Erwin's hands moments before. The spear connected just below the pillar we were stood above, the spider's dead body hung in the center of it and the audience erupted in cheers.

"Oh my! That shot was incredible. There's no denying that this boy has won," said Arn.

"Screw the trial. You could have had people killed; people who weren't even a part of your stupid test."

Jale pointed his sword in my direction, "If I were you, I would watch my mouth, stranger," said the Master Warden.

"Well I guess you're not me," I shot back.

"Both of our promising young men have slain their creature so let us now invite our judges down to the podium to call the winner," said the announcer.

"Come," said Arn. He stepped between Jale and me and then led me down a set of steps to the lower level by the podium. Only then did I realize that the announcer had been talking into an orb. Like the one Danford had given us earlier.

As the coliseum workers removed the spider's body, both young men were called up to the podium with us.

Arn received the orb first so that he could cast his vote. "I would first like to say that both of these youngsters have handled themselves like men today." There were cheers from the audience, causing Arn to pause. "But of course, only one of them may earn their father's name. There is no denying that Erwin should be the one to earn the name of Glazur after that fantastic shot with his spear. A shot that likely saved my life." There was a round of applause for the boy and even I had to respect the courage that the he'd shown.

Arn passed the orb to me. "Hold it in front of your mouth as you speak and it will amplify your voice," he whispered.

"To reiterate what Arn said, I want to say that I respect both of these young men for their display of courage today." This time there was no applause, the crowd were confused about my appearance. "Before I get to who I think won the contest, I want to take a moment to say something about these trials." I felt the eyes of Arn and Jale bore me from each side. "I've been in Aldeen for a few days and there are people in this region that I've come to respect. For that reason, I won't stand here and disrespect your traditions. Still, I want to ask you all if you feel it's right to subject your children to such dangerous tasks; just to prove that they are men. As someone who has trained for years to become, what you may call a warrior, I can tell you that forcing a young man in a situation that tests his manhood, will lead to many of them feeling inferior to others." I was beginning to hear displeasure among the audience at my words. "I want to stress that having the mother's name be attached to a failure, only degrades the strong women in society who work as hard as men do. Why should someone feel like a loser for having their mother's..." A tomato pounded my forehead and I staggered backwards. Cabbages, carrots and other vegetables followed as the audience let their displeasure be known.

Jale attempted to grab the orb from my hand but I whacked his hand away. This resulted in the two of us coming chin to chin; staring each other down. At this, the crowd roared with excitement, urging us to duel right there on the podium.

CHAPTER 22

"YOU DARE PISS ON THE NAME of Lord Jerrus with your blabbering?" said Jale. We were so close that I felt his hot breath circumvent around my face.

"I don't know your Lord. I just know how people should be treated." My fingers locked around the hilt of my sword, ready for any sign of attack from the Master Warden. I wouldn't aim to kill him, but I would defend myself if he took it there.

Then a sound derailed all trail of thought. The chanting from the crowd muffled as the buzzing noise became louder. It was as if someone was equalizing sounds in my head. Something told me to reach into my pocket, and that's when I pulled out a glowing orb. The orb blinked.

I walked to the edge of the podium and as I looked back over my shoulder, I saw Jale jumping off the opposite side.

"Wait, where are you two going? I need my vocal orb back," said the announcer.

"Sorry," I said tossing the other orb over my shoulder. I jumped from the side of the podium, landing atop one of the walls on the stage and continuing my way down to ground level.

"We want the duel! We want the duel! We want the duel!" The crowd repeated as I ran towards the central exit. Nothing would have made me happier than fighting for human rights in Relaun. But there was a bigger fight waiting. Retgar was awake, and now it was time to take action against Flurwick.

As I marched up the path towards the warrior's guild, Finian was taking large joyful strides in front of me. He was unaware that I was behind him so I tapped his shoulder.

Finian whipped around looking alarmed, until he saw my face. "Ah, there you are, Brandon. I take it your orb worked then," he said.

"It sure did. Where did you disappear to earlier?" I asked him

"I was going to ask you the same. One minute you were at me side and the next you'd vanished," he shrugged, "I'll tell you what though, I got me hands on some charged up Medius Stones. We can do some interesting things with those."

"That's if we aren't sent to a dungeon somewhere after they find out you've been thieving."

"How do you know I didn't pay for them?"

"Because I feel like I've known you for a whole lifetime already," I said, giving him a suspecting sideways glance. Finian chuckled, and we soon found our way to the gates of the guild hall.

"There you are," said Danford. "Come on, follow me; for there has been an assembly called. We have all Highwell's guild leaders gathered to hear Retgar's retelling of his ambush."

We were led to a large circular room with beautiful white and gold decor. The surrounding walls had upper floors with balconies; meaning, the room was also designed to have onlookers. At the center of the marble floor was a bowl shaped crater with a centerpiece statue floating above it. The golden statue was a man in robes with his right arm stretched outward. Above his hand was a glowing orb that lit up the area.

"The statue is of Lord Jerrus." Finian commented, as we approached the group of people who stood aside the statue. Master Retgar was seated on a chaise, topless with bandages over his upper body. Next to him, the hazel eyes of Evangeline found me. I tried to avoid staring into them. When I smiled she looked away.

Seconds later I realized why, as Blok was stomping

his way to the center of the room, escorted by two armored guards.

"What is that Mutano doing here?" Retgar asked. His voice was strong despite his injuries.

"Blok here, saved Corwy while you were away, sir," Finian responded. "Tore apart an entire horde of Undead he did; incapacitated them so that they could be burned."

"Well, it seems everyone is here that needs to be," came the voice of a lady. "I am aware we have a traveler here." Her hand strayed in my direction. "So let us all introduce ourselves as we speak. My name is Egith, Archmage of the Mages Guild. I command all of the Mage guild halls in Relaun," she said. With all the talk about Elves and magic, I had expected the leader of the Mages Guild to be of Elven race. But I suppose it made sense that the region of Aldeen would want humans at the forefront. Egith wore a long red robe with yellow outlines. An interesting assortment of jewelry graced her dark skin. Large golden bangles dangled from each of her wrists. I'd seen a decent number of black people during my time in Relaun, and it made me happy to see that humans of all ethnics were so unified.

"Beside me is Arjon—Grandmaster of the Warriors Guild, Hilda—master alchemist and lead hunter, and Robern—lead merchant. Sir Eldhert of the Farmers Guild is currently away from Highwell on business. You of course, already know Master Retgar, and Evangeline has already introduced herself. I must say that her talent for healing has me wondering why Corwy's guild would remove her."

"Lady Arch-mage, you flatter me." Evangeline curtsied.

"Before we hear from Retgar, I would like the traveler and his friends to introduce themselves and let us know why they have come all the way to Highwell."

"My name is Brandon Wardson." I nodded. "I owe you the truth. The truth is that I am from a galaxy known as the Milky Way. It is an arrangement of worlds where many species live. In this galaxy, people are able to travel between worlds using ships. To govern this galaxy, we have an organization called the Galactic Alliance. And that Alliance deploys marines to keep order in the galaxy. A marine, is the equivalent to what you call a warrior here in Relaun."

The wrinkled eyes of Egith bulged under her head wrap as I spoke. "This concept of many worlds entwined in a single space, it is so enticing. Please continue."

"Well. I was on a mission to find one of my superiors named Jonathan Flurwick, and one of my colleagues Natalya Carrick." Though I did not look, I felt Evangeline's eyes on me. "They had gone missing while on their own quest. When looking for them, I ended up falling into a black mist and when I came out of the other side, I was here in Relaun."

"And it was me who found him," said Finian. "The name is Finian Glaed, I work for merchant, Dalice Engreen in Corwy." He said, poking his chest out.

"Enough!" Retgar slammed his hand on the arm rest. If the man felt any pain, he made sure not to show it as he stood. "This Flurwick you speak of was named during the ambush." He pointed at me.

"Retgar, are you saying it was people like this traveler that attacked you?" asked Arjon, the Grandmaster of the Warriors Guild.

"I was attacked by Exul forces, and although I despise the Exul clan, they were clearly acting on behalf of another party." Retgar eyeballed me with the one pupil he had; the other eye being a solid ball of white. This was the first time I had looked at his face without his helmet. His thick gray beard showed his age. He had a chiseled physique and I stood as if he was proud of his body. "I heard them say *Flurwick needs the artifacts. Focus on securing the artifact; it matters not whether they die.'* This leads me to believe that the Exul were being led by your superior; which makes me question why you should be trusted."

"It is a reasonable concern," said Hilda, the master alchemist.

I readied myself to respond, but it was Evangeline who cut in before I could say a word. "Back in Corwy, I fed him truth serum. I was as cautious as each of you is now, but his truths were merely questions about the whereabouts of his comrades. We can trust this man."

I nodded. "May I also say that Flurwick's minion killed my partner? He then took many lives that I came to care for back in Corwy. I wish nothing more than to take him down before he has a chance to carry out his plans."

"Something tells me we can trust him," said Egith.

"Well, I suppose it saves me having to slip him some truth serum of me own then," said Hilda.

Finian walked a few steps in front of me and shook his head. "As leaders of Aldeen, I would expect you all to be focusing on what's important instead of deliberating over conclusions that have already been drawn. The fact of the matter here is that this man, Flurwick, is after the artifacts. It's time that we figure out why."

There was a pause before Egith stepped forward and bowed her head. "I agree with the boy," she said.

"I'm a man now actually," Finian retorted.

Egith continued to speak as if she hadn't heard Finian. "Let me tell you a little history about the artifacts so that you understand the dangers that may lie ahead; should they end up in the wrong hands."

CHAPTER 23

EGITH LOOKED INTO MY EYES as she spoke. Her level of devotion came across like a historian teaching the only person willing to listen. "It's believed that The Elders created Relaun three thousand years ago. They were gods. Gods who lived among their children and helped shape the lands into what we have now. The race of The Elders may differ based on who you ask. But my belief is that some of The Elders were human and some Elven. How other species came to be is but anyone's guess." She shot a quick glance over at Blok. "The Elders were graceful enough to bestow a fraction of their power to their children. Magic was their gift to the people fortunate enough to live in their world. But not everybody can be trusted with such power, so only the chosen would be born with the privilege to use this gift."

"I've heard these theories. What about the artifacts?" said Finian.

"Patience," Egith held up a finger, "the traveler must hear this if he is not from Relaun."

"Agreed," I nodded. "I want to hear this. It may help

me understand what Flurwick is after. Please continue."

"At the heart of Relaun is an island with eight giant crystals. We call it the Island of Crystalline. The crystals are wedged into the soil of the sacred land and they are what grant us all the ability to use our magic. The eight crystals represent each type of magic that species of Relaun are able to manipulate. We have elemental magic which consists of fire, ice, lightning and surface. We also have healing, death, force, and mind magic. All of these make up the types of magic you have seen here in Relaun." Finian yawned. "These crystals are sacred, and must never be breached. To make sure of this, The Elders ensured that it is impossible for anybody to get close to them. From the moment you make it to the Island of Crystalline, you will feel your body deteriorate. The energy emitted from the crystals will tear your body apart. Furthermore, there is a barrier around the crystals that will prevent contact with any living creature."

Some theories were forming in my mind but I needed more to go on. "I sense a *but* coming," I said.

"But; a common theory is that there may be a method of getting to the crystals. Nobody has ever attempted it and survived." At this point, everyone in the room was eager to hear more, despite the fact that some of them were already in the know about the island. Even

Finian became less animated, his face relaying an expression of deep thought. "The artifacts are belongings left behind by The Elders. The location of these artifacts has changed numerous times over the years. Some have even been lost and recovered. Currently, there are four known Elder artifacts in existence, and one of them we have here thanks to Master Retgar. In our possession we have the Runes of Aktarth, three magical runes belonging to Drellea Aktarth, one of The Elders. The Runes of Aktarth were in Corwy temporarily as we recently exchanged them with the Elven kingdom in Lainunia. They now have The Flask of Irithrel in their possession."

"Hang on, so if we're counting the runes as one artifact here, and the flask as another. Where are the other two?" I asked.

"This is where the matter gets complicated. To the north west of Relaun, is a region named Thirion. It's named after Vyncis Thirion, one of The Elders who had a falling out with the others. As an act of rebellion, he secluded himself to one island and abused his powers of summoning by spawning beasts and abominations; beasts that still lurk in Relaun to this day. It's said that the Staff of Enellas is somewhere in Thirion. Though, nobody knows how it got there. As for the Altar of Jerrus, it is said to have been lost for a thousand years in The Garden City to the south of Aldeen."

"Bleeding cry!" said Finian. "How careless can someone be to lose something so valuable?"

"This is an unconfirmed myth, but gathering all these artifacts and presenting them before the crystals on the island is said to grant a worthy soul access to their true power."

A million and one thoughts came to mind at once. But only one theory made sense after hearing her tale. "Flurwick wants to get to the crystals so that he can take control of Relaun's magic and return to the Milky Way with it. That has to be his end goal here," I said.

"If what you say is true, then he will need to gather each of the artifacts. This will be no easy task and we already have the upper hand," said Retgar.

"Indeed, we have an entire region at our disposal that will begin to search for these artifacts as soon as we give them the word. Flurwick's gathering is insignificant in comparison. They will not survive Thirion, let alone the Elven Kingdom in Lainunia," said Egith.

"But if he enlists the Exul, the Undead and the Mutanos to his cause, won't he be able to put up a good enough fight?" I asked.

"That is certainly a frightening thought," said Hilda.

"We need to divide efforts," said Finian. "The Elven Kingdom must be alerted as soon as possible and then we need to have multiple teams on the hunt for the remaining artifacts. It's crucial that we find them before he does."

Retgar stared down Finian. "You might be right there young man, but I will not take direction from a Mothernamed."

Blok and I edged forward at the bluntness of the comment.

"Enough," Egith raised her hand. "This is not the time to bicker over names. The boy is right."

Finian looked from left to right. "What boy?"

Evangeline then stepped forward to speak. "May I suggest that the four of us head to Lainunia first so that we may persuade the Elven Kingdom to assist in gathering the artifacts?" Given her Elven roots, it was a wise suggestion, but I assumed that the government of Aldeen had other high ranking Elves to communicate with Lainunia.

Egith considered it for a second before replying, "I have no problem with this. You four have proved yourselves capable of such responsibility. Would anyone else object?" she asked. Retgar looked as though he wanted to open his mouth but decided against it. "Good, then you four will head to Lainunia to retrieve the flask."

Arjon, Grandmaster of the Warriors Guild turned to face Retgar. "Master Retgar, are you fit for duty?"

Retgar bowed. "Yes Grandmaster, the healer has done her job well. I feel like I could take on an entire legion." Beside me, Evangeline shook her head as if she knew better.

"Then I would ask that you lead a fleet of warriors over to Thirion to retrieve the Staff of Enellas," said Arjon.

"It would be my honor, Grandmaster, sir." Retgar raised a fist.

Arjon turned to face the door where Danford stood guard. "Danford, please send for the Master Warden," he said. My lip twitched and settled into a smirk as I thought about the heated exchange I'd had with the Master Warden earlier. Moments later, Jale stepped into the room and joined us under the statue of Jerrus. He bowed before the Grandmaster. When he straightened up he shot me a glance.

"Jale," Arjon said. "We have been discussing the elder artifacts. It has come to our attention that Retgar's attackers are seeking them. We must gather them before they do. Retgar will be leading a team of warriors to Thirion and I would like for you to lead another team to The Garden City."

"Your wish is my command, Grandmaster," said Jale. "These four have also agreed to head to the Lainunia to persuade the Elves to aid us in this quest." Jale's nostrils flared as he shot me another glance. "With any hope, the Elves may add to our armies. Both The Garden City and the region of Thirion are said to be dangerous places. Keep your wits about you and be careful." Arjon said in closing.

"What about Highwell?" I asked. "By now Flurwick knows the artifact is here. More than likely he'll be planning an attack,"

"And when he does, he'll have a full scale war on his hands. There's no place in Aldeen as guarded as the city of Highwell. We have the strongest weapons, warriors and mages at our disposal." This did little to reassure me, but I was sure they would at least put up a fight long enough for a counter-attack to occur. "When all of the artifacts are secured, we should gather them all here in Highwell." Arjon continued.

"I will ensure scouts are set up both outside of Highwell and around The Garden City so that Jale won't have any nasty surprises," said Hilda. "All of you are free to visit my alchemist shops around Highwell and claim as many vials as you need."

"We're dealing with someone cunning here. Flurwick will alter his plans once he realizes that we're all looking for the artifacts. Is there any method of communication that will allow us to update each other on our progress?" I asked.

I figured it would be a long shot but Egith asked Danford to open the door. She then held both of her arms out in front of her and her eyes rolled back inside of her head. Most of us stood confused for what seemed like minutes. Only the three other guild leaders looked on as though this was a common occurrence. We started to hear chirping and looked around to find the source of the noise. Seconds later, two falcons, one white one black, flew through the door and they each settled on one of Egith's arms.

Her eyes returned to normal. "Meet my precious falcons. Both birds are bound to me with mind magic. Orato is the white bird; he is able to understand speech and can relay spoken words back to me, and only me. Audette, the black bird, is able to observe what is happening and will also be able to plant images in your mind, letting you know what is happening elsewhere. I'll see to it that these birds fly between each region of Relaun and pass information between us. If you see the white bird, Orato, please talk to him. Audette doesn't need talking to but if convenient then allow her to connect with your mind and relay information. She will sit on your shoulder when she needs to do this."

"Okay, this may actually be more incredible than a smartphone," said Finian, making me laugh through my nose.

"This is exactly what I've been asking for," I said. "This will help us more than you could ever understand." Egith raised her arms and both birds flew out through the door.

"As this is an urgent matter, I would suggest that you all go and get some rest so that you may leave as soon as you feel up to the journey," said Arjon. "The stables have at least two dozen horses with force magic. The magic allows them to gallop at far superior speeds than a regular horse. Each person assigned a task in this room should take one. Master Retgar and Master Warden Jale shall split the rest between their fleets.

"Magical birds? Faster horses? All the potions I could want? You mind throwing in some weapons too?" asked

Finian.

"You've some nerve addressing yer leaders like that you know?" Jale snarled. "But I suppose I shouldn't expect anything less than another mouthy turd considering you're hanging with that one." Jale pointed my way.

I popped my knuckles in my palm. "If you have a problem, I don't mind settling it outside, Master Warden."

"We'd ought to rethink sending these men out on such important tasks if they're behaving like locals at the tavern," said Hilda.

"Hmph..." Arjon grunted. "Testosterone is all this is. It's healthy for warriors to want to knock each other about. Just don't jeopardize the tasks we have assigned you. As for the matter of weapons, you may visit the armory and take what you need. Danford can assist you in that regard."

"We wish you all good luck. If you need us then please visit our respective guild hall," said Egith.

All four guild leaders departed. A moment of awkwardness ensued as the four of us found ourselves alone with Retgar and Jale; both of them looking as though they were waiting for a moment to tear us to shreds. The presence of the Mutano might have caused them to rethink their actions.

Evangeline stepped towards Retgar and handed him a small jar from her pouch. "You must take these for the next two days. The blades you were struck with may carry diseases. These will stop you from being infected. Be sure to also apply the paste I gave you earlier to the wounds every day " she said.

Retgar said his thanks and we all left the room.

Chapter 24

LIEUTENANT-COMMANDER Jonathan Flurwick and Simon Cunningham stepped out of their Alliance shuttle and walked towards the dingy warehouse. The security system detected their presence and the A.I asked them to state their name and business.

"Flurwick; here to see Kura."

"Verifying that now," came the response from the A.I. The square OLED screen displayed a swirling icon as it waited for confirmation from its owner. Seconds later, the OLED flashed green and the door opened to admit them.

Inside, young people sat at computers with headphones over their ears; oblivious to anything happening around them. A few of them were playing video games. Others were highlighting lines of code and copying them into different documents. Flurwick and Simon walked right past the hackers and headed for the back room. Double doors shot open as they approached. The man, Kura, swung around on his seat as he heard them enter. On the giant screen behind him was some kind of Anime.

"Flurwick, my man," Kura said, rising from his seat. "I'm not sure what kind of shit you're getting into. I have no idea why a scroll full of doodles is so difficult to get hold of. It was a lot of effort getting past security at that museum."

"Kura, I asked you to shut your mouth about it. Hand it to me now." Flurwick held his hand out.

Kura took a pull on his vape mouthpiece and it glowed green as he dragged on it. "Flurwick, you military boys are good. We value you. You keep us all safe in the Milky Way and prevent intergalactic war," said Kura, blowing out smoke. "But a common trait I find with you marines is that you think you run the show; no matter what planet you happen to be on." Kura picked up a blaster from his desk. As he did this, several of his minions stood, each of them holding firearms. "Getting your damned scroll was a pain in the ass, Flurwick. So I'm not handing it over to you without getting my credits first."

Flurwick held up his smartphone. "Paying you isn't a problem, Kura. But I'm not going to foolishly handover that amount of credits without even confirming that what you have is the real deal."

At this, Kura looked at the girl to his right and

nodded. She turned to the high desk behind her and opened up a black box. She carefully removed the scroll, holding one of the bars in each hand. She then unrolled the scroll so that the contents could be read.

Flurwick glanced at the scribbles and diagrams on the scroll. He raised his eyebrows in response and the girl rolled the scroll back together. "Take his payment, Shad," said Kura. The man known as Shad walked towards Flurwick and stopped in front of him. He held out a small payment widget for Flurwick to swipe his phone. Instead, Flurwick shot a laser through the man's forehead that also tore through Kura's chest behind him.

"You bastard!" Kura gulped. "Kill him," he said before his body crashed to the floor. Simon began unloading his blaster on everyone in the room while Flurwick walked towards the girl. She looked to be in her early twenties. With every step Flurwick took towards her, she took a step back, until she was pressed up against the wall.

Flurwick picked up the black box containing the scroll and eyed the girl. "You shouldn't be hanging out with scum," he said, before blasting a hole through her head.

* * *

Finding my breath was hard as I palpitated between the sheets. The bed sheets were moist with sweat beneath me and I had the sudden desire to tear off my vest. When I moved, I realized that my joints were on fire inside. Immediately, I found myself in torturous amounts of pain.

"Brandon, what's wrong?" came Evangeline's voice from the top bunk. "Your breathing is irregular." The hazel eyes peaked from over the side of frame.

"I..." was all I could get out as I tried to steady my breathing. Beside me I heard snoring from Finian's bed. There was creaking as Evangeline made her way down the ladder. A jug full of water was being pushed to my lips.

"Drink," she said. My breathing seemed to calm more with every gulp.

"Thanks," I said.

I felt her hand on my forehead. "Are you in any pain?" she asked.

"My hips and elbows." I panted. "But it's normal, not serious." I lied. This was almost on the level of a sickle cell crisis—a term that represented the worst possible state for a sickle cell patient to be in. I took another sip of water and collected my thoughts. "Flurwick, I saw him in my dream. But it was more like a flashback of something that happened back in the Milky Way."

"Are you sure about that? Perhaps you're dreaming of him because you're anxious about what lies ahead."

"No," I shouted louder than I meant to. "This was way too clear of a vision to be a dream. I felt as though I was there, it was too vivid."

"Stop that racket will ya?" said Finian, turning over. His snoring soon commenced.

"What happened in this vision?" she asked.

"He was after some scroll. He hired some kind of freelancer to get the scroll for him. The scroll had these weird scribbles and diagrams, but Flurwick understood them. I could tell. He murdered the freelancers as soon as he saw where they were keeping it; even an innocent young girl."

"Hmm..." She sighed. "When you saw Flurwick in Relaun, didn't you say he tried his mind magic on you?"

"Yes," I said, twitching as I felt a sharp stab in my hip.

"It's possible that you have somehow gained his memory as a result of him penetrating your mind." She walked somewhere out of my line of sight. When she came back she had her right hand closed around something. "Remember when your girlfriend suddenly broke from her indoctrination and began calling for you to help her? It's a somewhat similar effect. Because I was breaking into her mind, she was able to briefly fight her indoctrination. In your case, the indoctrination failed, but increments of Flurwick's mind may have been planted in yours."

"She's not my girlfriend," I said, looking into those eyes that I found too hard to avoid.

"It matters not," she said.

"Will these...increments, affect my behavior moving forward?"

"I should hope not. But you must tell me if this happens again so that I may try to figure out a means to dispel the effect."

"Can't you go into my mind and fix it?" I asked.

She knelt beside me once more and her necklace flashed so bright I thought it would blind me. "It's not so simple. And my mind magic isn't the best." She tossed a powdery substance into the jug of water and handed it to me. "Drink up, this will help the pain and it will help you sleep. We only have two hours before we set out. It's important that you are well rested." Obeying her order, I gulped down the remaining water in seconds. It tasted tangy, but by now I was used to disgusting medical substances. I eased back against my pillow and felt it hit me instantly.

"Thank you, Eva," I said. "I haven't been looked after this much since I left Earth."

She smiled. "Tell me about Earth." She shifted her weight onto her buttocks and leaned her arms on the side of my mattress. I felt conscious of how close our faces were. It made me uncomfortable; yet, I was hoping she wouldn't move.

"It's a big world." I slurred, my head feeling heavy, "with many countries and regions. People there used to squabble over race relations and politics all the time. But in Earth year twenty-thirty-three, first-contact with an alien race was made on another world called Mars. Since making peace with an intergalactic race called Stowyths, the science and technology of Earth changed drastically. Now Earth is a hub for intergalactic entertainment and trading. People there seem happier these days. Besides my family I guess."

"What's wrong with your family?" she asked. Her

eyes were puffy and half open, as if she was also struggling to stay awake.

"Well...not only do they hate the thought of any kind of intergalactic mixing, but they also resent me for joining the Galactic Alliance. But I guess much of it has to do with them worrying for my health."

"That's understandable. Families can become attached."

"If only there was a way to tell them I'm being well looked after right now. I'm sure they'd be happy."

She giggled. "What would you tell them?"

Unsure of how to answer I looked into her eyes and drank in her appearance. My head weighed a ton. If I hadn't been feeling like a wreck, I may have held her soft brown hair in my hands. Something about the way her ears pointed out from under her loose blanket of hair gave her a harmonious look under the candle light. If I wasn't drifting away, I may have worked up the courage to plant a soft, slow kiss on her plump lips while staring into those hazel eyes I would then close my eyes and just feel her.

If only...

CHAPTER 25

FINIAN NUDGED ME AWAKE at around four in the morning. We ate breakfast at the guild hall and then it was time to gather our things before departing. Our destination was farther than the distance between Corwy and Highwell, but we were told that with magical horses we would reach the west side of Aldeen in three days; otherwise it would have been a week long journey.

Finian was adamant that we take the guild leaders up on their offer. We stocked up with weapons, potions, snacks and fruits. An extra cart was also supplied for us to attach to our horses. Finian had upgraded his bow to a sturdier model with fancy engravings around the upper and lower limbs.

Evangeline—who had stocked up on medical supplies—had ensured that I took my medicine after we'd gathered our supplies.

As the four of us made our way out to the stables, something I had been curious about came to mind. "Okay, so I know you're fast on your feet, Blok, but are you as fast as these magical horses?" The Mutano showed me his teeth, but I got the impression that it was more of a smile than a snarl. "I ask because if you're not as fast as them, you'll get left behind, right?"

"Ogesh is big; Blok get around fast." he said, pulling our carts behind him. He was attracting many eyeballs as groups of people parted to let us pass.

"What he means is... The Mutano region of Ogesh is almost as big as Aldeen and the Mutanos are trained from pups to be able to run from one coast to the other, in the shortest amount of time." said Finian, chomping on an apple. "Also, if you're wondering why we haven't encountered as many beasts on our travels, it's likely because Blok takes them out for us before we even encounter them."

"Blok takes other routes, go hunting, then find Finian, Brando and Elf girl," said Blok.

Evangeline sighed. "Would you mind not referring to me as *Elf girl?* I would appreciate it."

"You have to teach him how to say it." I smiled. "He can almost say Brandon now."

"So uhh," Finian chewed. "What was Eve teaching you to say last night then? Bit weird that she was asleep while kneeling next to you this morning." Finian chuckled so violently that chunks of apple flew from his mouth. Evangeline rolled her eyes and walked ahead of us.

"Give me a break; she wasn't teaching me anything."

"You sure about that? Because you could probably be taught how to look anywhere else but at her."

I wasn't a stranger to some banter but this conversation was an uncomfortable one. "I had a vision about Flurwick," I said, in attempt to sway the conversation. "Evangeline had to nudge me out of it, that's all."

"Vision?" he asked. Finian was quiet as I talked him through what I'd seen. He asked questions about the logistics of the situation that he didn't understand and I answered them the best I could. "Hold on, so Flurwick killed all those people just to get a scroll with some scribbles on it?" he asked.

"Yep," I nodded.

"Are you thinking what I'm thinking?" He tossed the remains of his apple into a bush as we approached the city gates.

"That the scroll probably had information about how

to enter Relaun?"

"Exactly," Finian said, clapping his hands. "The real question now is how could he have learned of Relaun's existence in the first place? And how is your world and Relaun linked?"

"The million dollar question," I said.

"The million what? Anyway, if Evangeline thinks this is happening because Flurwick went in yer head, then maybe you'll have more visions and solve this mystery by the time we gather all these artifacts."

Evangeline, who had been listening while strolling ahead of us turned to face Finian. "You shouldn't be encouraging such a thing to occur. These visions can have a significant impact on his mind."

"Ah, I'm sure he'll be fine. He's got us after all ain't he?"

She rolled her eyes once more. "Yes, he has us; a thief, a Murano and a mage who has been kicked from her guild, very reassuring."

At the stables the farriers presented us with our horses. We attached our goods and checked the map given to us by the Hunters Guild. The fastest route had been marked in red ink for us. They'd also circled taverns, inns and guild outposts that operated independently around Aldeen.

"We'll be taking a different path than the one leading back to Corwy; so once we get here." Finian placed his index finger on a point on the map. "We have to make sure we take the right-most path."

"Got it," I said.

"By the way, Eva, I didn't want to ask you in the city, but I managed to get me hands on a few charged Medius Stones. Once we get to a safe point, do you think you could have a go at infusing some of our stuff? We need any advantage we can get."

Evangeline said nothing for a moment as she mounted her horse. When settled, she looked down at Finian. "If this quest wasn't so important I would curse you for being a filthy thief."

"Seriously, Eva, are you me mother reincarnated or what?"

"I shall infuse your weapons for you," she said. "Now hurry."

"Blok see you soon," said the Mutano as he jogged his way down the bridge ahead of us.

"Poor Blok, he's probably starving," said Finian.

* * *

As we led our mounts, there was hardly any chance for conversations. Their speed was such that we needed extra concentration to lead them in the right direction. Riding the horse was an uncomfortable experience as our bodies were knocked all around by their momentum. The horses themselves showed no sign of reaching their physical limits. Evangeline had mentioned that their bodies were performing at the same pace as a regular horse but it was the magic inside them that carried them farther with each gallop.

We soon reached our designated rest point, where Finian once again begged Evangeline to infuse our weapons. "Show me the Medius Stones that you have," she said.

Finian presented a sack and tipped out the contents on top of a flat tree stump on the side of the dirt path. Dark rocks, similar in appearance to lumps of coal, glowed in various colors.

"The amethyst ones are lightning, the citrine ones are force magic and the sapphire ones are ice," she said.

"Hmm," Finian rubbed his chin. "What effect would

it have if I used force magic on my bow?"

"I am not skilled enough to tailor the magic to work a specific way once it is bound to an item. I can simply do the infusion and the effects will be undetermined. Perhaps the bow would force your arrows through the air faster, or perhaps the arrow you fire from the bow would knock its target through the air."

"That sounds pretty awesome," I said. Both Finian and Evangeline glanced at me, unknowing of my terminology.

"I'll play it safe and go for ice on my bow. At least then my arrows may freeze enemies in their tracks."

"Hand me the bow," she said. Finian handed her the bow and she placed it on the flat piece of stump. She knelt, and dirt smudged across her linen. The dark Medius Stone pulsed inside her hands as she held it on top of the bow. Evangeline's hands glowed a misty shade of blue and I could see shadows of her veins. The glow expanded over the bow and Evangeline's eyes rolled upwards similarly to how Egith's had when she summoned her birds. After about a minute, I noticed the stone crumble in her hands. Black dust fell over the stump and trailed to the ground. Evangeline stood and held out the bow towards Finian. The bow had a new shimmer.

"Incredible," he said, taking the bow from her.

"You going to give it a try?" I asked.

"Of course," he said. He walked a few paces forward to where he had a view of an expanse of land.

"Please, not the sheep," said Evangeline.

"Don't worry, I won't hurt the harmless creatures," he said. He pointed somewhere to the right of where the herd of sheep stood. "See that gargoyle on the boulders by the cave over there? It would no doubt attack us if it could see far enough to know we were here. That justifies him being my target." Finian took an arrow and drew it against the bow. The arrow flew through the air and hit its target on one of its wings. The gargoyle immediately attempted flight despite being struck on its wing, but then something magnificent occurred. The gargoyle froze solid atop the boulder it had been resting on. The effect lasted for around half a minute, before the blue frost shattered from the gargoyles body and the creature collapsed onto the ground.

"Hmph!" came a grunt from behind us.

"Bleedin' cry!" Finian shook. "At least give us some warning before you pop up on us like that, Blok."

"Blok sorry; Blok was killing amphadilles."

"It's a shame I didn't see those, I would have gladly

tested my new bow on them." Finian sighed. He then turned to face me. "Oi Brandon, you've got some weapons too. Why not have Evangeline infuse one of them for you?"

"But the sword I got from Baron already has fire," I said.

"What about the weapons you brought with you from the milky lands or where ever it is you came from?" asked Finian.

It had never crossed my mind to try and infuse my blaster. "You think it will work?" I asked, pulling the gun from my holster.

"I may as well give it a try for you," said Evangeline.

The logistics of how this would work baffled me. Finian's bow itself had been infused, which added a magical effect to any arrow fired from it. Going with the logic that an arrow was equal to a bullet—or a laser burst in my case—the magic would be lost once my ammo had been depleted. "These guns use ammunition," I said. "Think of ammunition as the equivalent to arrows. That means that once my ammo is gone, I won't be able to use this anymore. With that in mind, could I instead infuse my energy cartridge so that it will be able to fire magical projectiles?" I asked as I popped out the cartridge.

Evangeline smiled and reached for the cartridge. "You're asking for answers on something that has never been attempted. I can only try and then we shall test the result."

"As long as it causes you no harm," I added.

She placed the casing containing the energy cells on the tree stump. "Lightning seems to be a good choice for this," she said. She picked up the dark stone that was pulsating amethyst from the inside. She carried out the binding as she had with the bow; this time her hands glowing purple. When the glowing faded, she rose and presented me with the cartridge. It shimmered as I loaded it into the blaster.

"I don't see any more threatening creatures but I reckon we'll run into something you can test it on if we go a little further," said Finian.

Through the corner of my eye I saw a blue jumbo wiener sized finger with long black nails pointing to our left. "Over there," said the Mutano. "Blok smell stantis bear behind bushes."

"Ohh, a stantis bear. One of those will rip your head off if you get too close," said Finian, "unless you're Mutano of course."

"Well I don't plan on getting too close. Let's try

and catch it at a distance," I said. We rode our horses down a side path in the direction Blok had pointed. According to Blok, the bear was hiding inside a small patch of land enclosed in a circle of trees and bushes. We dismounted our horses outside a web of leaves leading into where the creature lurked.

"Shh," said Finian, pressing his finger to his lips ahead of us. "I see it; move slow." He moved into a crouch. Getting closer, I got my first glimpse of the monstrous bear. It stood at least seven feet tall on two legs. As we crept closer, it bent its body to the ground, moving its snout around.

"Bear is picking up scent," said Blok.

"This is close enough," said Finian. "Go ahead, Brandon."

Right as I aimed the blaster, the bear looked in our direction and roared. I pulled on the trigger and a burst of energy shot out the barrel. The bear staggered as a amethyst sheen pulsed over its body, lasting no longer than a blink. The bear's body twitched on the spot before crashing to the ground completely. Its body continued to twitch sporadically a couple more times before it remained completely still.

"There you have it," said Evangeline. "Your weapon

is now enhanced."

"Technology and magic," I said staring at the blaster in my hand. "Now that's a frightening thought."

"We better get a move on now. We can't afford to waste much more time if we want to get those artifacts before Flurwick does," Finian said. "It's a shame we don't have enough time to skin that bear. It would bring in some good coin."

We soon mounted our horses and set off once again.

CHAPTER 26

FOR TWO WHOLE DAYS we traveled through Aldeen; passing towns, ruins, ruffian hideouts and various wild creatures that we needed to slay before proceeding. At night we would find a place to camp and rest for a few hours. Finian and Evangeline had been impressed with the alarm function on my phone, but they quickly grew to hate it as it forced them out of their sleep. Once, Blok had roared at the sound of the alarm and threatened to destroy it.

One feature of my smartphone that my companions came to enjoy was the camera. We spent an entire thirty minutes in camp taking selfies and group shots by the surrounding forest. Though it wasn't exactly a time for pleasantries, I couldn't help but to be happy at capturing a moment of cheerfulness with them. One of my favorite shots was one I took of Finian, Evangeline and Blok. Finian struck a suave artistic pose, with his right arm folded over his chest and his left hand held up as if cupping something in his palm. He'd positioned his body to the side. It made him look like an artiste, or a poet. Evangeline was in the middle. She held her staff in her right hand, with the other arm relaxed against her side. She wore a warm smile under her loose brunette hair. The image captured two of her features that I adored the most. Her Elven ears pointed out from under her hair and her eyes shimmered without there being eye-glare in the shot. Her necklace glowed brightly under the light.

Next to her, Blok stood with a disgruntled expression on his face. He hadn't understood the concept of photos and didn't see why he needed to stand next to his companions for my amusement. He hadn't attempted to strike any kind of pose. He simply stood there and looked directly at me, expressionless. But to me, it was a perfect photo. It captured all the unique qualities of these individuals that I was beginning to consider friends.

Evangeline had seen to it that I took my herbs each day, and my pains were at manageable levels. I could feel the odd ache of my hips and knees every once in a while when I was tired, but beyond that, I hadn't felt anything too excruciating since the night I'd seen Flurwick in my dreams.

On the third day of our travels, Egith's black bird Audette visited us and chose to sit on Evangeline's shoulder. Evangeline stood still as the bird relayed images to her. It was also receiving updates from Evangeline on our progress. Audette soon flew away, making loud cackling sounds.

"Both Retgar and Jale have only just managed to assemble their warriors. It has taken days for them to filter the best men they could find in Aldeen. Both men will lead their warriors on their respective quest today," Evangeline told us.

"You can't be serious," Finian said. "At this rate Flurwick will already have the artifacts before they leave Highwell. And they call me incompetent for failing me test."

"That's the perk of being in a small squad. More co-ordination and less deliberating over things that don't matter," I said.

"I guess now we don't have to feel so bad about setting up camp two nights in a row," Finian said, as he mounted his horse.

"Audette showed me the path ahead," said Evangeline, "such a smart bird. It mapped out our path before coming to me. Showing me which paths we should take to reach the bridge sooner. We should arrive at the Lainunia Bridge in a few hours." She pulled herself up on her horse.

"Well, since the birds love you so much, I'll let you lead the way." Finian's hand swayed, inviting Evangeline ahead of him.

"One more thing," said Evangeline. "Egith also sent a message saying that the magic gates allowing passage from one region to another shall be powered up with Medius Stones. She wants us to ask the Elves to assist in powering up the one in Lainunia so that we may quickly return to Highwell with the artifact once we have it."

"Where are the rest of those gates anyway?" Finian asked.

"One was in Ogesh until the Elves destroyed it. I am unsure if one is in Thirion. That leaves two active ones that I know of; the one in Highwell and the one in Lainunia."

"I see "

"How does the mind magic from the bird work?" I asked. "Can it read everything in your mind, or only what you volunteer to it?"

"The latter," she said. "First it projects into my mind what it wishes me to see, then it shows me an image of myself. I suppose that's a polite way of asking me to offer up what information I deem worthy for the others to see."

"At least Relaun's method of communication shows respect for your privacy," I said, completely aware that I was going over their heads with the comment.

"They also respect our sleep." Finian shot, as he galloped after Evangeline. I steered my own horse next to Finian as we began to pick up speed. The Mutano had gone off to hunt since we'd awoken, but he would no doubt return in due time.

* * *

"By Jerrus! That's a long bridge," said Finian, as we came down the final stretch of hill at the west end of Aldeen. "And it's pretty high up; I don't like the looks of that."

"We will not be able to ride our horses on there. It's too dangerous," said Evangeline. "My force magic may help to keep the bridge still as we cross it, but I'm not powerful enough to stabilize it with the added weight of the horses."

"What about Blok?" I asked.

"Grown attached to him now have you?" Finian smirked. "I'm sure he'll be around here somewhere. I'm not sure how Mutano instincts work, but he always seems to know when to show up."

As we moved towards the cliff, our horses acknowledged that the end of the path was coming and slowed their speed. They came to a complete halt some thirty meters from the bridge and we climbed down. "We're going to need to wait for Blok, he's the only one I trust to carry our things and walk across at the same time," said Finian. "Perhaps we should have gone below and taken a boat across."

What I wanted to say was that it would probably be safer to take a boat if that was an option. I was then going to ask if arriving in Lainunia by boat would set us back too far in time. Before I could begin to speak, I heard a familiar burst of gunfire. The horse next to me to collapsed. The same sequence of events happened with the two remaining horses and the three of us responded by pulling our weapons.

"The bridge," Evangeline pointed with her staff in hand. The bridge was now rocking as if caught in a hurricane. The rope bound to the posts at the side of the cliff rocked itself out of place. There was a great roar as the bridge collapsed.

"Definitely force magic," said Evangeline.

My gun extended in my arms and I looked through

the scope to locate the source of attack.

The sound of clapping echoed through the air as Jonathan Flurwick walked along the outskirts of the cliff with his hands beating against each other.

CHAPTER 27

"I APPLAUD YOU FOR making it this far, Brandon." came the cold voice of Jonathan Flurwick. "You've discovered what I plan to achieve, and you've managed to amass an entire region to put a dent in my plans. With that level of dedication, I see how you were made a Sergeant so young. You'll surely be promoted again when you tell the story of how you took down the Lieutenant-commander that went rogue." Flurwick was taking small steps forward. "But will you even make it out of Relaun?'

"Don': come any closer," I said with my blaster drawn. "Why are you doing this? What do you hope to achieve by getting to the crystals?"

Flurwick smirked. He waved his hand sideways through the air and our weapons were jerked from our hands.

"Huh," Evangeline gasped. "Your magic, how can you be so powerful after just a week?" she asked.

Flurwick eyed Evangeline and continued to smirk. Lines ran across his forehead, under his graying pompadour. "When you share a bloodline with The Elders, magic is something that comes naturally here in Relaun."

The three of us glanced at each other as we processed what Flurwick had just claimed.

"How could that be possible?" I asked. "The Elders lived here in Relaun; a world separate from the Milky Way. You only entered Relaun a week ago."

"For such a capable marine, you lack common sense. Ask yourself how it's even possible for us to be here now. Do you think there has never been a link between our realms before?" he asked.

"How is it possible? And what's your goal?" I asked. My eyes lingered on my blaster that was sitting on the ground. There was no way this exchange wouldn't end in violence. Luckily, I still had my sword bound on my hip.

"While I would love to fill your dim minds, I must be leaving. I have a tribe of repulsive blue beasts to command," he said. "But don't worry, Brandon, your lover is here to see you again."

Flurwick wolf whistled. The pitch of the whistle traversed through the air. Suddenly, a large sword, with a broad curved blade flew to the ground in front of us. The sword stood upright, with the blade wedged in the dirt. When I looked up I saw a second figure stood next to Flurwick. Natalya reached out her arm and the blade wiggled in the ground, releasing itself. The sword then flew into her hands. I noticed a subtle citrine glint emitting from her gloves. Natalya was also wearing an Alliance visor that had an amber shimmer.

"Play nice, lovebirds," said Flurwick. As soon as Flurwick took his eyes off us, we picked up our weapons. By the time I looked back up I saw Blok standing before Flurwick. Flurwick twitched at the sight of Blok, but he did his best to suspend his shock. "Ah, I may get to test this out before reaching Ogesh. Thanks for volunteering yourself as a lab rat," said Flurwick, with his hand rising.

"Blok, run." Evangeline cried.

Finian tried to dash towards Flurwick, but Natalya's sword flew towards him, causing him to leap out of its way. The sword swung through the air like a boom-a-rang, almost slicing my head off; I ducked to avoid it.

As Natalya caught the sword, I saw her eyes locked on us through her visor, as if she remembered what had happened last time she'd come into contact with us. Her expression showed burning rage.

"Look " Finian pointed. Being distracted by Natalya had caused us to miss the moment when Flurwick was knocked down by the raw strength of the Mutano. The smirk didn't leave Flurwick's face as he got back up and proceeded to attempt his mind control. This time the Mutano was too slow to react as his body shuddered. His arms shook by his side. The creases in Flurwick's face showed how difficult he was finding it to take control of the Mutano.

Finian sent an arrow into Flurwick's hand, causing it to semi-freeze. It was a masterful shot because if the arrow had missed Flurwick's hand by a few inches then it could have easily hit Blok.

Flurwick held his arm out and after a few moments the ice melted around his hand. For a second, a short flame glowed around his hand.

Regaining his senses, Blok grabbed Flurwick and lifted him from his feet. When it seemed we had Flurwick where we needed him, Natalya's sword slashed the side of Blok's leg. Flurwick's body crashed to the ground as Blok let off an earth shaking roar. Blok knelt, holding his leg as blood trickled from the wound.

Flurwick used his magic to send a boulder crashing into the side of the Mutano. He then shot a yellow blast at the three of us that knocked us onto our backs.

After feeling the stiff creak of my shoulder, I turned my head to see Flurwick fleeing. Finian and I rose as fast as we could to take aim at him, but Natalya's sword flew towards us in a horizontal position, forcing us back to the ground.

"We must get rid of her," said Evangeline, as we knelt. "I won't be able to take command of her mind again because the accessory on her face wards off mind magic."

"She's making us miss our chance to get Flurwick,"

Finian snapped. "Blok could have ripped him to shreds if it wasn't for her."

"Let's handle her." I stood, facing my murderous ex-girlfriend. To our right, Blok lifted himself, shifting his weight on the good leg. He limped into pursuit to catch Flurwick, but judging by his lack of speed, he wouldn't catch him.

The three of us were now stood facing Natalya. Her eyelids creased to slits as she gazed at us with pure hatred.

"The sword is missing," said Finian, "Be careful."

There were three of us and one of her. I knew from experience that the best way to subdue an outnumbered target was to hit them from all sides. "Evangeline, focus on long-range offense and call out the sword if you see it. Finian, you go right, I'll go left." I slurred these commands through the side of my mouth. Natalya was trained to lipread, so I'd made it a habit to prevent my lips moving as much as possible. Regardless, I was sure she would be expecting us to do exactly what I had planned. I would need to find a way to catch her off guard.

Natalya smirked and challenged us to come at her with a hand gesture. This cockiness was exactly the Natalya I knew.

I glanced right at Finian and he nodded. We ran forward and through the corner of my eye I saw Finian roll to the right. As I picked up momentum I drew the sword from my hip and spun around, launching the sword at her while in mid-spin. I then turned and drew my blaster, taking aim at her body. The sword whizzed too far to the right for it to be of any concern to her, but with her distracted I shot a lightning burst her way. She swayed the shot, but then miraculously, I saw my own sword behind her, shooting towards her blind spot. It grazed the side of her visor as it came back to me; suspending itself in mid-air. I took the hilt and glanced around at Evangeline. She winked at me, with her staff raised in her hand.

Sparks flew from the visor as Natalya adjusted it on her head. Finian threw a magic pellet at her feet that froze her left foot to the ground.

"Sword to your right!" Evangeline yelled.

Finian and I dived to the ground as the sword shot by. It then flew into Natalya's hands and she chopped away at the ice in attempt to free herself. With an opening, I ran towards her, but she anticipated me and sent the sword swooping in my direction; giving me no choice but to swing left.

"Evangeline, use force!" Finian cried, as he threw a dagger towards Natalya's face. The dagger changed course before it reached her face and sliced into the opposite side of her visor. The impact caused the glass at the front to crack. It would impair her vision if she didn't remove it. Evangeline brought the dagger back into Finian's hands, before Natalya's sword had him repelling backwards.

To my left I saw the sword circle through the air, but I was now close enough to engage her. I jogged to her and dodged her right hook. Then I grabbed her wrist and held it down between our hips. "Submit," I told her. "It's over."

"The sword!" Evangeline cried.

The sword could have struck me. But something told me not to move. Instead, I looked Natalya in the face, trying to locate her eyes through the cracked glass. The sword flew towards me at a pace that seemed impossible to stop. Then, it halted right before tearing through my through my skull. It was then suspended in mid-air before me.

"Natalya, I know you're in there. Take off the visor and let's talk this through. I'm not your enemy here. Flurwick is the one tampering with your mind." The sword dropped to the ground and Natalya whipped her wrist from my grip. She reached up and popped the pressure cap at the side of her visor. It dropped before her and then I shot at the ice to free her foot.

"Be mindful, Brandon, she could still be tricking..." Evangeline began to say.

I held my finger to my lips, hushing her, but Natalya was agitated with the remark. She shot a look of hatred at Evangeline and her arm rose. "You!" she said, scowling at Evangeline. The sword flew straight for her.

"No!" I cried. Evangeline ducked the sword and immediately held out her hand, no doubt trying to control Natalya's mind again. "Watch out!" I pointed, as the sword whipped backwards, almost beheading Evangeline. Natalya pushed me off balance with both of her arms, and then she set off into a run.

"Natalya, please!"

I ran after her. The desperation to have her on my side pushed my aching limbs, as I thought about how I had just gotten through to her. Natalya had been herself again, but only briefly.

My body halted as I saw her approach the edge of the cliff and dive off. Her sword followed her down.

PART III

CHAPTER 28

"SORRY BLOK, THIS WILL STING," said Evangeline, with her hands full of green paste. She applied the substance to Blok's wound. Beforehand, she had used her magic to reduce the bleeding and close the wound as much as her magic would allow her. Then she used her supplies to sow the wound closed. Blok grunted as she rubbed the paste across the cut. "This will protect you from infection," she said.

We braced ourselves as our self-moving rowboat hit a large current. "I can't believe the Elves just left this boat aside the Aldeen coast. Doesn't that mean any old scrub could reach their kingdom?"

"The magic is much more complex than what you see. Somehow it can determine if the passengers on board have a worthy cause to reach Lainunia," said Evangeline.

Finian breathed in deep. "Whose magic is more complex, the Elves or Flurwick's?" The question brought silence with it. Flurwick had managed to escape and the reality was that even Blok may have been no match for Flurwick—who was capable of casting superior levels of magic than other mages. Even when it appeared that Blok had dominated him, Flurwick never lost his composure. He never once looked fearful.

"Do you believe he's a descendant of The Elders?" The question was directed at nobody in particular, but Evangeline had caught me gazing at her and decided to respond.

"I can't see how it is possible. The Elders are supposed to be Elven."

"Elven shmelven," said Finian. "Lord Jerrus was definitely human; no denying that. The Elves are all up their own arses, so of course they think there's no way that an Elder could be human. I believe at least some of The Elders were human, which means it's possible that they have human descendants. The question is how someone from his world is able to be of Elder blood," Finian nodded to me.

In all the years I'd known Flurwick, he'd never shown any signs of being the man he was here in Relaun. He'd been a man who took pride in his work. His name was respected among marines. Flurwick had even led one of the squads that eliminated a fleet of outlaws who vowed to overthrow the Galactic Alliance.

But then I remembered; "the vision," I said. "In the vision I had that night; Flurwick was determined to get his hands on that scroll. That must have been when he learned how to produce the portal that brought us to

Relaun. He was wearing an older version of the lieutenant's space suit; meaning he'd had knowledge about this place for at least a couple months."

"For that to be the case, it suggests that people have traveled between Relaun and your world before," said Evangeline.

"Perhaps," I said. A dozen theories came to my mind, but I had no idea where to start with articulating them. My body ached, and the cold breeze sent chills through my body.

"Brando shivers." Blok pointed.

"Very observant there, big guy." I responded.

"Please, use my cloak to cover yourself," Evangeline said, shifting through her things. Finian and I had placed a chest at each end of the rowboat, with Evangeline's sitting in the middle to keep the weight as even as possible. Blok's weight alone was no doubt the reason that the boat swayed so turbulently over the current. Evangeline tossed her ruby colored cloak over me.

"Why does he get special treatment then?" said Finian. I felt an uncomfortable conversation incoming.

"Brandon is sick," she said.

"Sick?" Finian snapped. "How sick? Are you going to die on us, Brandon?"

"Not yet. At least I hope not," I said. "It's a blood disorder. It means my body has limitations. But I try to cope with it the best that I can."

"Limitations?"

"Yes," Evangeline said, "with the way his blood cells produce, he struggles to get air around his body as easily as we do. This means he exerts himself easier. And I imagine it causes excruciating pain for him because the blood cells get clogged in his body."

"Really? You never show any signs that you're in pain," said Finian.

"Well, pain is such a normal part of my every day that I've learned to cope without always showing it," I said. "If I do show it, then it means I'm in a serious amount of pain that could kill me. But thankfully, I haven't had an episode like that in about a year."

"But you always seem so strong; like you can take a beating." Finian continued.

"Well," I said, thinking how best to explain the complexities of my condition. "The truth is; there really is no pain to me quite like the pain from my disorder. I do feel the bumps and bruises that we've acquired on our adventures, but only briefly. I suppose my condition has given me a higher pain threshold."

"That doesn't mean you're not vulnerable to all the strenuous activities we've been putting ourselves through." Evangeline cut in.

"Sounds like you chose the wrong line of work," said

Finian, crossing his arms and shivering as the sky turned a grim shade of black.

"I didn't want my condition to set me back from doing what I always dreamed of. It's been tough to live with. Especially being around guys that have the ability to push themselves to limits far above what I can achieve."

I felt Evangeline's hand rub against my knee, comforting me. I looked over at the hazel eyes that had become my weakness.

"Well, I would be thankful that you're not as vicious as that ex-girlfriend of yours," said Finian. As the words resonated, the hazel eyes turned away from me. The hand removed itself from my knee. "Speaking of which, I've never seen anything like those enhancements," Finian continued.

"That must have taken advanced magic," said Evangeline. It felt as though she was avoiding my eyes completely now. "The way her gloves were bound to the sword and the way she was able to command its power just by wearing the gloves. It was like a fusion of force and mind magic, and it's not something that's easily achieved. I would think that the Master Conjurer assisted in such infusions."

"And that fancy thing she wore on her face. That stopped you from getting into her head didn't it?" Finian asked.

"Yes. Flurwick had already taken command of her mind, so the visor would not ward against his own indoctrination. The visor would however, ward off any on-coming attempts to dispel her mind warp."

"But she fought the indoctrination," I said. "She was herself again. When you warned me about her, it pissed her off."

I glanced at Evangeline and she scowled back at me. "Next time I shall refrain from trying to help you. Clearly my concerns get in the way of what you truly seek."

"Hmph, Brando make Elf girl mad," came the Mutano's voice, as water splashed across our feet. Evangeline looked at Blok as if she wanted to re-open his wound.

"Do you two really have to do this now?" said Finian. "And while we're on this topic, I'm tired of you two acting like there's nothing going on between you. Just act on it and be done with it already."

My head snapped towards Finian. "I have no idea what you're talking about."

"Clearly," snapped Evangeline. "Did you see how disturbed he was when we found no sign of his Natalya below the cliff? There's no denying that they love one another dearly."

I cackled so hard that I triggered my hip pains. "Me and Nat? All that love is lost; believe me."

"It matters not. Our focus is securing the artifacts. We have no time to discuss such useless topics," said Evangeline.

"We're approaching land," Finian pointed. I turned to see the most exotic looking shore I'd seen in a long time.

We joined into a lake that seemed to blend into a forest of trees. At the side of the trees was a giant structure in the form of a face. Extra attention to detail was paid to its pointed ears. Water fell from its mouth, back into the lake below it. The surrounding trees were inviting and as the wind breezed through the many branches, a feeling of clam and tranquil was in the air.

"This place seems inviting," I said. When the rowboat stilled itself, we hopped out in turn. Blok groaned as he stood on his bad leg. Finian and I decided to lift our things from the boat in order to give Blok some relief.

"I'm sorry to say that you will feel some pain for a while," Evangeline told him.

"Blok had worse injuries. Blok fought in tournament," said the Mutano. Blok picked up one of the three chests, even after we advised against it. Finian carried his and I carried mine. With all of our stuff accounted for, we walked up the path, bordered by the most beautiful trees I'd ever seen. The bark was a pattern of layered rolls, with a completely smooth texture.

"Me arms are tired already carrying this thing. I wonder how far we'll have to travel to get to the capital," Finian wined.

Blok began sniffing the air vigorously. And then, out of nowhere a line of arrows landed sequentially before us, stopping us in our tracks. As I looked around, I saw numerous Elves sitting in trees with bows.

Five Elves walked towards us from the other side of the arrows. "I don't know who you lot think you are, but you're not bringing one of those on our lands," said one of the Elves, pointing right at Blok.

CHAPTER 29

"WE HAVE BEEN SENT ON an important quest by the Arch-mage of Relaun," said Finian, "we must speak with your king as soon as possible and we're bringing the Mutano with us."

The Elves spoke among each other in another language before one of the pack responded. "Mutanos are not welcome here, under any circumstances. If you wish to visit our kingdom as guests, you must first escort that thing elsewhere. Either that or we kill him for you." At this, Blok growled so loud that I felt the ground vibrate. The Elves took aim at him in unison.

"With all due respect to your lands," I said. "Blok here is not hostile to innocents. Blok doesn't hold grudges against other races based on a war that happened before you were all born."

"Other races?" said the Elf closet to us, who seemed to be the leader of the pack. "That thing is not a race. It is a filthy beast that should be slain."

Despite his injured leg, Blok barged past us, closing the distance between him and the Elven snob. I grabbed

Blok by the leather strap that kept his weapons in place. "Blok, don't do it."

The Mutano looked back at me with his teeth exposed. "If you harm them then you're giving them an excuse to keep treating Mutanos this way. We can't change their way of thinking by fighting them."

"Please understand," said Evangeline, "the matter which we must discuss relates to the ancient crystals. There are people wanting to bring harm to all regions in Relaun. If we don't act quickly, you may be allowing them to destroy Relaun."

There was silence, as if they were taking in Evangeline's words. Blok steadied himself, allowing me to release his leathers. He growled a few times, but I had a feeling it was from the pain.

The leader of the pack laughed. "A half-Elf, you don't see too many of those around here."

"Does that matter?" I asked. I watched as his eyes shot up and down my body. "You are a strange collection of individuals. But your body language tells me that you are telling truths. We will allow you access to the city, but only if you submit your Mutano for capture."

"Then there's no deal," said Finian. "Blok has done nothing wrong to you or anyone. He comes with us; otherwise you take responsibility for allowing Relaun to fall."

"We will not let a Mutano walk freely through Shavatha. And there's nothing stopping us from killing the four of you and then passing on your message to the king so that he may talk with your superiors."

"It's taken our superiors days to get a team together. I'm not saying this with arrogance, but we're the best hope that Relaun has right now," I said. "I know the threat personally. My understanding of them will give us an advantage."

Elven eyes shot between the four of us. Shining like illuminated marbles. "Either hand over the Mutano, or die, Ahnaf!"

"Ahnaf?" I asked.

"It means human," Evangeline responded.

"Bloody knife-ears," Finian said, shaking his head beside me.

At those words, every Elf in the pack shifted their aim to Finian. Although I disliked Finian's insult, I was getting tired of these hard-headed Elves. I raised my gun at their leader. "If the choice is death or handing over the Mutano, then I'll gladly choose death. Go ahead and try me," I said.

A cold breeze blew through the trees as we faced off against one another; waiting to see who would make a move first. I wondered what Evangeline's stance on this situation was. Did her Elven blood cause any internal conflicts for her? I wanted to look over at her, but I also didn't want to lose the intense staring match with the Elves.

A black glow began emanating from the Elf's bow and I heard Evangeline gasp. "No," she said.

"Blok will go with them," came the deep rumbling of the Mutano.

"What?" said Finian, "you don't have to, Blok. They're being idiots."

"Wasting time," said Blok. "Brando, Finian and Elf girl need to get item. Blok will go with Elf."

As I thought about how Blok's sentences were getting longer, he limped towards the Elves, putting himself in their line of fire.

"Hands behind your back, beast," said the Elf leader, stepping over the line of arrows.

"Hey buddy, he's choosing to let you take him in," I said. "Respect him enough to not call him a beast. And don't you dare think about hurting him either, you hear me?"

The man lowered his bow as three of his Elves moved towards Blok to tie him up. "You know nothing of our culture, Ahnaf. Do not give me orders in Lainunia as if you are supreme. Be grateful that we are granting you passage to the sacred city."

Blok was now chained around the neck. A rope tied at the end of the chain like a leash, allowing the Elves to tug at him as if he were a pet. "Now, you may follow us back up the hill, but be warned that we will not tolerate any disrespect. We will slaughter your Mutano on the spot if you disobey." Another group of Elves removed the arrows from the path. The leader of their pack soon turned and they began marching in the opposite direction.

I shook my head, as I glanced at my companions. "Poor Blok."

"I'd heard the Elves were up their arses, but I never imagined this," said Finian, "have you come across Elves as ignorant as them, Eva?"

She looked up at him with a hateful expression. "Do not talk to me, you inconsiderate buffoon," she said, before marching up the hill.

"Your knife-ear comment must have pissed her off," I said.

"Better me than you, ay?" said Finian, nudging my arm.

We walked up the hill; wondering how far away Shavatha really was.

On the approach to Shavatha, we came to a giant wall, inscribed with hieroglyphic symbolism of Elves. At the center of the border was a large opening, around twenty feet high. There was no denying that Elven architecture resembled ancient Egypt in every possible way. It was frustrating that I couldn't communicate these similarities to my companions.

The gate at the center of the border was operated by mind magic. In order to gain access, an Elf needed to place his hand on the hard wood and the door would open. But only if it knew the Elf resided in Shavatha or had business there.

The region of Lainunia was also home to wild Elves that operated independently from the kingdom. Judging by how pompous these Elves were, they clearly didn't want to mix with wildlings.

On entering Shavatha, it became even more apparent just how influenced the city was by Egyptian architecture. Although wood was widely available, the Elves went out of their way to craft buildings from mud-brick and stone. In the distance, I could see pyramids, erected over the grid of smaller buildings. Being here made Flurwick's words feel more plausible.

"Do you think there has never been a link between our realms before?"

Now I believed there was a deeper connection to Relaun

and Earth.

The crew of Elves that were escorting Blok began to stray a different direction from where we were being led.

"If you hurt him, then I swear I will torture each and every one of you." I threatened, while they were still within earshot. The Elves looked back at me with cold expressionless glances.

"Why do you need to sound so aggressive towards them?" Evangeline asked. "They have roles in their society, just as we do. It's not their fault that they've been taught to prevent Mutanos from roaming the city."

"To be fair, Eva, they did fire arrows at us and threaten to kill us," said Finian.

"Agreed," I said, "they could have handled the situation better. They welcomed us with hostility."

"Well, let's at least try to be more understanding. We cannot be too forceful when we address the King. It's important that we gain the support of the Elves. Flurwick will find it hard to stand against them."

"Well, how about you take the lead then. This is where your Elven blood will come in handy, after all," Finian said.

Evangeline exhaled deeply. "Are you suggesting that my talents haven't come in handy until this moment? Perhaps I should let his girlfriend kill you whenever she chooses to come and find him again." At this, Finian glanced over at me. I shook my head—defeated. This was neither the time nor the place for disagreements.

We learned through conversation that the Elf escorting us was a warden, named Tarthir. He was more welcoming towards us now that Blok had been taken away. The Elf removed his helmet, revealing his bushy brown hair. The man had a slim frame, a common trait that I'd noticed about Elves. Another common trait was their olive skin, and glossy eyes.

Before long, we reached the outskirts of the city. We walked to a pillared palace with open access on all sides. In the middle section, the king sat in a high chair full of jewels.

"E'missi," said the king, in a deep commanding voice.

"E'missi, my king," said Evangeline, as she curtsied. A moment ensued where Tarthir and the king talked in their native tongue. "Just so you're aware, his name is King Thagorrom," Evangeline told us, while the two men exchanged information. And then the king stood.

"Tahmhet," he said. "I will speak Anglish now," he continued as he began to descend the steps below his throne. King Thagorrom appeared to be young in age, with long dark hair that draped over his long sapphire tunic. "My warden has informed me that you come here with a request. He also mentions that you speak of someone who plans to gain access to the ancient crystals of Relaun."

"Indeed, your highness. We come at the request of the guild leaders in Aldeen to obtain the artifact that resides here in Lainunia. We must prevent them from being captured," Evangeline explained.

"Your name, my young one?" asked the king. I was thrown off by him referring to Evangeline as a *young one* because he looked as young as she did.

"My name is Evangeline Celestè, born in Aldeen."

"Yes, I can see you are a mixed child. But I can look at you and tell you are full of intelligence." said the king. Her olive cheeks turned a pale shade of red. "I must question why you believe it to be a good idea for the Flask of Irithrel to leave the safest region in Relaun. There is not a human in existence that can steal from a nation of Elves."

"With all due respect, your highness," I said. "I may not have been here long, but I've heard the tales of how brutal the war was between the Elves and the Mutano. The human in question is planning to take control of the Mutanos. If he's successful, I can almost guarantee he will swarm Lainunia in search for the artifact." The king watched me. I couldn't tell if he was considering my words, or if he was disgusted by my presence. "In that case, it makes sense to gather the artifacts elsewhere; as I'm sure this will be his last destination."

"Where are you from, human?" asked King Thagorram. I recalled my story as briefly as I could for the king; informing him of my name and profession. I even gave him a brief catch up on Flurwick. "Well, no wonder your armor is so unique. It is quite impressive," he responded.

"Thank you, your highness."

"Answer me this, Brandon. Does this Flurwick that you speak of know that you're already here in Lainunia?" The king asked. I understood his point immediately. Answering him would be a direct contradiction to the argument I'd already imposed.

"I know what you're getting at. He does indeed know that we were seeking the artifact. But he doesn't know if we will be successful, especially because he ordered someone to have us killed before we got here."

"A man with a plan so grand does not carry on without considering all possible outcomes." said the king.

"He's right," said Evangeline. "Flurwick can't rule out the fact that the artifact may make it back to Aldeen. And Aldeen might just be the most vulnerable place to keep them all. Perhaps we should have them all gathered here instead."

"Are you serious, Eva? We have strict orders. We can't go changing the plan now," said Finian.

"Where we gather the artifacts doesn't exactly

matter," I said. "What matters the most is having your support so that when it comes to fighting Flurwick, both the humans and Elves are on the same page. The priority at this moment is securing the artifact and getting the gate open that will allow us to move back and forth to Aldeen quickly. Once our forces unify, we can discuss the safest place for the artifacts."

"That's right," Finian shot at Evangeline. "If people are able to nip between Lainunia and Aldeen in an instant, it won't matter where the actual battle takes place. We'll be able to respond to Flurwick's attack whether it's here or there. The gate is one of the most important tools we have."

"Distortion has been felt in Relaun's magic," said the king. "This falls in line with the timeline you have given on when Flurwick arrived here. We have little patience for human politicking. Your rulers are only known for slowing down procedures with pointless deliberations. If Flurwick chooses to bring disorder to our magic, then the Elves will deal with him alone."

"This is no time for supremacy," I snapped. "We must unify if we have any hope of stopping Flurwick dead in his tracks. We can't give him any opportunity to maneuver."

My outburst angered them. From the sidelines it seemed as though Tarthir was ready to strike me down. For a moment the king was silent. I was sure that I could see Evangeline's eyes burning me in my peripheral vision, but I didn't care. I was growing tired of ignorance. "If you're so desperate to secure the artifact then you will resolve an issue we are facing, to prove your worth," said the king.

"We have no time for tests or trials," I said.

"Then you will be without the artifact. For helping with this matter will take you to where the artifact rests."

"Then we will help," said Evangeline, "please tell us what we must do."

"Tahmhet, my young half-breed," said the king. "My adviser, Niserie Thaalnas here," he pointed to a beautiful Elven woman in a tight hooded robe. "She is one of the most powerful sorceresses in Lainunia. The potency of her mind magic is matched only by one other being in Relaun. Please speak with her to know more of what we ask. If you succeed, we will power up the gates."

"Tahmhet," Evangeline curtsied.

"Far'aedzo," said King Thagorrom, as he excused us with a wave of his hands.

CHAPTER 30

"WE DON'T HAVE TIME TO be fixing their leaks you know, Eva," said Finian.

"We are in their kingdom, and if this matter concerns Niserie, the famed sorceress, then helping them will be beneficial to our cause," she said. "And given your rudeness to the king, its only right we do everything we can to earn their trust."

Finian was ready to snap back, but I had no patience to hear them bicker. "Finian, let's hear her out and see where this goes," I said. I felt my body tiring and I was full of aches.

"E'missi," came the high pitched voice of the sorceress, Niserie Thaalnas. She removed her hood as she spoke. "In Anglish, it is hello."

"Hello." we said in unison. Only Evangeline shook Niserie's hand.

"It is my pleasure to meet you Lady Thaalnas. I have heard much about your work."

"Thank you, Evangeline," she said. Evangeline seemed taken a back at the use of her name.

"A brief overview for your companions who know

nothing of me...I work with the kingdom here in Shavatha. But my origins are from a town called Varghaanaire. It is to the far south." As she explained, I couldn't help thinking how poetic her voice was. "It is there where I grew up with my younger sister, Var'ae, the most powerful mind sorceress in Relaun. We were both gifted with magic from a young age, and with me being the older sibling, she aspired to be as talented as I was." As she spoke, I could see her history playing out vividly in my mind. It wasn't magic or anything; it was the fact that her voice was so captivating to hear tell the story that you felt as if you were being placed at the center of it. "When I was twelve, she was ten. At this age our parents were planning to separate so my father could seek his desired profession in the city. The deal between them was that each would keep a child. My father would take me to Shavatha with him while my sister stayed with my mother in Varghaanaire. This disturbed my sister and me; we could not fathom being apart from one another."

Evangeline sniffed. "Luckily, we had six months together before the departure went ahead as planned. We would read ancient scripts handed down to us from our town elders. Inside we would learn of exciting ways to use magic. And grand achievements made through the ages. There was one story about Elves who were able to communicate through the mind at vast distances. It was then that we decided to practice our magic every day until we were able to use mind magic to this level."

"There's no way that could be possible for such young mages," said Evangeline.

"It should not have been possible, no. But somehow we were able to achieve telepathic communication in less than two months." Evangeline's mouth fell open. "But at that time we were only able to test it within the town of Varghaanaire. She would be on one side of the town and I would be on the other. Not only could we talk, but we had begun to share visions and memories with each other. Finally, the day came when we were to part. We cried the entire day. As I departed with my father, and sat in our carriage, we stayed connected in our minds until we could not communicate any longer."

"I'm guessing you reconnected though," I said.

Niserie smiled, and the beauty of it caught me off guard. "On her seventeenth birthday, I felt a ringing sensation in my mind so powerful that I believed it would kill me. It turns out that some filthy male had set her up so that he and his friends could have their way with her. This sparked a rage so powerful within her that it somehow reconnected our minds," she beamed. "Magic works in mysterious ways."

"I hope those vile pigs were dealt with," said Evangeline.

"Oh they were. Var'ae's burst of rage was from anger at being deceived, not fear. Those silly boys found out firsthand what it's like to play with fire, literally." She glanced at Finian. Finian looked away, and I saw his face turn beet red. He had been glaring at Niserie lustfully; no wonder he was so quiet throughout this story.

"Now you have the back story. So let me bring you up to speed by telling you what you must do. Being connected with our minds has made my sister and I valuable assets to the region. We are capable of relaying information quickly through our minds and this has led to significant expansion of both north and south Lainunia. Years back, we decided to have the artifacts stored in Varghaanaire because my sister's mind magic has far surpassed my own. She is capable of sensing dark intentions from anyone who gets within miles of the region. She would be able to alert me in seconds, and I would respond by sending forces who would reach before the threat even arrived. But, I have been unable to connect with her for the past week and a half."

"What could be preventing you?" I asked.

"I do not know. And to be completely honest with you, I was willing to abandon Shavatha tonight and head there to see for myself. The King has forbid me to leave the city, and for good reason. But I cannot help but worry. We haven't even had any travelers from Varghaanaire since I lost connection. And I paid some travelers to visit there but I never heard from them again. There's no way for me to find out what has happened to her. But you three have no ties to Shavatha and you're well equipped to deal with any danger."

By now, I was willing to do anything to help reconnect her with her sister. "I have no problem heading over there to help you. I hope we'll have you and your sister united in no time at all."

"Thank you," said Niserie. "We will have an enhanced carriage to bring you there. Just walk outside the border to find it. You will reach when the skies become dark." Niserie walked over to me and held a necklace in her hand; at the end of it was a blue topaz pendent outlined in silver. "When you find Var'ae, please give her this for me."

"No problem."

"I appreciate your genuine concern for my sister, and I will try my best to have your Mutano friend released. But, please understand that Elven people do not trust the Mutano people. So he cannot walk around freely, for some mage will attack him."

"Well, at least you call them people. That's something," I smiled.

Finian twitched as Niserie walked by him. She placed a hand on Evangeline's shoulder and whispered something to her. Then I heard her compliment Evangeline's necklace. "Is it magic?" she asked.

Evangeline blushed again and shook her head. "It's a family heirloom," she responded.

Niserie nodded and then she was gone.

* * *

"Tahmet," said Evangeline as she marched alongside me.

"What does that mean?" I said, looking down at her.

"It means, thank you."

"You're welcome," I said, "for what?"

"For showing empathy; Niserie saw great qualities inside of you. It made her trust us."

"Is that what she whispered to you?" I asked.

"Not quite," she smiled.

"Did she say anything about me?" Finian asked, trailing behind us as we made our way back to the town borders.

Suddenly, I felt breathless. I'd felt this feeling a few times in my life; mainly after strenuous training sessions. My head was light and my chest pumped in and out rapidly. My heart was in overdrive, trying to pump enough blood and oxygen around my body. "I—I—I need...to sit down for... a moment," I said, struggling to get the words out. I managed to find a bench at the side of one of the mud-brick houses. Evangeline presented me with some water she'd found in a bucket nearby.

"The Elves took our supplies. We had plenty water and medicine there. I'm sorry that I didn't ask for any when we were at the temple," said Evangeline.

I was mad at myself. Mad for having such a moment of weakness while an important task was at hand. It took around ten minutes for my breathing to become normal again. Finian and Evangeline were stood, discussing my health and whether I was capable of doing all of this traveling. At one point, Finian even blamed the Elves for running us around.

While they stood there, debating where they would take me to rest for the night, I rose to my feet and limped towards the gate without them.

CHAPTER 31

MY HIPS NIPPED ME as I limped to the oversized gate leading outside the city. Finian and Evangeline either hadn't noticed I'd got up from the bench or were pondering whether to give me some space. Elven guards in leathers—equipped with daggers— were eyeballing me by the gate.

"I take it you're the outsider that Niserie told us about." One of them said.

"That's a fact," I said.

"There's supposed to be three of you," he said. "We'll open the gate for you once you're all here."

"Can't you let me out now?" I asked, eager to avoid the awkwardness of standing here to wait for my companions.

"No."

"Brancon, there you are," said Evangeline from behind me. I turned to see them jogging towards me, full of the concerns that I wanted nothing more than to hide from. "Don't do that! We were worried about you."

"You make me sound like some lost child," I said.

"I don't mean to," she said. "I was just concerned

about your health, that's all." she was avoiding all eye contact as if she sensed my distaste.

"I'll be alright, we should get going," I said.

The guards opened the gate and once we trailed outside the city we saw our carriage waiting for us. Two Elves sat saddled atop white magical horses, ready to ride us to our destination. We climbed into the box-shaped carriage and sat; each of us claiming a side to ourself. My hips throbbed as I seated myself and I had to suppress a yelp. Evangeline sat across from me and Finian was to my left.

Before long, it was necessary to clench the sides of the carriage for support as we were rocked side-to-side by the bumpy ride across the dirt roads. A grunt escaped me as I felt a sharp sensation after being rocked to the side.

"Are you sure you'll be alright?" Finian asked.

"I'm fine." I snapped.

"We don't know what we're going to be facing once we reach Varghaanaire. If you need to rest up here in the carriage then it shouldn't be a problem," said Evangeline.

"Why does everyone talk to me like I'm some weakling? I've been living with this my entire life. I've found my own ways to cope with it, alright? So if I say I'll be okay, then I'll be okay." I said. I was sick of feeling inferior. Sick of being reminded how unlike other people I was. Sick of being treated like I didn't know what's best.

The pain was so normal to me that I was always willing to push through it. That's why it stung me every time other's suggested that I give up or sit out.

Evangeline leaned her body sideways across the carriage. She was looking out at the path, as the surroundings passed by in a blur. I tried to steal a glance at her eyes. I could have sworn I saw tears streaming down her cheeks. Finian was looking down at his hands that he had cupped together.

"Look," I said. "I'm sorry, alright. Being in the marines with a medical condition has given me a complex about my health," I said. Evangeline wiped her face against her handkerchief. Finian was looking up at me as I spoke. "Marines are encouraged to always give our all; no matter what. In the heat of battle, we're encouraged to fight to the death for the good of the galaxy. But whenever it comes to me, everyone changes the narrative. Instead, my comrades tell me I shouldn't be on the mission. Or that it's okay if I need to sit behind in the shuttle. I end up feeling like I'm not good enough, you know?"

"Yes, I know the feeling myself," said Finian. Only then did I think about how much he may identify with how I felt. He'd been told he wasn't good enough for the past four years; ever since failing his trial.

"We understand, Brandon. I guess, we've just come to care about your wellbeing," said Evangeline.

"You might not have realized it, with how occupied we've been, but we've been around each other for quite some time now," said Finian. "Believe it or not, I think we might actually be friends." he smirked.

"We're not just some people you're forced to complete objectives with. This experience has brought us together," said Evangeline. "Dare I say it, but I've even taken a liking to Blok." Her smile lit me up inside. "So, I'm sorry for caring so much about how you're feeling. I'm only human."

Finian raised an eyebrow at her. "Technically, that's not true." Evangeline rolled her eyes in response.

"You're right," I said. "I'm honored that you both consider me a friend. Please accept my apology for dismissing your concerns." I said.

"Aw come on! You need not apologize," said Finian patting me on my arm. "Oh wait, you're arm doesn't hurt or anything does it?" I smiled back at him, admiring his ability to lighten any mood. I reached out to shake his hand but he stared at me blankly. "A shake won't fix this. Come here," he said, embracing me into a man hug.

Now that I'd hugged and made up with Finian, it was impossible not to do the same with Evangeline. But as I got close to her, the carriage hit a bump, launching me right onto her.

"By Jerrus! At least wait until I've got somewhere to

go, you two," said Finian.

I forced my weight off of her as soon as I could, but her sweet scent made me reluctant to pull away. Equally, she showed no desire to shift herself away from me. Once I'd balanced myself, I leaned into her for the intended hug—ignoring the stabbing sensations in my hip. Her graceful scent massaged my sinuses; I could taste her at the back of my throat. And as I felt the sweat from her neck against me, and the cold of her necklace on my skin, I knew I was growing too attached to her. I didn't want to stop being this close. Seconds flew by before I managed to pull myself away from her.

"My apologies for snapping at you, Eva," I said.

As my body drew away from her, she whispered something in Elvish to me. "E'Leawae Uea," she said.

"What was that?" I asked, staring into those shimmering hazel eyes as I sat myself across from her again. She didn't reply, she only smiled back at me.

"Ready yourselves, outsiders," yelled one of the Elves riding the horse. "We'll be reaching in another half-hour."

"That was bloody quick." shot Finian.

"Those horses are powerful," said Evangeline, picking up her staff that had been resting on her seat behind her. She slid it into its holder and tied it to her back. "It does seem a bit soon though. Niserie talked as if it would take longer."

The sky turned an amber pallet as the sun set. There was still enough light see across the desert, but Niserie had said that it would be dark by the time we reached Varghaanaire, and I saw no sight of the town as the carriage slowed.

"You're going to have to walk about six or seven hundred yards that way to reach Varghaanaire," said one of the Elves, pointing across the expanse. A large sand dune prevented us from seeing exactly where the outskirts of our destination began. Meaning we would be going in blind.

"What? You mean we have to walk?" Finian exclaimed. "What's the point of riding us this far only to make us walk?"

"We don't know what dangers are lurking there and it's your job to find out, not ours."

"But you're bloody Elves. Magic is in your blood. Are you telling me you're scared of entering a town?" Finian continued. The Elves shot him mean glances before forcing their horses into a turn and trotting off in the opposite direction. "No offense Evangeline, but yer people are really giving you a bad name," said Finian shaking his head.

We proceeded on as instructed; treading carefully up the dune. Though my hips carried a fiery sensation, I wasn't going to let it stop me. Concentration was needed to control my breathing in a way where I wouldn't exert myself as easy.

Finian was oblivious to how calculated my movement had become, but nothing health related seemed to slip by Evangeline. Several times she made comments about our lack of water. It was likely she was also thirsty, but her sequential glances towards me revealed her concern.

"Over there!" Yelled Finian, as the town became visible upon reaching the downslope. "Not too far now. Ready your weapons I say," said Finian, drawing his bow. We had no idea what was waiting for us in Varghaanaire. But whatever it was, I hoped it was a simple domestic issue that we wouldn't lose too much time on.

"Look," I heard Evangeline say. Her index finger—with its sharp, pointed finger nail—came into my peripheral sight. "A water fountain, over there; let's stop for a short rest before we reach Varghaanaire."

"Righto," said Finian. "But just a quick drink, don't go drinking the whole fountain."

Once we reached the fountain, my thirst made me disregard Finian's urgency. One might think that I'd been starved of water for weeks the way I drank. The truth of the matter was that my body was always devoid of hydration. It was what often caused my pain and breathlessness. Without hydration, my blood cells could not carry oxygen around my body effectively. Evangeline—who'd already drunk enough of the water—stood by me, fully understanding this.

Finian stood with his body positioned towards Varghaanaire, arms folded. Eventually, I stood; satisfied with my intake of fluids. "That's some of the best water I've tasted since being here in Relaun," I said.

Finian looked back at me as if I'd said something bizarre. "Water? Taste? Water has no taste."

"Trust me, I've drank enough variations of water in my lifetime to tell the difference," I said.

"The fountain uses magic to block out sunlight and filter the water. I'd imagine that it's managed by the residents of Varghaanaire," said Evangeline.

"Enough about water, let's get a move on," said Finian waving us towards him.

Feeling refreshed, my speed picked up as I walked alongside my companions. Looking through the scope of my rifle, I saw no signs of movement between the arrangements of houses in the distance. "Something's definitely not right here," I said. "It's not that late yet, for it to look this vacant. With all those houses and structures, there has to be a few hundred people residing there. Surely it can't be that quiet."

"Now you say it, I do have a bit of a funny feel..." Finian's voice trailed off. As I looked to my side to see why, the last visible signs of the sun had fizzled away.

I turned a full three-hundred—and—sixty degrees and found that both my companions had vanished in thin air. I was now alone and stranded in the dark desert climate.

Stars dotted themselves along the sky. It was as if I had somehow entered someone's painting while they were still adding details to it.

And then, I heard the all too familiar sound of an Alliance shuttle. Looking up, I saw the shuttle hovering low, positioning itself to land. The situation felt natural; as if I'd been standing here the whole time and Relaun was merely a figment of my imagination. I turned to face the shuttle as it landed a few feet ahead. When the door lifted into the air and the heeled boots revealed themselves, I knew exactly who wore them.

Natalya Carrick was now standing before me.

CHAPTER 32

"NATALYA, WHAT'S HAPPENING?" I asked.

As she walked towards me, she smiled and her hips swayed with every step. "I've been looking for you, Brandon. It's time to go home," she said.

"Where is home?" I asked.

"Home," she said, "to the G.A headquarters. You've been so out of touch that we need to bring you back around your peers."

My mind was racing, and there was one question that my inner voice kept repeating; is it possible that Relaun had been a dream? It had been so vivid; so intimate that I was somewhat saddened by the thought of it never existing. "Why are you here? You wanted nothing to do with me," I asked, trying not to get caught up in my thinking.

Natalya walked closer, until she was within kissing distance. She looked up at me, her eyes scanning my face. "Did you really believe it was over? Please tell me you've been feeling the same sense of longing that I have. There wasn't a day that went by that I didn't think about calling you," she said.

Indeed, I'd missed her for months after our break up. There were countless nights when I wanted to hop on a ship to where she was stationed and let myself into her quarters as if no break up had ever happened. "It was only pride that stopped me from contacting you," she continued, "and the thought that you may have found someone else. That would only have hurt me more."

Inside, I was happy to know the longing had been mutual. I thought about how nice it would be to rekindle. How I'd missed curling up alongside her warm, athletic body after a hard day of training.

"Natalya," I said. My mind was intercepted by thoughts of Relaun, thoughts of Blok, thoughts of Finian and thoughts of Evangeline.

Had Relaun really been imagined? My heart was having a hard time believing it. And though Natalya stood before me—looking keen to revisit what we had—I couldn't bring myself to go along with it.

"I was somewhere else, Natalya. I had friends, companions. We were trying to stop…"

"Brandon, don't lose yourself to the Vortex," she said.

"The Vortex?" I asked. I'd heard of it before. The Vortex was an A.I virtual world constructed for educational and scientific purposes. That was before hackers had got their hands on it and turned it into a life-sucking fantasy drug. "No way, how could I have been hooked up to that thing? Why are we in the desert if that's the case?" I asked.

Natalya sighed. "This is exactly it," she said. Her lips tightened and her eyebrows were pushed together.

"What?"

"This is why it ended between us. You're not grounded in reality. You're too stubborn to see what's right in front of you," she said.

"What are you talking about?" I asked.

"You know what, Brandon? You should quit. You should demand your discharge and leave the Alliance. You're not cut out for this, and you're not even healthy enough."

"Hold up, what are you talking about?" I asked, reaching for her shoulder. As I grabbed for her, she pulled herself out of reach.

"Don't you touch me," she yelled. "Face the facts. You'll never make any real impact in the Milky Way. You're completely useless, Brandon. You'll never climb the ranks." She was intent on regurgitating every feeling of anxiety that I'd ever expressed to her. "Forget about us, you should settle for your chubby little knife-ear that you love so much."

Though those last few words had been disrespectful, it was not the obnoxious insults that caught me off-guard.

It was the fact that she had referred to Evangeline.

"Evangeline," I said. "Where is she?"

Natalya stepped back a few feet while looking me directly in the eyes. Her expression was hurtful and it didn't match the Natalya I knew. She cried; black tears streaming down her cheeks. "Fine, Brandon. If it's the Elf you want, then have her. Just know that she doesn't want to help you grow. She doesn't want you to get better. She wants you sick and at your worst," she said, before wiping away the tears. "Goodbye," said Natalya.

"Wait!" I cried. And then Natalya disappeared in a swirl of black mist.

Seconds later I heard sniffling behind me. "Natalya?" I called, spinning around. I was caught off-guard, as instead of the slim athletic frame of Natalya, I saw the short curvy body of Evangeline, draped in her leathered robes.

"I heard it all," she said. "I was a fool to think you actually had some interest in me."

"Evangeline, it's not like that. I'm trying to figure out what's..."

Evangeline continued her tirade, cutting me off. "My whole life I forced myself to focus only on improving my magic. I wanted to be able to pass on all that knowledge to the generation behind me. For that, I sacrificed any interest in the opposite sex." She sniffed so hard that I heard air pull mucus up her nose. "And then you came along, looking me in my eyes any time you thought I wouldn't notice. I was revolted at first, but then I began to care for you."

"I'm sorry, Evangeline." I pleaded. "I care for you also."

"Don't lie to me," she sobbed, "you love her."

"Evangeline," I said reaching for her. As my hand came near her shoulder, she stepped away, but not before my hand went right through her leathers. "What the hell?"

"E'Leawae Uea!" She screamed at me. As I suspected, this wasn't real. Something wasn't right. I reached out to her again, attempting to replicate the touch, but she side-stepped each attempt to make contact.

"Why don't you want me to touch you?" I asked.

"E'Leawae Uea!" She shouted at the top of her lungs. I lunged for her, attempting to pull her into a hold. Instead she disappeared into a puff of smoke while the words *E'Leawae Uea* repeated in the air, with her voice.

For a moment I stood there, unsure how to proceed. Then, as if I'd needed time to digest it, I came to understand what those Elven words meant. "E-Leawae-Uea, Evangeline," I said.

My eyes closed and I breathed in as I thought back to our carriage ride. Whatever was happening right now couldn't be real. But back on the carriage she had said it, and it had been real.

"How pathetic," said a voice I knew too well by now. I turned to find myself face to face with Jonathan Flurwick.

Chapter 33

"STILL PUTTING YOUR HOPES ON LOVE, Wardson?" asked Flurwick. "It's what makes you weak. Love, and your little medical condition," he said.

"Where are we, Flurwick? What's happening here?" I asked. Whatever the cause of this disturbance, I was sure that Flurwick was at the heart of it.

"I am not the cause of this, Wardson. Believe it or not, you are," said Flurwick, wearing his sadistic smile. I was no longer in the mood for his mind games. I was eager for an explanation.

"Perhaps if you use your head, the explanation may not be so hard to find," he said.

"Dammit!" I said. "Are you reading my mind?"

"Reading it?" he chuckled. "Wardson, I am in it." His voice echoed in my head.

"What? But how?"

"Maybe it's not just your mind. I must say that there's a vast pool of knowledge here, all up for grabs."

And then it hit me. The reason we were being sent to Varghaanaire. Niserie's sister, Var'ae, had powerful telepathic abilities. "Bingo," said Flurwick, "right on the money there, Brandon."

"What's happened to her? I barely even made it into town."

"I suppose having such powerful mind magic drove her crazy. To be quite honest with you, I've felt her mind for some time. I was simply unable to access it. It's almost like having a storage unit full of sensitive data within your reach, but you don't have the biometric identification needed to access it," he said. I was trying to stop myself from thinking in order to prevent him grabbing too many of my thoughts. "But as the Master Conjurer continued to advance my powers, I sensed her more and more. Sometimes I even caught glances of what was in her mind. But I could never gain full access to it, not until right now; through you."

"Through me?" I asked.

"Yes, Wardson, start thinking and stop asking questions. It's right here in your mind, your fat little Elf has already discussed this with you."

I gripped my sword. "I swear, I will slit your throat if you keep disrespecting her."

Flurwick roared with laughter, doubling over himself. "How do you plan on doing that when I'm in Ogesh and you're all the way in Lainunia?"

I registered what he had said about being in Ogesh, but I tried to not dwell on it. Instead, the memory he'd referred to now came to mind. When I'd seen the vision of Flurwick obtaining the mysterious scroll, Evangeline had said that Flurwick's previous attempt to take control of my mind had left some kind of imprint on it. Some form of connection between us.

"Yes, Wardson; now you're thinking. It's a bit messy really, to think that I'm now accessing Var'ae's mind through yours. But I must thank you. For now I've obtained the last bit of information I need to fulfill my plan."

"You've figured out how to get to the crystals and leave Relaun?"

As Flurwick stared at me, I saw nothing but pure evil within his eyes. Perhaps it was a representation of his new found power consuming him. "No Brandon. In fact, I could leave Relaun anytime I want. But what I'm seeking is the full destruction of Relaun; because only then, will I be able to bestow its power to its unfiltered potential."

"No," I said, as the realization hit me. "I don't know how, Flurwick, but I promise that I'm going to find a way to stop you."

Flurwick laughed. "I'd like to see you try."

Now that Flurwick's intentions were clearer, I wanted to end this. I wanted to get out of this weird inception before he could gain too much from it.

"By the way, Wardson; thank you for giving me the

visuals of Highwell. I will be sending forces there to claim my artifacts as soon as possible. Too bad you and Var'ae will be lifeless carcasses by the time it happens." Flurwick held out his hands and then my head exploded with pain.

I heard myself screaming and I felt the impact on my knees as my body's weight came crashing down onto them. The pain was worse than anything I'd ever felt. So much so that I knew I couldn't withstand it. This was it, Flurwick had won. I struggled to lift my head; I was eager to look the treacherous scumbag in the eyes before I died.

My head was too heavy to lift. I could only raise it high enough to see the blue topaz pendent that must have fallen from within my armor. I stared at it as the silver sparked in the starlight. If I was to die while observing such an elegant piece of jewelry then so be it.

Somehow, the pain was numbing itself and Flurwick cursed.

"Bollocks! How could this be?"

A new voice was sounding off in my head now. "*Sesthaehr,*" came the repeated whisper of a woman. With the pain in my head fading, I was now able to look up at Flurwick, who appeared to be as curious at the sound of the voice as I was.

The lines on his forehead wrinkled and he exhaled deeply. "Everyone wants to help you, Wardson, but this time you won't get lucky." Flurwick raised his hands again and they began emitting an amber glow.

Something in my consciousness told me to look back down at the pendant. I took it one step further and grabbed it, holding it within my palm. As soon as I did this, the stars disappeared and the world went completely black.

CHAPTER 34

MY TONGUE FELT DRY and my body was damp with sweat when my eyes opened. When light hit my eyes, they stung profusely. I blinked until a wooden ceiling came into focus.

"He's up," Finian cried. Evangeline dashed to my side, followed by a woman I didn't recognize.

"How long have I been out?" I groaned, as I sat myself up.

"It's been at least five hours," said Finian. "It's morning now."

"Here, have a drink," said Evangeline, passing me a jug.

I took quick repeated gulps, eager to get rid of the dryness on my tongue. Then I addressed the elephant in the room. "Var'ae, is that you?" I asked the Elven woman who was peeking over Evangeline's shoulder.

"It is I," she said, bowing her head. "And I must offer my thanks for freeing me from my mind." Only then did I see that she was wearing Niserie's necklace.

"We both got caught up in her mind too," said Finian, answering one of the questions I'd wanted to ask. "We were forced to face our deepest anxieties. I saw myself get exiled from Aldeen for being an immature boy that couldn't pass his trial; and for failing to save Relaun from Flurwick. Then the Elves beheaded Blok."

"But it seems that your experience was much different to ours," said Evangeline, looking down on me. And then I wondered what her anxieties had been.

"Indeed it was," said Var'ae. "Your experience started out as your friend's did, along with the locals in this town. You were forced to see your anxieties play out in your mind. But, it seems that Flurwick was able to exploit you, to enter my mind and take control of the magic."

"Why was your mind acting like this first place?" I asked.

"It was my mistake," said Var'ae with her head bowed low as she spoke. "For the past few months, I had been trying to expand the range in which my mind could project. I was perhaps too ambitious with my capabilities. I'm already considered the most powerful user of mind manipulation in Relaun, but that was not enough for me.

Eventually, my expansion techniques began to work."

"How do you expand your powers like that?" I asked, curious if she'd been entering people's minds without permission.

"I am able to sense thoughts and emotions from other living beings. Whether animals, humans or Elves. I do not need to enter anyone's thoughts directly. I am able to simply feel that the thoughts are existing. Don't worry; I won't enter the thoughts of people around me unless it's warranted." It was spoken as if she'd read my mind. And based on what she'd said, I hoped she actually hadn't. ' As I was saying, my expansion started to work, and I sensed thoughts and feelings across Aldeen. Then, over a week ago, I felt strong emotions; the type of emotions that lead to death and destruction."

"Flurwick?" I asked.

They all nodded and Var'ae continued. "For nights, I deliberated on whether I should try to access the source of these feelings. Doing so would be a violation, and it's something I have strong feelings about. But I felt this person grow in power, and then I felt him practicing his own mind magic in the worst possible ways. That is why I made the decision to penetrate his mind. Unfortunately, the move backfired and he was somehow able to ward off my attempts. This caused damage to my mind, and it's what caused me to trap myself and everyone in Varghaanaire, in our own heads."

"Where are the other residents of Varghaanaire now?" I asked, sensing that it was too quiet around us.

"Many of them are on the brink of death," said Evangeline. "But I have been tending to them and there's a good chance that a majority of them will make it. There were actually a few deaths before we got here."

"As you can imagine, I am disturbed by this," said Var'ae, her eyes watering. "I have already reached out to healers from villages close by who are on their way help." I wondered if she'd used more mind magic to achieve this. "But more urgently, I fear what may be coming next from Flurwick. He has learned too much from having access to our minds."

She was right, and these words caused me to swing my legs over the side of the bed. I didn't want to waste any more time. "How much knowledge could he have gained in that short space of time?" I asked, feeling the pain return to my legs as I put weight on them.

"We shouldn't assume he knows as much as he says. Even for me, it takes some time to search through even five memories or thoughts in a person's mind. Flurwick had access to two separate minds, and I fail to believe he could have obtained everything of importance from us," she sniffed. "But we also must think hypothetically and act on what he could possibly know. It's the artifacts that he desires, and the knowledge of getting to the Island of Crystalline. He has no doubt seen the knowledge I have acquired on the matter."

"What knowledge is that then?" asked Finian.

She looked down at him, as if wishing he hadn't asked. "It's a long story, human. I must first present you with the Flask of Irithrel. Then you must use the gates to get back to Highwell and set up defenses. I also recommend extracting the Runes of Aktarth from Highwell and keeping them in your possession."

"What? You want us to carry the artifacts?" said Finian, shocked. "That would make us a target."

"Moving targets," I said. "If we stayed on the move then it means Flurwick and his minions will have to exhaust their efforts to find us; which in turn makes them vulnerable to attack." Var'ae nodded as I spoke. "It's a common outlaw strategy in space. Put a high value hostage on a spaceship and fly him all around the galaxy and make the Galactic Alliance have to work overtime to find him."

"And you have both a Mutano and a skilled mage here to help you stay protected," said Var'ae.

"It's a good strategy, but we'll have to see if your kingdom and the guild leaders of Aldeen will agree," I said.

"We also have to hope that the others were able to secure the remaining artifacts," said Finian. "I wish one of those darn birds would visit."

"I sense no triumph in the two locations where the artifacts are thought to be. All I can sense in Thirion is feral creatures. I think those artifacts have yet to be discovered."

"Can you sense anything in Ogesh?" I asked. "Flurwick mentioned going there to brainwash the Mutanos."

"Ogesh is to the far east of Relaun. Unfortunately my capabilities don't stretch that far," she said. "Even with Aldeen and Thirion, I cannot sense emotions across the entire regions; only the parts closest to Lainunia." Var'ae walked to the window and peered outside. "The healers are here. Now we must depart so that we will reach Shavatha as soon as possible."

"You're coming back with us?" I asked.

Var'ae turned to face me, her bright blue eyes beaming. She shot quick glances between me and Evangeline before responding. "Yes. I must unite with my sister and persuade the kingdom to take this threat seriously. You heard what Flurwick wants."

"What's that?" asked Finian.

"He wants to destroy Relaun completely," I told him. And I saw the most fearful look that he'd ever shown.

The healers faced a tough challenge. There were only a dozen of them in a town full of a hundred sick people. Fortunately, some of the sick had come around and were now conscious. Once they were back to their full strength, they would be able to assist in the effort to restore their fellow locals. Var'ae's mother was away from the town during the disturbance so she had no blood ties affected. She did however have many friends and students that hoped to learn her methods of telepathy. Her concern for them had her pacing back and forth between buildings.

Before long, Var'ae was ready to depart. As we prepared our things, I'd picked her brain with more questions on my mind.

"With this connection that Flurwick was able to exploit in my mind, could he access it again?" I'd asked her. She'd told me that it was unlikely because it was her own manipulation of my mind that had opened up the connection. She'd said that it may be possible for him to get into my mind again if another mage was weakening it. But I would have nothing to worry about if I was in full control.

Var'ae also confirmed to me that it had been her sister's pendant that gave her the willpower to shut out Flurwick. And that seeing the pendent through my eyes strengthened her defense against his invasion. In fact, she told me that she'd almost been able to destroy his mind. That he'd somehow been able to ward her off at the last second. This had worried her, for it meant that Flurwick's powers were threatening. If he were able to master these powers, then it would be troublesome for us all.

The Flask of Irithrel was an oval shaped bottle with blue scales. It had a round cap on top that couldn't be removed unless the flask was united with each of the Elder artifacts first. The flask was loaded into Var'ae's chest, which Finian and I carried to the stables for her. Two curtained carriages awaited us, each with a horse of its own. "Are they magical?" asked Finian.

"They are," Evangeline confirmed, "I sense much power from them."

"These horses are fast, and I'm able to communicate with them so they will know where to go," Var'ae explained.

"Why are we taking two carriages though?" asked Finian, "we could fit into one."

Var'ae shot quick glances between the three of us. "Once we make it to Shavatha, things will change," she said. "The war on Flurwick will begin. This ride back to the city will be our last chance for downtime. It seems to me that there is need for some of us to have private conversations," said Var'ae. It took a sideways glance from Evangeline for me to realize what she meant. She'd seen into our minds, so she had to know of our untapped feelings.

"What do we need to discuss, Brandon?" Finian smirked.

"You will be traveling with me." Var'ae told him. "But I will be making contact with my sister so that she is informed and ready before we make it to Shavatha."

Once our things were loaded into the carriage, it was time to board; and as I helped Evangeline climb into the carriage, I felt like I was suddenly floating on water.

CHAPTER 35

THE CARRIAGE ROCKED SIDE TO SIDE as the horse dashed along the bumpy stone path, near to where our escorts from yesterday had dropped us off. "So," I said, breaking the lingering silence inside the carriage.

"So," she mimicked while crossing her arms.

"Things are getting pretty serious now, it seems," I said.

"Serious in what regard?"

I realized that my comment could be interpreted in a different way. I had been referring to our pursuit of the artifacts and taking down Flurwick. "I meant with Flurwick. And everything that happened in Varghaanaire," I replied.

"Indeed, there's little time left for stalling. We will have to face things head on now; whether the kingdom and the guild leaders give us permission or not," she said. And her eyes lingered on me for so long that I forgot to respond.

"—Yeah, couldn't have said it better myself," I said. I bit my lips as my mind started racing. This was the only time Evangeline and I had been alone together since walking through the woods that night when she'd been captured. That's why there was so much intensity in the air. I couldn't take this awkwardness between us anymore. It was time to address the elephant in the room. I wasn't sure if my feelings towards her were mutual, but I had a deep desire to tell her my thoughts, just so I wouldn't have to hold onto them anymore. I decided to first ask her the personal question I'd been meaning to ask. "So, what did you see when you were swept up in Var'ae's mind warp?"

She averted her gaze from me and stared down at her exposed toes in her strappy sandals. She then crossed her legs. Her beautiful lace necklace caught my attention as light bounced off it while she moved.

"People died," she said, "people all over Relaun. There was a plague and I was working hard to find a cure to reverse the effects. But I couldn't do it. I was limited in my knowledge of ingredients. And then I figured out the cure once the last person in the village had died. I had caught the plague myself, so the only person left to benefit from the cure was I."

"Wow, that's more harsh than what I experienced," I added.

"And..." she paused. "And then you arrived." She looked up at me and I caught myself in a nervous twitch. "You were sick, but not with the plague. Your blood had clotted in your chest and you were in danger of dying. I gave you numerous formulas and you fought through it. You survived."

"Well, I guess it symbolizes how much you care about people's health. Even if you can't save them all, at least you saved someone. Though, I would have chosen for the village to be cured over myself." I was shooting verbal diarrhea at this point. The tension was making it hard for me focus on what I wanted to say.

"And then," she continued.

"Oh, there's more? How long were you out of it?"

She looked up at me. "Visions and dreams are exempt from time We see them in short flashes, but interpret them as if they are occurring in real time," she explained. "Your case may have been different because of Flurwick."

It made sense, but I was eager for her to continue sharing what she had seen. "I see. Sorry for the silly questions, please continue," I said.

"You left me," she said. "Natalya came and you left with her. And then I was alone. Sometime later I had awoken. Likely around the time you'd helped Var'ae shut out Flurwick from her mind."

I was unsure how to follow up with this revelation. If the effects of Var'ae's mind warp were to trap us in our anxieties, it meant that Evangeline saw the prospect of me leaving with Natalya as something she feared. Along with the incapability to help dying people.

"Before Flurwick tapped into your mind, I'm sure you saw other things. What were they?" she asked.

I wanted to lie; to not mention Natalya at all. But it would mean having to get creative with an alternate story on how Evangeline herself had appeared in the vision. Unfortunately for me, I was lacking in creativity at this moment.

"I—uh—I was back in the galaxy. It seemed as if I was on a planet all by myself. Then, a shuttle that we use for transportation dropped from the sky. Natalya came out of it." At the mention of her, Evangeline's head turned to the side. "She—uh—she made me feel as if I'd been dreaming about Relaun the entire time. As if all of this had been a figment of imagination. She told me it was time to go home."

"You'd like that, wouldn't you?" said Evangeline, and I felt my insides flood with guilt.

"Wait, let me finish," I said. "At first I thought it was real. But when I started thinking about Finian, about Blok, and about you. I started to resist her. I knew I couldn't have imagined all of this, because inside I felt so strongly about you." Evangeline's eyes closed and she was biting on her lip. "Natalya was antsy with me when I started resisting. And then she made a remark about you. That was when I knew that you definitely were real, and that my feelings for you were true. It hit me like a shot in the heart to hear her insult you." Her eyes found me again. There were no tears, just the shimmering hazel bulbs that had become my weakness.

"She insulted me, and mocked my medical condition. She disappeared, and then I was face—to—face with you. You were mad at me. You said you used to be revolted at how I always stared into your eyes. But then you'd developed feelings for me. You told me that you used to only concern yourself with improving your magic until I came along; and then you became interested in me. But you said it had all been for nothing, because you believed I only wanted Natalya."

Evangeline smiled. "Var'ae's mind is powerful," she said, as she brushed some of her hair over her pointed ear. "She was able to uncover our mutual feelings and play them off against one another."

"So you mean, that's actually how you feel?" I asked

"Every bit of it is true," Evangeline said. She was twitching her foot and I felt butterflies as it brushed against my shin.

"Before..." I began, trying to compose what I was going to say, "before you faded away, you repeated those words. The words you whispered in my ear."

In addition to her foot twitching, she had now started beating her fingers over her knuckles while her hands were clenched together over her knees. "E'Leawae Uea," she said, trying to mask a giddy smile.

"Yes, that."

"But I'm not telling you what it means," she said. Her smile was sending me over the edge; I could no longer stand it. I got up and shifted over to her side of the carriage. As I sat next to her, moving closer, she turned her head sideways towards me. Her hands balled into fists. She didn't pull away from me and she showed no sign of resistance. I took her chin in my hand and I pressed my lips against hers. Immediately, her hand rubbed against my bearded face. She leaned into me with a longing that told me she'd been waiting for this. Her lips tasted as sweet as fruit, and her hands were cotton soft as they stroked my puffs of facial hair.

"E'Leawae Uea" I said, breaking apart. She stared back into my face as if she was watching something incredible play out before her. I saw the hazel eyes become watery before she pulled me back to her and locked her lips against mine.

"By The Elders!" We heard Finian cry in the distance. We broke apart, afraid that Finian's bark had been in reaction to us. By the sounds of the rickety carriages, Finian's was further ahead than ours was.

"Do you think he's okay?" I asked.

"If he was in any danger, we would be hearing it now," she said, pulling me back towards her. It was the most carefree I'd seen her.

* * *

"Brandon?" said Evangeline, rubbing her hand against the tight puff of curls that had become my hair. The feeling of holding her in my arms and being blanketed by her warm naked body was indescribable.

"What's up?" I answered. The moment was so perfect that I was able to forget the nipping pains in my hip.

"What will happen if you have to go home?" she asked. It was something I hadn't thought of an answer for. At the back of my mind I'd thought about the many different outcomes of this mission. I'd thought about Flurwick being able to gather the artifacts before us; being able to exact his plan. I thought about dying while trying to stop him. But what would happen if we somehow succeeded in stopping him? Would I be trapped here in Relaun forever? Would there be a way to get back to the Milky Way? Would I be happy settling in Relaun?

"I haven't really thought about it," I said. "But I guess if our mission is to take down Flurwick, there may be no going home. He's the key to entering and leaving here for me." There was silence for some time, as the two of us were silently questioning our future together. "But I don't want to think about that now. I want to enjoy your presence."

She turned in my arms and pecked me on the lips. "I suppose this is the last chance for us to be selfish. I wish we could have been more open with our feelings before now."

"You should have pulled me aside one of those times I stared into your eyes like a creep," I smirked.

"Oh please, that was the look you gave every piece of Elven flesh. I deduced that it wasn't exclusively for me."

"With the other Elves, it was more acknowledging their differences," I said, stroking her arms. "But with you, it was infatuation."

Evangeline smiled and proceeded to rub my hips, as if she could tell there was pain there. Several silent minutes passed as we stared at each other, completely enamored.

"Brandon! Eva!" Finian shouted from the other carriage. "We're approaching Shavatha. Ten minutes, be ready."

"Well, I guess all good things come to an end," I said, sitting myself up, feeling the stabbing sensations.

"Please, let's not hide this. I want us to be open and free in our love," said Evangeline. "It will be important. We must show that Elves and humans can bond. There has been too much separation between races," she said.

"Do you really think I can go without holding you in my arms now?" I said. She smiled at me and then we dressed ourselves. As I forced my legs into my skinsuit, I thought about how my love for Evangeline had developed in a matter of weeks. In a short space of time she had filled the emptiness inside my heart. And I would push my body beyond its limits to preserve this feeling.

CHAPTER 36

IT WAS HARD TO COMPOSE MYSELF as I helped Evangeline fasten her pullover armor piece. Now that we were at the stage of sharing our desire for each other, I couldn't contain the excitement that flowed within me. But it was time to be sensible, as the fate of Relaun was in our hands. I couldn't let the side of me that wanted to sweep her back off of her feet run rampant at this moment.

We bound our weapons and took a lingering look at one another before we stepped out of the carriage—hand in hand. Finian was stood outside, greeting us with his intense gaze. His eyes shot to our linked hands, but when he spoke it was not in regard to us. "Audette visited me," he said. "Highwell is about to be attacked at any moment. There are forces heading in from two directions."

"Oh shit, and if he went into my mind deep enough, it means he knows exactly where the artifact is."

"Let us enter the city," said Var'ae, as she emerged

from the carriage. "I have spoken with my sister and she has told me that the gate is ready." Var'ae handed the flask to Finian and he pocketed it in his pouch. We followed Var'ae as she granted us entry to Shavatha. We were immediately greeted by Niserie, who teared up at the sight of her younger sister. After exchanging hugs and small talk, the two sisters faced us. Niserie was beaming at Evangeline. We still hadn't separated from each other, and it felt as though both sisters were pleased to see us so comfortable in our love.

"Thank you for your assistance, you don't understand the joy it brings me to see my sister again," said Niserie. "Please follow me." We obeyed her and trailed behind, as she continued speaking. "I have sent the wardens to escort the Mutano to the palace. The gate is close by and fully powered on both sides; it seems your guild leaders are eager to recover another artifact."

"They've got bigger problems than that right now. There's an entire legion outside of Highwell," said Finian. "I saw Undead, Exul clan and rogue mages."

"Yes, I have shown King Thagorrom the images from the bird," said Niserie. "But the King wants the Flask to remain here, and for you to return to Highwell and bring the Runes of..."

"I don't give a rat's piss what the king wants," Finian snapped. "We're not wasting time on silly politics anymore. We're going to defend Highwell and then we're going to put a stop to Flurwick once and for all."

"Darling, I understand your anger," said Var'ae. "If the King resists our pleas, I will distract him and allow you to pass through the gate; as we discussed in the carriage."

I shot a sideways glance at Finian, who raised his eyebrows at me.

Blok was waiting for us at the palace with two wardens stood close by. The Elves couldn't keep their eyes off him. It was as if they feared he would attack at any moment. Blok stood against a pillar on the opposite side of the room, returning their stares.

"Get over yourselves, this is not the time for racial pride," said Niserie. We reacquainted ourselves with Blok, checking him for any signs of hurt. Evangeline checked his wound and was happy to see that the scar had reduced in size. I wondered how fast Mutano skin rejuvenated in comparison to human skin.

"Elf girl and Brando hold hands now," Blok said, as if this was the most important revelation since his incarceration.

"Yeah, at least I don't have to hear their pathetic bickering anymore," said Finian, right before the King made his entrance.

"The kingdom thanks you for restoring Varghaanaire," he nodded. "In light of the new details, we would like you to now hand over the Elder artifact for safekeeping."

"Absolutely not," said Finian.

"Flurwick may know all there is to know about Highwell and Shavatha," I said. "We can't keep the artifacts stationary any longer. We have to keep them with us so he won't be able to track them down so easily."

The King took an extended blink before his response came. "I assure you that unlike the humans, we are able to deal with any attack on our kingdom."

"That's great, your honor. But the artifact is staying with us, and we must now leave to defend Highwell." I said.

"The humans speak true, my king. Please see reason," Niserie pleaded. There was silence for a few moments and you could cut the tension with a knife.

Niserie opposing the King's viewpoint seemed to be a rare occurrence in Shavatha.

The King's head rose until he was looking down at us with his chin in the air. "Guards, please seize the artifact."

"No!" Niserie cried. A dozen armed Elves surrounded us and we responded by grabbing our own set of weapons. Blok positioned himself as if ready to pounce on the first Elf that dared rush us. In the distance, I could see more Elves on the high ground, taking aim with their bows.

Then, the King raised his hand and it glowed. Evangeline gasped and held onto me in preparation for whatever he was about to cast.

"You will not!" We heard Var'ae scream, and before we knew it, her own hand was glowing amber. All of a sudden, the Elves dropped their weapons and stood straight with their arms beside them. The King sat down on his thrown.

"You actually did it," said Finian.

"I am not happy that it has come to this, my dear. When word spreads that we used our magic against the King, it will be dangerous for us," she said, looking over at her sister. "I'm not much better than the enemy at this point."

"If this is what is required to save Relaun, then so be it." Niserie said. "You're not using your magic to cause destruction, only to prevent it."

Var'ae nodded before setting eyes on me. "You must go now. The gate waits in the next room. We will do our best to restore order here and I hope we can persuade our people to send help," said Var'ae.

Niserie walked over to Evangeline and handed her a small jar with some green leafy contents. "Var'ae told me to prepare these for you on your way here. When the time comes, you will know what to do with them."

Evangeline looked surprised, but took them without hesitation. "Thank you, lady Niserie. It has been a pleasure to meet you both."

We exchanged departing hugs with the sisters. Finian and Var'ae seemed to have shared a more intimate hug than the rest of us. "Alright, let's get a move on," said Finian.

We made our way into the enclosed room nearby.

CHAPTER 37

THE GATE WAS A GLOWING WISP of energy that circled between two enormous wooden structures. Light from the circular energy bounced around the dim windowless room.

"Such a dazzling sight," said Evangeline. "The Elders left us wonderful treats." It really was enthralling to look at.

"Well, they apparently gave us Flurwick." Finian added.

I wanted to get a picture of the gate, but this wasn't the moment for it. "Alright, let's ready ourselves. We don't know what we'll find on the other side," I said. I clutched the hilt of the fire sword in case we were immediately ambushed after emerging. There would be no time to aim my blaster in that scenario, but I could at least thrust the sword at an attacker.

"Well, let's go for it then," said Finian. He tapped Blok on his bulky forearm and the Mutano stared down at him. "Wanna take the lead?" he winked.

"Let's head in at the same time," I said. "Whatever

happens, happens to us all." They agreed and we all stepped forward. As we got closer I could feel the energy radiating, like facing a fireplace. I took a deep breath and then we glanced at one another before walking right through the center of the swirling wisps.

At the blink of an eye, we found ourselves in a large room full of fancy brickwork. "That was much quicker and a lot less painful than I expected," said Finian.

"Blok smell mage in next room," said the Mutano.

"Friendly, I hope," said Evangeline.

"Guild leaders," said Blok. We walked up a small corridor and into the neighboring room; where we found the guild leaders standing in front of a large rectangular windowpane.

"It's too bad Master Retgar and Warden Jale have yet to return," said Arjon, the grandmaster of the Warriors Guild.

"We made it," I said. They each turned on the spot with fear on their faces. Arjon had his sword drawn ready to attack. Immediately, I regretted startling them.

"Ah, it's the young strangers," Egith smiled. "I knew we could count on you to get the gate up and running. Did you manage recover the artifact from the Elves?"

"We did, and we almost got zapped to oblivion for it," said Finian. "Is this the guild tower we're in?" he asked, walking to the window and observing. It took half a glance at the scene below for Finian's expression to shift completely. "By The Elders!" he exclaimed. We followed him to the window and looked down on the hundreds of Undead forming outside the gate. The horde was vast, far outnumbering the ones that had invaded Corwy.

"We have our defenses ready and I've been working my falcons overtime to spread word across guild halls all over Aldeen to send help."

"Good call," I said. "Finian says it's not just the Undead we have to worry about. And also, Flurwick may know exactly where to look." Egith nodded as I spoke. "Speaking of which, we should secure the runes as soon as possible and keep them on the move with us."

"There's no need," said Arjon. "If we focus on blocking the horde, surrounding them and closing in, there's no way they'll get as far as this tower."

Arjon's statement brought back memories of hardheaded superiors in the Alliance that had thrown away marine lives. I was tired of such superiors downplaying threats and foolishly endangering others, while they watched on in comfort. I pulled the trigger on my blaster and shot an apple that was stacked atop a fruit bowl across the room. There were several yelps as the apple glowed—thanks to Evangeline's enchantments—and then exploded into a thousand pieces.

I turned to face Arjon. "You see the precision on my firearm? Flurwick and his people are brandishing weapons more lethal than that. In which case he'll have no problem rolling through your defenses and finding his way right here."

"The runes are down the hall and to the left," said Egith, her fingers touching her parted lips. "Hilda, please go with the young man to secure the runes," she said nodding towards Finian. Hilda and Finian left the room together.

"Are you sure we should trust them with such a thing?" Arjon asked, as if I wasn't stood beside him. He still didn't get it.

"Judging by how seriously they are taking this, yes. And Brandon here knows the dangers well. We must trust them on this."

Finian soon returned with the runes. They were wrapped in a cloth, which he deposited in his pouch. He then handed the flask to me to carry, as it made more sense to have them separated by person.

"It's happening," Hilda pointed, "they're approaching the gate." We all gathered before the window to watch as the horde marched forward. Members of Exul clan were walking alongside the Undead as if they too were mindless carcasses.

On the inside of the gate, Highwell's army had set up barricades and archers positioned themselves on rooftops and watch-posts to shoot down on the horde. I saw mages in robes casting white objects in front of the warrior formations and around the high sturdy doors that separated us from the threat. "What are the mages doing?" I asked.

"They're putting up barriers," said Evangeline. "It's part of the healing family of magic. It requires much power from the mage for the barrier be strong enough to ward most forms of attack. I've never been great at them myself."

I was about to ask if these barriers would be strong enough to prevent them penetrating the doors like they did in Corwy, but I had my answer before I could summon the words.

The gate and the walls surrounding it collapsed with a terrifying blast. Though we were in the guild tower, the impact almost sent us to the floor. The horrific sight brought confusion, as we felt like the tower itself had also been hit. Watching the guild leaders flail on the ground in terror added to the feeling of despair. Arjon's face drowned in fearful tears. Evangeline was squeezing my hand and looking on at the flames surrounding the mess that had been the town gates moments before. Finian stood in front of the window, his head moving rapidly, taking in every movement below.

"We must go and fight now," Finian said.

"Agreed," I said. "That blast came from an Alliance weapon, and by the looks of it, it's enhanced with magic." I could tell as much by the over-effectiveness of the blast and the ongoing glints surrounding the wreckage. "Highwell's army aren't well informed enough to know what they're facing."

"Look," Evangeline pointed. The Exul mercenaries were using magic to out the fires, allowing the Undead to pass safely into the city. Blok had seen enough, he'd marched towards the stairs and the three of us followed behind him; before Egith stood before us and blocked our path.

"I will not stop you from helping. It's clear we need your expertise now. But I have some advice that may prove useful," she said.

"We welcome your guidance." I nodded.

"For this many Undead to be acting in unison, there must be someone nearby controlling them. Seek that person or creature out. For defeating this person will make the Undead weaker."

My companions and I glanced at each other and nodded in agreement. We then rushed down the stairs as fast as possible. The stairway felt infinite and I had to control my breathing as not to exert myself.

* * *

Flurwick's minions were now flooding their way through the array of streets and alleyways. Many of the Exul warriors were breaking into buildings, dragging people out and torturing them. We incapacitated each threat we came across, but there were too many for a squad of four to engage. The guild forces did their part as best they could; attacking groups of enemies head on. But the enemy had spread so much throughout Highwell that it was impossible for defenders to be everywhere at once.

"This is terrible," said Evangeline. "If it's the artifacts they're after, why terrorize these innocent people?"

"Because that's the easiest way to get the guild leaders to give up the goods," I said, watching Blok dismember several Undead. "It's hard to walk by watching this, but we have to do as Egith said and focus on finding the controller. If we try to assist in every battle we'll never make progress."

"You're right, but what in the name of Jerrus is that screeching noise?" Finian asked.

When Evangeline looked at him with curiosity, I knew I wasn't the only one who wondered. "What screeching?" I asked.

"You can't hear that?"

"We can't; come on, let's keep moving. My guess is that the controller must be somewhere behind the horde." We persisted on, occasionally needing to slaughter Undead attackers. Evangeline's staff attacks were doing wonders, stopping them in their tracks with focus fire. I hacked at them with my fire sword when they got too close, and I was now plastered in brown, Undead fluids.

"Okay, I'm sorry," Finian said, as we turned into another alley. "That screeching is too loud for you not to be hearing it now. Is it all in me head or something? Has some filthy mage worked their magic on me?"

I looked at Finian with a brow raised—wondering what he was talking about—until we heard sounds of an Undead squirming and its flesh being ripped apart. The sound was coming from around the corner. We all assumed that it was Blok—who was taking apart the Undead as if their existence offended him. That was until the creature appeared on all fours right before us, its eyes locked on Finian.

"The Pardu!" he yelled. "It's found me."

CHAPTER 38

"IS IT HOSTILE?" I asked, as the Pardu's eyes scanned us; studying our every move. The eyes followed my hand as my pinky finger linked around Evangeline's—something that had become a subconscious norm. The Pardu's acknowledgment of our movements made me feel uneasy.

"I can't believe it's here, in front of us," said Evangeline. "Legends say that the creature has lived for thousands of years, and could even be linked with The Elders in some way." She looked over to me, her hazel eyes still melting me inside. "It is known to be hostile. Every scholar who survived an encounter with it has said it attacked them ferociously. And with no sound coming from the creature itself, it can kill you in an instant if it wishes to."

"It doesn't want to," said Finian. The Pardu was now in a full on stare-down with Finian.

"Is it the magic you casted on its fur?" I asked Evangeline. "Is that why it's not attacking?"

"It must be; and the screeching that Finian heard, it explains why only he heard it. He must still have the fur on him."

"It's hurt," Finian said. "Look at its side. He has some bruising."

Indeed, the feline had taken a beating. It wore a large black mark on its right side. Its fur looked singed, but at the center of the bruise was a laceration surrounded in dried blood.

Evangeline gasped. "It's had healing. There's no way it could have survived such a wound without help."

"It's showing me something," said Finian. "Wait. It's the Master Conjurer from Corwy. He's somewhere close by. It's him that's commanding the Undead."

"The Pardu is connecting with you through mind magic?" Evangeline asked. "Imagine the secrets it must know about Relaun."

"Sadly, we don't have time to get the full history lesson. If the Pardu knows where the conjurer is, we have to get there now," I said.

"It wants us to follow it," said Finian. The Pardu turned in the opposite direction and looked back at us, like a cat trying to get its master to follow him to the unopened can of food. Once it saw that we were following, it picked up its pace.

We chased behind the Pardu as it raced through the streets. We watched the creature sink its teeth into straying Undead, dragging them by the ankles, allowing us to finish the kill. Finian shot numerous creatures with his bow and Evangeline continued blasting away oncoming attackers before they could get too close. Once or twice I shocked members of the Exul with my blaster for harassing innocents.

And then, before we reached the center square, a bunch of civilians ran in our direction, screaming; almost knocking us to the dirt.

"Spider!" A woman cried.

"Someone please stop this," came more yells. *"Maybe that feline will kill it."*

Finian turned his head to speak. "It's big. The Pardu can tell from the monster's scent that it's a larger than usual Undead arachnid."

"How much of its mind can you see?" Evangeline asked, stepping out the way of a civilian.

"Only what it shows me."

"None of us is scared of spiders, right?" I asked.

"I used to have pet spiders back at the barn," said Finian. "Cats kept eating them though."

"Domestic spiders are much less a threat than wild ones. We must proceed carefully," Evangeline said, taking the lead. I thought back to the arachnid I'd seen during the Trail of Becoming at the coliseum. The agility of that spider was intimidating. I could only imagine what we were in for now.

Screams trailed through the air as we turned onto the center square. And then we caught our first glimpse of the towering arachnid. It was knocking Warriors all over the square with its front legs while spitting a purple substance from its mouth. I felt the creatures' weight each time its legs slammed onto the stone surface. Despite its weight, it moved as if weightless.

"This isn't going to be pretty," I said. "It's fast, and it can attack from almost any direction. Getting a good vantage point may be tough too. And that venom can reach long distances." I was making these judgments based on what was in front of me, as well as what I had seen at the Trial of Becoming. "Finian, you go left and I'll go right. Between us we have both ice and lightning, let's aim for its legs from each side until we can get a clear shot at the face."

Finian and I nodded in agreement.

"I will do what I can to help the injured warriors and remove them from the area." I was relieved to hear that Evangeline wouldn't be putting herself too far into harms reach.

We crept towards our agreed directions, eager not to waste time. One thing worried me as I saw warriors tossing spears and arrows. The arachnid was deflecting the magic as if not fazed by it. I wondered if my blaster, assisted by its Radox energy and magic, would be enough to get its attention. I climbed atop a high wooden post and gazed down the monster.

Once Finian had positioned himself atop a shed, he began to fire down upon the spider's legs. The legs glowed sapphire, while freezing momentarily on the spot. Seconds later, shattering ice was heard as giant shards flew out from the arachnid, almost catching Evangeline where she stood. Finian faced the monster with his mouth wide open as it turned its attention to him.

I took aim at its hind legs and opened fire, but the shots deflected. "Shit," I said, as the spider shot venom towards Finian. Thankfully it had missed him.

With complete silence being its advantage, the Pardu flew at the arachnid from behind, leading us to wonder where it had launched itself from. It positioned itself on the spider's dome and then slammed its claws right into one of the spider's eyes.

The spider's monstrous wails were piercing, as it spun frantically around the square, smashing its surroundings in the process. The Pardu's body came crashing into the legs of the wooden post on which I stood, causing the structure to collapse in on itself. My armor had protected me from taking any major damage, but being an inch or so in the wrong part of the collapse and I would've been seriously injured.

When I recovered from the shock of falling, I dug through piles of wood in search of the feline. Blocks of wood then shifted beside me and the feline hurled itself out of the wreckage. Its tail swayed behind it as it stared at the spider, baring all its teeth.

"No!" Evangeline cried. My heart skipped at her voice—I was worried she'd been hurt—but I saw her looking up in terror. When I followed her stare, I saw a gush of venom shooting through the air, arcing downward at the Pardu's position. It was as if this brief moment was captured in slow motion, as I followed the venom's course through the air. Right before it was about to make contact with the feline, a solid frame stood in front of the Pardu to take the hit.

"Blok!" I cried. "What are you doing? It's venom."

The Mutano side-eyed me, completely undaunted. "Venom not hurt Blok," he said.

At some point during this exchange, Finian had made his way back to ground level and came dashing towards us. "The Pardu wants us to leave with it. It says time is running out," he said.

"We can't let this thing destroy the city," I said, watching the spider wail in pain at its loss of an eye.

"Go," said the Mutano. "Blok will kill spider."

"I've managed to assist the warriors and commoners in getting away," said Evangeline, walking towards us with her staff held out cautiously.

The Pardu sprinted towards a path to our left. At the same time, Blok had lifted a spear from the ground and lobbed it towards the spiders face. The spider deflected it with its front legs.

"Come on," said Finian. "We'll let him handle this. He's trained to fight spiders since he was a little one."

Finian jogged towards the Pardu. Evangeline and I followed behind him and when I glanced over my shoulder, I saw Blok running fearlessly towards the arachnid.

Chapter 39

THE PARDU LED US UP a narrow, rocky path outside the city walls. Our feet were splattered by water from the falls beside us. Something about walking along the large blankets of water falling to the river below was soothing.

The creature slowed to a halt as we approached the opening of a cave. An emerald glow from the Pardu's feet caught my attention.

"What is it doing to the surface?" I asked.

"He's making our footsteps silent," Finian answered. "The conjurer is inside that cave."

"Such a marvelous creature; I can't believe it's on our side," Evangeline said.

"We must stay behind him. Each step he takes will silence the patch of ground he has stepped on for a few seconds."

"Understood," I said, lining up behind Finian. We walked behind the Pardu as instructed, until we found ourselves inside the cave. It took seconds for my eyes to adjust to the dim surroundings, but below I could see firelight. We continued to step down a slope until we could see a person sat with their back towards us. His legs were tucked in as if he was in deep meditation.

We moved in behind the man and stared at one another, unsure of how to proceed. I kept quiet, not wanting to alert him.

Luckily for us, it was him who spoke first. "You have returned, Ezzan," he said, in a raspy voice while he remained seated. "Highwell must be torn apart until he receives the artifact. I saw you challenge me through the eyes of the spider. Why must you continue to oppose me, Ezzan?"

"The Pardu wants us to save him. To make him see reason," said Finian, breaking our silence.

The conjurer grunted. "You made a new friend, I see."

"What do you mean?" I whispered in response to Finian's previous statement.

"Yer friend Flurwick has completely corrupted the conjurer's mind. He believes he's doing right by following Flurwick's orders. He's commanding the Undead horde with his mind and magic, and no matter what the Pardu does, he can't force him to see reason."

"But why does the Pardu care so much for him?" Evangeline asked.

"His name is Ezzan," said the conjurer as he rose to his feet. "He bares the mind of the Elder, Vyncis Thirion."

At these words, Finian and Evangeline both looked down at the Pardu in awe. "It's an Elder?" asked Finian.

"Not quite," said the conjurer. "Ezzan isn't Vyncis himself. To put it simply, Vyncis created Ezzan so that he would share his own thoughts and feelings. When Vyncis was nearing death, he sought a way to make the creature live eternally with his thoughts. The creature won't share with me how this is possible, but using his own life-force, Vyncis cast a powerful healing spell that would keep Ezzan's body alive forever. Only a wound inflicted upon the creature by another entity can kill it."

The conjurer turned to face us. His movement was slow. "As you can see, Master Flurwick has had a go at doing so," he pointed towards the Pardu's wound. The conjurer was a tall, frail man. His gray hair and beard were long and unkempt. His skin was wrinkled and his fingernails were long and yellow. Despite his lack of care for his appearance, the conjurer looked to be the type of man with immense knowledge and wisdom.

"How is it that you know so much about the Pardu?

And why didn't you protect him from that bastard Flurwick?" Finian shot, his fist balled in front him.

"I recognize you from Corwy, my boy. You are the one who failed his trail are you not?" the conjurer asked.

"I didn't ask you whether you knew who I was," Finian snarled.

The conjurer examined us through his dark shadowy eyes. "As you know, my accomplishments with the Corwy guilds are well recognized. I have made countless magical discoveries through my willingness to travel the wilds and challenge wild creatures and rogue mages. On one of these outings, I had been curious to discover what had slaughtered a giant serpent that had claimed countless lives of guilders venturing outside of Corwy's walls. I took members of the Hunters Guild with me during my search. It became clear to me that something or someone was planting clues to send us in the wrong direction. So I used my gift of summoning to create a temporary threat that would lure out the serpent's murderer. With the hunter's following one of the false leads, I waited in the depth of the woods, watching my creation disturb the wilds. And then I saw it. I could never have heard it, but there, before my eyes I watched as the creature of legend pounced upon my ogre."

The Pardu's eyes became glossy as the conjurer told the story. "And then, it was as if the creature sensed that the ogre was artificial," the conjurer continued. "Immediately it looked in my direction, knowing that it had been deceived. It launched itself at me and I was prepared to face my death while looking at something so mystical. But the creature stopped before biting me to death and chose to connect with my mind. 'Nice trick,' it told me. From then on, the Pardu became my secret partner of the wilds. It taught me things. I learned new techniques that enhanced my capabilities far beyond what I was capable of before."

"Touching," said Finian, "clearly Ezzan here is attached to you. Why betray him by working for that scum Flurwick?"

The conjurer shook his head. "Do not speak poorly of Master Flurwick."

"He is no master, Sir Lockwood." said Evangeline. "Please do not speak of him highly. It brings shame to what the Mages Guild represents."

"My dear, Evangeline, expert at healing; you must understand that Master Flurwick is here to elevate us. With the artifacts he will deliver us to the worlds of excellence that we have wrongfully been exiled from."

The Master Conjurer—or Sir Lockwood as Evangeline had called him—was now reminding me of religious extremists back on Earth. But one thing he'd said stood out to me. "Exiled? What do you mean wrongfully exiled?"

Sir Lockwood eyed me up and down before responding. "You wear their attire, young man. Thus, you must know that those of us living in Relaun are the people who were casted away from your reality. Master Flurwick has shown me the wonders of your civilizations with his mind. And now he aims to merge our worlds so that magic and technology may live in unison. For, The Elders made the selfish mistake of casting us away here, to hide our magic from existence."

The expressions on my companion's faces showed me that we were all experiencing the same thoughts. "Let me get this straight," I said. "Are you telling me that The Elders sent all magical beings here to Relaun?"

"To cleanse the universe, yes,"

"Are you saying that magic originated where he's from?" Finian asked, pointing in my direction.

"Indeed it is so."

There was little time to fully process this theory.

Highwell was under attack and it was time to put this situation to bed. "Even if what you say is true, the fact of the matter is that Flurwick intends to do bad things with his magic. There's no way that his intentions are good," I said.

"Do you think it's right that generations of our people have been subject to entrapment, with no choice in the matter?" asked Sir Lockwood, through piercing eyes.

"Equally, do you think it's right to tear down towns full of innocent people at the command of Flurwick?"

"Brandon makes a strong point, Master. This is unlike you. You have been subject to Flurwick's mind control," said Evangeline.

"My dear, imagine the resources you would have to enhance your healing abilities in their worlds," he said, pointing at me. "Your talents would be far more appreciated. You would have more purpose than to heal wolf bites."

There was no denying that Sir Lockwood was making sense in his argument. But it was the senseless murdering that contradicted his reasoning. Those contradictions made it all too easy to pick him apart. "Instead, she now has to heal those who have been wounded by your onslaught of Undead," I said.

Lockwood snarled. "This is a necessary step. The guild leaders would never support Flurwick's vision. They must fall and they must give up the artifacts. Only then can the people of Relaun be released from their constraints."

"Ask yourself this," I said. "If all Flurwick wanted to do was help you and the people of Relaun by freeing you, then why would it be necessary to kill so many of you in the process?"

Sir Lockwood's eyes glowed right before he hurled a ball of fire at us. Evangeline and I had to leap in opposite directions to avoid being hit. "I told you!" he yelled. "The ignorant rulers of Relaun would never agree to such a thing. It would take months to convince them that Flurwick's claims were correct. Do not insult me with your foolish questions."

Landing on my chest had knocked the breath out of me. I looked over at my companions and saw Finian aiming an arrow right at Lockwood. Evangeline was staring over at me. I held up my hand to let her know I was okay but in reality I was struggling to get my breath back. The Pardu now stood in front of Evangeline, baring its teeth at Sir Lockwood.

"Do not cross me, Ezzan, you know it must be this way," said Lockwood.

"Hey asshole," I said, pushing myself up to my feet to face him. "I can understand your desire to see the Milky Way. But putting this much faith into Flurwick is your biggest mistake." Lockwood looked as if he were ready to attack me again. "Because Back in Varghaanaire when we were trapped in Var'ae's mind, he told me himself that he could leave Relaun any time he wanted."

"Lies!" he barked. Flames started to spread across the floor, stemming from the camp fire behind him. The streams of flame parted around where he stood. Slowly the flames rose beside him and formed into the shape of a dragon's head.

"No lies, conjurer," I continued, trying to keep composure. My goal was now to keep him angry; because angry people made mistakes. "He could take you to where I'm from any time he pleases. But do you want to know why he's choosing not to leave? Well, he told me himself that he wants to know how to destroy Relaun on his way out. Because only then will he be the sole and most enhanced magical user in existence."

After an immense stare-down—in which I expected

Lockwood's dragons to blanket me in fire—he turned his attention to the Pardu. "If what he claims is true, I want to see it."

The Pardu leaped over to me and stared into my eyes. My vision went blank and inviting warmth came over me. Something told me the Pardu was asking permission to access the memory, and I don't know how exactly it happened, but I granted him access. All I can remember doing is thinking the word 'yes' in my mind. I then recalled the memory of speaking to Flurwick in Var'ae's mind—being careful not to let my thoughts stray on anything I didn't wish to share. After what felt like a couple seconds, the creature was staring back at the Master Conjurer. The dragon flames behind him had grown in size, as if he was ready to burn us alive at any moment. I took a step back and encouraged Finian and Evangeline to do the same. The closer we got to the cave entrance, the better.

Lockwood stared at us in turn. His eyes were glossy and they'd lost the intensity they'd had moments ago. "Is it really possible that I've put my faiths into someone who planned to deceive me?"

Evangeline sniffed. "Sir Lockwood, with all due respect; I must say it is a disappointment to know that you so willingly chose to follow such a man. I am aware that your mind has been tampered with, but not to the same extent as..." she paused. "Natalya's was. Therefore it's clear that you allowed him to command you, without challenging his control. Your determination to see another world allowed you to submit your mind and your powers to him; when you could have instead fought him. He was surely weaker than you at the time."

Tears trickled down Lockwood's face. He closed his eyes and breathed in. "I am sorry, Evangeline, I have failed the guild; and Relaun as a whole." Lockwood held out his arm and pulled up the sleeve on his robe, revealing a large tattoo on his forearm. He held his hand over the tattoo and waves of dark smoke poured out from his hand. The tattoo glowed for a moment before it faded.

"The Undead!" yelled Evangeline. "What have you done?"

Lockwood looked up at Evangeline and smiled. "Your Mutano fiend just slaughtered the spider, but I have now commanded the remaining Undead to kill each other and the Exul only. It's likely that the defenders of Highwell will destroy what is left of them."

"Is there no way to stop the Exul without it leading to more death?" I asked.

"I do not have command of the Exul. They are acting on Flurwick's own control. The Undead will fight them, and perhaps the warriors will be able to subdue some of them without resorting to murder."

"Sorry, Ezzan," said Finian. "I'm happy to see yer friend has done right, but how can we possibly let him go free after this?"

"Is that what it wants?" I asked.

"Yes. It sees the good in Sir Lockwood and believes that Flurwick is the cause of this. He doesn't want to see Lockwood harmed now that we have made him see sense."

"That should be up to the guild leaders to decide," I said.

"Agreed," said Evangeline. "I would like for his fate to be decided by the mages."

"None of that is necessary," said Lockwood. And then the dragon flames began to encircle him.

"No," I stepped forward. As I moved closer to him, another ball of fire shot past me. The Pardu also tried to leap towards Lockwood but found itself walled off by flames.

"As a man regarded so highly in the guilds, this must

be the punishment for allowing such a conspiracy to unfold," he said. Somehow the flames weren't burning him yet. "I let the possibility of seeing new worlds excite me. To the point that I taught such an evil man the worst kinds of magic possible. I enabled this man to carry out such a heinous plan against my own people. I failed to realize that although we have been trapped away from the unlimited potential of the universe, it's the freedom that the people of Relaun hold that matters the most."

"There is no need for this, Sir Lockwood. You have a depth of knowledge that the guild must continue to benefit from; even if you must face imprisonment." Evangeline cried.

"One more thing, stranger," he ignored Evangeline and looked at me as the flames started to burn his robes. "Simon Cunningham is at the tower now. He is seeking the artifacts. He was accompanied by members of Exul and some Undead, but the Undead have begun ripping apart his Exul guards. You must stop him before he harms the guild leaders."

I glanced at my companions as we registered this. Then I locked eyes with Evangeline. "Do it now," I said, knowing that she was thinking the same thing I was. She held out her hand and streams of water began pouring out in Lockwood's direction. It seemed like it would work, until he responded with his own magic.

"Go now!" he yelled, as one of the flame dragons swirled in our direction, expanding in size as its flames illuminated the cave walls.

Evangeline's burst of water wasn't plentiful enough to combat the flames, as she was clearly the weaker mage when it came to elemental magic. We had no choice but to flee. The heat from the flames was set to boil us alive.

"Let's go!" I cried.

Through the dancing flames before us, there was a brief moment when Lockwood stared at Evangeline with shock in his eyes. "Oh my! The enchantment," he cried, right before the flames blanketed his body completely. Lockwood's finger extended outside the fire, right before flames rose up over his face. Evangeline stood staring back at him with her mouth agape, as Lockwood fully disappeared behind the flames with a fit of screams.

"What enchantment?" asked Finian.

I turned towards the exit. "Out, now!" I yelled, yanking on Evangeline's inner-elbow. We ran to the exit and I pushed Evangeline's body ahead of me to ensure she got out. My lungs were filling up with smoke and I felt my body begin to weaken from lack of pure oxygen.

It happened in a blur, but soon enough; the three of us hit the dirt beside the waterfall, coughing up smoke while crawling out of the way of more smoke.

"Ezzan!" Finian called, as he sat up.

"Did he get out? I didn't even see him." My eyes scanned the area, looking for any sight of the feline.

"I can't sense him anymore," Finian said with sadness.

"Such a waste of life, we have lost a powerful mage, and perhaps a legendary creature," said Evangeline, brushing dirt from her hair. "And for what?"

"Well, we got him to stop the Undead at least. We should head back right aw..." Before I could finish my sentence, the ground shook as a rippling crash came from the city. A wave of smoke clouded the air, climbing over the city walls. "What the!"

"Come on, I can't deal with any more losses today," said Finian, marching ahead.

CHAPTER 40

AS WE MADE OUR WAY back towards Highwell, there was a sense of unspoken dread among us. On top of that, I felt completely spent at the day's events. The new revelations had my mind working in overdrive, and the silence told me that the others were thinking along the same lines.

"So, magic came from the Milky Way, huh?" I said.

"And so did The Elders it seems," said Evangeline. "Going by what Sir Lockwood said, it would seem that they felt magic was too damaging for your Milky Way. Relaun is a means to contain magic in its own world."

"And so we're nothing but an experiment?" Finian said. "I always had a strange feeling that there was something more than Relaun out there; that we were suspended in one of many realities. Thought it was just me being depressed at being a failure, but I was right."

"You're not a failure, man,"

Evangeline grabbed my hand and held it tightly. "But what does all this mean for Relaun's future? Even if we stop Flurwick, what will happen?"

"That's a bridge we'll have to cross when we get there," I said.

"Indeed," she said. "Let's focus on taking Flurwick down for now. Whatever comes after will come."

A bird's cry came from the sky and as we looked above we saw Audette swarm down upon us. Evangeline extended her arm, inviting the bird to land. "Oh dear," said Evangeline. "Blok, no."

"What happened?" Finian stomped.

"The one called Simon; he fired some large projectile at Blok. It collapsed a building onto him. We must find him before its too late."

Finian's face went pale. "Come on, let's hurry," he said, sprinting forward.

When we made it past the wrecked entry into Highwell, it was hard to see where the ruin began and ended. Steamy debris obstructed our visibility. I stepped over many Undead carcasses. The spider was sprawled at the center of the city, its gigantic legs spreading across a number of alleyways. A giant pipe was lodged through the spiders face. Blok had saved another human settlement from total destruction and now his own life was in danger;

if it was still there at all.

"Blok?" Finian called, as we stepped cautiously through the ruin. "Can you hear me? Can anyone?"

"Be careful not to draw too much attention," I said. Simon was no doubt still at the top of the tower. At any moment he could fire another rocket.

"You two should go and save the guild leaders," said Evangeline. "Leave me to tend to Blok and the survivors."

"I don't want to leave you until I know you're safe," I told her.

"And I feel the same way about you every time you risk your life. But right now the situation is bigger than us." She was right, of course.

"Over there," Finian pointed. Through the mist was a faint silhouette of a person pulling someone from a pile of stone. The body being lifted was bulky. We ran forward and I almost tripped on a large slab of stone in the process. An Elven male with long white hair was struggling to hold Blok's weight as he placed the large blue arm around his shoulders.

"I recognize him," said Finian. "It's Alwin the Alchemist. One of the most gifted alchemists in Relaun. It's him that brewed the poison that I used to kill the Amber Monkey with."

"This is your friend, is it not?" said the Elf, finally managing to lift the Mutano. Finian ran ahead and placed Blok's other arm around his own shoulders. "I saw the three of you together that day you pushed Retgar through the city."

"He is with us, yes," said Finian, through struggled breaths. "I know all about your work."

"Yes, Alwin visits Corwy often," said Evangeline, stepping forward to check the severity of Blok's condition. "Please, Mister Alwin, do you have somewhere to treat the wounded? He is in bad shape, but I can save him."

"I have converted my shop into a rescue center for the time being. It's close by."

Evangeline took a step towards Finian. "Please, let me help you carry him. You two must save the guild leaders."

Once Evangeline had secured half of Blok's weight, Finian joined my side. "Be careful, Eva," I told her.

"Make sure you come back to me," she smiled. Finian and I nodded and turned to face the tower.

*** * ***

"I can't believe we didn't see this here last time," I said, in reference to the elevator we'd entered on our way into the tower. A pile of Undead and Exul bodies had been piled up by it, catching our attention as we snuck into the building. The elevator was merely a platform built with wood and steel. It used force magic to elevate us as soon as we'd stepped past its iron barriers. What worried me about the elevator was the rickety noise it made as it rose up the tower. Surely someone would hear us coming.

"How do you people survive without magic?" Finian asked.

"Technology, my friend; we created our own magic."

"Do you think Relaun and your universe could ever exist together? Assuming we manage to stop Flurwick."

I didn't know how to answer the question. If magic ever merged into the Milky Way, I fear it would tear the galaxy apart. There were countless stories about interspecies kidnapping after the humans of Earth made first-contact with the Stowyths. After the Alliance was first formed, species in the Milky Way feared the abilities of others, and desired to have the same abilities. Some species would kidnap beings from other races and carry out genetic experiments in attempt to gain these abilities. Throwing magic into the mix would skew the balance of the galaxy. The humans of Earth always feared a galactic war, and a person like Flurwick unleashing his power would bring that fear to reality.

"I would like to hope so. But I'm not so sure my people are ready to accept that all of this is possible," I said.

Finian crossed his arms. "I've been an outcast for a long time, Brandon. But these last two weeks or so have made me feel like I matter. No matter what happens, do you promise we'll be friends forever?"

"You've had my back so many times that it's not even a question," I said. But in the back of my mind, I doubted the possibility of us continuing to know each other.

We soon made it to the top floor where we heard wailing and sniffling cries.

"Just five more minutes and you're toast, witch," came the voice of Simon Cunningham. "Unless he comes with our artifacts; and if I see your birds hovering around again, I won't hesitate to shoot them out the sky."

"He's waiting for us," I whispered. Looking around,

I noticed Exul bodies littering the corridors; with Undead body parts scattered among them—burned to a crisp. Black singes stained the rugs and walls; revealing that someone had come through the area torching everything in sight to finish the Undead. Perhaps it had been Simon himself.

"I'm going to go and confront him," I said. "You wait behind and then if you hear him getting the better of me, save my ass, alright?"

"No way, I want in on the action," said Finian.

"But if you stay behind then it fools him into thinking I'm alone. It gives us an advantage. You'll be able to swarm in at any time and catch him off guard." Finian's raised eyebrows told me he needed further persuasion. "Plus, you should look around to see if there are any surviving Exul or guild leaders."

"Fine, go ahead," said Finian, lacking in enthusiasm. It was his eagerness to prove himself that made him resistant to my idea. But this was personal between me and Simon. Plus, nobody else in Relaun understood the capabilities of a G.A marine.

Simon's position was given away by shadows on the floor as I crept towards entrance of the room. Judging by the angle of the shadow, he was standing in front of the large window. The same window he'd fired a rocket blast from moments ago. His back faced me as I peeked into the room. Egith was curled on the floor sniffing beside Arjon's lifeless body. Blood spilled from a number of holes in his chest. Simon had murdered him with a shotgun.

"Stand down, Private," I said, edging into the room and holding up my blaster. Maybe I should have shot him while he wasn't looking, but the marine in me needed to know where his mind was before engaging him in combat. It was honor for my fellow marine.

"Ah," he said, turning on the spot. "Sergeant Wardson finally arrives." He wore a sadistic smile. "You done befriending useless Elves and Relaun locals, Sergeant? Because if so I'd like it if you'd hand over your artifacts."

"Why do this?" I asked. "You and Charlie showed such promise in the Alliance. You were both earning the respect of your peers and superiors."

Simon sent a ball of saliva shooting to the floor. "And if you haven't noticed, I've been recruited by a superior for this life-changing operation. Why don't you join us? It will do wonders for your career." Simon's voice was much raspier in comparison to his brother's.

"Do you think Flurwick actually cares for your future, Cunningham? He told me himself that he plans to destroy this realm as soon as he gets what he needs to do it."

"And I'll be right there with him when he does it. You and your sexy little ex-girlfriend are welcome to join us if you wish."

His mention of Natalya meant that she hadn't been in contact with Flurwick or Simon since we fought her by the border. "And then what?" I asked. "What happens when Relaun is destroyed and we're back in space? Are we supposed to carry on like everything is normal between us?"

"Then we change the Milky Way for the better. Your loyalty may be with the Alliance, but they're not as clear-cut as you think they are, Wardson. With the magic we'll have, we can change the galaxy for the good of all humans."

"Just humans?" I asked.

"I'm getting bored here." Simon spat. "Either you hand me the artifacts—" he aimed the shotgun at my head. "Or I blow you to smithereens."

The tightness of the room gave him a deadly

advantage with a shotgun and it made me uneasy. Simon was also wearing a synthetic suit with energy shields. I wondered if these shields would dispel the effects of Evangeline's enchantments on my blaster. Galactic Alliance gear had never been optimized for magic after all.

"I'm not giving you a thing, Cunningham," I said. As his finger moved over the trigger, I shot my blaster at his chest. The lightning caused him to twitch, confirming that magic worked against his defenses. I moved in and slammed my fist into his face, flooring him. I kicked the shotgun across the room and it slid to where Egith was curled up.

By now it seemed the lightning affect was wearing off and Simon had regained full movement. I stood above him, holding my gun at his face. "Stand down, Private," I said. My plan was to restrain and interrogate him, but these thoughts were interrupted when Simon's foot connected with my gut and sent me flying across the room.

Simon got to his feet while laughing. "I see you've had some enhancements on your weapon, Wardson. Well Flurwick saw to it that my suit was also enhanced. The arms and feet on my suit possess force magic. Now, where are the artifacts, Wardson? Are they in your little man-bag?"

As Simon approached me, we were interrupted by

footsteps coming from the hall. A man emerged, dragging Finian by the collar. "Sir Cunningham, I found this skinny little runt snooping around outside," said the Exul warrior.

"Aha, I should have known you wouldn't be alone, Wardson. But something told me your pride would get the better of you and make you want to protect your friends. I guess you'll never be a good enough marine to save lives." Simon clicked his fingers at me, "Come Alex, pick him up and disarm him."

The Exul warrior dropped Finian and made his way over to me. As he bent over to grab me I stunned him with an uppercut that sent him falling backwards. My fingers secured the hilt of my fire sword and I swung it outward in Simon's direction. Simon raised his arm to block the swing, but my sword sliced the suit's underarm open. Flames erupted from the arm and Simon quickly waved up and down to put it out.

Simon snarled. "Time to die, Sergeant."

His fist came flying at me but I backed away to dodge it. Evading his advances was necessary for my survival, because with his enhancements, any hit he landed would send me flying across the room.

The Exul warrior made it back to his feet and he too

was advancing on me. I found myself ducking and weaving blows from both men. The more I did so, the more difficult it became. One of them would make contact soon enough. I swung my sword again, causing them to back up. Space is what I needed; to maneuver and to figure out a plan of action.

"Give it up, Wardson, the odds are against..." Simon started, until I swung the sword at his face, causing him to jump backwards. The Exul dived in to tackle me during that split second, but I was a step ahead of him. I leaned back and used my arm to hurl him across me. He landed on his back beside Egith, groaning.

Taking advantage of the momentary distraction, Simon swung his foot towards me and connected. The blow sent me flying towards the entrance, right where Finian was lying.

"Brandon," Finian whispered behind me.

"Yea?" I grunted.

"Just give me a moment and I'll be able to help." His shaky voice told how much pain he was in.

"I've got this," I said, as Simon made his way towards me. Then I saw Egith doing something behind him. Her hand was placed on the Exul warrior's face, as if trying to counter the effects of mind magic that had been put upon him. Simon, who saw my eyes lingering, looked behind him and saw what was happening.

"You! Stop that now," Simon said, dashing towards them. I got to my feet and ran after him. Part of me wanted to pick up my blaster that had fallen when he'd hit me the first time, but I wouldn't have had enough time to save Egith. I slammed my shoulder into the back of Simon, causing him to hit the window ledge beside Egith. My body throbbed violently and I was beginning to break out in critical levels of pain. It was only adrenaline and determination keeping me going.

Simon elbowed me in the face and I felt something crack, before blood trickled to my mouth. As I stood there, pressing my hand against my nose, I saw Simon go for his shotgun. Egith raised her hand and a citrine colored blast sent the gun flying across the floor, out of Simon's reach.

"You bitch!" he yelled, raising his arm at her. I grabbed him by the neck to catch his attention once more, and he he responded by lodging a fist into my chest, sending me flying to the center of the room.

The pain was too intense. Along with the agony from where he'd just hit me, every joint in my body felt like they were about to break apart. There was no way I could get back up.

Simon stood over me and pulled the bag housing the flask from my waist. He tossed it beside him and knelt over me. "Time to sleep, Wardson," he said raising his fist above my face. The blow—enchanted by force magic— would splatter my head against the stone floor. This would be the end of me.

But before Simon could land the blow, I watched his head jerk backwards and his body weight shift from me.

I tilted my head against the stone floor and took an upside down glance behind me. Finian was holding the shotgun in his hands; his mouth wide open in shock.

PART IV

CHAPTER 41

WHEN I OPENED MY EYES, I saw the inside of a tent, and I heard Evangeline rustling around nearby. "How's your pain?" she asked, as I sat myself up.

"I'm feeling a lot better now. Whatever you gave me worked wonders." I stretched my body, feeling the throbbing sensations. The pains continued to plague me, but Evangeline's painkillers had done their work and taken the edge off. She'd also healed the broken nose I'd suffered by Simon's hands. Every now and then I felt the nasal bone click, but the remedy she'd made me drink had it feeling just as it had before I'd suffered the blow.

"I mixed it using an Opus plant," she said, referring to the painkillers. She stroked my shoulders and I wondered if an Opus plant was the Relaun equivalent to opium. It certainly sounded like it.

Loud conversations from beyond our tent blended into one large white noise. After Finian had ended Simon Cunningham, Egith arranged for me and Arjon to be carried down to the coliseum, where the entire city would gather to treat the wounded and register the dead. My body was in such bad shape that I was struggling to walk. I'd been given a stick to help me limp around. "How long was I sleeping?" I asked.

"Just under two hours now, I think. The clocks have yet to chime again."

"What did I miss?"

"Blok is back on his feet. He's helping the guilds clear the streets of debris and what remains of the Undead. I tried to warn him against moving around so soon, but Mutanos do not listen."

"I'm glad he wasn't killed. We're lucky to have you patching us up." I pulled her in to sneak a kiss.

"By The Elders!" yelled Finian, tearing his way into our tent. "I can't take this anymore; it's too much." He sat before us, crossing his legs. "Oh, I'm not interrupting am I?"

"Not at all," I said, straightening my posture.

"Tell us what plagues you," said Evangeline.

"Ever since Egith told everyone that it was me that killed the invader, everyone keeps coming up to me and praising me. Thanking me for saving them and their families." Finian's hands swayed as he spoke.

"It means they're grateful," I said.

"But I'm not used to such praise. I'm the failure, remember?"

"Except you were never a failure," I said. "That's just what ignorant people thought."

"But Brandon, what I did wasn't honorable. I'm haunted by visions of that man's head splitting open as I shot that awful thing of yours."

"That was not my thing, and it's called a shotgun." I understood how traumatizing it must have been for him to use such a weapon in a world where they didn't exist.

"But I killed a man, and it was terrifying." he said, shaking his head.

I edged forward and patted him on the shoulder. "Hey, you did what you had to do, and you saved my life. You saved the people of Highwell. I know it's hard to live with these things, but what you did was necessary."

"I...I guess. But now they're going beyond thanking. I overheard the guild leaders talking about making me Champion of Highwell. Me and me Dad would get a house and everything."

"And this is a bad thing, because?"

"I dunno—I just dunno," he shrugged. "All of this feels inhumane. Killing each other, for what?"

"That's a question for Jonathan Flurwick; because he's the reason we're here. He's the reason all those people died in Corwy, and here in Highwell."

Finian said nothing more as he lost himself in thought.

* * *

Evangeline pulled me outside the tent as she needed to speak with me in private about something. We left Finian to hide in the tent so that he could escape the hundreds of people wishing to offer their thanks. "It's cold out here. Let me make us a hot drink," said Evangeline, igniting the pot outside of our tent with her hands, "any requests?"

"I have an acquired taste for Gorvey bush tea," I said.

She smiled and placed the contents into a mug for me. She was right, the weather was bitter. I pulled the robes she'd given me around myself, tightening it around my commoner clothes. And I clenched the walking stick tightly, distributing my weight onto it as I followed her along the wet streets.

Despite the chill, Highwell residents strolled around

the coliseum visiting one another; checking on the wellbeing of their friends and family. Children played, swinging sticks at one another, recreating the city-wide battle that had happened hours prior. Two children even argued over who would be playing as Finian Glaed. Some of the children were throwing small balls of flame at one another. This caused Evangeline to lecture them about practicing magic with no mage guardians around.

Soon enough me and Evangeline found ourselves in a vacant alleyway where we couldn't resist stealing a moment to get close. "We should be careful. I almost spilled my tea all over you." I said, as I looked into those eyes.

"For you, I can take a little hot tea over me. And anyway, it means you would have to clean me up."

We lost our mugs as we stood kissing and touching; absorbing every part of our bodies. It lasted until I grunted in pain; which meant nothing to me, but meant everything to her.

"Stop," she said, pressing me away. "I shouldn't be pushing you like this."

"No, I'm fine." I said, limping towards her.

"This is what I need to discuss with you," she said. Immediately my mind started racing; wondering if I would lose another lover because of my lifelong burden. "Do you remember what Niserie gave me?" she asked.

It took seconds to recall the small jar full of leaves that Niserie handed over to her before we went through the gate. "Yes, I remember; why?"

Evangeline took a deep breath. "While I was brewing medicine to treat the injured, I decided to try and brew a separate concoction to treat your condition. I used the Pocan Broadleaf that Niserie had given to me. But that leaf possesses agents that can seriously harm humans. This meant that I needed to add a few more ingredients to offset these agents."

I stroked a hair away from her face. "Baby, do you mind speaking in English?" I smiled, "or Anglish"

"I made an Elixir to treat your condition," she smirked.

I pressed my lips against hers again. "You didn't have to go through all of that for me," I said, "but I appreciate it. You're the woman I've needed my entire life."

"But..." she said.

"Uh oh....what's the but?"

"I am unsure of the side-effects. I know that taking

the elixir should grant you days of living a pain free life. It will increase the fetal haemoglobin in your blood and reduce the sickled shaped blood cells that it produces now. In other words, you will function like a normal healthy person while its effects last." The thought of living a normal pain free life was something I never thought was possible for me. "I am concerned however, because the way in which the elixir works means that you would be unable to produce children while it is in your system."

Having children was something I'd never given much thought to. Sickle cell is a genetic condition that can be passed down through genes, meaning there were many women who would avoid breeding with me completely. But at this moment, I couldn't see past being with Evangeline. She was all I wanted, and it was much too soon for us to think of children; especially with Flurwick still to be dealt with. And even after confronting him, if we made it out of the situation alive, would we still have a future together? "But, I would be able to have children once it's out my system right?" I asked her.

"I assume so," she said. "But also, I believe that once the elixir does wear off, your sickled cells would return and multiply. Meaning you would suffer immense pain for some time after the elixir stops working."

The side-effects as she described them didn't seem worth the risk for me. Sure, my body had its limits, but it had carried me this far. "Are you suggesting that I should take it?" I asked.

"That is your choice. I have no means of testing it because I have made it for your condition only."

"Why did Niserie give you the leaves in the first place?" I asked.

"Well, I apologize if you feel it was inappropriate, but Niserie, Var'ae and I communicated mentally a few times. I was curious about the extent of their magic. Niserie learned how much I adored you; even before we had our beautiful carriage ride. They saw how concerned about your health I was all the time, so Niserie saw to it that the hunters gathered some of the Pocan Broadleaf."

My thoughts strayed as I stared into her eyes; the sounds of distant footsteps are what brought my mind back to the present. Evangeline allowed me some time to stand there thinking, knowing that this was a major thing to consider. "I may have suffered, but I've made it this far. I will hold off on taking the elixir, because right now you are all I need. You alone, allow me to summon the strength I need to keep going." Evangeline tip-toed and planted her lips against mine.

Loud cheers were now erupting from the coliseum. We decided to head back and see what the commotion was.

* * *

On approach to the coliseum we saw a large crowd surrounding a group of men. The men were screaming words that only began to make sense the closer we came.

"A man should not return to his home to find a city of ruin. I should not be returning to hear that my guild leader has fallen to these invaders." It was Jale Enchcroft, the warden I'd argued with at the trials. "We have what that bastard wants," he said, pointing down at a flat block standing in front of him. He had found the Altar of Jerrus. "Now, I promise we will lure him out and use all our strength and power to send that wicked man to the darkest depths of Relaun." The crowd roared in approval.

Finian and Blok were among the crowd of people and we took our places among them. Jale seemed to notice us as we stood in front of a group of locals. "The birds have told me that Highwell is standing because of these strangers," he said, pointing in our direction.

"Here we go." I breathed, expecting round two of

our face off.

Jale walked towards us and we locked eyes. For a moment, it seemed as if the entire crowd held its breath. "It is time that I put my arrogance aside and thank those that looked out for my home while I was unable to," he said. "Thank you, stranger," he said, extending his hand.

I embraced him. "Call me Brandon." Once again the crowd applauded.

Jale then turned his attention to Finian. "And this young man possesses more heart than the most seasoned of warriors. I thank you from the bottom of my heart for avenging Arjon."

"Don't mention it, sir," said Finian, locking arms with Jale I'm sure he meant his words quite literally.

The people of Highwell continued to express their gratitude, but even above their loud chants we could hear the falcons—Orato and Audette—chirping in the skies above.

"Blok also thanks Evangeline," said Blok.

Evangeline placed a hand on her chest. "You learned how to say my name?"

"Blok learn. Blok also buy Evangeline a gift because the guild paid coin."

"Man, you're kind of making me look bad here,

Blok," I smirked. Blok handed her a large box which she opened immediately. Inside was some kind of golden arm brace with engraved symbols.

"Oh my, is it a magic ward?" she asked.

"Yes, Blok buy magic ward for Evangeline for saving Blok life."

Finian chuckled. "If only Elf and Mutano relations were always this civil."

"Blok also bring whiskey and ale for Brandon and Finian," he said, pulling a large bottle from his pouch.

Evangeline pushed his hand away. "Absolutely not! Brandon is banned from drinking that stuff until he's better."

"Can't I have just one little..." I chose not to finish asking the question as Evangeline scowled at me.

"Brandon!" Jale called from across where we stood. His expression was stern. "Egith has important news for us. We must all gather at the announcer's podium," he said.

CHAPTER 42

EGITH, JALE, HILDA, FINIAN, EVANGELINE, BLOK and myself were now gathered at the announcers' podium. Egith had named Jale interim master of the Warriors Guild but he wasn't too thrilled. He was still torn over the loss of his master. We stood in a circle at the podium, awaiting the new revelations from Egith.

"Now, onto the matter for which I summoned you; my falcons have brought me news on Flurwick's whereabouts and what he has accomplished. I would like to ask permission to access your minds so that I may share what my birds have shown me."

"No objections, ma'am," I said. "I'm sure we all want to take this asshole down."

"Then close your eyes so that you may see."

The darkness of my eyelids faded into an image of Flurwick standing before an army of Mutano. They were stood, observing something that we couldn't see. Whatever was the object of Flurwick's fascination was glowing before his eyes. His face was lit up in a dozen different hues, as if he was stood before a street full of neon signs. The image panned around until we were behind his newly acquired army and it was then that we saw a field full of crystal shards; shards of every color, in different sizes.

The image faded.

"Keep your eyes closed," said Egith, "there is more."

We caught a glimpse of Master Retgar, beside a gigantic monster he'd slain. The creature had a long tail, scales, wings and a lizard-like head. Around Retgar, the forest trees were white and the grounds full of snow.

The vision cut before we again saw Retgar; this time with blood flowing from his penetrated armor. He was in some kind of cave with markings along the walls. He reached for something and the view panned to reveal a staff. He grasped it but then cried in agony as his hand was burned to a crisp.

The scene transitioned again, and we were now looking at Flurwick marching with his army alongside an endless narrow river. As the view panned around, we saw them walking towards a giant gate, much like the one we'd gone through in Lainunia. Flurwick wore a smug expression as he walked through the gate with his legion following behind him.

The scene transitioned, and now Flurwick was outside another gate in the middle of a blizzard. It was the same area in which Retgar had slain the monster.

Flurwick was in Thirion.

"Open your eyes," said Egith. "As you can see, Master Retgar is in danger and Flurwick has found a gate we did not know of that has granted him access to Thirion. Retgar was unable to grasp the Staff of Enellas, because only a mage may hold it. But it is said to be a powerful artifact, and we must not let Flurwick get hold of it."

"How does Ogesh have all those magic shards?" asked Finian. "It was an entire field full of them; I've never seen anything like it."

Blok stepped into the middle of the podium and his eyes closed as he took a deep breath. "Blok must break Mutano oath." Finian, Evangeline and I glanced between one another.

"The war," he continued. "The Mutanos were wrong to hurt humans. Blok will never forgive Mutanos for harming humans."

"Good to know at least one of you sees sense," said Jale. Despite our peace, I wished he would keep his mouth closed.

Blok ignored the interruption and continued. "But the Elves, they knew the Mutano secret."

"Which was what?" asked Hilda.

"To the far north of Ogesh, a garden has magic shards. The shards grow plenty. Mutanos knew of garden, but swear to never speak. Mutanos not like magic. My ancestors not want magic shards to be used by Elves or humans. But during war, Elves use invasion as a reason to enter Ogesh and defeat Mutanos. After defeat, they take all crystals. But after many years, the crystals grow back. All Mutanos believe that Elves do not know that the crystals grow anew. And now, Mutano chief made oath that Mutanos must never speak of the crystals."

For a moment everyone was silent—processing what Blok had told us. "Judging by how large that garden was, the Elven kingdom could have been utilizing the crystals for years," said Evangeline, "perhaps decades; without ever needing to hunt for new shards throughout the lands."

"It's possible that securing those shards boosted their kingdom." Egith added. "At a time when the humans of Aldeen were scared of being invaded by the Mutanos again, imagine how much coin the Elves made selling enchanted weapons and defenses to us."

"One more thing," said Blok. "The garden is the only place in Relaun where the Death Shard grows; a shard for dark magic. Flurwick must now hold this."

"By The Elders!" said Evangeline. "We cannot let him hold such a powerful means of destruction."

"I thought it wasn't possible to hold crystal in your possession." I said. "I thought something like that could kill you."

"That is true of most people. But there is recorded history of the Elves being able to retrieve a full shard from the grounds and live to tell about it," said Egith. "It requires powerful mages to accomplish. But with a Death Shard, I hear that it's more practical to contain it inside something."

"Is Flurwick really so powerful?" asked Hilda, her eyes bulging.

"With a Master Conjurer mentoring him, I wouldn't be surprised," said Egith, "which is another reason we must enter Thirion and stop him; for if he has both the Staff of Enellas and this Death Shard, then he has unimaginable power."

This was it. Now was the time to put Flurwick down once and for all. There could be no more stalling. With an army of Mutano and these new powers at his disposal, Flurwick could gather the rest of the artifacts with ease. I'd been in Relaun long enough to know how much of a danger he was becoming. "How long will it take us to get to Thirion?" I asked.

"It took Retgar over a week to travel there," said Egith. "But we have the advantage of being in Highwell; the closest city to Ogesh."

Blok turned away from us and pointed into thin air. "Ogesh is north; fast by boat."

Egith nodded. "Indeed. We can travel to Ogesh and take the same gate that Flurwick did. But please, Blok...how far into Ogesh is the gate?"

Blok turned back to face Egith and shook his head. "Blok was never told about gate." We heard Hilda sigh. "The image showed area of Ogesh Blok has never seen. This can only be The Valley of the Chief. A place only the chief and his chosen may enter. Mutanos will be killed if they are caught sneaking in. The valley is forty-minute walk, if humans walk fast like Blok."

"I'm sure I can give you a run for yer coin when it comes to speed," Finian winked.

"Are you telling me that your lot were also hiding magical gates?" Jale snapped. "It's secrecy like this that has left us so vulnerable to attack."

"We can't have expected the Mutano to tell us their secrets. Especially when the Elves already took what they needed from their lands." said Egith. "In any case, it matters none. We can fix Relaun politics once we have eliminated Flurwick. We must gather an army of warriors and mages at once to venture out. Hilda, Jale, I will need you two to assist in gathering our forces."

"As you wish," said Jale.

"My birds will give me a clear view of the path so we can prepare for any resistance." Egith walked to me and my companions. "The rest of you must ready yourselves.

As was the case before, you have full access to any supplies you may need in Highwell."

Egith looked me right in the eyes. "Brandon, once we get to Thirion, I want you to lead us all; for it is you that understands the enemy more than any of us. Relaun is counting on you."

The pressure of those words mounted me. But I was eager to finally end this mission—once and for all; even if it meant being stuck in Relaun. "We'll get him, I promise." I saluted.

CHAPTER 43

MANY WARRIORS AND MAGES were injured during the invasion of Highwell. This meant that the number of capable bodies were slim. Despite their injuries, the majority of them were willing to offer their services; the ones that could still walk and wield a weapon at least. Protecting their land mattered more to them than their own wellbeing. I understood their devotion to their hometown, but Jale worried about having too many weaknesses in the army.

Finian was gathering supplies for us, while Evangeline said she had an important errand to run. Blok was planning a route to Ogesh with Egith and I was stuck helping Jale carry the Altar of Jerrus out of the coliseum.

Egith and Hilda had agreed to have the altar left in the tower. That way we wouldn't have all the artifacts in one place once we made it to Thirion. In the event that Flurwick—by some means—seized the runes and the flask, he would be slowed down by the need to travel back here for the altar. Besides, the altar wasn't exactly easy to carry.

"Forces from other towns in Aldeen are on their way to Highwell as we speak," said Jale. "They'll defend this place while we're gone."

We knelt to drop the altar so that Jale could unlock the door. "Let's hope nobody comes knocking on Highwell's door once we leave," I said. "These people have dealt with enough already."

"Aye," he said in agreement. At the top of the tower, mages were cleaning rooms that had been violated by Simon and his minions. There were even unassisted mops and brushes cleansing the room that we had fought Simon in. The room was still a bloody mess and it would take some time for it to appear like new.

Egith had instructed us to place the altar in a hidden trapdoor that only a few people knew of. We located the trapdoor in a room across from the magic gate.

After stashing the artifact, we made our way back down the tower. Jale told me about all the powerful creatures lurking in Thirion that could make our mission problematic. I asked about the dragon-like creature that Retgar had been standing above in the visions.

"T'was indeed a dragon. Legends tell that both fire and ice dragons lurk in the lands," said Jale, as we stepped out the doors. I started daydreaming about how insane it would be to write a report for the Alliance, telling them that I'd followed Flurwick into a world full of Elves and dragons. Relaun became more and more surreal the longer I stayed within it.

Jale turned to close the front door but was startled when the door slammed itself shut. "Must be the winds," he said.

Back at the coliseum an immense debate ensued. There was concern over whether the army should be equipping themselves to defend against magic or the raw strength of the Mutanos. "Don't think of this as one large battle." I told them. "Instead, we should split our numbers into individual units that will focus on different objectives. Each unit should be optimized to deal with both magic and physical resistance." They looked at me as if what I'd suggested was unheard of.

Jale seemed irritated by the suggestion. "Egith wants him in charge when we reach Thirion, so we'll take his advice," he said, with a hard swallow. "We also need some units to focus on tearing down the Mutanos, while others will lure Flurwick away and seclude him."

"That job should be ours," said Finian, who was tugging on two large chests.

"Whatever you say, champion," Jale nodded. "The remaining units will engage the Mutano army and divert their attention. We'll need archers to scout for deadly creatures that could tip the balance into their favor." Jale faced his army. "Now, let me assign you all on your roles."

As Jale handled the assignments, we stepped away as if we were the cool kids separating from the do-good nerds. Some of the men in the front-lines were eyeballing us for doing so; but the way I saw it was that we'd earned the right to operate as an independent unit. Egith herself had gone as far as to ask me to lead the operation once we found Flurwick.

We moved to our tents and began preparing ourselves. Blok had advised us to wear heavy armor and headgear in preparation for the Mutano army. With that, I'd decided that it was time to finally adopt some Relaun armor. I wore my skinsuit underneath to help my blood flow, but over it I wore metal shin, arm, and waist guards. Then I wrestled a chain mail over my head—adding an additional plate of metal over my chest to protect from penetrative weapons. A sudden feeling of invisibility came over me, like I could withstand any physical attack that came my way. I would put my helmet on once we were in Ogesh, but something in my head told me to also have my breather ready as a precaution.

"You look like one of us," Evangeline said, glaring at me.

There was a clanging of metal as I pulled her to me. "Well, I already feel like I'm one of you." I planted my lips on her forehead.

"Excuse me," came a voice outside the tent. "I have a delivery for Brandon Wardson, friend of the champion." A man wearing the mages emblem on his overcoat was stood holding the handle of a cart.

"For me? Who is it from?" I asked, emerging from the tent opening.

"From the guild tower sir. We confiscated the invader's weapons and by order of Master Hilda, we have enchanted one of them. She instructed me to return them to you as you know the correct way in which they should be used."

I peered into the cart and saw both the shotgun and the rocket launcher that had belonged to Simon Cunningham. "What kind of enchantments do they have?"

"The weapon used by the champion to defeat the invader is infused with force magic. The larger weapon used to collapse the hostel has a fusion of thunder and surface magic. This enchantment was already on the weapon when we found it. We fear it may be too powerful but we're allowing you to make the judgment call on whether to use it in the coming battle."

The weapons could become a difference maker. Personally, I always preferred being as lightweight as possible. The thought of carrying either of these weapons was daunting for me; even though the shotgun was designed to be lightweight. "May I make the suggestion that the weapons be loaded onto our boat and carried to Thirion with us? Once we are there we can decide on when and how to use them."

The man nodded. "I shall see that it is done."

"Father!" We heard Finian cry from across the coliseum. I tapped the courier on the back in thanks and then ran over to find Kover hugging his son. At least thirty warriors and mages surrounded him. "What are you doing here?"

"Word got to Corwy that my boy saved Highwell and that help was needed to defend the city. I decided I would come at once."

We greeted Kover and for some time he spoke on the state of Corwy. People had been living in fear of another attack ever since the Undead had invaded. The attack on Corwy had felt so long ago. Kover told us that after Highwell was attacked, messengers had arrived in Corwy and several other towns with orders from Egith to send men.

With new bodies available, another debate was sparked as Jale wanted to add some of the men from Corwy to our army. Others felt as though these men should remain in Highwell to defend it. In the end, only ten of the Corwy men joined our army.

Finian spoke with his father for some time and his mood seemed to improve over being honored as the Champion of Highwell. "How's young Filip doing?" he asked his father.

"Filip is doing great, thanks to you. He's so full of energy, he reminds me of you in many ways." Kover smiled. "Before I left, I managed to convince the new Inn Keeper to take him in and look after him."

Before long, Egith appeared. "The boats are ready. We mustn't delay this any longer."

Finian frowned, as he stared back at his father. "I believe in you, son. Do us proud and come home safe," said Kover. "Good luck to you all," he said, shaking our hands one by one.

An argument erupted on our galleon after Finian overheard one of the warriors complaining about having a champion who couldn't pass his trial. "We all fight to keep Highwell safe on the daily. Patrolling bandits and slaying creatures that stray too close," said the warrior. "It should be one of our own that's named champion."

There was so much I wanted to say to this argument, but Finian needed no back up. "I didn't ask for any of this ye prune. All I did was follow me heart; and if that was enough for me to be named champion then maybe it means you're lacking one."

"The trials exist for a reason," the man said, stepping towards Finian. "If we let any flimsy street rat with a mother's name earn such a prestigious title then what do us tried and true warriors have to strive for?" As he turned to face his companions he rammed his shoulder into Finian knocking him off balance. Finian got his footing back fast and pulled the man back towards him.

Finian struck the man's jaw, putting all his body weight into it.

They traded blows, as the warrior's companions cheered their friend on. The warrior started to get the better of Finian so I edged forward, but before I could reach them, a wave of water came splashing onto the deck, covering the fighters and stopping them dead in their tracks.

"Enough," came Egith's voice; her staff angled in their direction. "I don't know how things are managed in the Warriors Guild, but whilst you are in my command you will not talk down on those with a mother's name." The warrior shook himself, sending sprinkles of water flying. "Furthermore," Egith continued. "The champion shall have a say on all future trials in Highwell; for he will be appointed on the committee."

"I want to abolish the trials completely," said Finian.

Egith glared at him. "This is not a matter to discuss now. We must focus on what is ahead."

Rainfall and wind made the waters violent as waves splashed high over the sides of the ship. Blok had taken a rowboat for himself so that he could reach Ogesh ahead of us and try to eliminate any lurking threats. We worried whether he's be safe in such a small boat given how bad the weather was, but Finian reassured me once again that Blok's Mutano blood would carry him.

I visited Evangeline on the lower deck as she was preparing potions and poultices. After noticing that I had yellow eyes, she shoved a jug of water in my hands, encouraging me to drink as much as possible to avoid going into battle dehydrated. While I drank, my eyes followed her around the room. I never thought it was possible to find someone who understood my own needs more than I did.

It was then that I felt some eternal sadness about what was to come. Could it be that this would be the last chance for me to enjoy the company of my new friends? The uncertainty of what was to come was worrying. To take my mind off of my anxieties I decided to recalibrate my blaster.

Once we had all come down the gangway at the coast of Ogesh, Jale organized a headcount. Looking back at our army, it was surprising that so many of us were able to fit in one Galleon.

"Blok killed some orcs," said Blok, meeting us at the coast. "Path to the valley should be clear."

We soon pressed on, pushing through an array of

lifeless plants. The air of Ogesh felt thicker and my breaths were deeper.

Gloomy smog filled the atmosphere. Many creepy wails, chirps and screeches were heard as we marched through the vegetation. Blok's ability to catch scents from afar alerted us on anything deadly that was incoming. Whispers came from among the warriors and mages. "Are we really following the lead of one of them?" someone said. At this point I didn't have the energy to call out ignorance.

"Valley ahead!" said Blok, as we came to a large sloping path. "Blok does not know path to gate now."

"It's alright, Blok, we'll have to use our intuition from here," said Finian. We came to a large slope that would require us to slide down. The problem was that large boulders and sharp bits of wood stuck out at various parts of the downward slope. Sliding down would be dangerous, and we could lose some of our numbers in doing so.

"How long would it take for us to move around and find another way in?" Jale asked.

"Two hour' to walk around other side." Blok answered.

"Mages," said Egith, walking in front of us. "If you

are trained in advanced force magic then gather beside me. We will form a barrier to guide ourselves down."

The mages lined up side-by-side and a citrine-colored aura floated in the gloomy air. First they asked that any carts and supply chests be handed to them so they could use their magic to send them down the slope. There was concern about the objects being destroyed by the descent, but the mages proved to be talented enough to see our belongings safely down.

With our supplies down, Egith instructed us to stand behind the group of mages. We lined up in rows, so that once one row of people had fallen, the next could follow without there being too much congestion. At her count of three, my row dropped down, putting our weight on our knees and elbows. Dirt sprayed in every direction as we descended. When we came too close to the boulders, wood and rocks, the magic steered us around them. There were a few near misses when there was limited space between the obstruction and other bodies, but the magic guided us all the way down until everyone had made it unharmed; safe for a few scratches.

Blok, who didn't need or want the magic, was already at ground level waiting for us. He had slid down the slope on his own accord. "This is the place from vision," he said. Indeed we could now see the endless river from the falcon's vision.

We pressed on, with many of us turning our heads at the faintest sound. The air was too still, and the area too spacious. Nobody would admit it, but we were shitting ourselves with fear.

And then, a turbulent voice made us halt in unison. "Name yourself, Mutano!" The voice was amplified in a way that could not have come from a single body.

"What in the name of Jerrus was that?" asked Finian, as he turned in each direction, searching for the source.

Blok was motionless; rooted as if in deep thought. "I am Blok," he said eventually.

"As the spirit of Aezelin, I am to destroy you all. For, Chief Hegu of the Uomba tribe has not granted you the privilege of entering the valley."

Concerned looks spread from within our army. Being threatened by something we couldn't even see made our efforts seem redundant.

"But—" the spirit continued. "Hegu has broken an oath by allowing outsiders to walk through the gate. Aezelin shall let you and your followers pass if you agree to slay Chief Hegu and return alone to claim your new role as chief." Aezelin had put strong emphasis on the word 'alone'.

Blok stood silent for a time; perhaps processing the fact that he might become the chief of his tribe. "Blok accept," he said finally.

"Then continue on to the gate. It is close," said Aezelin. "The human leading Hegu has disabled it. One of your followers must find a means to activate the gate." Several of us glanced at Egith. Her unwavering confidence told us that she had come prepared. "Know that you have also broken an oath by bringing these people here." Aezelin continued. "I have not decided whether the oath you have broken shall cancel Hegu's. For this reason, when you become Chief, I will allow a Mutano from another tribe contest your leadership. The winner of this duel will be named the true Chief of Ogesh."

Blok's only response to these words was a short grunt.

"Proceed, Mutano." Aezelin said.

After some time, in which Finian stuck by Blok's side for moral support, we finally reached the gate. Like the one in Lainunia it consisted of two giant engraved stands. Two rounded cylinder shaped metal containers stood beside each stand. Egith stepped forward, followed by a few of her mages. They filled each container with a number of charged Medius Stones. A large glowing energy began to circle between the two stands. It was now exactly as it had looked in the vision from the Falcons.

The mages turned towards us and Egith spoke. "It is time."

CHAPTER 44

WHEN MY FEET TOUCHED THE icy surface of Thirion, a chill hit my bones and made me stir. The cold would not serve me well. My companions and I glanced at one another, confirming our safe passage. We cleared space for the army that would follow us and the number of bodies that emerged from the gate grew in size as the seconds ticked on.

Soon enough, Egith came strolling towards us. "My birds are scouting as we speak. I will know which direction to head in soon." Her shiver confirmed to me that it was every bit as cold as I felt. Sometimes I wasn't sure if it was just me.

Warriors were now walking forward, carrying supply chests and crates. "Finian, I have a suggestion," I said, spotting the crate carrying the enchanted weapons of Simon Cunningham. I picked up the shotgun from the crate and presented it to Finian. "It may traumatize you to see this again, but now it's enhanced. You should carry this. You are an expert marksman, but close combat will be necessary here. This will come in handy."

Finian's gaze lingered on the matte finish. "Please," he

said, "bind it to me." He turned to the side to allow me to do so. He was becoming quite encumbered with arrows already at his back, and the pouch carrying the artifact. Luckily, this specific model was designed to be as weightless as a pistol with an advanced energy source from Jupiter powering it.

"And Blok, you should carry this," I said, pushing the cart containing the rocket launcher. We can have someone else push the cart behind us, but I want to show you how it is used. I knelt to lift the launcher and handed it to Blok. He shouldered it naturally, as if remembering how Simon had held it before collapsing a building on him. "I give this to you because you're strong enough to handle it with ease and eat the recoil."

"Recoil," said Blok, highlighting the word that he clearly didn't understand.

"Yes, recoil. The kickback that occurs after shooting the weapon," I said. "To aim it, all you have to do is look through the sights here." I pointed. "Then press on the trigger here." I held his enormous finger over the trigger so he understood.

"Boom," said Blok.

"Yes, it will go boom. But only use this at a distance, if the situation calls for it. Look at it as a last resort if things don't go our way. And be careful, because it's infused with two types of magic."

"Blok hate magic." He tossed the launcher back into the crate and I shuddered at the possibility of it firing as a result of his rough handling.

"I know," I said, patting him on the back. "But we need to make use of any and every tool at our..."

"East," said Egith, cutting in. "In that direction," she pointed. Audette was sat on her shoulder. "Flurwick is in the cave seeking the staff. His Mutano army is on guard outside."

"We'll need to figure out a way to sneak around the Mutanos to get to him," I said. Evangeline looked disturbed, as if realization had only just hit her on what we were facing. "Are you alright?" I rubbed her shoulder as everyone marched on.

"Yes," she blinked. "I was lost in thought, that's all. Please tell me you're feeling alright. It's not too late to take the elixir," she said.

I threw an arm around her and kissed her forehead. "I'll be fine. Let's head on."

Jale led us through the icy expanse. Forests surrounded us and the occasional howls and shuffles that came from within them had us on edge. Finian spoke of rare creatures that are said to lurk in Thirion. "I've always wanted to see a giant musk ox," he said.

"You'll see it alright. Right before it sticks its horns through your bony frame," one of the warriors chuckled.

"Bony as I may be, I'm still your champion," Finian retorted.

The ice became thinner as we found ourselves moving uphill. Soon, it was cotton soft snow that crushed beneath our boots. Flakes of snow sprinkled over us like seasoning. It felt like every muscle was coming into use as the uphill walk became steeper. My breathing became rapid, as my body craved more oxygen. I was suddenly becoming anxious that I'd let everyone down at a crucial moment. Second guessing myself was something that I frequently did in life or death situations; and I somehow managed to always persevere. But the stakes hadn't been this high in a long time.

"Halt!" came Jale's voice as we made it onto even ground. We all formed behind him, as the outlines of the Mutano army came into view. The Mutanos were marching through the snow, led by a single figure. Blok pushed his way to the front of our pack to stand beside Jale.

"If a battle breaks out, we must be ready to separate from it to seek out Flurwick," I said to my companions.

"There will be so many casualties, I cannot imagine walking away and leaving them behind," Evangeline said.

Finian side-eyed her. "Well I suppose you can stay and help if you want, but we have a set plan. The army knows the risks of this battle and they will do what they must so we can stop Flurwick."

Evangeline shot quick glances between Finian, the approaching Mutano and myself. "Well I suppose I will stay and assist them. But you two must be careful, as I won't be there to heal you." A feeling of hurt bit me inside at the thought of being away from her. I tried to put aside my selfishness and remember that it was better to help many, rather than a few.

I grabbed her hand and squeezed it. "Look after yourself."

"And you." she nodded. "I was thinking that since you will be seeking out Flurwick, you should leave your artifacts with me to avoid giving direct access to them."

"Good call." I said, taking the flask from my pouch and depositing it into her supply bag. Finian followed suit with the Runes. "Just be careful."

"You forget that I have magic on my side," she said, "I will be fine."

The Mutano army now stood meters from our own.

Their size was jarring when stood directly in front of us. The only object towering over them was a giant carcass of the dragon that Master Retgar had slain—I'd only just realized that it was there. Snow blanketed the carcass, including its wings that angled upwards. The creature seemed much larger in person than it had done in the vision from the birds.

"Blok!" said a Mutano from the front of their pack. There was no denying that this was Chief Hegu. He wore a feathered head bonnet and there were numerous markings over his leathery blue skin. He carried a spear at his side that was planted in the snow.

For some time the Mutanos stared at Blok. "Is this a staring contest?" asked a warrior standing nearby.

"The Mutanos speak to each other in their heads, remember?" said Finian. "It's the closest thing resembling magic that they have."

"Besides mysterious spirits that threaten to kill entire armies, of course," I added.

Chief Hegu pulled his spear from the ground and held up his fist. "Hegu not care if spirit talk to Blok. The Uomba have united with the Hetha tribe. We will kill Blok and his weak humans."

"They will not stop," said Blok, turning to Jale. "I

must kill Hegu. Only then will Mutanos see reason."

Jale nodded. "Then let us..."

A spear had landed beside Jale before he could finish speaking. The Mutanos charged forward, advancing on our army. Warriors raised their shields as mages shot spells from their staffs. The army of Mutano was suddenly knocked back from an invisible barrier that the mages had thrown up.

"Not one of them was knocked off their feet," said Evangeline. "Such strength; the barrier will not hold long, it will require incredible strength of magic to keep that barrier up."

Archers from our backline began shooting. Their arrows arched over our heads, as if by magic. Mutanos that were struck pulled the arrows from their bodies, completely unscathed.

Evangeline jumped, as Hegu stepped through the visible outlines of the barrier. "They're through!" yelled Jale, as the Mutanos stepped through and started striking our front lines. Hegu's spear clanged against Blok's axe.

Egith was pouring flames into the horde, causing them to spread and thus creating space for our army. Evangeline was using force magic to knock weapons out of their hands, but she had knocked a few from our own warriors in the process.

Mutanos were then nearing Finian and I. Finian shot ice arrows from a safe distance but the enchantment was not slowing them down. "I never realized just how tolerant they were to magic." Finian yelled over the cries of war. "It takes multiple arrows just for the ice to affect them. I can't even fire fast enough to slow them." Finian pulled the shotgun from his waist, while I took aim at one of the approaching threats with my blaster. "Brandon, do I really have to kill again?" Finian asked, keeping his eyes on the oncoming Mutano.

"Right now, its kill or be killed," I said, steadying my aim on the target. "Do not hesitate, or you're putting us at risk."

With its eyes locked on us, one of the Mutanos charged in to close the distance. I fired the blaster and my shot hit him square in the face; his body contorted as the lightning took effect.

Another one of them dashed forward and Finian's shotgun blast was so powerful that even I recoiled standing next to him. The force magic enhancement sent the Mutano body flying across the battlefield, leaving trails in the snow.

"By The Elders!" Finian exclaimed. "Your world must be out of control," he said.

"Especially if merged with yours," I replied. "Come on, we should use this as an opportunity to sneak past."

We edged around the outskirts of the brutal fray. Sorrow filled me as I watched a Mutano impale a mage with his sword and lift him up as if he were food on a fork. I wanted to stay—to protect these people—to watch over Evangeline. But finding Flurwick before he could get the staff was necessary.

We hid in bushes white with snow and from behind them we ran alongside the enormous numbers of the Mutano. Eventually we slowed and glanced ahead in search of a cave entrance. And then my heart skipped as a gigantic shadow slid across the floor and an earth shaking roar came from above.

"Whoa," I gasped, as spiky wings expanded on the shadow below. I looked up to see a dragon gliding over the battlefield.

CHAPTER 45

"OH DEAR," SAID FINIAN, as we watched the dragon pour flames down on the battlefield. Many in our ranks were burned alive as we stared up at the flying beast with bewilderment. "What are we going to do?"

Seeking out Flurwick was a priority but there was no way I could leave Evangeline and the others behind, knowing that they were on the verge of being scorched. "Come on, we have to help them," I said, pulling Finian.

We ran back to the heart of the battle where the two colliding armies were scrambling in panic. Some Mutanos and humans diverted their attention to the dragon as it circled among the clouds. Others continued to fight each other as if there wasn't now a greater threat.

"Fire your arrows," I told Finian, as I extended my blaster. "I'll shoot with you to get its attention. Hand me your shotgun and then I'll shoot it once it dives in. Make sure you get out of its range once it swoops in."

Finian looked at me, knowing it was an act of suicide. "Actually, I will use the shotgun. I've taken a liking to it. Besides, you need to live so you can take out Flurwick." He nocked an arrow and took aim.

"Whatever happens," I said, "know that you're a true champion."

Finian winked. "They shall never doubt us Mothernamed again," he said, before firing an arrow into the air. I followed up with a shot from my rifle. The dragon showed no sign of hurt, but it registered the attack and set its sights in our direction.

"Here she comes," I said, transforming my rifle back into its blaster form. As I took aim, I felt my body ache and a familiar frail feeling took me. It was only adrenaline that fueled my survival instincts as I opened fire while the dragon descended towards us.

Finian threw his bow down and readied the shotgun, but before the dragon could come within shotgun reach he was tackled by a Mutano warrior.

"Are you kidding me?" I yelled. I took aim at the Mutano who was now strangling Finian. It took five shots before the Mutano shuddered. He fell beside Finian and twitched until his body stiffened.

A wave of red hot death was rushing towards us now. I hurled myself on top of Finian and we threw our combined body weight together across the snow; rolling as a single unit, trying desperately to avoid the dragon's blanket of fire. When we were sure that we had escaped its area of attack, our bodies separated and we looked around to see where the dragon had gone. It had somehow vanished.

"He'll be back." I panted.

"Can you believe that Mutano? Fighting us despite the fact we we're all about to be burned alive." Finian raged. "I can't have been the only one that saw Mutano warriors lying as burned as a Corwy roast."

"I don't understand it either; but come," I said, forcing my body up. "We have to be ready for the dragon's return."

"I lost the blooming shotgun," he said as we ran back to the center of the battlefield. Finian's eyes located where he'd dropped his gear and he dashed towards a lingering bed of flames to retrieve them. We then found ourselves ambushed by another Mutano. My body was on the verge of shattering as one of their fists crashed into my shoulder. Snow cushioned me as I fell, and before I could reorient myself I heard the familiar blast of the shotgun. Green particles from the magic rose from the shotgun barrel like smoke.

"Brandon, I love this thing," said Finian. "Are you alright?" he asked, helping me to my feet.

"I've been better," I panted.

And then we heard the roar of the dragon again. Looking up, I saw the creature positioning itself for another dive. "Same strategy?" I asked. Finian nodded and then I took aim.

Before I could get in a good shot, we noticed a large spear-like projectile flying right for the beast. The object tore through its right wing, causing sparks of fire to fly from its mouth. The dragon descended through the air at an angle.

"It's the Elves," said Finian, pointing to our left. A group of Elves were stood beside the forest. Niserie stood with her hand held up to the skies. "It was an icicle. Niserie fired an icicle at it," Finian announced, much like a commentator might.

"Let's move, it's coming down fast," I said. We parted and tried to clear as much space as possible for the dragon's fall. Soon enough it collided with the snow and the ground rumbled beneath us. A few Mutanos, who were adamant on fighting, had been crushed by the beast. Its claws had dug themselves deep into the blanket of snow which halted the creatures slide. Then, the dragon roared with anger, raising its uninjured wing high into the sky. Humans and Mutanos that surrounded the beast were met with balls of fire. Some were knocked back by its good wing as it thrashed around.

"Now is our chance to take it out; while it can't fly," I said.

We edged our way towards the dragon, but we were still met with conflict from the Mutano army. That's when the Elves stepped in. Mutanos were suddenly sent flying, and their attacks were blocked by powerful barriers and wards. Soon, the Elves were fighting side by side with us.

As we came closer to the beast, Finian readied the shotgun. "Any chance you can keep it still while we…" he had tried to ask Var'ae, but before he could get the words out he'd had his breath knocked right out of his lungs as the dragon's tail knocked us back across the field.

I was grateful for the thickness of the snow, for it softened our landing. By now, my body felt ready to fall apart. Most of my pain was internal, but the various bumps were adding to the agonizing throbs.

"Bleeding cry!" Finian grunted. He patted snow from his furs and stared over at the beast. "Is that Blok?" he pointed.

I looked over to see the silhouette of a Mutano standing atop the dragon that Retgar had slain. The Mutano held an Axe over its shoulders, and it was positioning itself to dive onto the living dragon. It was definitely Blok.

"I will catch its attention," said Niserie. She ran ahead, blasting any contesting Mutanos off of their feet with her force magic. Then, she let out a screeching cry as she held her arms out, summoning another icicle. Her leg was stretched outward and she put every ounce of her physical strength into the hurl. The dragon's side was grazed by the icicle, and once again it roared. It turned to face us with burning anger in its eyes.

"Come on then ye' ugly flame bucket," said Finian, brandishing his new favorite toy.

Behind the beast I could see Blok's silhouette diving. What happened next I didn't see, as the dragon's body blocked the entire event from our sight. But we felt the earth-splitting cry of the beast as its agony vibrated under the snow. Sprinkles of flame fell sporadically around us.

"Look." I pointed. Blok—who was miraculously back on the ground unscathed—was now pulling the rocket launcher from the cart. He came running towards us, getting around the wounded dragon unnoticed. Only a Mutano could run at that pace holding such a weapon.

"Ah," said Finian. "There he goes coming up with a better plan "

"Watch out, Mutano!" Niserie cried, as the dragon spewed a wave of flames behind Blok. She saved Blok by waving her hand and making a wall of ice shoot up from the ground, blocking the dragon's fire. "Hit it now Mutano, for it will melt that ice in no time." Blok did something I'd never seen him do; he gave Niserie a thumbs up before taking aim through the sight.

When Blok shot the dragon with that enhanced rocket launcher, it was as if the entire world collapsed. The skies darkened and lightning ripped through the battlefield, settling right at the spot where the rocket had struck. The ground quaked, forcing us on our backs again. We no longer heard the dragon's roars and I was sure there was no more life left in the beast. Either that or the thunder had drowned out every other sound on the field.

Finian and I watched one another—side by side on the ground—through concerned eyeballs as the thunderclap continued. Finally it calmed, and once we were sure that Blok hadn't brought about an apocalypse, we pushed ourselves up to our feet. The dragon's body lay lifeless and adjacent to the remains of its friend. Its mouth was wide open, with its giant fangs exposed. Blok, who had been kneeling, rose to his feet and nodded towards Niserie.

"Brandon, I wish that you understood how revolutionary it is to see such camaraderie between an Elf and a Mutano," said Finian, nudging my arm. The warmth of the moment was enough to ignore the surge of pain I felt in my elbow after his nudge.

But the moment of triumph didn't last, as Chief Hegu's spear went flying into Blok's shoulder.

CHAPTER 46

"GOOD MUTANO," The Chief clapped. "Blok always a good Mutano. Blok leave Ogesh when Hegu tell him to. Blok only know how to follow order. Now Blok must follow Hegu command or die."

Blok's jaw was clenched tightly as his hand closed over the spear stuck inside his shoulder. "Hegu told Blok to leave Ogesh because Blok love human. But now Hegu follows the command of a human." he grunted.

"You dare speak against Chief Hegu?"

"Blok already told Hegu; the spirit of Aezelin has chosen Blok," said Blok. And then he somehow mustered the strength to pull the spear from his shoulder. Watching the act was enough to make me stir. "Now, Blok must kill Hegu and unite the tribes."

"Even Mutanos can dream," Hegu chuckled. The two Mutanos pounded their chests, perhaps as a sign of respect. Then they approached each other, legs squatted and bodies leaning in like two wrestlers after the bell had rung.

Mutanos surrounding the duel took it as a sign to continue fighting, despite the fact that their numbers had dwindled. Fatigue had set in with our own army, and they'd used the crash of thunder as a moment for recovery. Now they were being forced to continue fighting, as the Mutano warriors approached them.

"Please, let us not harm them," came Evangeline's voice. "If we resist, they will see that it is no longer worth fighting. Only their chief has been mind-warped, the rest of them are acting on the chief's orders."

"We will not back down," Jale yelled. His surrounding warriors cheered and charged in to fight the Mutanos head on. Mages stood on the outskirts, pouring in defensive spells to prevent the warriors being instantly pummeled.

"This will be over soon enough," said Finian. "Now the Elven arcane warriors are joining the battle," he nodded. "They are warriors that channel their magic into their attacks. They are incredibly powerful, and their army is what allowed the Elves to win the war." Looking over Finian's shoulder, I saw leathered up Elves carrying an array of different weapons; swords and shields, double daggers, maces and lances. One Mutano warrior towered over one of the arcane. He closed his fists together and swung them down upon the Elf, but the Elf used a shield to deflect the blow. The Mutano was knocked back on impact and then the Elf lodged a sword in the Mutano's abdomen. As blood oozed from the Mutano, it turned from purple to crystal blue. The wound was filled with icy frost as the Mutano collapsed.

"See... When normal mages use magic, you can see them putting physical strength into it to enhance it. Just like Niserie with the icicles," said Finian. "Arcane warriors focus on physical attacks and then insert magic, making it more devastating. They spend every waking day training to enhance both their physical and magical abilities."

"Impressive," I said, shivering inside my armor.

"Are you okay, my love?" Evangeline had now found her way to us, and I embraced her into a hug.

"I'm fine." I lied.

"Please, let's encourage them to stop. They will listen to a champion."

"Not exactly a good idea when the Mutanos don't understand the meaning of backing down," said Finian. "They wouldn't stop to let me kill that thing." He pointed to the dragon's carcass, and we caught a glimpse of Blok trading blows with Hegu. Hegu was using Blok's crippled shoulder to his advantage. Our Mutano friend had no choice but to keep backing up as his one good arm limited his ability to counter-blow. Soon enough, Hegu would have him backed up towards the dragon's body and Blok would be in serious danger. I grabbed my rifle, ready to assist.

"Brancon," Evangeline snapped. "We have to stop. There are too many casualties. Let's focus on finding

Flurwick."

"Oh my," said Var'ae from behind us. Following her eyes, it looked as though she was staring at Evangeline, but further on I saw Hegu's body folded over Blok's good shoulder. Blok lifted Hegu off his feet and turned with great difficulty as Hegu thrashed around. Then, Blok found the strength to toss Hegu over the giant exposed fangs of the dragon, impaling him. For a short time, Hegu's body quivered until it remained completely still.

Hegu was no more. Blok had won. He was now the chief of his tribe.

"Yes big man! Yes!" Finian chanted. Every Mutano on the field stood still to acknowledge the death of their chief. Some were murdered by arcane warriors that refused to stop. The humans however, were drained enough to seize another moment of rest.

"What now?" I asked. "Will they stop fighting?" My question was answered immediately, as Blok turned to face the Mutanos. He pounded his fist on his chest and slowly, Mutano warriors followed suit; pounding their chests as a sign of peace and co-operation.

"Thank The Elders for that," said Finian.

"We better continue with our original plan," I said, patting his shoulder.

What I heard next made my heart jump. Evangeline let out a heart wrenching scream before diving into the snow and then a sword came spiraling where she had just stood, almost killing her.

When I looked around to see where it had come from, I saw Natalya running forward.

CHAPTER 47

I FORCED MYSELF IN Natalya's path as she bolted for Evangeline. She did not slow. Instead, her arm rose as she continued dashing towards me.

"Brandon, the sword," I heard Finian cry. Immediately I hit the snow, realizing that her sword was about to boomerang its way through me.

Natalya caught it and stood above Evangeline. "No more," she said, as he held her sword at Evangeline's neck; but Evangeline fought back, hurling snow at Natalya's face using force magic.

Natalya staggered and I rose to subdue her. With one hand pressed against her shoulder, I used my other to stretch her arm behind her back. "Stand down, Natalya." It took every resistance in me not to rip her arm from its socket.

"You idiot!" she screamed. I flipped her arm and then threw her to the ground. My knee was now holding her in position. Truthfully, I wasn't sure how long I could hold her. My body was feeling weaker by the minute. A mix of cold and exhaustion had accelerated my painful symptoms.

"I thought I'd gotten through to you, but still you won't back down. Don't make me put you down for good." I told her.

"Brandon, stop," said a voice in my head. "It's Var'ae. I must tell you…" came the Elf's voice. But her words cut short, for now something worse was approaching the battlefield.

Shouts of "it's him!" echoed all around. My head turned to where everyone was staring; and then I saw him. Flurwick was walking down a slope, holding a long, jeweled, golden staff. He wore a hooded robe over his skinsuit. The hood was covering his gray pompadour.

"Elves, attack him! You are powerful enough in volume," Jale yelled.

At some point—I'm not sure when—I had released Natalya. She rose alongside me, looking on with concern as she watched Flurwick approach with a snide cockiness to him. "No," she said.

Elves and human mages began sending elemental projectiles at Flurwick. He held out the staff and every bit of magic was deflected. And then we saw Egith march to the front of our ranks. She held up her own staff, as if inviting Flurwick to a duel.

"She will lose," said Niserie.

Egith had fiery determination in her eyes, and it made

me believe in her. "You may think you hold true power," she said. "But the power is only as strong as the person wielding it. And your desires make you weak."

"My desires are only to restore order in the Milky Way." Flurwick huffed. "I'm simply fulfilling what is required. I am undoing the greatest mistake in history, and you are all a product of that mistake."

"Enough," said Egith. She swung her staff around in the air and it emitted white magical energy. She used her left hand to hurl an ice blast at Flurwick but he dispelled it with fire from his staff. Egith's right hand continued to command her own staff and she appeared to be building a barrier for herself.

"Let's skip the warm up," Flurwick smirked. Egith's eyes glowed; right before she gripped the staff with both hands and spun in a three-sixty-degree motion. Dim citrine waves erupted from her staff and traveled at speeds I couldn't follow. The magic hit Flurwick and staggered him. And then the falcons—Orato and Audette—flew in above Flurwick, circling far above his hood.

"The birds are casting mind magic on him," said Niserie. "Sister, do you know what it is?"

"It would seem they are trying to interrupt his mind; to pause his actions."

Flurwick's body stiffened. His face showed discomfort

as the birds continued to circle above him. Flurwick was vibrating so much that his hood flipped backwards. "He can't fight it," said Jale. "We should attack him head on while the effect lasts." At Jale's words, several of his warriors stepped forward.

That was when I noticed the expression on Flurwick's face change. In one instance, his lip was pressed into a thin white slash but then his eyes squinted as the thin lips curved into a hard smile. A flash of light erupted before us, and before we knew it, we all found ourselves rooted to the spot, unable to move.

"What the heck is going on?" I growled; my lips struggled to move. Flurwick had resumed full control of his body, and with a wave of his hand a bolt of darkly colored magic shot into the skies, catching the two falcons. Both birds fell onto the snow with a loud squishy thud.

"No!' Egith cried; she was also rooted to the spot.

"Perhaps your Elven friends know this already," said Flurwick as he approached Egith. "But one of the perks the Staff of Enellas grants the right user, is the ability to attack through barriers. You see, the power of this staff is unmatched in the right hands. And being that I'm a descendant of The Elders, I am granted its true power."

Flurwick approached Egith and in one sweep of the arm, he cast a crystallized shard that tore through her chest. Spit flew through my lips as I watched her quiver. I wanted nothing more than to lunge for him and tear him apart, but all I could do was twitch. Tears fell from my eyes as Egith's body fell. Seeing someone with such strength of character fall made the situation hit home.

Flurwick turned to me, smiling. "It's over, Sergeant. Everything I came for is within my grasp."

The altar was still in Highwell. The only artifacts he had within range were...

"Eva," I whispered. Trapped within the magic, I was unable to look over at her. My worry was that she would be harmed for what she possessed. I had to stall him for as long as I could. Until perhaps the magic wore off and the Elves would be able to ambush him.

"You don't have all the artifacts," I said, fighting the stiffness of my lips.

"Are you sure about that?" he said. Flurwick turned away and pointed in the distance. Beyond the gray cast sky and the thick chunks of snow pelting down around us, two figures could be seen. Their faces couldn't be identified at this distance, but it seemed they were both pulling something.

"Shit," I said under my breath, as the realization dawned on me. Someone had secured the altar. They had made it across to Ogesh and gone through the gate. And they would now deliver the altar right to Flurwick. Other muffled curses and cries could be heard around me as my companions registered what was happening. Even Natalya gasped beside me and I wondered if she had been screwed up by all the mind warping.

Flurwick turned to face me once more. "As you can tell, Wardson, my altar is here; as are the rest of my artifacts." he beamed. "So then," he said, while turning his attention somewhere else. Even with my inability to move my head, I could tell he was now facing Evangeline. My heart kicked into overdrive.

"Don't you touch her," I shook. I felt my body jerk as if my rage could suspend the magic. When I tried to move again I was met with discomfort as the magic continued to lock me in place.

Flurwick was laughing. "Wardson, trust me. I don't need to touch her." Flurwick waved the staff in a circular motion. "You are free, my dear."

My eyes locked onto Natalya beside me. I waited for her to make her move; to snatch the artifacts from Evangeline. The woman I'd thought I'd loved, taking from the woman I knew I'd love forever. But what I saw shattered my soul into a million fragments.

Through my peripheral vision, I watched Evangeline marching through the snow; walking to Jonathan Flurwick.

CHAPTER 48

"EVANGELINE, STOP!" I cried. My soul burned at the sight of Evangeline pulling her pouch from her shoulder and holding it out for Flurwick obediently.

"This is what I wanted to say," came the voice of Var'ae in my head. "I realized it when Natalya attacked her. I saw the truth inside Natalya's mind. She knew that..." Var'ae's words were cut abruptly from inside my head.

"Uh-ah, there will be none of that, Elf," Flurwick said, with his staff raised at her. "I'm sure Sergeant Wardson would like to hear this one from the horse's mouth," he said, as he took the artifacts from Evangeline's pouch and deposited them into his own. Flurwick slid his fingers down Evangeline's face and I closed my eyes because it was too much for me to bear.

"How about you go give him a demonstration, seeing as you love him so much," he said. I heard her footsteps as she approached, and my eyes opened to meet hers. Seeing the hazel eyes I'd come to love were now making my blood boil. As she stood before me, with her eyes beaming,

I could see that the woman I knew wasn't the one looking at me. Evangeline had been tampered with.

"You see, Wardson, it's all in the necklace," he said. I looked down to see the lacy necklace shimmer. "It was crafted by the conjurer and me. Of course, Lockwood didn't know who would wear it. Originally, I intended for Natalya have it so I could continue to control her. You see, the necklace uses what's called triggered warping. Think of it as magical programming." Flurwick's revelation and the sight of Evangeline's eyes were causing me so much grief that I closed my eyes to shield myself. "I am able to tell the necklace when to warp the wearer's mind, and which actions I wish for them to carry out. I can ensure that the wearer will never remove the necklace. Outside of these triggers, the wearer will operate as normal. As you can tell, it's the perfect way to create a mole."

The necklace; now it all made sense in my head. I remembered the expression on the conjurer's face right before he'd been covered by his own flames. *'Oh my, the enchantment'* he'd said, before he was burned alive. That was the moment when he'd realized that Evangeline was wearing his own creation.

"I'm going to kill you," the words escaped without me realizing I'd said them.

Flurwick laughed in response. "Isn't it interesting how love brings about murderous emotions? But anyway,

Wardson, as you can tell, I'm quite proud of it. You see, I knew that you'd seek out the artifacts to stop me. And in doing so, you would come into contact with the Elves. Your good friends Var'ae and Niserie there have mind magic far superior to anyone else in this shithole. This meant I would need precautions to ensure the necklace would prevent them from detecting her triggers. It took me and the conjurer an entire night of infusing mind crystals before the warding was powerful enough. Lockwood even had a small fragment of Death Shard handy to infuse into the necklace and make its effects stronger."

"When," I said, forcing the word through my lips. "When did you get to her?"

"Step aside my dear," said Flurwick. As I opened my eyes, Evangeline moved between me and Natalya. Looking over at Flurwick, I now saw two men standing either side of him. One of them was the Exul warrior that had fought alongside Simon Cunningham in Highwell. It took a moment before I recognized the other man, but soon I realized that it was the mage Evangeline had fought when I'd strayed away from camp to find her; the night she had been captured.

"It was shortly after news came to me that you and your friends had defended Corwy. My scouts saw your darling strolling down a path all alone. Confident enough

427

in her magical abilities to think she could hold her own. Lyndon here, who was already under my command at the time, was able to capture her. He sent word that he'd captured an Elven mage coming from Corwy and I immediately came to visit. I must say that that you have a talent for selecting women with spunk, Wardson. The knife-ear put up quite a fight as I tried to enter her mind. But when I broke through her barriers, imagine my surprise when I saw you featuring so predominantly. She'd only known you a couple days, but already you'd left an impression on her. That's when I knew I would use her to steer you in the path I wanted." Flurwick turned away and gave some kind of signal to Lyndon.

All of a sudden, I felt my body release from the magic. Flurwick hadn't noticed, as he was looking down upon the altar. When I looked around me, it seemed everyone else was still in stasis. How had I come free?

Thoughts rushed through my mind. I was now free to attack if I wanted to. But as a sole attacker, I could be slaughtered in seconds with the power Flurwick wielded. I decided to keep him talking in hopes that the others would come free. I stood as still as possible—trying to maintain the same awkward pose I'd been in during stasis—despite feeling the throbs in my joints. My body's weight was being distributed to my legs again now that the magic was no longer holding me. With the weight pressing against my limbs, my pains grew tender.

"Why?" I asked, trying to mimic the difficulty in speaking that I'd had previously. "Why go through all this when you already had Simon, Natalya and the Undead?"

Flurwick looked back at me and I feared that he'd figured it out. "The real question is why not? By manipulating your lover I could control your feeble attempts to stop me. Meaning I would have total control of the situation; whether my minions succeeded or not." he smiled, and then he continued pacing from side to side. "You see..." His free hand waved as he spoke. "The triggers I programmed into her necklace would make her committed to serving your medical needs. Even more committed than she already was. I made it so she would pander to your weakness; to make you more and more comfortable. I used the attraction you had for each other as a means to pull the wool over your eyes; all so that you would be well equipped to seek out the artifacts for me. I didn't care who died in the process, whether it was you, Simon or Natalya. As long as somebody brought them all to me, it didn't matter who did it."

Around me, I could hear my companions sigh woefully as Flurwick spoke. "Evangeline's necklace would insure that her every action would be geared towards securing the artifacts in some way. That's why when you were in Highwell she sought to find a means for the altar to be seized after your party had left." Flurwick placed a hand on the Exul's shoulder. "She saw to it that this Exul warrior was freed, right under your noses."

As tears ran down my face, I resisted every urge to lunge for him. "And then, she saw to it that you and your pathetic Corwy boy handed over the other two artifacts to her. Because you see, Wardson..." Just then Evangeline turned to me and placed her hand around my throat. I felt a chilling sensation bite my neck. I struggled to breathe. "The necklace is more powerful when she is near me."

Just as I felt I would suffocate, Evangeline ceased the magic effect but her hands remained on my throat. Out of nowhere, an image came into my mind. Evangeline was planting an image there. An image of an arm brace; it seemed familiar to me. And then I remembered it was the magical ward that Blok had gifted to her. She had planted it on me when my eyes were closed; when I couldn't bear to look into her own. I hadn't felt her plant it on me because of the magic that had held me at the time. This ward had to be the reason that the magic binding me was now gone. And Evangeline was showing me what she had done. But did this mean she still had free will? Or was she still under his control?

"That's enough, dear," said Flurwick. Evangeline removed her hand and stood facing me. She looked as soulless as she had done moments ago. "Now, I have everything I need to end this. But I have one more task left for your beloved half-breed, Wardson. You see, for me to obtain the celestial matter on the Island of Crystalline, I need another mage. Drinking from the self-refilling Flask of Irithrel makes its drinkers immune to to the crystal's radiation. Once I'm on the island, the Altar of Jerrus must be positioned at the correct co-ordinates. The Runes of Aktarth must be slotted into the altar in the correct order to open up the sealed entrance to Relaun's core. And then a mage must wield the Staff of Enellas to dispel the barrier surrounding the entrance. That is what Evangeline must do; all while I secure the celestial matter and restore magic to the Milky Way. And then I will absorb the celestial body with the Death Shard to become the single and most powerful person in existence. Our Galactic Alliance will be no more, Wardson." Flurwick stared at me and I got the sense that his monologue had ended. By the looks of things, my companions were still trapped. Weighing the situation, the odds were stacked against me, but now was the time to act.

Flurwick turned his attention to Lyndon and placed a hand on his shoulder. "There is a boat here," he said. No doubt he was using mind tricks to display the location of the boat. "It is close by. You and the Exul must take the altar there and place it inside the boat. I'll be there in a few minutes; after I have my fun."

I wasn't sure what Flurwick's idea of fun was going to be, but I knew that I wasn't going to stand around and find out. As Lyndon and the Exul knelt to grab an end of the rope tied around the altar, I grabbed the butt of my blaster. I watched their bodies rise, and watched Lyndon position himself to pull the altar. When I aimed my blaster, a gasp escaped me as I felt the pain in my shoulder. I endured the throbbing sensation and forced my arm to comply. With Lyndon's skull at the center of my scope, I pulled the trigger and watched as the lightning powered projectile made his head jerk. His body fell forward onto the snow.

Through my scope, I watched Flurwick turn to me. I didn't hesitate to pull the trigger a second time.

Chapter 49

FLURWICK HELD UP HIS STAFF and deflected the lightning projectile so that it would return. My reflexes didn't disappoint me, as I was able to anticipate this and pull a combat roll to dodge it. This resulted in the shot hitting one of the Highwell warriors, who screamed in agony as the lightning rippled around his body. The stasis was keeping him still, but his cries saw no boundaries. "I'm so sorry," I said.

"Why would you do that, Elf?" said Flurwick. "I'm about to grant you the pleasure of seeing the most beautiful and sacred sight in Relaun, and you defy me?" Evangeline looked at Flurwick like a child full of regret after disobeying their parents.

"Looks like your necklace isn't as powerful as you thought it was," I said. He scowled, and slowly the scowl transitioned into a snide, sadistic smirk. A glint of amber caught my eye, and then before I knew it, Evangeline's hand whipped across my face. While I was stunned from the slap, she pulled the magic ward from my wrist with so much force that I heard it snap.

"Eva..." I started to say. But before I could finish, I found myself surrounded in a snowy blizzard. She was forming all the snow descending from the skies into a circular cocoon around my body. The temperature was lowering to levels more freezing than it already had been.

My body could not withstand the chill. Freezing temperatures were my weakness. The cold would narrow my blood vessels, and the cells would clot faster; bringing my body into a state of crisis. I shivered amid the snowy vortex, trying to step my way out. Pellets of snow lashed my face so hard that I struggled to keep my eyes open.

"Stop!" I cried.

And then I felt the snow cease. At my command, the blizzard had vanished. My eyes opened to find Evangeline staring at me with her arm still held out.

"Stupid Elf, you will not listen to him. You are under my command." Flurwick yelled. I was blasted off my feet and I met the ground with a hard thud. When I looked up I saw Evangeline running at me with dark colored magic flowing from her hands. When the magic caught my body, I felt torture like I'd never felt before. It was pain; pain that was the closest imitation of a sickle cell crisis. It felt as if my body was burning and being hit with high voltage lightning all at the same time. I heard myself screaming, but I had no idea how loud my cries were. "Eva!" I let out in an extended cry, "please."

Again, she stopped hurting me. "Eva, you have to listen to me. Take the necklace off." I pleaded.

"If you keep listening to him, I will kill you both," said Flurwick. "Obey me!" Evangeline moved her hands in a circular motion, and then flames shot up from the ground, melting the snow. I then found myself trapped in a circle of fire that seemed to be closing in on me by the second.

"Lieutenant-commander!" I yelled, getting onto my feet. "Or should I even call you that?" I turned to look Flurwick in the eye, through the flickering flames. "You're a disgrace to all marines. There you stand, hiding behind your new found power. But you're not even brave enough to fight a lower ranked marine one on one." Flurwick's eyes tightened. "Well, I guess I can die with the knowledge that Lieutenant-commander Jonathan Flurwick was nothing more than a coward; a coward who turned traitor because he needed magic to feel an ounce of significance."

"On second thoughts, Elf, you may stop," he said, and then the flames dissolved. "Go and wait for me by the boat, and help my friend here load the altar." Evangeline obeyed and walked over the Altar of Jerrus, where the Exul warrior had stood watching us. They began walking down the hill, pulling the altar behind them.

"This wasn't part of the plan, Wardson." Flurwick turned the staff sideways and released it. Somehow it was able to suspend itself in midair, unassisted.

"I should be on my way to see my mission through. But how could I deny a fellow marine the right to die an honorable death?"

I clicked my knuckles and stood in my fighting stance. I wasn't sure if my body was up to this, but my intention was to stall him long enough for my companions—who were becoming mere pieces of furniture around us—to be freed from the magic that held them.

Flurwick removed his cloak and tossed it to the ground. "I thought you'd already suffered enough shame and embarrassment by having the woman you love fall into my command," he said. "But if you wish for me to strip you of your manhood, then so be it."

He was closer now. I walked forward to close the remaining distance; happy that he had presented me the chance to vent my frustrations. And then we were so close that I could see the gray stubble around his face.

"Are you going to salute me, Serg..." Flurwick's head whipped backwards as I socked him squarely on the nose. Without giving him time to react, I hit him with a flurry of follow up shots.

Out of nowhere I was winded, as Flurwick's hand slammed into my chest. He'd hit me with force magic that sent me flying backwards. Flurwick pressed his hand against his face and stared; his nose clogged with blood. "Nice shot, Wardson." He raised his hands and then my body was being pulled forward towards him. His fist struck my jaw with so much force that I felt whiplash. I tasted blood in my mouth.

"You see," I groaned, now on my knees. "You can't fight me without magic." With great agony, I forced my body back onto its feet.

For the first time, Flurwick seemed flustered. He glided towards me, at a speed too fast to dodge, and then his fist lodged itself into my abdomen. "Fine, Wardson," he said as I doubled over, panting. "You want a man-to-man fight? Well if it shows you how pathetic your career in the Alliance is, then so be it."

Flurwick lifted his knee towards my face, but I threw out my arm to block him. He threw a right hook as I straightened my body, but I blocked that too. It was then that I knew I was faster than him. Flurwick staggered as I struck him with a three-punch flurry. Any minute now he would use his magic to save him from embarrassment; but I didn't care. My fist lashed his cheek again; that was for Elentos. And then again; that was for Egith. And then once more; that was for forcing Evangeline to play with my heart.

Flurwick threw another hook and I ducked it. With my back arched, I threw my weight into his body and tackled him off his feet. Just as I was about to continue pounding him I felt the familiar sharp throb in my shoulder. The pain was now so excruciating that I yelped.

Flurwick took advantage by whipping the back of his hand across my face, knocking me away from him.

"Sorry, Wardson; on second thought, I must be getting on with my mission," he said, walking to where I lay. "But don't worry; I'll leave you with something to remember me by."

He leaned over with his hands glowing a citrine hue that represented force magic; right before I felt the most amount of pain I'd ever felt at one time. Flurwick's fist slammed into my chest in rapid succession. The magic he used allowed each blow to dent my armor until he was making direct contact with my chest. My ribcage was on the verge of shattering. With my joint pain still running rampant, the combined level of pain was sending me into a state of shock I couldn't sustain. It was time to die, or so I thought. Every blow was knocking more breath away from my body.

My head turned, as it became too heavy for my body. And before my eyes could close, I saw arcane warriors moving alongside Var'ae and Niserie. The Elves were free. One of the Elven mages appeared to be going for the Staff of Enellas, right behind Flurwick's back. Eager to keep Flurwick occupied, I summoned what strength I had left to insult him. "C-coward."

His eyes bulged and I was sure he would hit me with one final blow to claim my life, but instead he spun around. "Filthy Elf!" he yelled. Unable to move or reposition myself, I missed what happened next. All I heard were loud cries.

"Oh my, Brandon," Var'ae said, as she knelt before me. She placed her palms on my chest and then I felt tingling sensations within. "I cannot heal you fully. Your body will need to heal itself somewhat, but I am trying to put your bones back into position and close the internal wounds that have been penetrated by them." Indeed it had felt like my bones were tearing away from my flesh as she worked her magic. Flurwick had done a number on me. He'd cracked my ribcage in many places. But Var'ae was talented, because soon enough all I could feel was the joint pains.

"Brandon, I'm sorry about Evangeline. But you must understand that the woman you know is in there. It was she who freed you from the stasis. She placed the ward on you to weaken the magic. And then she dispelled the stasis from you without him noticing." I listened, but the words didn't mean much to me at this moment. Heartache was something I didn't need. "Evangeline loves you. It's just that his control overrides her actions; for as long as she wears the necklace, she cannot help herself."

There was a loud blast in the distance that caused Var'ae to jolt.

"I wanna see." I groaned. "Show me what is happening."

She placed her palm on my forehead and I saw through her own eyes as Flurwick waved the staff. Several arcane warriors were being burned alive on the spot. Some had survived the fire blast, thanks to their defenses. Around us, other Elves were freeing human and Mutano warriors from stasis.

"Enough," Flurwick cried. "I'll show you power like you knife-ears have never seen in your lifetime."

The staff twirled in his hands until it became still in a vertical position. Flurwick screamed and amethyst auras erupted around him. Elves were shooting magic at him to no avail. "I can't believe it," I heard Var'ae say. "He's summoning."

"What?" I asked. But Var'ae now stood, and I could no longer see what was happening. Everything went dark. For a second I believed it was my demise, but I heard the confused screams from my companions as a purple energy pulsed in the sky.

"Niserie, come. We must form a barrier," said Var'ae nearby. What followed, felt like a hallucination. The energy in the sky formed the shape of a dragon, which was larger than the one Blok had slain. It roared, before it took a dive through the sky, coming down towards us. Sounds of thunder ripped through the air as the hollow dragon descended on us. Before the dragon could make contact, a white bubble formed around us. The dragon seemed to pass right through the barrier, and the ground shook fiercely as it plummeted down.

The dragon had dissolved into the ground like a ghost, leaving a violent storm behind it. The whole of Thirion seemed to shake, and bolts of lightning whipped through the sky. The sisters' barrier shielded us from the brunt of the storm.

Soon, the ground stopped quaking and the skies faded back to normality. "You saved us," I heard Jale say minutes later. "But now he is gone. He has escaped with the artifacts."

And with those words, my eyes finally closed.

CHAPTER 50

"WE CAN'T STAND HERE and allow him to reach the island," said Jale. My consciousness had returned, but I wasn't ready to open my eyes. They had placed me on layers of blankets, but I could feel the cold slush of snow bleeding through the fabrics beneath me.

"By now he is too far in the waters for us to catch him, and our bodies cannot withstand the energy from the crystals. We will disintegrate before we even get close," said someone, with an Elven accent.

"So, what? It's over? We're going to let him seize this power and destroy us with whatever he finds on the island? We must at least give our lives to stop him."

"But then what if he returns from the island?" said another Elf "That would grant us another chance to stop him. If we all rush to the crystals and sacrifice our lives, then we shall have a weaker defense."

But Flurwick would not return from the island. Once he'd captured the celestial matter from the island, he would vanish back to the Milky Way. Only I stood any chance of defeating him there. It had to be me and me alone who stopped him. And if I died, then so be it.

When I sat myself up, my chest was fragile and my joints still throbbed. The large group of warriors and mages near me were so engrossed in their conversation that they didn't pay me any mind. Nobody was even looking in my direction.

The skies had returned to their normal gray, snow had stopped falling, and the barrier that Var'ae and Niserie had thrown up was no more. Looking around, I saw Finian and Blok standing beside the two sisters. They had laid me beside the forest, slightly outside of their view. It was a bad idea to have my body rest on top of the snow with no source of heat. But I couldn't expect them to understand my pain triggers. The only person in Relaun who understood how to take care of me, had been using her empathy against me.

It had been a while since I'd felt like an outcast in Relaun. This realm and the people within it had welcomed me. In a matter of weeks, I'd felt like one of them. But now the realization dawned on me that I didn't belong here. Flurwick, despite his evil intentions, was the one link to my reality.

As quietly as possible, I struggled to my feet. The pain in my hips nipped at me as I shifted my weight. I bit my lip to prevent my cries of pain and after a final look at my friends, I limped away.

To avoid being seen, I slid myself down the hill, before circling around to where Evangeline and the Exul warrior had pulled the Altar of Jerrus. The thought of Flurwick controlling her, burned my soul as I followed her footsteps. Her small feet were imprinted in the snow alongside the trail of the altar, which they had dragged behind them.

Each step I took felt like I was being stabbed in my hips. The desire to kill Flurwick allowed me to endure these sensations. I had none of Evangeline's pain remedies, and none of her medicine to deliver oxygen around my bloodstream.

And then I remembered the elixir she'd brewed for me. I reached into my pouch for it and considered it in my palm. The red fluid bubbled inside the clear glass vial. If this elixir had been exactly as she described, then drinking it would cure me of all my symptoms for at least a couple of days. It was more than enough time for a final stab at killing Flurwick. But could I trust this? Knowing that she had been largely under his control. Var'ae had said that she was able to function as herself when she wasn't commanded by the necklace. But Flurwick had also made it clear that the necklace would influence her to use my illness as a means to appease me. For all I knew, she could have added a secret ingredient to the elixir that would act as a kill-switch.

Anger consumed me as I thought about her. I couldn't believe that the love we had shared for one another had been manipulated. Sure, true love rarely blossomed after a few weeks, but it had felt like an anomaly. Like we had always belonged together and had finally found each other.

I thought of those Elven words—E'Leawae Uea—and then I lost control. I threw the vial, feeling the sharp pain in my shoulder. The vial smashed against a large boulder; the red fluid staining the point of impact. Pieces of glass sprinkled under the light. I would not face Flurwick using this elixir that Evangeline had brewed under his command. My body was aching all over, but so be it. At least I was in a state that I fully understood. I'd lived with this pain my entire life.

"Don't forget," said a voice. I turned to see Natalya approaching. "There's still another marine here."

"You knew," I snapped. "How long did you know he was controlling her?"

Natalya walked beside me. "I knew for sure right after you freed me from his control by the bridge that day. I recognized the necklace. After learning how you'd almost managed to free me in Corwy, he wanted a way to continue controlling me whenever he wasn't around. Just in case you and your girl ever tampered with me again.

But then they captured her. I didn't know about her capture until now, but when you returned me to my own consciousness, I saw the necklace and knew it was from him."

"You should have said something. Instead of jumping off a cliff," I said, glancing at the sword on her back. The same sword she'd used as a tool to survive her leap from the cliff that day.

"I was scared, and confused. I needed time to recollect my thoughts; to return to my original state of mind. So for that, I apologize."

"Apologies mean nothing at this moment." I grunted.

Natalya rubbed my shoulder. And I admit; it felt nice. I remembered falling sick during one of our dates. She'd taken me to her quarters and dosed me up on painkillers. As I lingered in a state of unconsciousness I remembered feeling her hands massage me. That had been one of the only times she'd shown affection. "You can't possibly be going after him in this state," she said.

"My state doesn't matter," I said. "Either I stop him, or I die."

"I'm coming with you," she said. "This is my mission too."

"As it is ours," came Finian's voice. He approached us from behind, alongside Blok.

"No. You guys must stay here," I said. "You must live,

because no matter what happens, this realm needs you."

"Aw stop yer yappin, Brandon. You're not going to stop us. Unless you fancy taking on the new Chief of the Uomba clan here," he said, nudging Blok.

"This will be suicide," I replied. "You know that, right?"

"And what's the other option? Wait for that bastard to destroy all life in Relaun?"

"Touché," I nodded.

"Two what?"

Somehow, Finian had managed to bring a smile to my face. "We have to get a move on now." The four of us continued on down a slope until we reached the coast.

CHAPTER 51

THE FOUR OF US SAT in the large rowboat as Blok paddled us through the sea. His strength had us gliding hastily through the waters. The Mutano's strokes were so disciplined that hardly any water splashed over the sides. Finian had been describing the events that unfolded after I'd passed out. He estimated that I'd been out for fifteen minutes or so. Some of the Elves had entered the same cave where Flurwick had retrieved the Staff of Enellas and they'd found Master Retgar's wounded corpse.

"We saw in the vision that Retgar was already wounded, but according to the Elven autopsy, it was magic from the staff that killed him. It seems the poor master was clinging on for dear life until Flurwick finished him off."

"That's one more person I need to avenge," I shivered, "assuming we live long enough."

"The odds don't seem great," Finian replied. "I wish one of us could at least do magic. Perhaps we should have gathered a few Elves."

"We'll make do with what we have," I said.

"Well," he glanced at Natalya. "At least we have her

sword trick. That's something."

"Why are you talking as if I'm not sitting right beside you?" Natalya asked.

"I'm half expecting you to slice me in two," said Finian. "How did you make it to Thirion anyway?"

Natalya's eyes closed, as if she were reliving a moment in time. "I spent some time in Lainunia with the Elves of Feroa." Natalya read the confusion on my face. "They are Elves of the wilds who believe that nature is god. They helped me reconnect with myself spiritually, and that is how I am able to think so clearly after having been mind-warped for so long."

"That still doesn't explain how you got to Thirion though," said Finian.

"I would have gotten to that; had you not interrupted."

Finian looked between the two of us, as if trying to picture us ever being together. "My apologies; continue."

"I remembered that Flurwick was planning to visit Thirion to retrieve the Staff as his final act before setting out to the Island of Crystalline. I knew it was there that I needed to go if I wanted to stop him. As a reward for slaying a vile beast that slaughtered Elves and animals in the forest, the Feroa Elves granted me access to a secret path that links Lainunia and Thirion. Even the Elven Kingdom doesn't know of this path."

"A secret path? Sounds like something they should know. What if unwelcome guests show up some day?" Finian asked.

"The path is watched by the Elves of Feroa, so that is unlikely to happen. They are both powerful and peaceful."

"Sure, until they're mind-warped. We've seen an entire tribe of..." I'm pretty sure Finian was about to use the Mutano as an example of how the Elves of Feroa could be manipulated, but he didn't get a chance to finish his point.

The four of us started to feel stinging sensations on our skin. I glanced at my hands as I held them at eye level. Their texture turned leathery and it felt as if the skin was detaching itself from bone.

"Crystals are close," said Blok. His skin hung from his finger as he pointed ahead. Indeed the crystals illuminated the skies above us like some festival. Seeing the enormous sized crystals slanting as high as the skies was the most mystifying thing I'd seen in Relaun. Their colors were vibrant and the glow brightened the night. If my body hadn't been falling apart, I might have felt moved enough to snap a picture.

"Well, I suppose this isn't such a bad way to die," said Natalya.

"I'm sure the thousands of beings before us, who wished to get close, would agree with you. Not sure if I do though," Finian slurred. Every inch of our body felt as though it was beginning to melt away. "Thiff if beg-inning to, hurth. I with we fought thif through mo," said Finian, struggling with his words. The skin on his forehead was dissolving, and beyond a bloody patch of flesh, his skull started to emerge.

"Something…coming." Blok said in low grunts.

My head struggled to swivel right as I looked to see what Blok was referring to. Something in the distance was floating towards us. "Th..Flathk," Natalya cried.

And then I realized. The object flying its way towards us was the Flask of Irithrel. It would allow us to drink its contents and become immune to the crystal's energy. Unfortunately for us, the flask was angling away from our boat and descending into the sea ahead of us.

Natalya screamed as her arm rose. Her gloves glowed, before her sword snapped out of its binding behind her. The sword glided through the air and miraculously, the sword caught the leathered straps that were bound to either side of the flask, right as it was about to hit the sea.

The sword rose and circled itself so that the straps would wrap themselves around tightly. And then it made its way back as Natalya cried in pain. It was causing her great effort to guide the sword while her body was disintegrating. Eventually, the sword came crashing down to the middle of the boat; the flask with it. Natalya fell from her seat, her weight making the boat sway.

"Qui', we-muth-try-to drink fro-it," said Finian. Blok was now leaning at the front of the boat, with a hand placed on each side of the boat to balance it. "I-thall let her drink firth. She deserve' it the moth after tha'," Finian slurred. He struggled to unbind the flask from the sword.

"No time," I grunted. I felt as though my body would give away any second. Finian nodded and abandoned his attempt to unbind the flask. He opened the flask's cap and held the sword in one hand and the flask in the other. I forced myself down with a cry of pain. My fingers found Natalya's mouth, and I opened them with all the strength I had left. Finian leaned the flask and Blok moved forward to hold Natalya's head up. Finian poured the fluid into her mouth, and I used my other hand to rub her throat, hoping she would swallow.

Seconds later she leaned forward coughing, completely independent of our own support. It took seconds of gagging before she became aware of the situation. "Oh my, my skin is repairing," she said.

"Help," I wailed, turning over to my back; ready to die at any moment.

"Sorry," she said. The illuminated sky was my focal point as I came closer to unconsciousness. The last thought that came to my mind at that moment was returning home to Earth, with Evangeline by my side; a thought that would never come to fruition.

And then I felt my body being lifted and supported by large hands. The flask was being pressed against my lips and the fluid was poured down my throat. I felt the cool liquid running down my throat, and suddenly, my body's natural instincts kicked in as I registered that I needed to swallow. The next thing I remember is coughing against the boat's surface. The liquid burned. It was like drinking gasoline.

"Brandon, are you okay?" Finian asked.

As he asked, I felt my skin revitalizing itself. "I'm good," I said, my shoulder throbbing. "The flask, how did it get here?"

"I don't question it." Finian replied, after drinking from the flask himself. "I'm just glad we're alive." He passed the flask to Blok.

We'd each drank from the flask and now our flesh was slowly revitalizing. "Be ready," Blok said, after about a minute. "Close now."

I peered over the side of the boat to see the bright ambient island a short distance away. Evangeline stood holding the Staff of Enellas. From the end of the staff came a bright beam of energy that linked itself around the crystals. At the center of the island we saw the altar placed in front of the crystals, with the runes glowing on top of its surface. Flurwick was nowhere to be seen, but

Evangeline was staring our way.

CHAPTER 52

"EVANGELINE," I CALLED, as I stepped out of the boat and onto the sand. She stood completely still with the staff clutched in her right hand, but her eyes sparkled at me. Her lip was trembling and tears fell down her cheeks. "Why?" I asked. I didn't exactly know what I was asking her. It just hurt to know she hadn't been acting on her own instincts.

Evangeline held up her right hand, and then the Flask of Irithrel came flying from the boat into her hands. That meant, "it was her!" I said. "She sent the flask to us."

"Brandon, she seems to have some level of control beyond what the necklace tells her to do," said Natalya. "Perhaps you can get her to stop what she's doing. Maybe Flurwick will be trapped below if it works."

"Can't we just snatch the necklace from her?" Finian asked.

"You can try, but I bet it will force her to attack. When I was under Flurwick's influence, Brandon's voice alone was enough to trigger something deep within me. To make me subconsciously aware of my true thoughts," Natalya said. "I suggest speaking with her first."

I breathed in deeply as if using the fresh air to cleanse my heartbreak. "Evangeline, please listen to me," I said, taking a small step forward. I grunted in pain as I felt my knee pop. "Please put the staff down."

Evangeline sniffed. "Tell me, are you feeling pain?"

My pain was the last thing on my mind at this moment. Relaun and the Milky Way were depending on me. "That doesn't matter. Please, drop the staff."

"Tell her," said Natalya.

I glanced at Natalya sideways. "There are more important things than my pain."

"Evangeline is strong. I know firsthand that she knows her mind magic well. It's possible that she knows of some loophole that will override her commands from the necklace. Don't forget that Flurwick made it a priority for her to appeal to your sickness. Because he thought that would allow her to earn your trust."

"Worth a shot, Brandon," said Finian. "If it doesn't work we'll snatch that necklace from her."

I faced Evangeline again and looked into the eyes that I once hoped I could wake up to each day. "I'm in insufferable amounts of pain," I said.

Evangeline dropped the staff and time seemed to slow as it fell. Some kind of energy based barrier was forming at the center of the crystals, where Flurwick had entered.

Evangeline began walking to me, but as she reached

the midpoint in front of the crystals, she was blasted from her feet by some invisible force. The staff then rose and suspended itself in midair; just as it did in Thirion. And then Flurwick emerged, with a large glowing ball of energy floating above his hands.

"So, the fat little Elf betrays me again," he said. He raised his free hand and it glowed. Evangeline's screams followed, and they traumatized me.

"Stop that!" I cried, running straight for him, only to be lifted into the air and slammed back down against the sand.

"Enough of your antics," said Flurwick. As I attempted to sit up, I watched him grasp the ball of energy with both hands and yell. The sky erupted with thunder and lightning and soon our bodies had become still. We were stuck, once again in some kind of stasis.

"I must admit, Wardson, your attempts to stop me are admirable," he said, as he paced around our bodies; the glowing orb floating above his palm. "For that, you will not die by my hands. It's the last good deed I have to offer to the Galactic Alliance, before I return to the Milky Way and dismantle the organization. But sadly, you will still die."

Flurwick stood before me and extended his free hand. A sharp migraine like sensation crept into my head. "My plan is so grand that I want my former colleagues,

Brandon Wardson and Natalya Carrick to understand the extent of it before they die. I have opened up your minds; only the two of you, because I care nothing for your pathetic companions. You may ask any question you like as I talk you through this revolution. Speak to me with your thoughts."

'Eat shit,' I told him through the mental link.

Flurwick laughed. "Wardson, if there's one lesson you should have learned in your life, it's to never follow an organization so blindly. They only sent you after me because you're expendable with your ailment." Although I knew he was trying to mess with my psyche, it was actually plausible that the Alliance would do such a thing. "Never complete missions so obediently for a powerful institution that has its own objectives. For you see, I learned what the Galactic Alliance kept from us."

'And what's that?' I asked.

"There once existed a planet in the Milky Way called Yoyvis. Sometime before the humans existed on Earth, the galaxy had magical properties, Wardson. At some point, these properties formed into what I hold in my palm now. This celestial ball of energy is what permits the existence of magic." He waved the ball of energy in our faces, and I felt the heat radiating from it.

"It's impossible to tell when this happened in history, but somehow a planet was formed around this celestial energy. Yoyvis. It was on this planet that The Elders were born."

'And how did they get here?' I asked.

"Uh-ah, Wardson, let's not skip ahead. On Yoyvis, humans occupied the planet alongside the Elves, for many generations. Yes, Yoyvis had humans long before Earth did." This had been the most calm I'd ever seen Flurwick. Clearly he was feeling happy in his accomplishments. "Like Relaun, not everybody possessed the gift of magic. Elves were able to pick up the magic naturally, but with the humans, it was more of a genetic trait. But like on Earth, the humans were eventually able to manufacture and create technologies."

Flurwick stood and began pacing again. "There are several theories about what happened to Yoyvis, but there is no way to truly understand what contributed to its demise. With their technological capabilities, the people of Yoyvis were able to detect a devastating force in space that was making its way to them; a force that would destroy their planet. They'd only had one prototype vessel that could evacuate them from the planet, and they weren't even sure it worked. This vessel was limited in size. It's written that only two-hundred of them were able to evacuate, and only ten of them were Elven."

'Why so few of the Elves?' Came Natalya's voice in our heads.

"The spaceship was an invention of the humans, so they had priority."

'Typical.' I said. *'What was this devastating force?'*

"There is no way to tell. But Yoyvis was for sure destroyed by it. The Elders believed that the mix of magic and technology on the planet had cursed them to the point of extinction. Remember that fact, because it will come into play again. As for the ship, it landed on Earth, thousands of earth-years ago. Luckily, the Yoyvis people had managed to extract this piece of the planet's magical properties before the planet was destroyed. It meant that they were able to continue using their magic."

'Does that mean you can't use your magic without that thing?'

"To put it simply, Wardson, this energy must exist somewhere within a realm or galaxy for magic to be used." It took a moment for this fact to sink in. "That brings me back to their theories. See, as the Yoyvis people toured Earth in stealth, they realized that civilizations were on the brink of creating technologies much like their own. This caused a panic in the Yoyvis people. They believed that magic and technology both would make the galaxy unbalanced. The people witnessed earthquakes and tsunamis, and these natural disasters only intensified their fears. So, after years of deliberation, it was decided that the Yoyvis clan would banish away magic in the Milky

Way, to a separate realm where magic could exist without impacting the known universe. And here it is. Relaun is the manifestation of that vision."

'But how?' I asked.

"There are tools that exist in the Milky Way, Wardson. Powerful things that I still don't understand. But once I return, perhaps I will discover new possibilities. All I can tell you about the creation of Relaun is that all the Elves agreed to enter the realm, along with a hundred humans. The Elders, as they are called, were simply the most talented magical beings in Yoyvis. They understood magic like no others had, and they also had technology on their side. That is how they were able to create things. Like the Mutanos, and all the beasts you've come across here."

'If more of the Yoyvis people remained on Earth, you can't be the only descendant.' came Natalya's thoughts.

"You are correct; there are more descendants of The Elders; in the Milky Way and even here in Relaun. Of course, nobody else but the Alliance and I, are aware that magic even existed in our galaxy." So much of what Flurwick was saying was a shock to the system that I hadn't registered the fact that my employers had knowledge of magic too. It angered me. "Here in Relaun, the Elven King is born from The Elders' bloodline. I'm simply the only descendant that was willing to seek out my true power." Flurwick stood still and faced us. "After all this bonding, I almost feel bad for having to kill you. Are you sure you wouldn't like to join me on my conquest?"

I glanced over at Evangeline's body. I saw a glint of the necklace under the illuminated sky. '*Not in your wildest dreams, asshole.*' That was the only fitting response I could think to give him.

Flurwick grimaced. "Well, it was nice knowing you both."

'*What will happen to us?*' Natalya asked.

"As soon as I leave here, the people of Relaun will no longer be able to use magic. Theoretically, the realm may be able to exist without this energy, but I will soon encapsulate it and then use the Death Shard to destroy it, while also absorbing its properties. The magic energy will live inside me, and only I will be able to cast magic. I will become a god, while Relaun crumbles to pieces. And then, with all the Medius Stones I have collected, I will form an army and grant them magical weapons, much like yours." he pointed at Natalya. "But enough talking, I must go."

Flurwick walked to the center of the island, close to where the altar sat. We watched as he placed some kind of device over his index and middle finger. The glow of the device told me that it was something from the Milky Way, a technical item. He used the device on his fingers to draw glowing shapes in the air. His strokes were practiced, as if he was drawing the symbols from memory. He finished by drawing a large circle and the shape sizzled, sounding like a piece of meat on a barbecue.

"That last entryway I created did not work as I'd intended, Wardson. Your entry to Relaun was not what I wanted. This time there will be no room for error." A large misty circle manifested itself where he'd drawn. "Too bad I can't bring the staff with me. These artifacts will not carry over to the Milky Way." Flurwick then walked over to a large sack that I hadn't noticed before. "I must be thankful to my former Exul minion for bringing along all these Medius Stones."

'Where the hell is he now?' I asked, referring to the Exul warrior who'd assisted Evangeline with the altar.

"Probably drowned by now; he was slowing us down and with this large sack of stones on board, there was need to relieve ourself of some weight." he smiled.

Flurwick approached the portal. "Well, this is it. Enjoy death, comrades." Flurwick stepped through the portal, foot first, until his body had dissolved.

Total darkness followed after Flurwick left Relaun.

Even the once vibrant crystals had faded.

"I can move," said Finian. "I could hear everything he said, but I couldn't talk."

"Shut up!" Natalya snapped. "Look," she pointed. Beyond the darkness, we could see the outline of the portal, still open. "I've heard Flurwick mention this portal before." She was speaking so fast that it was difficult to understand her. "When I was under his control; he mentioned that it stays open for sixty seconds. Right now he thinks we're still trapped. We have to go after him, and fast."

She didn't need to tell me twice. I forced myself onto my feet, refusing to let the pain stop me.

"Evangeline!" Blok grunted. My heart jolted as I looked over at Evangeline's body.

"We have to carry her, Brandon. I know you're angry about what happened, but it's not her fault," said Natalya. Blok ran to where Evangeline's body lay, and hoisted her into his arms.

As I thought about my companions entering the Milky Way, something occurred to me. "What about oxygen?" I asked Natalya. My breather was around my neck, ready to be pulled to my mouth and activated at any time. But I feared for my Relaunian friends.

"We better hope we're going somewhere with oxygen mills," she said. "Come! No more talking."

Natalya approached the portal first. "See you on the other side, Sergeant," she saluted. And then she dissolved through the portal.

"Let's go through together," said Finian, "quickly."

We approached the front of the portal and faced each other. Blok was significantly larger than the portal was, so I feared he would struggle getting through with Evangeline. "Blok, pass her to us. We'll carry her through and then you follow," I said.

Blok carefully shifted her body into our hands, and then I noticed he'd removed her necklace. With the pain, I struggled to bear her weight on my arms, even with Finian there to balance it out. The thought of not being strong enough to carry her disturbed me.

"Bleedin' cry!" Finian exclaimed. "This bloody thing is closing. Come on, let's go." Then we could see the glowing edges of the portal closing in on us. In a burst of fear, we shifted our weight and fell backwards through the circle completely.

CHAPTER 53

MY BODY SLAMMED against the ground and immediately I felt the difference in oxygen. I knew right away that there was an oxygen mill. My eyes remained closed, and as I felt the constant throbs around my body, I wished that I could lie here forever.

"Brandon!" I heard Finian call.

"Finian," I breathed, "welcome to my reality."

"Blok," said Finian. "Where is Blok?" That was enough to make me open my eyes and swing my head left to right. I saw Natalya sitting up on my left, and Evangeline was sandwiched between Finian and me.

"Shit!" I leaned up. "Where's the portal? He must be coming now."

"It's gone," said Natalya, now standing. "He didn't make it. I'm sorry."

"Blok, me dad...and everyone. What will become of them?" Finian sobbed.

"I promise Finian, we'll do everything we can to find a way to get them back." I breathed. Looking around, I realized that we were on Nurvoa; the same planet in which this chaos had begun. I felt sadness that Blok hadn't been able to join us. He would now be stuck on the dark island, alone. Perhaps he would sail back to Thirion and rejoin our legion. Sadness filled me, as I imagined the state of confusion they must all be experiencing.

"How!" came Flurwick's enraged voice. We glanced around, looking for where he stood. And then Natalya let out a screeching yell as a bolt of dark magic hit her. The blast knocked her off her feet, leaving her body sprawled over the blood red dirt of Nurvoa. "How did you manage to make it through?" Flurwick appeared a few feet away from where we had landed.

I pushed myself up to a kneeling position. "Magic may make you powerful, Flurwick," I panted. "But nothing is stronger than raw determination." I was through with the talking. It was time to hit Flurwick with everything I had. I would exhaust all adrenaline left within me to push my crisis-struck body to its limits. As I ran towards him, I pulled the fire sword bound to my leg and swung it forward, aiming for his neck. He blocked my arm with his own, but before he could use his free hand, I clocked him upside the head with a left hook. I continued to strike him, feeling the swelling in my knuckles.

Flurwick recovered from his stagger and grabbed me by the neck. He lifted me off my feet before slamming me so hard that I felt the ground crack beneath me.

"You see this, Wardson?" he said, towering over me.

In his hand was a long glass case with a black crystal that had sharp edges on each side. The case was perhaps to protect Flurwick from its intense magical energy. "This is the Death Shard. Before you disturbed me yet again, I was about to use it to absorb the celestial energy in the container, over there." he pointed. My head swiveled enough to see a gray container with clear glass at its center. Inside it, the celestial energy glowed. "But since you and your friends are eager to die by my hands, you can be the first to fall victim to the Death Shard."

The hand with which Flurwick held me, started to glow a dark color and I felt my throat tighten. "You see, if a mage has a piece of Death Shard in their possession, it grants them the ability to use death magic, also known as dark magic." Flurwick was explaining all of this while I was feeling all the oxygen being cut from my body. "But it only works if you have the Death Shard on you. Evangeline was able to use dark magic on you earlier because the necklace contained it," he smiled.

Before I blacked out completely, I watched his arm shoot up to halt an incoming arrow from Finian. Moving his arm had disrupted his attempt to kill me. "You can have this back you pathetic piece of waste." The arrow grew flames as it raced back towards Finian. My head was unable to move far enough to see if it had hit him, but I heard no yell or cry from my friend. Instead, Flurwick's mouth fell wide open and he rose to observe something.

"Go away, you stupid lizards!" Flurwick yelled. "I won't hesitate to obliterate you all." Dozens of Drekarth dived in and surround Flurwick. He responded with magic. Magic blasts shot in every direction and each one collapsed one of the Drekarth.

And then he hit one of them with a powerful blast of energy. The obsidian shade of the blast told me he'd used the Death Shard's power. It was the first time I'd heard the creatures make a sound, but I knew from the high screeching that it was a sound of pain. The rest of the Drekarth retaliated by piling onto him.

Flurwick yelled as they clung to him, their numbers growing. Suddenly, Flurwick sent a large glowing blast up vertically, that caused dozens of Drekarth bodies to fly in the air. They sprinkled in every direction. The impact of his blast had even knocked me further along the expanse of dirt.

"I told you..." Flurwick yelled, as he zapped several of them with spells. "To leave me be."

Finian, found his way into my line of sight. "Brandon, are you alright?"

"I've..."

"Been better, yeah, I know." he smirked. "I was going to ask you what in the name of Jerrus those creatures were, but now I want to know what that giant building in the sky is." He pointed up. "Because it looks like it's about to fall down on us."

"Son of a bitch," I panted. "It's an Alliance ship. We're saved! My friends are coming."

Flurwick had noticed the ship too. I saw the panic on his face and he cursed obscene words. Then, he sprinted to his container. He took one look back up at the ship as it descended. His face showed immense hatred as he eyed the Alliance emblem. And then, using his enhanced speed, he bolted out of sight with the container trailing behind him.

"What a bloody idiot," said Finian. He leapt to his feet and sprinted to where Flurwick had stood moments ago.

"Finian," I gasped. Worried that he'd run after Flurwick. But he soon returned to me holding the glass case that contained the Death Shard.

"Looks like this is ours now," he smirked. "Those creatures seem friendly; didn't even stop me as I picked it up next to their friend's body."

As the ship began to hover below ground, I knew it was only a matter of time before they spoke. "This is the Alliance," came the projected voice over loudspeaker. "We are now landing. Disarm yourselves or we will open fire."

Finian stared down at me in confusion. "Just throw down your bow, and then stand with your hands in in the air." I told him. "They won't harm you. They need to be sure we're not hostile. I will identify myself once they leave the ship. You may need to help me to my feet so I can talk to them."

Finian did as I instructed. Before long, I heard the familiar mechanical sound of the ship's ramp lowering. "There are three of them," said Finian.

"Identify yourself, human," said one of the marines.

"Fellow marine," I yelled as loud as I could. "I am Sergeant Brandon Wardson. I am suffering from a medical crisis. My friend here is going to help me to my feet. We are not hostile."

"Affirmative, our Comm-link has identified you and Natalya Carrick."

I winked at Finian, as he looked down on me, completely oblivious. "Help me up," I told him. Finian crouched down and placed my arms above his shoulders. As I grunted, I watched one of the marines lift Natalya across his shoulders, while the other lifted Evangeline. The third marine made his way over to us.

"Man, am I glad to see you," I said, recognizing the man as Commander Pearson. The same man who'd mentored Joe Elentos. The same man who'd put together my mission to seek out Jonathan Flurwick. Pearson was easily identifiable at a distance by his long blond curls.

"I don't know what you've been up to, Wardson, but you've sure had the Alliance working overtime," said

Pearson.

"I'll tell you all about it. Just get me some damn morphine."

And then my heart jumped, as I saw Pearson pull handcuffs from his utility belt. Pearson slapped the cuffs over my wrists. "Sergeant Wardson, I am placing you under arrest for galactic-wide conspiracy and treason." I couldn't believe it. "Do you want me to read you your rights?" he asked.

I shook my head in defeat. One of Pearson's partners came beside him to slap cuffs on Finian.

"You believe I'm guilty, Commander?" I asked him.

"All I know, Sergeant, is that Charlie Cunningham made a shit ton of claims against you. You'll have to take it up with internal affairs."

And so, the marines I thought were going to help me stop Jonathan Flurwick for good, rounded us up like criminals. All I could think, as I sat in the prisoner's compartment of Pearson's ship—called the Lapwing—was that this was the worst possible way to introduce my friends to the Milky Way.

THE END

Brandon and his friends will return in Realm Blender Book Two. The ETA is early 2020.

Read *Starfade – A Realm Blender Novella* for a fun lead up to Book Two.

Acknowledgments

This book is for all the sickle cell sufferers out there who often feel inferior, misunderstood or as though no one out there can understand their struggle.

I have to thank my mum, Vanielee, for working hard all these years to ensure I always had a place to rest in my times of pain. Without her, I wouldn't have had the time or place to express my creativity.

Thanks to all my closest family members for supporting me through the years: Greg, Grandad, Kiesha and my Grandmother (Rest in peace).

These people have played an important part of my upbringing: Carmen, Michael, Robert, Colin, Oliver, Kieran and the Blackman family, Anette, Shirley, Mark, Murray, Jenny, Masha, Aunty Daphne, Uncle Beanie, Kieran Todd, Kyle Ross, David, Una, Nicky, Lisa and everyone else who has been an important part of my life.

When I go through hard times, there are a few people that I consider to be my support system. We share the good and the bad with each other; and I can't go a day without the jokes these people provide: Carl Ebanks and Rameez Quadri (thanks for being super supportive friends). Richard Bailey, Edward Velazquez, Ilesha Knight,

Asad Quadri, Dana Abercrombie, Tony Polanco, Anthony Frasier, James G, Fergus Mills, David Jagneaux, Tatjana Vejnovic, Max Moeller and Torrence Davis. I couldn't stomach life without you all.

To James Kennedy, thanks for always being supportive. If only you knew how much you helped me with this book. I'll explain the story someday.

Much love to my family in America: Dad, Aunty Dawn, Niccle & Tracey.

Thanks to Garrett Glass for showing me everything that was wrong with my writing and helping me to slowly improve. I hope I didn't let you down.

Thanks to Clement for the encouraging words.

Much thanks to Tunde and Kaye for understanding my work needs over these past few years.

Thank you to Chris Matz for your kindness.

Thank you to Julienne for being the first to officially call me a writer. That's what gave me the confidence to begin putting this book together.

Thank you to Annabel (Anzy) for providing inspiration along the way, and mental support as a fellow sickle cell sufferer.

And thank you to Maureen Scarlett and Hyacinth for all the medical support and advice they've offered over the years.

And thank you to the Sickle Cell Society.

About the Author

Gary Swaby is a digital marketing manager, book blogger and winner of the 2015 Floella Benjamin Achievement Award. He currently lives in Luton, England.

After suffering with sickle cell anemia—a lifelong disease that only affects a small minority—throughout his youth; he quickly realized that most people didn't understand him or what he was going through. Feeling alienated, Gary gravitated towards movies, video games books and computers. During moments of pain and recovery, Gary spent a lot of time daydreaming.

When Gary was older, he quickly realized that all the times he spent daydreaming was a sign that he was meant to write. He couldn't let his ideas go to waste any longer.

The idea for the Realm Blender series came after a life-threatening sickle cell crisis, in which Gary could have died. He'd longed to write a Sci-fi Fantasy story, but he'd also wanted to write a memoir to spread awareness about sickle cell. Gary decided he would fuse the two ideas and create a Sci-fi Fantasy adventure with a sickle cell warrior as the protagonist.

Follow Gary on Twitter at: @GarySwaby and check out his blog **www.garyaswaby.com** for more info on sickle cell and his book projects.

Thanks for reading! Please add a short review and let me know what you thought!

Please also sign up to my mailing list at:

www.garyaswaby.com

9 781916 006621